A DAY
LIKE
TODAY

A DAY LIKE TODAY

JOHN HUMPHRYS

WILLIAM
COLLINS

William Collins
An imprint of HarperCollins*Publishers*
1 London Bridge Street
London SE1 9GF

WilliamCollinsBooks.com

First published in Great Britain in 2019 by William Collins

1

A catalogue record for this book is
available from the British Library

ISBN 978-0-00-741557-1 (hardback)
ISBN 978-0-00-741559-5 (trade paperback)

Typeset in Adobe Garamond Pro
Printed and bound in Great Britain by
CPI Group (UK) Ltd, Croydon

MIX
Paper from
responsible sources
FSC™ C007454

This book is produced from independently certified FSC™ paper
to ensure responsible forest management.

For more information visit: www.harpercollins.co.uk/green

For Sarah

Contents

Part 3 – *Today* and Tomorrow

A DAY
LIKE
TODAY

Prologue

In which I answer the questions in the way I choose …

JH: Good morning. It's ten past eight and I'm John Humphrys. With me live in the studio is … John Humphrys. It's just been announced that he's finally decided to leave *Today* after thirty-three years. Mr Humphrys, why leave it so long?

JH: Well, as you said it's been thirty-three years and that's—

JH: I know how long it's been … far too long for the taste of many listeners, some might say. It's because your style of interviewing has long passed its sell-by date, isn't it?

JH: Well I suppose some people might say that but—

JH: You suppose some people might say that? Is it true or not?

JH: I'm not sure it's really up to me to pass judgement on that because—

JH: What d'you mean you're 'not sure'! You either have a view on it or you don't.

JH: Well I do but you keep interrupting me and—

JH: Ha! I keep interrupting you! That's a bit rich. Isn't that exactly what you've been doing to your guests on this programme for the past thirty-three years and isn't that one of the reasons why the audience has finally had enough of you … not to mention your own bosses?

JH: I really don't think that's fair. After all it was only politicians I ever interrupted and only then if they weren't answering the question.

JH: You mean if they didn't answer YOUR questions in the way YOU chose—

JH: Again that's not fair because—

JH: Are you seriously suggesting that you didn't approach every political interview with your own views and if the politician didn't happen to share those views they were toast? You did your best to cut them off at the knees.

JH: That's nonsense. The job of the interviewer is to act as devil's advocate … to test the politician's argument and—

JH: And to make them look like fools and to make you look clever. It's just an ego trip, isn't it?

JH: No … and if that were really the case the politician would refuse to appear on *Today*. And mostly they don't—

JH: Ah! You say 'mostly', which is a weasel word if ever I heard one. Isn't it the case that when they do refuse it's because they know you will deny them the chance to get their message across because all you want is a shouting match?

JH: Not at all. They're a pretty robust bunch and I'd like to think they hide from the live microphone because they don't want to be faced with questions that might very well embarrass them if they answer frankly and honestly.

JH: I'm sure that's what you'd like to think but the facts suggest otherwise don't they? And when they do try to answer frankly, you either snort with disbelief or try to ridicule them.

JH: Look, I wouldn't deny that I get frustrated when the politician is simply refusing to answer the question, and I'm sure the listeners feel the same. It's my job to ask the questions they want answered and if the politician refuses to engage or pulls the 'I think what people really want to know …' trick, then it's true that occasionally I do let my irritation show.

JH: Nonsense! The fact is you have often been downright rude and that is simply not acceptable.

JH: Well … we agree on something at last! You're absolutely right when you say being rude is unacceptable and I admit that I've been guilty of it – but not often. In my own defence I can think of only a tiny number of occasions when it's happened and I regret it enormously – not least because it really does upset the audience. One of the biggest postbags I've ever had (in the days before email which shows you how long ago it happened) was for an interview in which I really did lose my temper. The audience ripped me apart afterwards and they were quite right to do so. If we invite people onto the programme we have to treat them in a civilised manner.

JH: So we've established that you're not some saintly figure who always occupies the moral high ground. I suppose that's a concession of sorts. But what I'm accusing you of goes much wider than that. Of course you have a responsibility to the audience and to the interviewee but you also have a wider responsibility. Let me suggest that when people like you treat politicians with contempt you invite us, the listeners, to do the same. And that's bad for the whole democratic process.

JH: Once again, I agree with you. Not that we treat them with contempt, but that programmes like *Today* might contribute to the growing cynicism society has for politicians and the whole political process. But which would you prefer: a society in which politicians are regarded with awe and deference, or a society in which they are publicly held to account for their actions by people like me who question them when things go wrong or when we suspect they might be misleading us?

JH: Not for me to say: I'm the one who's asking the questions this time remember! But what I'm asking you to deal with is a rather different accusation. If people like you, who've never been elected to so much as a seat on the local parish council, don't show any respect to the people the nation has elected to run the country … why should anyone else?

JH: But that's not what I'm saying. Quite the opposite. I can't speak for my colleagues, but I have huge respect for the men and women who choose to go into politics. I hate the idea that for so many people politics has become a dirty word. Henry Kissinger once said ninety per cent of politicians give the other ten per cent a bad reputation. The wonderful American comedian Lily Tomlin put it like this: 'Ninety-eight per cent of the adults in this country are decent, hard-working, honest Americans. It's the other lousy two per cent who get all the publicity. But then – we elected them.' Yes, that's funny, but it's wrong. One of the greatest broadcasters of the last century, Edward R. Murrow, got closer to it when he chastised politicians who complained that broadcasters had turned politics into a circus. He said the circus was already there and all the broadcasters had done was show the people that not all the performers were well trained.

JH: In other words you regard political interviewing as a branch of showbiz rather than your high-flown pretension to be serving democracy!

JH: Look, I'm not going to pretend that we don't want our listeners to keep listening and if that means we want to make the interviews entertaining as well as informative I'm not going to apologise for that. After all, the BBC's founder Lord Reith said nearly a century ago that its purpose was to 'inform, educate and entertain'. But you'll note that he made 'entertain' the last in that list. Ask yourself: what's the point of doing long, worthy and boring interviews if nobody is listening?

JH: Ah ... so now we get to the nub of it don't we? It's all about ratings!

JH: Of course it's not 'all about ratings' but obviously they matter …

JH: … because the higher they are the more you can get away with charging the BBC a king's ransom to present the programme!

JH: Ah ... I wondered how long it would take you to get onto this because—

JH: I trust you're not going to deny that you've been paid outrageous sums of money over the years for sitting in a comfy studio asking a few questions when somebody else has probably briefed you up to the eyeballs anyway?

Prologue

JH: That's not entirely fair is it? You know perfectly well I spent years as a reporter and foreign correspondent in some very dangerous parts of the world. And anyway are you really saying the amount a presenter gets paid shouldn't be related to the size of his or her audience? That's rubbish!

JH: Ooh … touchy aren't we when it comes to your own greed! Have you forgotten it's the licence payer who foots the bill and the vast majority of them earn a tiny percentage of what you take home?

JH: Yes, I am a bit touchy on this subject and that's partly because for various reasons I got a bit of a bum rap when BBC salaries were first disclosed back in the summer of 2017. And anyway I volunteered several pay cuts as you well know …

JH: Yes yes yes … we all know you're a saint but I'm afraid we've run out of time. John Humphrys … thank you.

JH: And thank you too. And now I'm going to tell my own story without all those impertinent questions …

PART 1

Yesterday and *Today*

1

A childhood of smells

By the time I joined *Today* in 1987 I had been a journalist of one sort or another for thirty years and I'd been exposed to pretty much everything our trade had to offer. I had been a magazine editor at the age of fourteen – though whether the (free) *Trinity Youth Club Monthly Journal* with its circulation reaching into the dozens properly qualifies as a magazine is, I'd be the first to admit, debatable. I'd had the most menial job a tiny local weekly newspaper could throw at a pimply fifteen-year-old – and that's not just the bottom rung of the ladder: it's subterranean.

At the other end of the scale I had written the main comment column for the *Sunday Times*, the biggest-selling 'quality' news-paper in the land, for nearly five years. I'd had the glamour of reporting from all over the world as a BBC foreign correspond-ent – not that it seems very glamorous when you're actually doing it. I'd had the even greater (perceived) glamour of being the newsreader on the BBC's most prestigious television news programme.

And I had reported on many of the biggest stories in the world: from wars to earthquakes to famines. I'd seen the president of the United States forced out of office and the ultimate collapse of apartheid. I'd seen the birth of new nations and the destruction of old ones. So on the face of it I had done it all. But, of course, none of it properly equipped me for the biggest challenge in broadcast journalism: the *Today* programme.

Presenting a live radio news programme for three hours a day, day in and day out, is bound to test any journalist's basic skills, not to mention their stamina. You need to know enough about what's going on in the world to write decent links and ask sensible questions. You need enough confidence to be able to deal with unexpected crises.

You need the stamina to get up in the middle of the night and be at your best when people doing normal jobs are just finishing their breakfast and wondering what the day holds in store. And you need to be able to do all that with the minimum of preparation. Sometimes no preparation at all.

But thirty-odd years of trying to do it tells me you need something else. You need to know who you are and what you can offer to a vast audience that's better than – or at least different from – your many rivals. My problem when I started was that I had no idea what I was offering. I had done so many different things I wasn't at all sure who or what I was.

Was I a reporter?

I'd like to think so. Reporting is, by a mile, the most important job in journalism. Without detached and honest reporting there is no news – just gossip. At the heart of any democracy is access to information. If people don't know what is happening they cannot reach an informed decision. I like to think I did the job well enough. I had plenty of lucky breaks and even won a few awards. But I was never as brave as John Simpson or as dedicated as Martin Bell and I never had the writing skills of a James Cameron or Ann Leslie. I did not consider myself a great reporter and knew I never would be.

Was I a commentator?

Positively not. Columnists may not be as important as reporters, but they matter. The best not only offer the reader their own well-informed views on what is happening in the world, they cause them to question their own assumptions. They make the reader think in a different way. I very much doubt that I managed that.

Was I a newsreader?

Well, again, I was perfectly capable of sitting in front of a television camera and reading from an autocue without making too many mistakes. Not, you would accept, journalism's equivalent of scaling Everest without oxygen. Whether I had the gravitas to command the attention and respect of the audience is another matter altogether. Probably the greatest news anchorman in the history of television news was Walter Cronkite, who presented the *CBS Evening News* in the United States for nineteen years when it was at its peak in the 1960s and 70s. Cronkite not only had enormous presence and authority, he had a relationship with the viewers that any broadcaster would kill for. It can be summed up in one word. Trust. He was named in one opinion poll after another as the most trusted man in America. He also happened to be a deeply modest and decent man.

As for me, back in 1987, I was just a here-today-gone-tomorrow newsreader who was about to become a presenter of the *Today* programme and who had not the first idea what he had to offer its enormous audience. I tried asking various editors who had worked over the years with some of the great presenters what I needed to do to make my mark or, at the very least, survive. Most of them gave me pretty much the same answer: be yourself.

As advice goes, that was about as much use as telling me to write a great novel or run a four-minute mile. How can you 'be yourself' if you don't know who or what you are? How can you impose your personality on the programme if you're not quite sure what it is? It's not as if you can pop out and buy one off the peg.

'Good morning, I'm looking for a radio personality.'

'Certainly sir, anything specific in mind?'

'Well, it's for Radio 4 so nothing too flash. Obviously I need to be trusted by the listeners and I suppose it would help if they liked me.'

'Of course sir, wouldn't want them gagging on their cornflakes every time they heard your voice would we? But when you say "liked" do you have anyone in mind? Dear old Terry Wogan maybe? Or a bit more on the cutting edge, if I may be so bold? Perhaps a touch of the Chris Evans? It's always a little tricky designing a personality if the customer doesn't have a specific style in mind.'

'Yes, I can see that. How about the trust factor then?'

'Just as tricky as likeability in a way, sir. Takes rather a long time to earn trust.'

'Of course … So what about "authority"?'

'Sorry to be so negative sir, but that doesn't come easy either. Bit like trust in a way … takes time and depends on your track record.'

'Hmm … I think what you're telling me is that you don't actually have anything in stock that would give me a *Today* programme personality eh?'

'I'm afraid so. Perhaps I could offer sir a suggestion?'

'Please!'

'Why not stick with what you've got and then pop back in … shall we say … five years or so and we'll see whether it needs a little adjustment?'

'Thank you … most kind of you.'

'Not at all sir … is fifty guineas acceptable …?'

Had such a shop existed in the real world I might very well have popped back – not after five years but more likely after a week. Because I learned something very quickly, and it's this: a curious thing happens when you present a live radio programme such as *Today* for several hours on end, mostly without a script or without any questions written down. You discover that you have no choice but to 'be yourself'. There is so much pressure that there is no time to adopt somebody else's persona or even to think about creating a new one for yourself. And that can be a blessing and a curse. In my case it is both.

* * *

A Childhood of Smells

Those of us who practise daily journalism need to be able to write to a deadline. You either master that skill or you find another way of making a living, and I can make the proud boast that I have never missed a deadline. Very impressive, you might say, given how long I've been practising this trade and how many deadlines I have faced. You might be rather less impressed if I reproduced here some of the rubbish I have written over the years as the clock ticks down – but that's another matter altogether. The rule is: never mind the quality … get it done and get it done NOW!

I've lost track of the number of times the 8.10 story on *Today* has suddenly changed and another story has taken its place, meaning that I've had only three or four minutes to write the introduction. In the pre-computer days it meant hammering away at the typewriter in the newsroom, ripping it out of the rollers as the clock ticked down and then running like hell into the studio with it. That, by the way, is always a mistake. I learned the hard way that you might save five seconds if you run to the studio, but when you drop into your seat in front of the microphone you will be unable to speak for the next thirty seconds because you are out of breath. And you will sound very silly.

I like to think I had a pretty rigid routine when I was presenting *Today*. I would skim the newspapers in the back of the car that picked me up at about 3.45 a.m. so that by the time we got to New Broadcasting House I had a rough idea of what was going on in the world. Then I would log on to my computer, heap praise on the overnight editor for the invariably wonderful programme he had put together (or not as the case may be) and would set about writing my introductions – or 'cues' as we call them. Then I had my breakfast sitting at my desk – a bowl of uncooked porridge oats, banana and yoghurt – while I started to think of the questions I'd be asking my interviewees over the next three hours. So by the time I got into the studio, I had lots of questions written down just waiting to be asked.

In my dreams.

Look, I KNOW it made sense to do just that. I KNOW I should have done what most of my colleagues did, which was read the briefs that had been so painstakingly prepared by the producers the day before and had the structure of the interview written down with some questions just in case the brain went blank at a crucial moment. Something which, I promise you, happened more often than you might think. So why didn't I do it? God knows. I always ended up finding another dozen things to do that seemed infinitely more important at the time but never were.

It meant that at some point in the programme I would realise that I hadn't the first idea what vitally important subject it was that I was meant to be addressing with the rather anxious person who had just been brought into the studio. Every morning I promised myself I would be more disciplined in future and every morning I failed. I tried to justify my idiotic behaviour by telling myself that interviews are better if you have no questions written down. After all, we wanted our audience to feel they are listening to a spontaneous conversation rather than to some automaton reading from a list of prepared questions. But there was a balance to be struck and I invariably erred on the side of telling myself it would be alright on the night – even when there was a tiny warning light flashing in my brain telling me I might be about to make a fool of myself.

I remember one torrid morning when everything that could go wrong did go wrong. The radio car broke down en route to the interviewee. The person who was meant to be operating the studio for the guest in some remote local radio station had a ropy alarm clock that had failed to go off so he never turned up. The politician who was meant to be coming into Broadcasting House had changed his mind at the last minute. The stand-by reports prepared for just such an emergency had all been used. We were on our last tape. About the only things that didn't go wrong were the microphones in the studio, but that wasn't much consolation because at approximately fourteen minutes to nine we had no one left to interview.

And then, just as I was planning to fall off my chair clutching my chest, thus leaving it to the other presenter to deal with the crisis and being able to blame him if he failed, my producer shrieked into my headphones. There were approximately five seconds to go before the report we were broadcasting reached its end – just time enough for him to tell me: 'We've got the leader of the Indian opposition on the line and—'

And that was all he had time to say because then my microphone was live and I was broadcasting to the nation. In theory. Instead I was left to ponder not only what the name of the Indian opposition leader on the other end of the line might be but what might have happened on the subcontinent to cause my colleagues in the newsroom to set him up for a live interview. In short, I had not the faintest idea who he was nor why I was interviewing him. In the milliseconds available I ran through the options short of staging that mock heart attack.

There were only two. I could play for time and say something like: 'Good morning sir and many thanks for joining us. May I say what an honour it is that you have given up your valuable time to join us this morning on such an auspicious day for your great country …'

A fairly uncharacteristic approach to a politician on *Today* I grant you, but the strength of it was that if I said it sufficiently slowly it would give my producer a vital few seconds during which he might just possibly be able to tell me why the hell I was talking to whatever-his-name-was. The weakness of the plan was that maybe nothing auspicious had happened and the mystery guest in New Delhi would decide he was dealing with a raving lunatic in London and hang up.

So I went for the opposite approach, gambled that we tend to interview foreign opposition leaders only when they are out to make trouble for their country's government, and tried this:

'Many thanks for joining us … it seems the government is facing a pretty serious crisis eh …?'

And then I prayed. If there was no crisis I was toast. It was a fifty-fifty gamble and luck was with me.

'Yes indeed …' he began. And that was enough. The opposition politician who ducks the chance of taking a swipe at his government has yet to be born and he was away. The rest of the interview was child's play.

That sort of thing happens all the time on *Today*. Scarcely a day goes by without a presenter having to go off-piste for one reason or another. It comes with the territory and, obviously, any live radio presenter who can't think on their feet would be much better getting a rather less stressful job. Rudyard Kipling wrote a pretty good job spec for *Today* in the first verse of his poem 'If':

> If you can keep your head when all about you
> Are losing theirs and blaming it on you;
> If you can trust yourself when all men doubt you,
> But make allowance for their doubting too;
> If you can wait and not be tired by waiting,
> Or being lied about, don't deal in lies,
> Or being hated, don't give way to hating …

I especially like the line about not dealing in lies – can't imagine why it puts me in mind of certain politicians – but I'm not so sure about 'being hated' and 'giving way to hating'. It raises the tricky question of how much presenters should worry about the way they are perceived by the listener and takes me back to my search for a 'radio personality'. Presumably if you are a so-called 'shock jock' anchorman of the sort they seem to specialise in on the other side of the Atlantic, being hated by a large chunk of your audience is an essential qualification. Perhaps not so much for a *Today* presenter. But is the opposite true in the more civilised world of Radio 4? Is it important to be liked by the listener? I've never been quite sure about that. I like to think that so long as you're doing your job reasonably competently you will be tolerated. Well … up to a point. Sometimes you get just a tiny hint that not everyone loves you. I got more than a hint from the broadcasting critic on the *Observer* one Sunday morning. He wrote that if he ever found himself sitting next to me at a dinner party he would probably drive a fork through my hand.

So I turned to some fan mail to cheer myself up and there was this:

Dear John,
Some people ask me what I live for. Well I tell them that I live for the day when Mother Nature finally takes the old codger that you are out and releases the rest of us of suffering your miserable existence. For the sake of humanity, may you rest in peace, and the sooner the better. When you are finally dead heaven will descend on earth and disease, starvation, inequality and suffering will all be things of the past and there will be much merriment and rejoicing in every corner of the globe.
    Thank you

It's the polite 'Thank you' at the end of that letter that I cling on to. And I suppose it's nice that someone out there thinks I have it in my power to make the world a better place – albeit by dying.

The overriding priority of BBC news is to deliver information and try to analyse what it means – but there's no point in doing a brilliant interview if nobody is listening. Getting the balance right is never easy compared with, say, a Radio 2 show where entertainment is what matters. Someone like Terry Wogan knew exactly what buttons to press. He presented himself as a loveable old Irishman with an endless supply of easy-going charm. His gentle, self-deprecating sense of humour hid a quick wit and a sharp mind but what mattered above all else was that the audience liked him. His vast army of TOGs ('Terry's Old Geezers or Gals') were invited to believe that he was just like them really: just one big happy family. The genius of his radio persona was that the audience could imagine sharing a glass of Guinness with him, enjoying a chat and probably agreeing about pretty much everything. In truth Terry was a complicated man tortured by the same demons that afflict most of us, but that's not what the adoring listeners heard.

Of course *Today* presenters want to be liked – don't we all? – but life is not like that. And certainly not in the world of journalism. One small test of my own humanity (if not necessarily likeability) came on a morning when I was scheduled to interview a senior political figure about the war in Iraq. She was in our radio car rather than in the studio so I'd had no chance of a quick chat in the green room before the interview. If I had, we'd have aborted it there and then. Within roughly thirty seconds of going live I realised she was drunk. It was 7.20 in the morning. The listeners might have thought she sounded a bit slurred but would probably have assumed she'd just got out of bed or was maybe a bit hungover. I knew her well enough to know the truth and that she was capable of saying anything. I pretended there was a problem with the radio-car connection and ended the interview very quickly.

Was that the right thing to do? Certainly not if I were being strictly faithful to the (unwritten) journalists' code. I should have exposed her frailty and allowed the audience and her political masters to reach their own judgement. It would have almost certainly finished her career. But I liked her and respected her both as a politician and as a human being. I might have asked myself in those few seconds whether the world of politics would have been better off without her and concluded it would not – but I probably didn't. The fact is, I acted on instinct and I agonise about it still – as I do with another similar interview for slightly different reasons.

This happened at a party conference in the late 1980s. The difference is that it was a pre-recorded interview with a prominent Northern Ireland minister late one evening for use the following morning. Party conferences don't have too much in common with Methodist temperance meetings. There are many parties and receptions and a great deal of drink is taken. The minister had taken too much. Far too much. He or his advisers should have refused to do the interview but they didn't.

What he said was pretty incendiary and would almost certainly have had a seriously damaging effect on the peace process, which was going through a tricky time. Should we run it? I talked about it at some length with my editor and in the end we decided not to. Again it was not an easy decision. It might well have made headlines the next day, but what's a headline in the context of a vicious conflict that killed and injured many thousands of people?

All of which makes me appear as a saintly soul whose only wish is to make this world a better place. The reality is that self-interest played a pretty large part in my calculations too. Experience told me that presenters tend to win more brownie points with the listeners if they are not seen to be behaving like total thugs. I'd had a taste of how much the good *Today* listeners disapprove of such behaviour following an interview with John Hume I did in my early years on the programme.

At the time he was the leader of the Social Democratic Party in Northern Ireland, a formidable and brave politician who went on to win the Nobel Peace Prize. And I was rude to him. I interrupted for no good reason, told him he wasn't answering the questions without giving him a chance to do so and generally behaved like a pub bore after one pint too many. Those were the days before emails when the postman arrived with the mail in a sack. The day after the Hume interview there were several sacks dumped in the *Today* office – almost all filled with letters from angry listeners. I survived – only just – and I'd like to think that I learned a lot from that ghastly interview. But that's for others to judge.

* * *

I suggested earlier that I had a problem deciding on my 'radio personality' – assuming it existed outside my own imagination.

What I did not decide on my first morning in the *Today* studio was that I would set out to be the stroppiest Welshman on the airwaves. And, contrary to popular assumptions, I do not set out when I interview someone to have an argument – even if it's with a politician. But I cannot deny that I enjoy arguing. Nor would I deny that I approach people in power – all of them – with a pretty strong dose of scepticism. Whether that is a good thing or a bad thing is for others to judge, but either way it's not my fault. And I have that on pretty good authority. Aristotle is quoted as having said: 'Give me a child until he is seven and I will show you the man.' If he was right it must surely mean that our parents are bound to have a profound influence on us – one way or another.

A few years ago one of our leading universities offered me the chance to become 'Professor' Humphrys: a very tempting prospect for a grammar-school boy whose single academic achievement had been a handful of O levels. I even managed to fail woodwork. My father never quite forgave me for that. I accepted the university's offer immediately but imposed one condition: I would close down the department in my first week. The offer was withdrawn. The department was (what else?) media studies.

Maybe my response had been a bit childish and maybe I'm wrong about the value of a media studies degree. I'm sure that many bright young people have left university with them and gone on to great things. I'm equally sure that they would have succeeded without a media studies degree. I simply do not believe that you can learn to be a journalist. I'm with that late, great reporter Nicholas Tomalin who said the only qualities essential for success as a journalist are rat-like cunning, a plausible manner and a little literary ability. Tomalin wrote in a pre-digital age and he would have been forced to add to that list today the ability to understand and navigate the world of social media. I would add insatiable curiosity, and something else: a good journalist needs, in my book, to be contumacious.

A Childhood of Smells

Not a word, I concede, that one hears every day but it's been around a long time and apparently we have St Benedict to thank for it. He applied it to people who 'stubbornly or wilfully resist authority'. The punishment for it 1,500 years ago was excommunication – which is fair enough I suppose if you are in the business of founding the greatest monastery in history. You can't have monks calling into question the supreme authority of the Catholic Church, can you? Equally, in my rather more humble view, you can't have journalists who do the opposite: who accept supreme authority without questioning it. Or any other kind of authority for that matter. And that is not something you can learn. You are either contumacious or you are not. I am, and I have my father, George, to thank. Or to blame.

He was born into a working-class family in Cardiff in what we would now call a slum but was pretty standard housing for people like them in the early years of the last century: a tiny back-to-back terraced house with an outdoor lavatory and a tin bath in front of the fire. He was, by all accounts, a bright and rather wilful child who loved reading and running. But his disobedience was to cost him his eyesight.

Like most youngsters in those pre-vaccine days he caught measles – a particularly bad dose – and my grandmother was told that on no account was she to let him out of the house. He was to be kept in a bedroom with the curtains drawn. The next day she had to go shopping, leaving him in the house alone with strict orders to stay put. Obviously he didn't. It was a glorious winter's day – bright sunshine after some heavy snowfalls – and there were snowballs to be thrown and snowmen to be built. The temptation was too great for him. The sun reflected off the snow and that, coupled with the poor nutrition common in working-class families at that time, did massive damage to his optic nerve. For the next couple of years he was blind. His education effectively ended when he was twelve.

Gradually his sight began to recover enough for him to get an apprenticeship and he became a French polisher. He got a job with the firm where he'd served his apprenticeship and, confident of a steady income, promptly proposed to my mother. She accepted. The job lasted barely a week. My father took great exception to something the foreman had said to him, punched him on the nose and he was out on his ear. The dole was not an option – he was far too proud to take what he called 'charity' anyway – so he set about building up his own business.

There were always people in the richer parts of Cardiff who wanted a table or a piano polished and, one way and another, he made enough money to keep hearth and home together – with my mother doing the neighbours' hair in the kitchen and me doing a paper round before school and my older brother making deliveries for the local grocer. We also tramped the streets of the posher suburbs sticking little circulars through letter boxes advertising Dad's services. I've never been sure if it was worth the effort but at least it gave me an idea of how the other half lived.

Obviously we didn't get paid for it but there was some compensation. I carried two bags – one for the leaflets and the other for any apples hanging temptingly near the garden walls. It's always puzzled me that my friends and I would not have dreamed of stealing apples from a shop but I think we must have seen scrumping as a victimless crime. And anyway there were always far more apples than the posh people could possibly eat. Or so we reasoned. I also made a modest income from our own neighbours: selling them little bundles of mint door to door which I picked from the backyard where it grew in the ashes thrown out from the coal fires. Twopence for a small bunch: an extra penny for a bigger one. I always sold out. That was where my entrepreneurial career began and ended.

We were told endlessly what was wrong and what was right, and not just by our parents. For those of us who went to Sunday school, the vicar reinforced the message. There was a clear line of authority running through our tight little community, with the vicar and perhaps also the GP at the top. Perhaps it was a small-scale reflection of the wider world, in an age when we deferred to figures in authority, when elites told us what our responsibilities were.

My father had an abiding dislike and distrust of the clergy mostly, I think, because they thought they were a cut above ordinary people like him. That can probably be traced to an experience he had as a young man when he was staying with his aunt at her little cottage in a Somerset village, not long after the First World War. They were about to sit down for lunch when the door burst open and the vicar strode in. Without so much as a by-your-leave or a 'Good morning' he demanded to know why my great-aunt had not been at the morning service. She did a little bob and stammered an apology. She tried to explain that she seldom had visitors and that she'd been preparing lunch for her nephew whom she hadn't seen for a year and who had come from a long way away. She said she would be sure to turn up for evensong. He was having none of it. He did not even glance at my father but barked at his auntie: 'See that you do and don't let it happen again!' Then he turned on his heel and left.

Instinctive deference – unearned deference – is dying if not dead. Its defenders say it has taken respect with it but I doubt that. Over the years I have received countless letters (invariably letters) blaming me and my ilk but I suspect we were reacting to, rather than creating, a change in attitudes to authority. Richard Hoggart, who was one of Britain's most respected cultural critics, thought that attitudes to authority, whether religious or lay, really began to change at the end of the last war – when the soldiers came home and the women, who'd been forced to work in the factories, decided they didn't want to go back to the old ways.

I behaved according to the rules of my community when I was growing up, but I think (perhaps thanks to my father) it instilled in me not just deference to authority but a questioning attitude to it too. I don't like being defined or told what to do, whoever is in charge. I even have a thing about wearing identity tags at work. Once, during the Gulf War, when BBC security was at its tightest, I was rushing to the studio with a few minutes to spare and a man in a peaked cap stopped me at the door.

'You can't go in there,' he told me sternly.

'Why not?'

'Because you're not wearing your ID.'

'But you know who I am and I'm on air in two minutes.'

'Sorry. No ID, no admission.'

'OK,' I said, 'you do the bloody programme.'

Mercifully, he gave in. Yes, I know I was being petulant and he was just doing his job but I thought at the time I was striking a small blow for freedom. Today, I suspect I was just being difficult because I don't like authority.

Mine was a childhood of smells: the horrible smell of the chemical Mam used for perms and the even more horrible (and probably dangerous) fumes from the chemicals Dad used when he had to polish furniture in the kitchen – which was often. One of the tricks of his trade – I was never quite sure why – was to pour methylated spirits onto, say, a tabletop, wait a few seconds and then set fire to it. There'd be a great 'whoosh!' Job done. Remember … this was in the kitchen where my mother cooked and the family ate. Even worse, because it was so noxious, was his use of oxalic acid. The crystals were boiled up in a baked beans tin on the gas stove and the liquid used as a very powerful bleach if he needed to lighten the colour of a particular piece of furniture. The fumes got into the back of your throat. God knows what they did to your lungs. My mother suffered the most and died a relatively early death. The doctor said her lungs 'just gave out'. Unsurprising really.

Dad would have had an easier life had he been a bit less stroppy. He hated 'snobs' – a word that encompassed a vast range of people – and he hated authority in all its manifestations. Almost all. There was one exception. He did a lot of work at Cardiff and Port Talbot docks polishing the officers' quarters on the banana boats and iron-ore carriers. I sometimes worked with him as an (unpaid) labourer and was always surprised to see how he treated the captain. He even called him 'sir'. That was a word I'd never heard him use.

His politics were perfectly balanced. He hated capitalism – specifically those who got rich from it – and inherited wealth. And he hated socialism. When he turned up at a really grand house to do some work he would always ring the bell at the main entrance, and if he was ordered to use the servants' entrance – which happened from time to time – he would tell them to bugger off and walk away. He was, as he unfailingly pointed out, a skilled craftsman. He was absolutely NOT a 'servant'. The fact that he needed the work took second place to his pride.

He had a special place in hell reserved for the bosses of large companies, specifically the ship owners and the banks, who hired him to do a job and did not pay him for at least a couple of months. I decided long ago that when I become prime minister the first law I shall propose will be one that forces all companies to pay their bills within one month – except in the case of one-man firms like my father's in which case it will be one week. Why not?

Dad hated royalty too. He was the only person in our street who did not go to see the Queen when she visited Cardiff soon after her coronation, even though her motorcade passed down a road only a few minutes' walk from our house. 'Why should I?' he'd demand. 'She's just another human being ... she's no better than me.' He was thrown out of his club because of her. It was a busy Friday night and the only spare seat was beneath a portrait of her. 'Buggered if I'm sitting there!' he announced. And that was the end of his club membership. He hated socialism equally. He regarded trade union leaders as dangerous and their members as dupes. The welfare state was an excuse for lazy men to live off hard-working men like him. He made an exception for women who had lost their husbands in the war or were struggling desperately to bring up their children. The Man from the Board, with his large notebook, intrusive questions and prying eyes, was hated by everyone in our street. If you applied for benefits you had to prove your need. One of our neighbours, who'd been widowed and was struggling desperately to bring up her two children, told my mother how he had demanded to know why she had four chairs around her kitchen table when there were only three in her family, her husband having died in the war. The Man from the Board said it would count against her when 'the office' reached a judgement on her case. Obviously my father hated him too.

The curious thing was that Dad never admitted we were poor – even when there was no work and we were really on our uppers. I remember one night – I was probably seven or eight – being woken up by him screaming when he should have been snoring. My brother told me he was having a nervous breakdown – not that he really knew what that meant. I understood much later that he was at breaking point because he didn't know how he was going to put enough food on the table for all of us. I *think* what I understand now is that he regarded himself as a failure and that was more than he could handle.

In fact, we kids never really went hungry. We knew when times were hard because there would be lamb bones boiled for a very long time with potatoes and onions for dinner (meaning lunch) and sugar sandwiches for tea (meaning supper). In better times meals were strictly regimented. I can remember exactly what we had for dinner every day of the week. It almost never varied and it gave me my unshakeable conviction that the cheapest meat is the tastiest.

Scrag-end of lamb neck made the perfect stew, and point end of brisket the perfect roast – so long as you left it in the oven for about six hours. It was at least seventy per cent fat but that was fine because my father preferred fat to lean meat – especially when it was burned to a crisp. I can't imagine it was terribly healthy food, but he made up for it by drinking the water the cabbage had been boiled in. And, yes, it was just as disgusting as it sounds.

A Childhood of Smells

Tea was slightly more flexible, especially in summer when the allotment was producing lots of lettuce and other salad ingredients. Funny how the middle class came to discover the joy of allotments for themselves in later years. Unlike the working class who grew the food because they needed it, the middle class grew it for the pleasure of it. Nothing was wasted in our house. I mean nothing. Stale bread was soaked in water and used to make bread pudding and, on the vanishingly rare occasion when one of us left some food on our plate for dinner it would be served up again for tea. Obviously there was no fridge, but that didn't matter because nothing stayed around for long enough to go rotten. On hot days the milk stood in a saucepan of cold water. It worked.

My father's nervous breakdown did not last long. He was not a man to show emotion of any kind. In the language of the time he 'pulled himself together' – almost as though his breakdown had been a fault in his character. I'm not sure the word 'counselling' existed in those days, possibly because there were so many men who had survived the war but were still suffering from what we would now call post-traumatic stress disorder. We had no language for PTSD then.

My favourite uncle, Tom, had fought in the Great War and was still suffering horribly. He had been gassed in the trenches, shipped back to Britain and put to work in the docks. Unbelievably, given the state of his lungs, his job was offloading coal. The coal dust completed the job that the gas had begun. His lungs were wrecked. He was never again able to lie down to sleep because his lungs would fill with fluid. His life had been hellish enough anyway.

He and Auntie Lizzie had one child, Tommy – or 'Little Tommy' as everyone called him even though he was a very large man. His brain and his face had been terribly damaged at birth and he had the mental age of a toddler and no speech. In fact, he had nothing – except an unlimited supply of love from his utterly wonderful parents. Whenever I went to his house Little Tommy would bring out the photograph albums and point gleefully at every picture of me and my siblings and parents and look terribly proud of himself for having made the connection. Then he would laugh uproariously.

Uncle Tommy and Auntie Lizzie had a hard life by even the harshest of standards. Desperate would be a better word. Their one constant worry was what would happen to Little Tommy 'when we are gone'. But I never once heard them complain. Yes, I know that's one of the oldest clichés in the book but so what? It happens to be true. Whether their lives might have been improved if they had complained we shall never know.

My father's proudest possession was a medallion he won representing Glamorgan on the running track. He carried it with him in his jacket pocket everywhere. He was a first-class sprinter but two things held him back: his eyesight and his poverty. It's not easy to race if you can't see the man in front of you clearly. A friend of his told me how Dad once ran off the course and into a barbed-wire fence alongside the track. He kept going. He always did. But poverty proved to be a bigger problem. He had been selected to run for his athletics club in a meet some fifty miles from Cardiff. He had no money and so the club paid his bus fare for him. But those were the days when athletics was a strictly amateur sport and when the Amateur Athletics Association got to hear about his subsidised bus fare he was banned. Like Uncle Tom he did not complain. Unlike Uncle Tom he got angry.

I am sometimes told how remarkable it is that I made such a success of my career in spite of my poor background and having to leave school at fifteen. But of course that's nonsense. I succeeded not in spite of it but because of it. And anyway I had some huge advantages. My mother was one of them. She left school at fourteen without a single qualification and had never, as far as I could tell, read a book in her life. Not that there was much time for reading with five children and no little luxuries such as a vacuum cleaner or washing machine or fridge. The only time I remember her sitting down was when there was darning to be done. Mostly socks as I recall.

She seldom expressed opinions – certainly never political ones. But she was utterly, single-mindedly determined that her children should have the education that was denied to her and my father. That meant that, unlike the other kids in our street, we were forced to do homework. It also meant that when the *Encyclopaedia Britannica* salesman came knocking on our door Mam made my father buy a set.

It cost a shilling a week and the salesman called every Saturday morning to collect the payment. It was the only thing my parents ever bought on the never-never. She told us one evening that the woman who lived opposite had paid for a holiday on the never-never. She could not have been more shocked if the neighbour had sold her children to the gypsies who came to the door every few weeks selling clothes pegs.

So precious were the encyclopaedias that my father built a bookcase especially to protect them. It had glass doors so the neighbours could admire them. Sadly, the doors had a lock and he was the key holder so when he was out – which was most of the time – we kids couldn't use them. That might have seemed rather to defeat the reason for buying them, but even if we had never opened them they sent out an important message. Knowledge was important. It was empowering. My parents wanted their children to have something they could not have dreamed of in their own childhoods: access to everything they wanted to know beyond the grinding poverty of their own lives. Hence the homework.

There were two rooms downstairs in our house: the kitchen with a coal fire in it where we cooked and ate and washed (dishes and selves) and a tiny front room where no one was allowed except at Christmas and for homework. At least a couple of hours a night. That was when the encyclopaedias came out of the bookcase.

My parents were utterly determined that we would pass the eleven-plus and go to high school – we didn't use the term 'grammar school' then – but beyond that, I don't think they had any real ambitions for us. There was just the unswerving certainty that if we went to high school we would have a very different life from theirs. And we did pass – all of us. My younger brother Rob and I went to Cardiff High, which was regarded as the best school in Cardiff, if not in Wales. I hated it from the day I joined until the day I left.

The headmaster was a snob and I was clearly not the sort of boy he wanted at Cardiff High – far too working class for his refined tastes. I remember being beaten by him because I was late one morning. I tried explaining to him that it was because I had a morning newspaper round and the papers had not been delivered to the shop as early as usual because it was snowing heavily, which also made it difficult to get around on my bike. I tried to suggest I could not let down the shop's customers and we needed the money from my job, but he was not impressed. The pain from the beating did not last long, but the anger never faded. Some years later, when I had started appearing on television and was considered something of a celebrity, I had a letter from the school. Would I accept the great honour of making a speech at the annual prize-giving? I replied immediately. Yes of course, I wrote, and then I added a few lines about what I proposed saying. The invitation was swiftly withdrawn.

By then the various chips on my shoulder had been firmly welded into place. Growing up in the immediate post-war years in Splott (an ugly name for a pretty ugly neighbourhood) I'm not sure children like me were really aware of being poor. We knew there were rich people, of course, but we simply did not come into contact with them. The man who owned the timber yard a couple of doors up from my house had a car, and that put him in a totally different class way beyond our own imaginings. It wasn't, I think, until some of the neighbours got television sets and we were able to see inside the houses of middle-class people like the Grove Family (the first TV soap opera in Britain) that we realised the gulf between them and us.

A Childhood of Smells

I remember clearly the first time I was invited for tea in a middle-class home and how surprised I was that the milk came out of a jug rather than a bottle and the jam was in little cut-glass bowls. There was even a bowl of fruit on the table for anybody to help themselves. An old friend of mine, the brilliant comedian Ted Robbins, always says you could tell someone was really rich if they had fruit in the house even when no one was ill … and if they got out of the bath to have a wee.

Envy was one thing. Anger was something else again. Anger not because they were richer than us but because of the sense that some looked down at us for being poor. People like my old headmaster, and the hospital consultant I was sent to see when I was thirteen because I had developed a nasty cyst at the base of my spine. I was lying naked face down on a bed when the great man arrived, surrounded by a posse of young trainee doctors. He took a quick look at my cyst, ignoring me completely, and told his adoring acolytes: 'The trouble with this boy is that he doesn't bathe regularly.' Mortified, I lay there, cringing with shame and embarrassment and hating the arrogant posh bastard and all those smug rich kids surrounding him who were sniggering at the great man's disgraceful behaviour.

The resentment had been building for a long time. I was barely six years old when it began. It was a Friday lunchtime (dinner time) and although it was seventy years ago I remember it in terrible detail. I had been sent out to the local fish and chip shop to buy dinner. This was a huge treat – the closest we ever got to eating out. All the more special because it happened so rarely and only ever on Fridays. I got back to the house, clutching the hot, soggy mass wrapped in newspaper, vinegar dripping through, the smell an exquisite torture of anticipation. When I stepped into the kitchen my small world had changed for ever.

Dr Rees, our local GP, was there. This in itself was an extraordinary event. He visited very rarely – only when one of us was literally incapable of walking to his surgery – was always handed a glass of whisky by my father who kept a half-bottle in the cupboard for just this purpose, and never stayed more than a few minutes. This time he looked different and so did my parents. They were white and visibly trembling. The tears came later for my mother. I never saw my father cry. The doctor had just told them that Christine, my baby sister and the apple of my mother's eye, was dead. She had been admitted to hospital the day before, suffering from gastroenteritis.

That is not a disease that kills people – not even in those more clinically primitive days – and for as long as he lived my father believed she died because we were poor. How can I make a judgement on that? All I know, because he told me years later, was that he and my mother had not been allowed to visit their dying child in hospital and, had they been middle class, things would have been different. She had been put in the 'wrong' ward and nobody spotted how ill she was. My mother would have spotted it had she been allowed to.

She never recovered from it. She had been blessed with a head of magnificent raven hair. It went white almost overnight. She had been strong and confident and healthy. She lost all that when Christine died. Eventually, of course, she came to terms with the loss. People do, don't they? But she was never the same woman, and my father's resentment and anger towards what he saw as the ruling class grew even stronger.

Their one consolation was their surviving children – especially my younger brother Rob, who was born five years after Christine died and took her place in my mother's affection if not in her memory. As for me, I found another reason to rail against the establishment some years later.

My career had prospered and I was living overseas. On one of my weekly calls home my father told me he was desperately worried because he had been summoned to an interview with the tax man. It was a serious matter. He had been accused of fiddling his taxes. I knew this to be total nonsense. My parents were as honest as it is possible for two people to be. And anyway, my father earned so little from his one-man business he scarcely paid any taxes. That, it turned out, was the problem. My mother was summoned with him because she kept his accounts – such as they were. She told me some years later what happened.

She and Dad had been made to sit on two hard chairs in the inspector's office and he sat behind his desk. He handed Mam a copy of her accounts and told Dad to swear they were accurate and that they would be in very big trouble if they were not. Dad said they were. Then the inspector said:

'The accounts show you have earned very little money indeed. If that is so, would you explain how it is that you and your wife were able to take very long holidays not only to the United States of America but also to South Africa? And don't try to deny it. We have checked out the information handed to us and it is accurate in every detail.' Presumably some jealous neighbour had snitched.

Dad told me what happened next:

'Your mother leaped to her feet and she looked that man straight in the eyes and said: "My son lived in America and he lives in South Africa now and he sent us the tickets and paid for both holidays. My son is the correspondent for the BBC. And if you don't believe me you can watch him on television!"'

I talked to Mam about it in her closing years. She told me it had been one of the proudest moments of her life.

You can add that tax inspector to my blacklist of authority figures. It is a long one and, I fear, still growing.

2

The teenAGE pAGE

I was seven when I knew that I wanted to be a reporter. I'd like to claim I was inspired by grandiose visions of speaking truth to power and enthralling my millions of readers with eyewitness accounts of the great events that would determine the future of humanity. The reality was rather more prosaic and a lot more embarrassing.

In post-war Britain poor families like mine did not squander what little spare cash they had on buying books and there was no television, and so much of my spare time was spent reading comics – mostly *Superman*. Vast bundles of second-hand comics were sent to this country from the United States as ballast in cargo ships. They ended up being sold for a penny or two in local newsagents and then getting swapped between one scruffy kid and another. Superman, as all aficionados will know, took as his human alter ego a chap called Clark Kent and Clark Kent was a reporter. Ergo: reporters were akin to Superman. I would break free from my grim existence in the back streets of Cardiff and save the world into the bargain by becoming Superman. And Lois Lane – adored by everyone who read the comics – would be my girlfriend.

You might say that for a very small boy that logic was perfectly understandable. Not so much for a grown adult maybe. But no matter, when I left school at fifteen I had only one ambition and that was to get a job on a local paper. There wasn't much alternative. The monster of media studies had yet to be created.

No, you learned on the job – if you were lucky enough to get one. I got mine by lying, or, as we journalists prefer to describe it, through a little creative embellishment of the facts. My years in school had been, to put it kindly, undistinguished and highly unlikely to impress any prospective boss. But I'd been told that the editor of the *Penarth Times* – a weekly paper in a small seaside town a few miles outside Cardiff – was more impressed by athletes than brainboxes. So I allowed him to believe that I had often been first across the finishing line when Cardiff High School staged its cross-country races. It was technically true – but only because I was so hopeless at running that I was never selected to compete and instead chose to cycle alongside the real athletes shouting encouragement (or abuse). My deception worked.

'Just what reporters need,' huffed the editor, 'plenty of stamina and determination!' I still feel a twinge of guilt – but only a very small one.

I learned a great deal during my two years on the *Penarth Times*. For a start: how local papers stayed in business. The good people of Penarth were far more likely to buy it if their names were printed in it, so one of my regular jobs was to stand outside the church after a funeral or wedding and take the names of everyone who had attended. That taught me something else. Accuracy. By and large our readers asked little enough of the paper, but if their name was spelled incorrectly my editor would hear of it. They would demand an apology and a correction the following week. He would not be pleased.

Another skill I developed was how to stay awake in the local library, which was where I spent very large chunks of my time leafing through past issues of the paper in the hope that I might find something interesting enough to fill the 'Penarth 50 Years Ago' column. There almost never was anything interesting, so I filled it with boring stuff instead. Nobody seemed to mind – I suspect for the very good reason that nobody read it.

My biggest contribution to the survival of the *Penarth Times* was on a more practical level. I became an expert in operating a

Flit gun: a hand pump you filled with insecticide and squirted at flies or other nasty insects in the house. It was a lifesaver for the *Penarth Times* when the printers went on strike. The proprietor had refused to shut the paper down. He rampaged around the place declaring that he wasn't going to allow a couple of bolshie inky-fingered troublemakers to deprive the good people of Penarth of their democratic right to be informed about the local council's latest pronouncements or who was the latest miscreant to be fined five shillings for urinating against a wall in the town centre after a pint too many. So the paper would be printed without them.

Sterling stuff, but not without one or two difficulties. It didn't help that none of us had the first idea how to operate a printing press, even something as modest as the one owned by the *Penarth Times*. It wasn't exactly one of those thundering behemoths I was to encounter on daily papers years later – the sort that made the whole building shudder when they roared into life – but still way beyond our ability, as was the typesetting. So instead we used just typewriters and stencils and an ancient duplicating machine. The problem was that the paper had a habit of sticking to the roller. My job was to stand beside the machine with a Flit gun filled with water, and give it a quick squirt when it happened. It worked a treat – even if it did end up looking like an extremely amateurish version of a parish magazine. Mercifully the strike didn't last long: the printers had made their point and good relations were restored.

Sadly, the strike had done nothing to dampen our boss's enthusiasm for establishing a publishing empire – albeit a modest one. Penarth's population was tiny compared with Cardiff's. It had a morning and evening paper (the *Western Mail* and *South Wales Echo*) but no weekly, so the boss decided we should fill the gap with a new weekly newspaper called the *Cardiff & District News*. It was a brilliant idea – or might have been except that we had no budget.

One feature of the paper was a double-page spread headlined, in huge type, 'the teenAGE pAGE'. It was my job to edit it and, because there was no money for reporters, to do all the reporting as well. I did not complain – mostly because my editor would not have listened but also because I used my fancy title (I called myself Showbiz Editor) to blag free tickets for all the big concerts in Cardiff. Since it was the capital city of Wales it attracted lots of big stars and I usually managed to persuade the promoters to fix an interview for me with them. I won't pretend they were memorable interviews, but when you're sixteen and discovering (or hoping to discover) what sex was all about, that wasn't really the point.

A casual 'Fancy meeting Cliff Richard next week … or Billy Fury or the Everly Brothers?' would surely work miracles with girls who had been way out of my league even before I was struck down by late-onset chickenpox and spottier than a Dalmatian. The theory was sound – I'd be able to bask in reflected glory – but I failed to spot the obvious flaw. The girls did indeed fall in love – but not with me.

My greatest professional triumph was to set up an interview with the one star who put all the others in the shade. She was Ella Fitzgerald, easily the greatest singer of her generation. It was also my greatest disaster. The interview was scheduled to happen in her dressing room before she went on stage with another musical giant, Count Basie, and his orchestra. When I arrived at the theatre I was not so much paralysed with nerves as the exact opposite. I was hyperactive, bouncing from one foot to the other, waving my arms and speaking much too loudly. And when I was finally ushered into the presence I was overwhelmed: hopelessly star-struck.

There she stood, magnificent in her glittering stage gown, and utterly terrifying. She was a living legend at the height of her powers and I was an awkward teenager in total awe of her – so awkward that as I advanced towards her my elbow caught the corner of a mirror, which fell from the table and smashed to pieces. Smashing a mirror was said to be bad luck at the best of time. Smashing a mirror in the dressing room of a star minutes before she was about to go on stage put it in another category altogether.

She glanced across at me. 'Get that fucking kid outta here!' she snarled. And they did. Within a second I was surrounded by her heavies. My feet literally did not touch the ground. They took my elbows, lifted me about a foot off the floor and deposited me outside the dressing room with the big star on the door. So ended my career as a showbiz reporter.

Many years later when I was working in New York for the BBC I (almost) met my other musical hero: Duke Ellington. He was performing for a small, invited audience in the Rainbow Room at the top of the Rockefeller Center in Manhattan and I wangled an invitation. I was determined to shake the great man's hand and be able to claim in years to come that we'd been old mates, so when he left in the interval I followed. He was headed for the gents' toilet. I stood at the urinal next to him and tried to strike up a conversation. And I froze. I suppose I can boast that I peed alongside the greatest jazz musician of all time but the truth is I was so intimidated by his presence I couldn't even manage that.

As for my career on the *Cardiff & District News*, it did not last long. Apart from writing most of the paper (stealing stories from the *Echo* and *Mail*) I also had to deliver it. Physically deliver it, that is, to the few newsagents in Cardiff who had agreed to stock it on the strict condition that if it didn't sell they got their money back. I was too young to drive, so the publisher hired the services of a nice old lady who owned a pre-war Ford Prefect. She and I would pile the newly printed papers on the back seat and sail off to Cardiff. The following week we would repeat the journey, each time collecting the unsold papers and dumping them in the boot. Logic dictates it is impossible, but I have always believed that we took back more newspapers than we had delivered the previous week. The *Cardiff & District News* did not live to see the year out. I don't think anyone noticed.

I had hit seventeen when that happened and decided it was time to leave to work on my next newspaper, the *Merthyr Express*.

It was also a weekly, but there the similarity ended. Penarth was prosperous and so prim and proper in those days that it may even be true that it was the inspiration for the old gag about its residents believing that 'sex is what coal comes in'. Merthyr was a tough industrial town with a glorious past and not much of a future. It went from being the most prosperous town in Wales to the poorest. There was still coal mining in the South Wales valleys but towns like Merthyr were living on their histories. And what a history.

At the peak of the Industrial Revolution, the Welsh valleys were producing vast amounts of coal and iron. Merthyr had four great ironworks (one of them was said to be the most productive in the world) and – maybe Merthyr's proudest boast – the first railway. The locomotive was designed by the Cornish engineer Richard Trevithick – Stephenson's *Rocket* came later – and it managed to haul twenty-five tons of iron and a few passengers too.

So there was plenty of money being made, but not much of it found its way to the wretched souls slaving for a pittance in the ironworks and the pits as they created the wealth for the mighty ironmasters and pit owners to enjoy. The great Victorian essayist Thomas Carlyle wrote of 'those poor creatures broiling, all in sweat and dirt, amid their furnaces, pits and rolling mills'.

The area where most of them lived became known as 'Little Hell' – and for good reason. If their jobs didn't kill them there was a pretty good chance they and their families would be seen off by the cholera and typhoid which thrived in the open sewers. Flushing toilets were a stranger to Little Hell. A century after Carlyle, when I was reporting for the *Merthyr Express*, I had my own tiny taste of what the miners he had written about all those years ago had to endure. To this day I marvel that any of them managed to survive.

To drop in a cage to the bottom of a deep mine is not an experience for the faint-hearted. The speed of the descent through total darkness is terrifying, made worse by the grit that flies through the air, stinging your face. And when you get to the bottom all you can think about is how quickly you can get to the surface again. The idea that these men could spend a third of their lives down there was simply incomprehensible to me – as was the massive physical effort it had taken to create this and every other deep mine in the valleys.

I suppose I had imagined in my childish ignorance that once a mine had been sunk the miners immediately found the coal waiting for them to hack away and get it hauled to the surface. But first, of course, they had to dig out the thousands of tons of rock and waste to form the tunnels that gave them access to the black stuff. I looked up at the roof of the tunnel we were walking through to get to the coalface. All that stood between us and instant death were the ceiling props these men had put in place. If they got it wrong they died. And, of course, vast numbers did die: some from roof falls, many more from the deadly gases that could seep into the tunnels and reach the coalface.

Carbon monoxide was one of the big killers until, in 1913, someone had the brilliant idea of taking canaries down the mine. If the canary keeled over, the miners knew they had to get to the surface fast. Canaries were still being used until only a few years before I first went down a mine in 1961. An even bigger killer was methane.

An old miner told me what it was like to be working at the coalface and hear a loud bang. It happened to him once and, mercifully, turned out to be a relatively minor incident – a few injuries but no one killed. Even so, I struggled to imagine the sheer terror as he and the men with him raced back through the tunnel, not knowing whether the blast had brought down the roof ahead of them so they would be trapped. Perhaps rescuers would break through the fallen rock to save them. Perhaps they wouldn't and they would die, as so many miners had, when their oxygen ran out or the attempt to rescue them brought more rocks crashing down and crushing them. Fatal accidents were commonplace.

Every miner in the Welsh valleys had his own story to tell of disasters that nearly happened – and those that did. The worst – only a few miles from Merthyr – killed more men and boys than any other mining disaster in the history of British mining. It was in 1913. Nearly 950 men were working at the Senghenydd colliery when a massive explosion ripped it apart and 439 were killed either by the blast itself or the poisonous gas that had created it.

Like most reporters working in the valleys in the days when almost every village had its colliery and every colliery had its share of tragedies, I was occasionally ordered by the editor to knock on the door of a grieving widow. I dreaded it. How could such an intrusion be justified at such a time? But never once was I sent away. Invariably I was invited in, given a cup of tea and shown photographs of the dead miner while the widow talked about what a wonderful man he had been. I seldom saw a tear shed – and I have always wondered why. Perhaps it was because women who married miners lived with fear from day one. They were prepared for the worst to happen. They knew, too, that even if their husband survived, his retirement would be a short one. The biggest killer of all was not the gas: it was the dust.

The first time I went for a drink in a miners' club I noticed that many of the miners coming in after their shift would have a pint of water plonked in front of them by the barman. I asked him why. His answer was obvious when you think of it: 'Waste of money buying a pint when your throat's full of dust isn't it? Makes sense to wash the dust away so you can taste the beer.' If it was doing that to your throat, I thought, what the hell was it doing to your lungs? The answer: pneumoconiosis or silicosis or any of the other hideous illnesses caused by a life spent underground breathing in the deadly dust.

Many years after I had left the valleys behind me I reported on the 1984–5 miners' strikes that brought the coalfields to a halt in a doomed attempt to save them from the cost-cutters and the hated Margaret Thatcher. I talked to many angry miners. But it was rare to meet a miner's wife who mourned the death of the industry. In all my years in South Wales I never spoke to a mother who wanted her sons to follow their father down the pit.

I was to see for myself the ultimate, unthinkable, price of coal: a disaster in so many ways worse than all the others because its victims, crushed or suffocated to death, had not chosen to face the dangers of deep mining. But that was a few years after I had left the *Merthyr Express* to return to Cardiff and take another step up the journalistic greasy pole.

I had been offered a job as a reporter on a national daily no less – though not exactly the giddy heights of Fleet Street. It was the *Western Mail*, the national daily of Wales. I'd like to report that pretty soon my name was up in lights, or at least writ large on the front page. Sadly it never was. Not once. My great mistake had been to bear the same surname as the news editor of the paper, though he spelled his with an 'e' which I affected to think rather vulgar. Mine, I claimed, was pure Welsh, which was complete nonsense. The truth was that an incompetent registrar had misspelled my surname on my birth certificate so my parents and older siblings were 'Humphreys' and I was 'Humphrys'. I pointed out to my news editor – a rather unpleasant bully with one of the most prominent beetled brows I had ever seen – that the different spelling would remove any confusion in the reader's mind, but he was having none of it. He ordered me to adopt a different name for byline purposes. I chose Desmond and so I became 'John Desmond' for *Mail* readers. (I had been christened 'Desmond John Humphrys' but contracted very severe hooping cough when I was little and was such a miserable child my mother decreed I should henceforth be known as John. She was not, she announced, going to have people calling me 'Dismal Desmond'.)

In spite of my new name, my brief time on the *Mail* was not particularly distinguished. But I suppose I must have done enough to impress someone because, my editor told me after I'd been working there for a year or so, I had come to the attention of 'London'. He seemed almost as surprised as me. For a young provincial hack, 'London' was not just beyond my wildest dreams. It had not even figured in them. Until now.

The *Western Mail* and many other papers, including the mighty *Times* and *Sunday Times*, were owned by the Thomson newspaper group. My editor told me the *Sunday Times*, no less, was thinking of giving me a job and I was to go to London to meet both its managing editor and news editor over lunch. I was terrified – and totally intimidated. I'd been to London only twice in my life and I had never eaten in a restaurant anywhere near as grand as Simpson's in the Strand, which was where they took me. Nor had I met such imposing journalists before.

My own recollection of the lunch was more of trying to remember which knife and fork to use and agreeing with everything my hosts said rather than making a serious attempt to impress them with my journalistic brilliance. I had no doubt they would send me on my way with a pat on the head and a patronising 'perhaps you're not quite ready for the big time just yet' and, had they done so, I suspect I'd have agreed and felt rather relieved. But they didn't. They offered me the job of reporter on the paper's brand-new Insight section. This really was the cutting edge of national investigative journalism. Insight, which exists to this day, was to become one of the most respected institutions on one of the most respected newspapers in the world. On the train back to Cardiff I wondered when I would wake up from this ridiculous dream.

The next day I told the *Sunday Times* I didn't want the job.

Like so many things in life it happened because of a chance encounter. When I got back to Cardiff from London I'd gone to meet a few reporter friends for a drink in our favourite pub to do some serious boasting. One of them, Norman Rees, had left newspapers to work for the new commercial television station TWW. He out-boasted me. Newspapers, he told me, were old hat. Television was where it was at. He made it sound amazingly glamorous and exciting. I'd be famous – plastered all over everyone's TV screens, the prettiest girls in Cardiff throwing themselves at my feet wherever I went! Why didn't I join him? He promised he could persuade his editor to give me an interview if I was up for it. I was and he did and I got the job.

The *Sunday Times* were furious. They told me I had wasted their time (not to mention a fat bill at Simpson's) and my name was on their blacklist. If I ever so much as dreamed of working for Times Newspapers again I could forget it – which made it all the more gratifying when, thirty years later, I was invited to write the main comment column for the *Sunday Times* and did so for five years.

It's fair to say that Norman had rather overplayed the glamour and excitement bit. TWW was among the first companies to get a commercial television licence. It broadcast to South Wales and the West Country – a ridiculous cultural mix given that the two regions had virtually nothing in common apart from the Bristol Channel – and it was also among the first to lose its licence. That did not come as a great surprise. Most of us thought its owners were far more concerned with selling exciting new adverts. showing perfectly made-up housewives, with just a few stray blonde hairs escaping from their Alice bands, glowing with pride as they told us how happy they had made their hard-working husbands by discovering how to make the perfect gravy. Not to mention the sheer joy of washing dishes, knowing that it would make their hands just as soft as their face – which would make those hard-working husbands even more proud of them. Ah … the glory days of television advertising.

It might have been sexist garbage, but the profits poured in. Charging a fortune to broadcast commercials was so much easier than trying to produce insightful television programmes. The Canadian publishing tycoon Lord Thomson, who owned TWW and half of Fleet Street, famously called it a 'licence to print money' and so cross was he when they lost their licence that they abandoned the station months before they were supposed to. I suspect few tears were shed by the viewers.

My own contribution to TWW was limited but it taught me a lot – such as not getting drunk at lunchtime on Christmas Eve if you were live on telly that night. I did – and when I leaned in closer to try to read the autocue I fell off my chair. No one in the studio or the newsroom seemed to care very much – possibly because they were all as drunk as me. I also learned that nothing in the whole world is more scary than drying up on live television. I did it twice. It's the most extraordinary sensation – as though you are floating just below the studio ceiling looking down on a young man whose body, tongue and brain have become totally paralysed.

The first time it happened I was trying to interview the most famous broadcaster in the land, the ultimate smooth-talking Irishman Eamonn Andrews, and the second time I was interviewing the finest rugby player Wales has ever produced, Bleddyn Williams. Bleddyn rescued me but Eamonn just smiled and waited for consciousness to return to me, which it did after an hour. Or maybe it was only five seconds. Either way, the scars remain.

One memorable (for me) story was the disappearance of a middle-aged man who had vanished from his home in Cardiff without trace for no apparent reason. An everyday event, perhaps, but this was local telly and 'man disappears' was news. So I was sent off to interview his wife. She was a nurse – clearly in great distress – and she greeted me warmly, sat me down with a cup of tea and talked at length about her fears for what might have happened to her beloved husband. She shed a quiet tear and my heart bled for her. Some months later he turned up. The police found him underneath the patio on which I had been sitting taking tea with the loving wife who buried him there after she had murdered him.

By now I had been a journalist for the best part of ten years. I was to practise the trade for another fifty years, travelling the world, reporting on many of the great events that would come to define the century. I would, in the words of the old cliché, have the great privilege of occupying a ringside seat at history. I would watch an American president forced to resign in disgrace. I would report on earthquakes and famines and wars around the globe. But nothing would compare with what happened just a few miles from where I was born, on 21 October 1966. I was still a young man who had barely set foot outside South Wales. I watched a community deal with a tragedy I still struggle to comprehend. It left me with memories that will never fade, an immense respect for the strength of human beings faced with horror beyond comprehension and a lifelong distrust of authority.

On that terrible morning I had turned up as usual just after nine in the TWW newsroom, and I wandered over to the Telex machine that was always clattering away spewing out endless, useless information. One relatively small story had caught my news editor's eye. It reported that there had been a tip slide at Aberfan in the Merthyr Valley.

There was nothing particularly unusual in that. It often happened. The waste tips above the old collieries were notoriously unstable and shamefully neglected. They were slipping and sliding all over the valleys. Sometimes a slide would take the occasional miners' cottage with it, but mostly they just made a mess of the road and the land beneath. This time it seemed it might be a little more serious than that.

I knew Aberfan well from my years on the *Merthyr Express*. My closest friend on the paper lived there and I often stayed with him after we had drunk too much beer in his local. So I knew that there was a primary school below the tip and at that time in the morning it would have been full of children. But there was nothing in the PA report to suggest that it had been affected or that this was anything more than the usual minor slippage. Even so, nothing else of any news value was going on in South Wales that morning, so I suggested I might as well drive up the valley to take a look. It was only twenty-five miles away from Cardiff and if I thought the story was big enough to merit sending a film crew I could always phone in and ask for one.

As soon as I'd started driving up the valley I began to get the sense that something truly awful had happened. The steep sides of the Welsh valleys are lined with cottages, little terraced homes of drab grey squatting defensively against the hillside. You could tell which were the miners' cottages – almost all of them at that time – because it was the day of the week when they had their small piles of coal dumped outside. Cheap coal was one of the few perks of being a miner. Normally the women would have been busy shovelling it up and carrying it through their tiny terraced houses to dump in the small coal sheds at the back. This morning they were standing at their doors looking worried, peering up the valley in the direction in which I was driving. They knew something bad had happened and so, by now, did I. None of us could begin to imagine how bad. Here is how I described, all those years ago, what had happened:

Just after 9.15 a group of workmen had been sent to the top of the big tip that loomed above Aberfan, grey, black and ugly. There had been some worrying signs that it was sinking more than usual. A deep depression had formed within the tip like the crater in a volcano. As the men watched, the waste rose into the depression, formed itself into a lethal tidal wave of slurry and rolled down the hillside, gathering speed and height until it was thirty feet high and destroying everything in its path. From that moment the name of Aberfan has been synonymous with tragedy beyond comprehension.

It crushed part of the school and some tiny houses alongside like a ton of concrete dropping on a matchbox. And what that foul mixture of black waste did not flatten it filled – classrooms choked with the stuff until the building was covered and the school became a tomb. The moment the terrible news reached them, hundreds of miners had abandoned the coalface at the colliery which had created that monstrous tip and raced to the surface. And there they were when I arrived, their faces still black – save for the streaks of white from the sweat and the tears as they dug and prayed and wept. Most of them were digging for their own children.

Every so often someone would scream for silence and we would all stand frozen. Was that the cry of a child we had heard coming from deep below us? Sometimes it was and some were saved. I saw a burly policeman, his helmet comically lopsided, carrying a little girl in his arms, her legs dangling down, her shoes missing. She was a skinny little thing, no more than nine years old. Thank God she was alive. The men dug all day and all night and all the next day. They dug until there were no more faint cries, no more hope, but still they kept going. They were digging now for bodies.

I watched through the hours and days that followed as the tiny coffins mounted up in the little chapel. There is nothing so poignant as the sight of a child's coffin. By the end of it there were 116 of them. One hundred and sixteen dead children and twenty-eight adults.

When the miners finally stopped digging they went home to weep, to mourn, to relive the nightmare. To cherish the children who were spared. And later to show their anger at the criminal stupidity and venality of the officials and politicians who had allowed it to happen.

Never was anger more justified. The National Coal Board who ran the mines had – from a mixture of deceit and cowardice and fear of retribution – tried to claim that the tragedy was an act of God. It was not. It was an act of negligence by man. Criminal negligence. The politician responsible for the NCB, Lord Robens, a blustering lying bully of a man, had gone on television to say that the cause of the disaster was the water from a natural spring which had been pouring into the centre of the tip and produced the water bomb that finally exploded with such devastating results. The spring, said Robens, was completely unknown. That was just one of his lies. Not only was it known, its presence was marked on local maps and the older miners knew exactly where it was and what the danger was and they had been saying so for years. They were ignored. Mercifully, they had put their fears in writing and the letters, written by the miners and ignored by the NCB, were eventually produced at the inquiry into the disaster so the truth could be revealed for the world to see.

I was twenty-three when Aberfan happened. I have been back many times over the years and talked to the dwindling handful of bereaved parents and to the few children in the school who survived the disaster. And every time I wonder how they were able to recover from their grief and the nightmare of that terrible morning. But 'recover' is the wrong word. As so many have told me, you don't get over it … you just have to live with it. What is the alternative? To that, there is no answer.

What we owe the people of Aberfan
Today, 20 October 2016

When I drove here from Cardiff fifty years ago, the hills on either side of the valley were scarred with tips. Black and ugly and threatening. Now, as I look back down the valley from this cemetery, they're gone. Bulldozed away or covered with grass and trees. The mining valleys of South Wales are green again. The river that flows beneath me was also black and dead. And now it's clean and children can play and fish in its shallows. And the men of these valleys, unlike their fathers, do not end their day's work with lungs full of coal dust. I never met a miner who said he wanted his son to follow him down the pit. The nations owed miners a debt of gratitude for the wealth they helped create over the centuries. The mines have gone, of course, but our generation owes something different to the people of Aberfan. Respect for the courage and dignity they have shown for fifty years in dealing with unimaginable grief. But more than that. The children in these graves were betrayed by the men in power decades ago who refused to listen to their fathers when they warned them their little school faced a mortal danger. If Aberfan stands for anything today, apart from unbearable grief, it stands as a reminder for every journalist in the land of this: authority must always be challenged.

3

Building a cathedral

I was still in my early twenties when I was offered a job by the BBC. I remember feeling terribly pleased with myself. I was going to be based in Liverpool, the most exciting beat in Britain for a reporter in those days, with the Beatles and the Cavern club at one end of the news scale and dock strikes at the other. I was to work out of Castle Chambers, an office building in the heart of the city where the north-west Representative of the BBC was based. The Representative (I can never think of him without the capital letter) was a dapper little fellow called Reg. But only to his closest friends. To young pond life like me he was Major H. R. V. Jordan (Retd), JP, BA (Hons) and he was a very grand figure indeed.

Reg had an extremely large office with a well-stocked cocktail cabinet and two elegant young secretaries. Not one, you will note, but two. Their duties, it is accurate to say, were less than onerous. Reg graced the office a couple of times a week to sign a few letters, and occasionally drove up the coast to Blackpool for lunch with 'my friend, the mayor of Blackpool' in his large plum-coloured Jaguar and white cotton driving gloves before returning to his home in The Wirral.

Perhaps Reg's relationship with His Honour and one or two other municipal worthies in the north-west was, as he insisted, invaluable to the well-being of the BBC. Whether it repaid the considerable sum forked out by the unwitting licence payer is debatable. And he was not alone. There were many of them here

51

and abroad. Our Representative in the United States, where I was later sent to open a television news bureau, had a far grander suite of offices in New York and an apartment in the UN Plaza with stunning views over the East River that would not have disgraced the residence of a Saudi prince.

They were still building the Anglican cathedral in Liverpool when I arrived, the largest religious building in Britain, and the longest cathedral in the world. One of my first assignments was to make a film about its construction. It was a massive project, started some years before I was born. I interviewed one of the stonemasons who had been working on it all his life. Young as I was, and trying to make my way in the exciting world of journalism, I pitied the poor chap. Rooted to one place, always following the same boring routine. There I was, dashing everywhere, never knowing what I might be doing from one day to the next, master of my own timetable and destiny (news editor permitting). And here was this man, turning up at the same time, day after day, week after week, chipping out more stone blocks to lay on the other stone blocks he'd chipped out the day before and so on ad infinitum.

'Don't you get bored?' I asked him.

'Why should I?'

'Well, all you're doing is laying one stone on another year after year.'

'No, I'm not,' he said. 'I'm building a cathedral. What will you leave behind when you die?'

It was a fair point. Broadcasting disappears into the ether, leaving little trace behind. Those who ply the trade leave no lasting monument. My stonemason was still building his cathedral when I left. By the time it was finished, in 1978, I had become a foreign correspondent.

The wireless in our house had always been tuned to the BBC Home Service and when I was a young teenager I listened to *From Our Own Correspondent* with awe. I tried to imagine being one of those correspondents reporting from around the world

– but only in the way that my younger self had imagined being Superman.

Those were the dark ages for television news. There was no such thing as twenty-four-hour news, no satellite feeds or electronic cameras, and no smartphones. If an earthquake or revolution struck somewhere a long way away television news editors did not, as they do today, have their pick of endless footage filmed by eyewitnesses within seconds of it happening. The first thing they reached for was an airline guide. How quickly could we get a reporter and film crew there and, once there, how quickly could we get their film back to London so that it could be processed, edited and on the next news programme? It might be a day. It might be a week – or more. My first big foreign assignment – and, as it turned out, one of my most dangerous – was in the country now called Bangladesh. In those days it was East Pakistan. It took six months to get my most dramatic footage back to London.

The partition of India in 1947 remains perhaps the darkest stain on the history of the British Empire. For centuries Muslims and Hindus had lived together on the Indian subcontinent relatively peacefully. The creation of Pakistan for the Muslim minority led to a refugee crisis of biblical proportions. Fourteen million people left their homes either to flee violence between Hindus and Muslims or to seek a new home in a new country. At least a million – some estimates are double that figure – died in the violence that broke out. It was, by any historical measure, a shameful betrayal of a great nation and its hopes.

Pakistan was created out of two regions: one in the west and one in the east. East Pakistan was carved out of Bengal, which was part of India. The Bengali people living there refused to accept their status as Pakistanis. They demanded independence. Instead, they were savagely attacked by the West Pakistan military. Vast numbers died. When I arrived there in December 1971 the country was at war with itself.

I had been in the capital Dhaka for only twenty-four hours, and was asleep in my room at the top of the Intercontinental

Hotel when I was woken by what felt like an earthquake. There were thunderous explosions and the hotel seemed to sway. During the night India, which had opposed the creation of East Pakistan, had declared war on Pakistan. Indian warplanes were bombing the city.

I shot off to the airport with my camera crew to film the destruction, naively believing that the attacks had ended at dawn. They had not. We were filming the wreckage of what remained of the East Pakistan air force and the runway when the bombers with their fighter escorts returned. They had come back to finish the job and – or so it seemed to me in the terrifying hour that followed – to finish us off too. Thank God, there happened to be a fairly deep bomb crater quite close. We made a run for it.

It struck me then that all those scenes in the movies when fighters fire rockets and machine guns at targets on the ground were about as realistic as kiddies playing at cops and robbers. It's the noise that instils the fear. Not so much the gunfire and exploding rockets, oddly enough, but the noise of jet engines screaming above your head so close it feels you could reach up and touch them. I have never heard anything like it and nor do I ever want to hear anything like it ever again. I was terrified.

But we made it to the crater, jumped in and my cameraman started yelling at me: 'Piece to camera! Do a fucking piece to camera!'

Was he mad? We were about to die. Why would I want to do a piece to camera, and anyway what was there to say? But he wasn't mad – just much more experienced and battle-hardened than me. So I did. To this day I have no idea what I said – or, rather, screamed.

I learned a few things about myself and my trade as a result of that little episode. The first is that it is never wise to assume the bombers will not return to finish the job. The second is that it's not a bad idea if you're entering a battlefield to wear something a bit more protective than sun cream. And the third is that reporters have a different set of priorities from real people.

I imagine that the first thought most sane and rational human beings would have had would be something like: 'Thank God I survived!' My first thought was: 'Wow, we must have some bloody brilliant pictures!' My second thought, which became my first thought, was: 'And we were the only film crew there! This city is packed with foreign correspondents and film crews and we are the only one with pictures of the Indian air force attacking the airport!'

Pathetic? Yes, with the benefit of half a century in this trade I suppose it is. But it's not enough to know you have good pictures. What matters is that they must be better than anyone else's. And that explains what happened next.

I was back in my hotel room wondering how the hell we were going to get our film to London when Michael 'Nick' Nicholson knocked on my door. Nick was the opposition. He was the ITN reporter and the best in the business. Hugely experienced, clever, brave, resourceful, brilliant on camera and probably the most competitive human being I have ever worked with – which is saying something.

He was so far my superior in every aspect of our craft that I was mildly surprised he had deigned to pay me a visit – he'd ignored me until then – and even more surprised when he told me he wanted to help. He'd heard that we'd shot some decent stuff at the airport and said he had a small charter plane which was taking his own footage out of Dhaka to Burma where his agent would put it on a plane to London. Did I want my film to go too? You bet I did! The answer to my prayers. He might be the most ruthless operator in the business, but what a decent human being Nick was when his colleagues needed a bit of help. I told him I'd get the film from my cameraman, who was having a much-deserved snooze, when he woke up in an hour or so.

'No good,' said Nick, 'the plane is waiting to take off. I need it now.'

And then the little worm of doubt did its job. I told him my cameraman would be extremely cross to be disturbed and then I went down to the hotel lobby. The first journalist I saw was a friendly stills photographer: 'Ah, John, heard about the plane have you? It's been set up by the Americans ... probably leaving in a couple of hours. We're all using it.'

To his credit Nick managed to look a little sheepish when I told him I wouldn't be handing my precious film to him after all. Later that afternoon the plane took off headed for Burma with all our footage including my own. I treated myself to a large whisky and settled back to await the congratulatory Telex messages from my bosses in London. They never came – for the very good reason that the film took longer to get to London than if it had travelled by camel.

The country I had flown out to on 1 December 1971 was East Pakistan. When I flew home three weeks later East Pakistan no longer existed. The war lasted only thirteen days, one of the shortest wars in history, and Pakistan signed the instrument of surrender on 16 December. The new country of Bangladesh was born. The Bengali people, who had suffered terribly under what they regarded as the Pakistani occupation, went wild. It was the first (and last) time I had ever been carried shoulder-high through the streets of a city by a massive, cheering mob who regarded the BBC as heroes. Tragically, the Pakistan military had taken a different view. When we arrived in Dhaka we had recruited a local Bengali to work with us as guide and interpreter. One night he disappeared. We found him the next day in a ditch with his stomach slit open. Would he have been a target had he not been working for the BBC? It is impossible to know, but equally impossible not to feel guilt.

Everyone was at risk in that war-torn city and the Red Cross declared our hotel a protected zone. They draped a huge Red Cross flag over the roof and we foreign journalists who were staying in the hotel were asked to act as wardens. Our job was to stand guard at the hotel entrance and check all those who wanted to stay. There is something deeply unpleasant about having to search through the luggage of strangers just in case they happened to be terrorists with a bomb. Much more unpleasant when the war ended was watching how the Bengalis dealt with some of the defeated enemy. Vast numbers became prisoners of war, but some of the Pakistani forces' most notorious leaders were dealt summary justice in public. We decided we would not film some of the most gruesome punishments. Our judgement was questioned later by some colleagues and bosses, but my cameraman had no doubts. There are some things, he said, that nobody should see and he would not film them even if I ordered him to. He was right.

We were, by now, desperate to get home for Christmas and we went out to the airport to try to get a flight. We knew there wasn't much chance. The problem was that the crater we had sheltered in a few days earlier, plus several more, meant no commercial airlines had a hope of operating. We were told it might help if we lent a hand to some of the workers trying to fill in the holes so that at least some light aircraft might be able to operate. Parked at the edge of the runway was a small, ancient single-engine plane which might, just about, have been the very last remnants of the old East Pakistan air force. The passenger door had been removed and a large machine gun bolted to the floor. There was a young man standing next to it. We asked him if he was the pilot and when he said he was we asked him if he would fly us out – ideally across the border to Calcutta a couple of hundred miles away. He looked a bit dubious but he thought there was probably enough space between potholes to take off. We settled on a price, squeezed in around the machine gun and set off. We did a little praying, held our breath, wobbled a bit … and we were airborne.

The pilot seemed mightily relieved but still tense. He had no maps and nor, as far as I could see, much in the way of working instruments but after what seemed like a very long time he pointed out of the window: 'Look! Calcutta!'

Now it was just a matter of landing. Obviously there was no question of trying the international airport (they'd have probably thought we were the Pakistani enemy launching an attack) but our pilot said he knew there was a grass air strip somewhere – and so there was. The landing was, second only to being rocketed by the Indian air force, the most frightening moment of my life. It wasn't so much a landing as a series of crash landings, each slightly less shattering than the last. When we skidded to a halt on the grass strip I swear the pilot offered thanks to whichever god he worshipped. I said something like: 'Err … well done! Looked a bit difficult …?'

'Yes indeed,' he said, 'it was my first time!' It turned out that he had been a co-pilot and his instructor had yet to prepare him for a solo landing.

In September 1973 I was despatched to Chile to report on the bloody military coup that had just been staged. It was a big story. Democracy was a fragile flower in Latin America and the democratic government of Chile had been threatened for some time by those who opposed the policies of the socialist president Salvador Allende. Leading them was the man who was to become one of the world's most ruthless dictators: General Augusto Pinochet.

I happened to be in New York at the time and London ordered me to get to Chile post-haste. It was difficult. All the Chilean airports had been closed and no international flights were being allowed in. So I decided to get as close as possible and, with my film crew, caught the next plane to Buenos Aires – more than 5,000 miles south. Maybe we could drive across the Andes and into Chile by road. I was disabused of that idea very swiftly: far too dangerous and, anyway, it would take for ever. So maybe we could charter a light aircraft from Argentina. No chance. Again, too dangerous. The Andes are very big and very high.

There was only one way to get in – assuming the Chilean army would let us. I decided we should charter a jet and tell them we were on our way. That wasn't easy either. The only one on offer was from the Argentine state airline and it was a jumbo jet. I suspected my masters in London, desperate though they were to get footage out of Chile, would quibble at the cost. And the airline wanted the money up front. But there were many other foreign correspondents from news organisations around the world in BA also trying to get into Chile so we all met in my hotel room, agreed to split the cost, handed over our credit cards and I scuttled off with them to the airline's office. They made it clear that once the deal had been done we'd have to pay whether our plane was allowed to land or not. We were over a barrel so I paid up and a few hours later we all pitched up at the airport and prayed.

Late in the evening the word came through from Santiago: permission granted. At any other time the prospect of flying over one of the world's great mountain ranges in your very own jumbo jet would have been the stuff of dreams. But not in the middle of the night and not when you're worried sick about trying to catch up on a story that had broken days before. The champagne in the first-class cabin went undrunk. When we finally arrived in Chile we were greeted by the military – 'greeted' meaning that we were herded into the back of an open-topped troop carrier and driven into a subdued and fearful city. The fighting was over. The government had been crushed and the dictatorship led by Pinochet was in total control of the country.

We were allowed into the city's football stadium, now converted into a vast prison for Allende supporters. I wondered as we filmed them how many would still be alive the next day. We also filmed at the presidential palace, which had been stormed by Pinochet's soldiers. Allende's body had been removed long since. We all assumed he had been killed by the military. Years later his body was exhumed and it was established that he had killed himself with an AK-47 given to him by Fidel Castro of Cuba. It bore a gold plate with the subscription: 'To my good friend Salvador from your friend Fidel who, by different means, tried to achieve the same goals.' His daughter eventually told the BBC that Allende chose suicide rather than face being humiliated and used by Pinochet to further his own goals.

So I had my story. Now I had to get it back to London. The good news was that the airports had been opened. The bad news was that when I arrived with my 'onion bag' (the name we gave to the sacks in which we carried the cans of film) they would not let me on the plane. I tried everything – including begging and bribery – but the airport officials, closely watched by military minders, were adamant: they would not let me board the plane unless I handed the film over to be put in the hold. I had no choice. I reckoned that the chances of it getting through security, making it into the hold and reappearing at Heathrow airport were no better than fifty-fifty. At best. So I spent the next fourteen hours en route to London calculating how much money I had laid out in the past five days for a story that might never appear on the air. It was several times my annual salary. I waited at the conveyor belt in Heathrow. And waited. My own suitcase arrived and so did everyone else's. No onion bag. And then an angel appeared. She did not have a halo and she was wearing a British Airways uniform but I knew she was an angel because she did have the onion bag. She seemed a little surprised to be hugged by a tearful young man who hadn't had a proper night's sleep for a week.

Those, as I said, were the dark ages for television news. If, God forbid, there were to be another military coup in Chile tomorrow the pictures would start appearing on our television screens within minutes.

In fact, things had already begun to change when I was based in Washington in the mid-1970s. The first electronic news-gathering (ENG) cameras were appearing. They were great clunky things but they had one massive advantage over the cameras we'd been using since the first motion pictures were invented in the 1880s. No film. They transformed the way we covered stories. A roll of film on our news cameras lasted for just over ten minutes, so you had to be very careful when you switched on and when you switched off. And Sod's Law dictated that the moment you switched off was when the bomb blew up or the Queen slipped on the banana skin.

But you spent your life terrified that you would miss the one moment that mattered. You would also get a bollocking from the boss if you used too much film – partly because it all had to be developed, which took time back at base, but mostly because it was very expensive. And there was the other fear. The hair in the gate. No matter how careful the cameraman was when he loaded a new roll (always a 'he' incidentally: I never once worked with a camerawoman) he could never be a hundred per cent certain that a little hair had not managed to find its way into the gap between the film and the lens. You could tell when it happened if you were passing the edit suite just after the film had come back from the lab. The cry from an anguished reporter of 'Oh fuck! There's a fucking hair in the gate!' It made the film unusable.

No such problem with ENG cameras. No film: no hairs in gates. And, pretty soon, with the blessing of satellite transmission, no need to find helpful passengers in foreign airports willing to courier your film back to London so that it could be processed and edited. Why use passengers? Because by the time you got to the airport it was usually too late to send it by freight, and anyway passengers were much more reliable.

By the early 1970s geostationary satellites were in use and in May 1974 the world's first direct broadcasting satellite (DBS) was launched. So now we had pictures that needed no processing and a way of getting them back to London instantaneously – albeit very expensively in those early days. A ten-minute sat-feed from Washington cost $10,000. All that was overtaken with the birth of the digital age. Instead of lugging great onion bags bulging with cans of film and endlessly worrying about running out, you had a few tiny disks and virtually unlimited airtime in your pocket. One of the unintended consequences of that is the temptation when you're on an assignment to film pretty much everything that moves. So you end up back at base with endless hours of material all of which has to be viewed – and what no one has yet invented is the computer program in the editing suite that will eliminate all the boring stuff instantly and keep the good stuff. It's probably on its way.

The biggest problem facing the editor back home now is not how to get a story covered and the footage safely back to base, but how to distinguish between the mass of material that appears almost instantly on social media in one form or another. If it's a natural disaster – an earthquake or a tsunami – it's pretty straightforward. But if it is, say, a terrorist attack you have to know who was filming. The role of us broadcasting hacks has changed beyond recognition too – and I'm not talking just about the way reporters are used in television news.

In those days, as a foreign correspondent, I could put a report on a homeward-bound plane and wait for the call from the foreign desk, secure in the knowledge that several days might pass before I might be disturbed again. This meant the pace of news was entirely different from today. A film needed to be processed in a chemical bath for the print to be developed. Then the film had to be edited in the old-fashioned way: it was broken up into its constituent shots, and the strips of film hung up in the editing suite. The picture editor would edit the selected shots together on a Steenbeck – a reel-to-reel viewing machine. All this took time.

Today we all have telephones so packed with technology they can not only do the job of the camera but also replace the need for a satellite station. And along with the advent of digital technology came computerised editing, so it no longer takes 'real time' to do an edit. A thirty-second ENG clip would take thirty seconds to lay down for the edit. On a computer, it can be done in the blink of an eye.

All of this would have been the stuff of fairy tales in my early reporting years. Occasionally you will hear old hacks reminiscing about the good old days of black and white film and how vastly superior the pictures were when shot on a proper cine camera by a highly trained cameraman rather than by any ten-year-old with a shaky mobile, but the truth is we'd have given our eye teeth for it. Very little happens in one part of the world today without the rest of the world being able to see it minutes later. But I am not suggesting that this is an unalloyed blessing. Technology has solved many problems but it has raised many questions too about the role of international news organisations.

The BBC in particular has had to face the challenge of new technology by asking what it means for the way the organisation is structured and how best it can position itself to retain a big enough audience to justify the licence fee. It's made many attempts to get its structure right but somehow it never quite seems to work. Perhaps there is no right answer.

When BBC Television News moved from its early home in Alexandra Palace to the new Television Centre in London in the early 1970s there were no television foreign correspondents based abroad. There was a network of radio correspondents, but no foreign television news bureaux. You might think that the simplest answer to that would have been to train radio correspondents in the ways of television. I have yet to meet a good radio reporter who is not also capable of delivering a good television report. Then again, I'm not a boss. Bosses think differently. Many of them see their purpose as either building their own empires or taking over someone else's empire. That's not necessarily an ignoble aspiration but the effect on BBC News was that we ended up with two distinct empires – radio and television – and, almost half a century later, I'm damned if I can see why.

What happened in the BBC in the early 1970s was that two separate cultures were encouraged to develop: radio and television. That meant two different satrapies, each with its own boss, management structure and team of journalists – and crucially, each with its own budget. Television, for entirely obvious reasons, had much more money than radio and, equally obviously, was seen as more glamorous. Television wanted to create its own stars.

So a corps of television foreign correspondents was formed. In the early 1970s four were appointed to cover the world: one based in the Far East, one in Europe, one in East Africa and one in the United States. I won Washington.

In 1987, John Birt became deputy director general of the BBC, in charge of news and current affairs, and he tried to change all that. He had quite a fight on his hands: forcing radical change on an organisation, many of whose bosses enjoyed living in the past. It was more comfortable there. But he did it. He established the specialist journalist posts on which BBC News is still founded and insisted that correspondents should work for both TV and radio – he called it 'bi-medialism'. He also thought the BBC had 'starved' TV news of resources. He pushed news and current affairs together into one directorate. They did not go willingly.

There was 'no single and coherent overview of the BBC's journalism', he wrote later. Many of the news staff, he said, had 'long since ceased to think enquiringly'. It's fair to say that many of the news staff did not warm to him. But Birt was a man with a plan, which was unusual for the BBC. In the 1970s, he had developed his journalistic philosophy – what became known as his 'Mission to Explain'. He argued that there was a bias against understanding in television journalism. News and feature journalism, he wrote, both failed to put events in their proper context:

> Our economic problems for instance, manifest themselves in a
> wide variety of symptoms – deteriorating balance of payments,
> a sinking pound, rising unemployment, accelerating inflation
> and so on.
>
> The news, devoting two minutes on successive nights to the
> latest unemployment figures or the state of the stock market,
> with no time to put the story in context, gives the viewer no
> sense of how any of these problems relate to each other.

In 1989, as a sign of the new Birtist seriousness, *Breakfast News* replaced the *Breakfast* programme. The era of comfy sofas and chunky sweaters was over. Weekend television bulletins were put under the control of the editor of the flagship *Nine O'Clock News*, with its two presenters sharing the seven-day presentation duties, to try to invest the bulletins with greater authority.

Birt backed the launch of continuous news output and took money from traditional services to fund the twenty-four-hour news channel and BBC News Online. The BBC World news channel was launched, aimed at an international TV audience, originally under the name World Service Television and funded by advertising and subscription.

In some ways Birt's greatest achievement was to recognise the significance of the nascent digital revolution that was to change all our lives. He saw that the era when the family all sat around together in the evenings watching whatever it was that the BBC and ITV bosses saw fit to show them was coming to an end. Soon we would not dance to the tune of the mighty channel controllers: we would create our own schedules. And if we wanted to watch news, we would watch it when we chose to, rather than when the schedule dictated. The verb 'viewing' would be replaced by 'consuming' and the implications of that were clear. Viewers watched what they were given; consumers picked and chose when and where.

Birt decided that the BBC should launch new channels and new platforms. At the 1996 Edinburgh Television Festival, he said that without the resources to prepare for the digital age, the BBC would be 'history'. So whatever we may have thought about Birt at the time, he had a vision for our journalism and positioned the BBC for the technology of the future with uncanny accuracy. In 1997, when BBC Online was launched, there were fewer than 8 million people online in the UK as opposed to the tens of millions with a TV licence. *The Times* asked whether 'dear old Auntie, always regarded as a little dotty' had now gone 'completely bats'. A few years later it, and many other newspapers, were fighting to halt the march of BBC Online across their own borders.

Birt's impact on the BBC's foreign reporting is being felt to this day too. There are correspondents reporting more and more easily from nearly every corner of the world on scores of different news channels that broadcast 24/7. They can email their videos or radio reports or broadcast direct from their mobile phones. Everywhere you look, you can find news: on your phone, your computer, your watch, on Twitter, on the screen at the rail station, on aeroplanes. Never in the history of the human race have we been able to communicate with each other so quickly.

And yet, at the risk of seeming to hark back to a golden era, I fear we have lost something in translation. Yes, we no longer have to worry about putting the film in the 'soup' and waiting anxiously for it to re-emerge. Yes, we can cover the ground more quickly. Yes, we can report from any corner of the world.

But ever more news reported ever more swiftly, if not instantaneously, is not necessarily better. We need to feel the quality as well as the depth and speed of delivery.

4

A gold-plated, diamond-encrusted tip-off

When the first four television foreign correspondents were appointed in the early 1970s I was sent to the United States. My patch stretched from the northern tip of Alaska to the southern tip of South America. Pity we didn't have air miles in those days. Rather bizarrely, the BBC decided I should set up our news bureau in New York and not Washington. That didn't last long. Within days of my setting foot on US soil the biggest American political story of the century was beginning to seep out. A group of shady characters hired by Republican Party sympathisers had been caught breaking into the offices of the Democratic Party. The offices were in a building called Watergate. I had been sent to the States for a three-month stint. I was to stay for nearly six years.

I suggested earlier the qualities that reporters need as a basic minimum to survive in the trade: a modicum of literary skill, a plausible manner, and rat-like cunning. All those might help, but every reporter knows that what really matters is the ability to be in the right place at the right time. It's called luck. I've always had more than my share of it. You don't get luckier than fetching up in the United States just as Watergate was about to blow a massive hole in the side of the White House and threaten to wreck the US constitution and everything the presidency stood for. If the head of state could survive even though he was proving to be a liar and a crook, what exactly was the point of the great American constitution? This was a watershed moment in the history of the United States.

Like all the other foreign correspondents in Washington, I followed the story's every twist and turn with a mixture of disbelief and, in my case, fear. Disbelief that the most powerful man in the world could conceivably be brought down by such a third-rate bunch of bunglers, and fear that I simply did not have the experience, let alone the knowledge, of the American political scene to analyse every development and offer a remotely plausible prediction as to what might happen next. Pretty basic qualifications, you might think, for a correspondent reporting on the biggest story in the world for the most respected broadcasting organisation in the world. The fact is that I was, by any objective assessment, the wrong man in the wrong place at the wrong time.

The right man was Charles Wheeler, perhaps the greatest foreign correspondent the BBC has ever had. When I was still in nappies, Charles was a captain in the Royal Marines, second in command of a secret naval intelligence unit that took part in the Normandy invasion of 1944. He went on to become the longest-serving foreign correspondent in the history of the BBC. He was, quite simply, brilliant. A small man with a commanding presence, he had steely grey hair, piercing blue eyes, a brain the size of a house and a natural authority born of decades of reporting on crises around the world. When Charles delivered a report the audience trusted him. And they were right to.

The first time I worked with him was at the Republican National Convention in Miami Beach in 1972 when Nixon was nominated to run for a second term as president. We knew there were going to be demonstrations. Nixon was a divisive figure at the best of times and protests over the Vietnam War were still tearing the country apart. We suspected that the protests in Florida would turn violent and my film crew and I had equipped ourselves with gas masks in case the police used tear gas. They did. I put mine on and strode confidently into the fray, gas swirling around us, breathing my own filtered air confidently. Except that it was not filtered. Within a minute I was in agony. I had never used a gas mask before and nobody had warned me that they're not terribly effective unless you make certain that the bung is inserted at the point where the air gets in. Mine wasn't and I had not checked. The result: I was breathing in undiluted tear gas. By the time I realised what was happening and ripped the mask off my face I was a blubbering mess. Somebody told me helpfully after I'd recovered that it's possible to die if you do something that stupid. I never did it again. The other thing I learned from that convention was how to make the most powerful man in the world look an idiot – courtesy of Charles Wheeler.

National party conventions are awe-inspiring demonstrations of American politics at their majestic best and cringe-making worst. There is a bit of a gap in rhetorical brilliance between Williams Jennings Bryan in 1896 and Donald J. Trump 120 years later. The big issue at the 1896 convention was whether the United States should have gold coinage as well as silver. The moneyed classes said yes, the poor farmers said no. Bryan was on the side of the poor: 'Having behind us the commercial interests and the labouring interests and all the toiling masses, we shall answer their demands for a gold standard by saying to them, you shall not press down upon the brow of labour this crown of thorns. You shall not crucify mankind upon a cross of gold.'

What a phrase eh? Hard to imagine anything like it coming from the lips of some more recent candidates. Perhaps the most memorable sound bite from the Trump convention was the endless baying of 'Lock her up, lock her up!' from the floor whenever the name of Hillary Clinton was mentioned.

What made the Nixon convention of 1972 memorable for me was not so much the big speech itself as how it reached us. The party managers always make sure that the candidate's speech is distributed to the media an hour or so before the candidate himself delivers it. It is eagerly awaited. We were in the BBC office – perhaps a dozen of us including Charles Wheeler – when our copy was handed to us by a couple of Nixon's staff. Charles started to read it. He stopped, looked puzzled, and began again. And then he started laughing.

'For God's sake!' he spluttered. 'They've given us the wrong copy. This is Nixon's own personal copy. It's the one he will be reading from!' And so it was. Between almost every paragraph were instructions to Nixon as to how, exactly, he should deliver it:

Serious expression here
Look as if you really care
Smile! This is meant to be funny
Squeeze out a tear at this point ... VERY sad face!
Nobody believes this: show that YOU do!
Stern look at the delegates!
ENJOY this bit!

I may not recall every instruction in precise detail, but this was gold dust for Charles. One of Nixon's big PR problems was that so many Americans believed he did not have a sincere bone in his body. Not for nothing was he known across the nation as 'Tricky Dickie'. This would be deeply embarrassing. If he had to be instructed in how to react to words that were supposed to be coming from the heart, what would America make of it? Charles was scribbling furiously, trying to get as much of it down as possible, and then the inevitable happened. The door to our little office burst open and a posse of red-faced Nixon staffers barged in.

'Give it back!' they shouted.

'Not on your life!' we shouted back.

Then they saw it on the table and made a grab for it. Charles got there first. They tried to snatch it from his hands and he threw it across the office. Chris Drake, one of my radio colleagues, caught it and they tried to grab it from him so he threw it to me and I threw it to someone else. The farcical scene must have lasted for a few minutes and Charles (by now holding it again) tried to make peace.

'Look,' he said, 'I am going to report this and there's absolutely no way you are going to stop me. If you bring in security guards you'll get it back in the end but there's going to be an almighty stink. Freedom of the press remember? So leave it with me for another few minutes and I'll give it back to you.'

What else could they do?

An hour later Charles was sitting in front of a BBC camera not just telling his audience what Nixon had to say at the convention, but also what his team did not want us to know. This was television gold.

Part of the problem for any journalist covering the Watergate story – let alone a new boy like me, taking over from the great Charles Wheeler, who was being sent to Brussels – was trying to come to terms with the notion that the president of the United States, with his vast experience of politics, could have been so breathtakingly stupid as to destroy everything he had spent his life trying to achieve. And in such a crass manner. This was a man who had been written off by most of America when he was defeated by John F. Kennedy in 1960 and who had fought back in the face of an often viciously hostile press. The Washington establishment, who worshipped the ground Kennedy had walked on, regarded Nixon as a lying, scheming lowlife and they made no attempt to conceal it. They treated him with contempt.

But he won the presidency in 1968 and again four years later. I followed him and the Democratic contender George McGovern around the country in 1972 from one rally to another and the result was never in doubt. McGovern himself knew he had no chance. It was one of the biggest landslides in American history. I remember one rally in a Midwestern state that removed any doubts I might have had. We filmed McGovern getting off his plane and walking through the obligatory, but pretty sparse, crowd of supporters. Most were cheering but one of them was clearly not a McGovern fan. He hurled some abuse at the candidate as he walked past. McGovern stopped, went back to him, and said something that left the man silent and looking stunned.

Later I asked him what McGovern had said. 'He told me: "Suck my cock buddy!"' I swear he looked impressed. But a candidate who can do that knows he's not going to be president.

It was clear even to a novice like me that as the Watergate saga rolled on Nixon was in deep trouble. Once we discovered that he had been secretly recording everything that was said in the Oval Office we knew how deep. So did he. For me the most telling moment – and certainly the most surreal – came when he made a trip to, of all places, Disney World in Orlando Florida. It was November 1973 and the country was being rocked by a relentless stream of accusations – mostly unearthed by the *Washington Post* reporters Carl Bernstein and Bob Woodward – of endless clandestine and illegal activities by members of Nixon's administration. What nobody had actually said, explicitly, was that Nixon himself was a crook. He was, after all, the president of the United States. 'Crook' was not a term to be used lightly – and certainly not without copper-bottomed proof. And yet Nixon used that word himself.

'People have got to know whether their president is a crook,' he declared. A slight pause and then he went on: 'Well, I am not a crook. I have earned everything I've got.'

The room was silent. We journalists looked at each other open-mouthed. Had he really said that? Had he really invited the people of America to consider that he might be a crook but to take his word that he wasn't? And then to add the bizarre line about 'earning everything I've got'. It was as though someone had accused him of stealing the takings from a drug store. Instead, as we were about to learn over the coming months, what he had been trying to steal was the presidency of the United States.

I said earlier that the greatest blessing the gods can bestow upon a journalist is luck. My luck had already played a huge part in my getting the best story in the world by the time I was still in my twenties. But my biggest break was yet to come. And it happened because of yet another piece of luck.

A Gold-Plated, Diamond-Encrusted Tip-Off

When I first went to the States for three months to set up the New York bureau I left my family at home in Britain and lived in a small apartment in midtown Manhattan. But then, when I got the correspondent's job, I had to find a house big enough for my wife and two young children to join me – preferably outside the city but not too far. It wasn't proving easy. And then I fell into conversation with a wealthy businessman who told me that his mother had a house in the small, delightful town of Irvington just a few miles north of the city. Would I care to rent it? It sounds perfect, I told him. But then he described it. It was a mansion. The servants' quarters were bigger than our house in England. It was fully furnished down to the Steinway grand piano in the library and the Tiffany silver in the butler's pantry. The lawns ran down to the Hudson River.

I told him that not only could I not afford the rent, I couldn't even afford the heating bills. He looked shocked. 'No, no,' he said, 'we're not interested in making any money from it. Mother is living there alone with just the servants and we want to persuade her to move out for a year or so in the hope that she'll agree to sell the wretched place. It's just too big.'

So we did a deal there and then. He settled happily for my meagre BBC rent allowance and I rang my wife to prepare herself for a shock. That was pretty lucky. But the really big luck came when I met my neighbours. One of them just happened to be a Republican congressman called Peter Peyser. It may be overstating it a bit to say that I owe him my career, but not by much. The fact is that he was to give me the greatest gift a politician can bestow on a journalist: a tip-off. Not just any old tip-off. This was a gold-plated, diamond-encrusted tip-off that any journalist would have offered his soul for.

What Peter did was phone me on the morning of 9 August 1974 as the Watergate crisis seemed to be approaching some sort of climax to tell me he'd just come from a prayer breakfast at the White House. Would I perhaps be interested in what President Nixon had told him? I rather think I might be, I said. Well, he said, the president had told him he would be going on television this very evening to make an announcement.

With this president at this time there could be only one reason for it. Never in the history of the United States had a president been forced to resign but that is what Richard Nixon was planning to do before the sun had set over the White House. At least, that's what I told my editor in London as soon as I'd hung up on Peter. 'How can you be sure he's going to resign?' the editor asked me.

'I can't but …'

'You know how much a satellite feed costs? Ten thousand dollars – that's how much – and you can't be sure?'

'No, but it's worth every cent if—'

He finished the sentence for me: 'If you're right, maybe. But if you're not we'll be ten grand out of pocket and the BBC will be an international laughing stock and your career will be toast before you've even hit thirty.'

'And if we don't do it and Nixon resigns tonight we'll have thrown away a sensational scoop and it'll be you standing outside your local supermarket begging for a crust to feed your starving children.'

Maybe I didn't put it quite as strongly as that – editors are powerful people – but after a few minutes of heated discussion, he agreed and pretty soon I was sitting in front of a camera informing the British people that President Nixon was on the point of resigning. Twenty-four hours later, standing on the lawn of the White House, I understood the meaning of that old cliché so often applied to journalists: the privilege of a ringside seat at history.

A White House press pass entitles the holder to strictly limited access to the briefing room, and if you are ever foolish enough to try to stray off-limits without an official invitation the secret-service agents make sure you don't get far. But on that historic morning, as we waited for Nixon to make his last appearance as president of the United States and board the helicopter waiting to fly him to political exile, the rules broke down. I remember wandering into the Blue Room and spotting one of Nixon's two daughters sitting in a corner by herself looking out at the gardens of the great house. Five extraordinary years with all those memories: the triumphs and the humiliations and finally the most spectacular fall from grace any president had ever suffered. The journalist in me wanted to try to coax her into doing an interview – but the soppy father in me won. She clearly wanted to be alone with her thoughts.

Watergate and the downfall of the most powerful man in the world was – and remains – the biggest story of my career. Even as I write that sentence I question it. Bigger than the earthquake in Nicaragua which I reported in 1972? More than 10,000 people lost their lives, 20,000 were badly injured, 300,000 lost their homes. Bigger than mass famine in sub-Saharan Africa or revolutions in Latin America or wars on the Indian subcontinent? I reported on them all and neither I nor anyone else could even begin to put a figure on the number who died. Nobody died in Watergate.

And yet none of those massive human tragedies had even a fraction of the coverage given to the story of one flawed human being who tried to subvert an election by authorising a handful of shabby characters to break into the offices of his opponent and try to dig some dirt that might gain him a few extra votes in an election which, as it turned out, he won by one of the biggest landslides in American presidential history. What a supreme irony.

If Nixon had played by the rules he would have stayed in power for another four years instead of being thrown out in disgrace and quite possibly earned himself a place in the history books in the top rank of American presidents. Instead his name is synonymous with lying and deceit. And the name of an unremarkable office building in Washington has become the prefix for every serious scandal in the Western world ever since. It is the yardstick by which stories of political skulduggery are measured.

I stayed on in the United States to see Gerald Ford become president and then lose the White House to a relatively unknown peanut farmer from the Deep South: Jimmy Carter. Washington winters can be pretty miserable and Gerald Ford was about as boring as an American president can be. The most interesting thing about him was the claim that he was so dumb he couldn't chew gum and walk at the same time. True or not I was keen to get out of Washington and, ideally, spend a few days in the sun. It so happened that Carter had just begun campaigning in Florida. I persuaded my boss in London that he was an intriguing character and just about a dead cert to win the Democratic nomination. He fell for it. I got my few days in the sun to do the interview as well as the chance to boast about spotting Carter's potential before most of my British colleagues. Thus are reputations cemented.

But by then my family was getting restive. Or, at least, my wife was. My children were, to all intents and purposes, native Americans. They spoke with an American accent, knew every word of the 'Star Spangled Banner' and thought it perfectly normal that our delightful, friendly neighbours kept his 'n' hers pistols in their bedside tables. All they knew about the United Kingdom was that every time they went there for a holiday it rained. But I had promised their mother that we would return home before they went to secondary school and she was keeping me to that promise. A date was set. And then the big story (for the BBC at any rate) switched from the United States to another country on another continent. Two countries in fact: Rhodesia (as Zimbabwe was then known) and its powerful neighbour, South Africa.

BBC Television News had a problem reporting from South Africa. We were not allowed to open a news bureau there. The apartheid regime tolerated radio, but drew the line at letting in a television correspondent. Then, in 1976, they changed their mind. Nobody knew why. Maybe they calculated that if only the rest of the world could see what problems the country was facing they would change their hostile attitude to apartheid and remove the iniquitous sanctions. Whatever their reasoning the BBC leaped at the offer and I got a call from my boss Alan Protheroe.

'Hi John … looking forward to leaving Washington?'

'You bet! My wife is counting the days … packing the suitcases already.'

There was a slight pause and then …

'Umm … that's good. Just one slight snag …'

'Stop right there Alan! I've told her we're leaving the States and that's that.'

'Of course … of course … no question about leaving the States … it's just that I'd like you to make a bit of a diversion en route to London.'

The diversion was 8,000 miles.

5

A sub-machine gun on expenses

There were two huge and simultaneous stories on the African continent closely connected to Britain. One was the growing threat to the apartheid regime in South Africa and the fear that the country would collapse into lawlessness. The other was the bush war in Rhodesia, which would end with the sun finally setting on Britain's last colonial outpost on the African continent. I had first been to South Africa in the 1960s when the world was beginning to take apartheid seriously and opposition to it was gathering pace. The police and military kept an iron grip on the growing discontent of the black population – and a beady eye on foreign reporters like me who were trying to tell the world about the inhumanity of the system. When I returned in the 1970s the country was under siege.

My wife hated living there – partly out of fear of the knock on the door from the South African police. We were allowing a husband and wife to live together in our house in Johannesburg. That meant we were breaking the law and so were they. Their crime was that they were black and the shameful apartheid laws did not allow black couples to live together in 'white' neighbourhoods, let alone allow them to have their children living with them. If they wanted to live together legally as a family, they would have had to find a home in one of the so-called townships. The nearest to us was a squalid slum called Alexandria, or 'Alex' as everyone called it.

It was a hell on earth – an affront to the richest nation in sub-Saharan Africa. Raw sewage ran in the gutters and most of the shacks had no electricity or running water. The children looked as if they were permanently hungry or sick, or both. Most of the men had no work and their wives fought a hopeless battle to give their children a decent meal every day and, even more difficult, some chance of an education.

On the other side of the main road out of Johannesburg was a different universe: the white suburb of Sandton, known to everyone as the 'mink and manure' belt (the mink to cover the elegant shoulders of the women in the cold high-veld winters, the manure deposited by their children's ponies). I suspect they spent more in a month on their ponies than a family in Alex spent in a year – on everything.

Our own house closer to the city centre was typical of the homes in the smart northern suburbs of the vast city. It cost about as much as a modest semi in my home city of Cardiff but in Cardiff a modest semi did not come with verandas on all sides, nor a swimming pool in a beautifully tended garden shaded by a magnificent jacaranda tree and shielded from the obligatory servants' quarters by shrubs that seemed to flower all year round. It was, in short, a small paradise – but available only to those with white skin.

In our absurdly naive idealism my wife and I had agreed that when we moved to Johannesburg we would have no black servants. We were not going to turn into those ghastly whites whose lawns were immaculate thanks to the gardeners (black, obviously) who were paid a pittance to crawl over them all day plucking out every weed by hand or whose house servants called their employers 'master' or 'madam'. I recall with a shudder the first time we had dinner with a white couple, and on the table was a little silver bell. Our hostess would ring it imperiously to summon the next course or when she spotted something of which she disapproved. Not that they were all like her.

There were many, many decent white liberals who fought tenaciously to end apartheid and treated their servants with dignity and generosity but yes, of course, they had servants. And, of course, we too ended up with them. I say 'ended up'. It took roughly twenty-four hours. On our first day in our new home I decided to give the overgrown grass in front of the house a trim. I'd barely pulled the starter cord on the lawnmower before I was surrounded by a small crowd of young black men, jostling with each other to take over.

'Let me do that boss … you must not do that!' And so I did. They desperately needed work and to deny it to them just to parade my liberal credentials and indulge in a bit of virtue-signalling would have been both selfish and stupid.

The couple who ended up working for us and living with us were delightful and intelligent (they spoke three languages fluently) but I never did persuade them to call me John. It was always 'master'. It became almost a joke:

Me: 'Victor, my name is John so please stop calling me master.'

Victor: 'OK master.'

They were the children of apartheid and were permanently scarred by it in ways people like me struggled to understand.

For the whites of the northern suburbs, though, life was good – if you were able to accept that you, as a white person, were the superior race and black people existed to do your bidding. My wife could not. She hated having to send our children to posh private schools. We tried the local state school and pulled them out after one term. Like everything else in that disfigured country, the education system was racist to the core. At least the private schools did not teach history from a purely white supremacist standpoint.

She hated having to stand in the very short 'Whites/Blankes' queue at the post office while the 'Blacks/Swartes' queue stretched into the distance. She hated the way black people automatically stepped off the pavement to make way for whites. She hated the high walls, topped with spikes, of our neighbours' houses and the armed guards whom some of the more fearful residents kept in little huts outside their fortified gates.

There's no doubt that security was a worry, though, and we were endlessly nagged by friends to at least get a fierce dog – just in case. John Simpson, who was the BBC's radio correspondent when I arrived in South Africa and had become a close friend, offered me his dog when he returned to London. He was a very fierce-looking Rhodesian ridgeback called Titus – as strong as an ox but very good with small children, as John was anxious to point out. And so he was. But he had one slight flaw as a guard dog which John conveniently forgot to mention when he handed him over to me: he was terrified of black men – presumably because of something that had happened when he was a puppy.

I discovered it when I heard a gang banging on our gate one night demanding to see Victor about some unpaid debt and threatening to do him serious damage if he didn't pay up. I dragged Titus to the gate and he barked ferociously, straining on the leash. The men cleared off pretty sharply. They need not have. What they didn't realise was that he was not threatening them: he was straining to run away.

A few months later, when Titus and I were returning from our regular morning run around Zoo Lake I saw some black men standing at our gate. So did Titus. I tried to grab his collar but too late. He was running hell for leather in the opposite direction. Not for nothing are ridgebacks known as lion dogs. When their ancestors were used for hunting lions they were capable of running all day and all night – which is exactly what Titus did. We searched everywhere, put up 'missing dog' posters, even contacted the police (fat chance there) but after two days we'd begun to give up. Then the phone rang. It was a very elderly lady.

'Have you got a dog called Titus?'

'Well,' I said, 'we used to have but he's run away.'

'He's with me and his feet are all torn and bloody. You must come and get him.' Titus had run clear across the city and Joburg is a very big city. Thank heaven we'd put a disc on his collar with his name and our phone number.

My wife and I also found it difficult to live with the constant low-level hostility we met because I worked for the hated BBC – hated, at least, by Afrikaner officialdom. We represented the enemy. The British ambassador expressed it well when I asked him just after we'd arrived how we could expect to be treated.

'Well put it this way,' he told me, 'as the representative of Her Majesty's Government I tend to find myself going everywhere with my fists half raised.' For the most part, though, they left me alone to get on with my job. There was the occasional visit from policemen calling at my home with spurious claims that I had been seen driving dangerously or committing some other low-level offence, but it was pretty half-hearted stuff – presumably just to remind me that they knew who I was and where I lived. Potentially more serious was when the South African government demanded that the BBC recall me to London. They ordered their ambassador to make representations to the head of news at the BBC, Alan Protheroe, and a meeting was duly arranged.

Alan listened politely. The case was, on one level, unanswerable. Mr Humphrys, said His Excellency, was opposed to the South African government and its policy of apartheid. Difficult to argue with that, but was I getting it wrong? As Alan pointed out, the BBC would need hard evidence that I was failing to report accurately what was actually happening in South Africa before it would consider replacing me.

'Ha!' said the ambassador (as reported to me later by Alan). 'I shall give you one very concrete example of his inaccuracies. When he reported on the rugby match between the Lions and the Springboks in Durban just the other day he said the first try was scored by Grobelaar and it wasn't: it was scored by Geldenhuys. The man cannot be trusted!'

That was fair enough as far as it went – sport has never been my strong point – but my boss took the view that it did not necessarily prove I was unfit for the job of South Africa correspondent, all other things considered. And that was the end of that. A faintly ridiculous encounter, but with an important principle underlying it.

The ambassador was dead right when he said I had not been reporting from his country with the impartiality that the BBC demands from its journalists. Normally that might indeed be a sackable offence. Frederick Forsyth was sacked by the BBC in the late 1960s (or, if you prefer, allowed to resign) because he was sympathetic to the Biafrans when he was reporting on the civil war there. He had the last laugh. He tried his hand at writing a novel and the rest, as they say, is history. *Day of the Jackal* became a massive international bestseller and a blockbuster film, and there were many more where that came from.

But the principle stands. BBC correspondents are reporters, not commentators. We report the views of others, not our own. The BBC is, above all else, impartial. And yet ... there is one exception that overrides even that iron law. It was pronounced by the man whose shadow has hung over the BBC since he became its first director general in 1927: John Reith. The BBC, he said, is not required to be impartial as between good and evil.

In my view and – rather more importantly – in the view of the BBC, apartheid was an evil doctrine. It's true that I did not use my access to the BBC airwaves to denounce the National Party government of South Africa and demand its overthrow, but neither did I try to pretend that the way it treated the vast majority of South Africans was anything other than repugnant. Not that it was easy to have a sensible argument about it with those Afrikaners – and there were many of them – who believed as a matter of faith that they were superior to the 'kaffirs'. After all, they had God on their side. Their defence rested on the Bible. They liked to quote from the New Testament: 'God made all nations to inhabit the whole earth, and He allotted the time of their existence and the boundaries of the places where they would live.'

See? Apartheid means 'apartness' and all they were doing was enforcing laws that meant blacks lived apart from white. And, please note, God also allotted the boundaries of the places where they should live. How very fortunate in the case of the white people in Johannesburg that they should be allotted the rich, luxurious suburbs while those with a black or coloured skin were allotted the stinking slums. But, as God would no doubt point out, it wasn't HIS fault that white people would turn out to be so much better at accumulating wealth than black people. Which would also, presumably, explain why the whites should have the richest land in South Africa including (naturally) the gold mines, while the blacks should be banished to their 'homelands' – even if they'd never set foot in the godforsaken places.

To my enormous surprise I got the chance to challenge the country's president about all that in a television interview which I asked for but never, for a second, believed I would get. It was clearly a sign that, for all its arrogance, the government knew it had to start persuading the rest of the world that apartheid was just and essential for the country to survive let alone thrive. The president was P. W. Botha, popularly known as 'Die Groot Krokodil' (The Big Crocodile). He had earned the nickname: he had a thick skin, the sharpest of teeth and was totally ruthless. I tried suggesting to him that simple justice and humanity demanded all people should be treated the same, whatever the colour of their skin. Here's his reply: 'Simple justice suggests that you must allow a black man with his family to live a healthy, decent life. And you must provide work, where possible, for him, and not allow him to squat on your doorstep … and then, in the name of Christianity, say you've done your duty towards him.'

In one twenty-second answer Botha had used the three phrases that summed up the apartheid philosophy: 'allow a black man'; 'in the name of Christianity'; 'you've done your duty'.

There was not a scintilla of doubt in the minds of men like Botha that they were the master race and black people were a subspecies. Wasn't he worried that they might have had enough of being subjugated by their white masters? Wasn't some form of revolution inevitable?

'People have said so over a period of 300 years,' he told me. 'And, today, South Africa is one of the most peaceful countries in the world to live in.'

That, of course, was rubbish. Nelson Mandela might have been safely locked away on Robben Island, but the liberation movement he led was growing in strength. There could be only one possible outcome but it was to be several more years before Botha's successor, F. W. de Klerk, released Mandela from jail and brought an end to one of the great criminal political systems of the twentieth century.

The first rays of sunlight were breaking through the smoke haze of 100,000 coal fires rising into the cloudless sky above the biggest black township on the African continent. This was Soweto on a chilly April dawn in 1994. The following morning 20 million black South Africans would be free to vote in democratic elections for the first time in their lives. But the government had opened some polling stations a day early for the very old and disabled who might want to avoid the crowds the next day. I had driven out to Soweto hoping enough people would have taken the opportunity of that early vote to give *Today* a decent lead story. They had.

From every polling station great queues snaked into the distance: old grannies leaning on their sticks; old men in wheelchairs; young, heavily pregnant women. For an election that had not even formally begun this was already a turnout to gladden the heart.

I wanted to do a live broadcast into *Today* at 8.10 British time from a polling station. I chose an old woman to interview who looked as though she might deliver a lively couple of minutes and asked her: 'What will this vote mean for you?' Her answer was disappointingly low-key: 'I am very old. My life is coming to its end. For me, it means little,' she said. This was not what I expected or wanted. I waited and hoped there was more to come. There was. She patted the stomach of the young woman next to her.

'But for the young man in this woman's belly it will mean everything. He will have the dignity that has been denied to me all my life.' In that one sentence she encapsulated the achievement of perhaps the greatest African of the last century. I asked the pregnant women what name she would give her new baby. I think I knew what the answer would be.

Nelson. What else?

A couple of days later I stood in the dangerously overcrowded ballroom of the largest hotel in Johannesburg, deafened by the roar that greeted the arrival of her hero at his victory party. Nelson Mandela. The first black president of South Africa.

Over the years that followed Mandela would become the most respected and revered statesman of his time, his name a byword for courage and honour, humanity and humility. In towns and cities around the world public buildings and streets would bear his name and the Nobel Peace Prize was merely one of a thousand honours to be bestowed on him. Mandela's moral authority was unquestioned, his autobiography *Long Walk to Freedom* required reading for any who wanted to understand something of the triumph of the human spirit over adversity.

In these sceptical times when our leaders struggle to gain our respect it is tempting to suggest that no single figure can really be worthy of such adulation. Nelson Mandela, after all, was not unique. There have been other great liberation leaders. He was not a great naval hero like his namesake, or a brilliant scientist who changed the way we understand the world, or a Churchillian figure who led his nation to victory with the power of his oratory. He himself acknowledged that during his five years as president he failed to achieve one of the two great aims that he spoke of at his inauguration: to bring prosperity to black South Africans. The fact is that millions of them still live in the most appalling poverty.

But he did succeed in his other great aim: to reconcile a country divided by race for so long. To create a rainbow nation of people who would be, in his words, 'assured of their inalienable right to human dignity'.

To understand Mandela's achievement you have to go back to the old South Africa. When I first went to Johannesburg to set up a television news bureau for the BBC he had already been in jail on the notorious Robben Island for twelve years. The apartheid regime he had sworn to bring down was tightening its grip with increasingly draconian laws. The more isolated it became on the world stage, the more savagely its leaders reacted to protests at home. In 1976, high-school students in Soweto had staged a peaceful demonstration against apartheid and were met with murderous force. Hundreds were shot dead. I went back for the anniversary a year later and once again the police turned on the protesters with gas and guns.

Black people were not only treated as a subspecies of humanity, unfit to share the same schools or hospitals or post-office queues as white people, denied the vote and their basic rights as citizens. They were even denied the very citizenship of their own country. They were deemed to be citizens of bogus tribal 'homelands' created by the regime. Those who were allowed to live in the 'white' towns and cities could do so only in shacks in the gardens of the whites. Their sole purpose was to serve the needs of white people.

Mandela could have done what some other educated black people did: collaborate with the system or struggle to modify it. I remember a conversation I had soon after I arrived in South Africa with another very brave man, Archbishop Desmond Tutu. I asked him whether, given the apparent invulnerability of the regime, that might not be the wisest approach. 'Young man,' he said, 'we do not want to modify apartheid. We want to destroy it.'

Which was exactly what Mandela had set out to do when he took control years earlier of the youth wing of the ANC. He instantly became a wanted man and proved so elusive he earned the nickname 'The Black Pimpernel'. But he cut an unlikely figure as an underground leader: he didn't even own a pistol. Eventually he was arrested and in 1964 was convicted of sabotage, treason and violent conspiracy in the infamous Rivonia trial. His speech from the dock reverberated around the world. And in South Africa it removed any doubts as to who was the leader of the struggle. His words send a tingle down the spine to this day: 'I have cherished the idea of a democratic and free society in which all persons will live together in harmony and with equal opportunities. It is an idea which I hope to live for and to see realised. But, my Lord, if it needs be, it is an idea for which I am prepared to die.'

When he walked free from prison twenty-six years later Mandela's moral authority was unquestioned. In prison he had behaved with brave and stubborn dignity – he showed defiant respect even for the men holding him captive – and that dignity and quiet modesty never left him, however many honours an admiring world bestowed on him. Everyone wanted a piece of him, to share in the Mandela magic, and he seemed almost to be surprised by it all. I remember when he came to Television Centre many years later. He was approached by a South African musician who was performing in the studio. Mandela went to shake his hand, but the man bent down on one knee and bowed his head. Mandela shook his own head in disapproval. When I interviewed him he made me feel as though I were the person who mattered. Even for a cynical old hack it was hard not to be overawed by the man.

And never once did he seem to glory in his victory over the old regime. The contrast with neighbouring leaders could not have been more complete. President Hastings Banda in Malawi went nowhere without a great gaggle of adoring, ululating women wearing T-shirts emblazoned with his picture. He had me locked up once for asking what he deemed an impertinent question. And unlike Robert Mugabe, Mandela's former comrade-in-arms in the neighbouring Zimbabwe, Mandela did not use his new power to butcher those who had sought to destroy him. Instead he worked with them.

Back in the 1970s I'd had little enough idea what to expect from my posting to South Africa. In those dark days it had seemed inevitable that, sooner or later, the 20 million oppressed black people would rise up and demand equality – and that they would be met by overwhelming force, South Africa would descend into chaos and, ultimately, bloody civil war, taking the rest of southern Africa down with it. But it did not happen. And that, surely, was Nelson Mandela's greatest gift to his country and to his continent.

As for me, I'd had enough of living in foreign countries. I wanted to keep the promise I had made to my family and return to the country where we were born. So when Alan Protheroe said he was coming to South Africa to get briefed on what was happening in that troubled country and have a proper chat with me, I seized my chance.

Oddly enough, 'getting briefed' for Alan did not involve, say, visiting black leaders in Soweto to take the temperature of that volatile township or meeting stern-faced Afrikaans political leaders in the unlovely capital of Pretoria. It meant spending a couple of hours with a government official or two and the rest of the week exploring in some depth the state of South African cuisine and, naturally, its most famous vineyards while staying in some of the finest hotels the continent of Africa had to offer.

I was never quite sure why he was so interested in fine dining. He always had exactly the same meal: steak. And he always briefed the waiter in exactly the same way.

Waiter: How would you like your steak sir?
Alan: Well done.
Waiter: Yes sir.
Alan: Very well done.
Waiter: Yes sir.
Alan: Tell the chef that he must grill the steak until there is not a drop of blood left in it.
Waiter: Yes sir, I understand.
Alan: And when the chef is in tears because he will feel he has destroyed a perfectly good piece of meat, tell him to put it

back under the grill and cook it again. And then – and only
then – you can bring it to me.

But Alan knew his wine, which is why I left the big conversation
about my career until the night before he was due to fly back to
London from Cape Town. He had insisted on our final meal
being taken in the finest grape-growing area on the planet:
Stellenbosch.

The meal was magnificent (well … mine was) and the wine so
good that even my palate, which can just about recognise the
difference between a 1950 claret and a bottle of malt vinegar, was
aroused. And then, with the sun setting over the rolling, vine-
covered hills of Stellenbosch and the boss as mellow as big bosses
ever get, I took the plunge. I wanted to come home, I told him.
I wanted to reintroduce myself to my family, rescue my marriage,
do a job which meant I wasn't always waiting for the phone to
ring and having to rush off to the airport. I wanted a normal life.
Alan listened carefully and then …

'Fancy being a newsreader do you?'

Wouldn't I find it just a little boring? I ventured.

'Absolutely not! I've had enough of "announcers" reading the
news that other people write for them. You would not be just a
newsreader, you'd be the journalist who reads the *Nine O'Clock
News* and you'd be the BBC's first reporter to do it. You'd write
your own stuff and get involved in all the big decisions over what
stories are in the bulletin and how they're handled. You'd do live
interviews with the people making the news and you'd even present the big stories on location – not stuck behind a desk in a
studio. You'd be Walter Cronkite rather than Robert Dougall.
You'd love it. What do you think?'

What did I think? I thought I'd won the lottery. My life would
be my own again. No more being torn away from the bosom of
my family at a moment's notice. No more living out of a suitcase.
We'd be able to do amazingly exciting things together like arrang-
ing to see friends for dinner in a week's time and not having to

apologise at the last minute because someone had decided to stage a revolution somewhere a long way away. We'd be able to keep promises to the kids about a weekend at the seaside. We'd be able to lead normal lives – as a family. And I'd be on telly every night, recognised everywhere I went. Getting paid a fortune to open supermarkets and making brilliantly witty after-dinner speeches. And making BBC history into the bargain. Alan ordered another bottle of wine to toast my new future.

The toast turned out to be a little premature. I should have known better. Never trust a boss when he makes a promise after a couple of bottles of Stellenbosch's finest. At first everything went according to plan. It was agreed that we would be leaving for home – but not until I had covered the last act in the Rhodesian independence drama.

In 1965 the Rhodesian prime minister Ian Smith had rocked the British government 6,000 miles away by issuing a unilateral declaration of independence (UDI). His country had run its own affairs for half a century, but remained a British territory. No longer, said Smith. It was now an independent sovereign state. The British colonial governor in Rhodesia called it treason and fired Smith and his entire government. Smith ignored him, threw him out of the country and told Britain to go to hell. Britain was outraged, declared UDI illegal and persuaded the Commonwealth and the United Nations to bring in economic sanctions, the first time the UN had ever done so. The Royal Navy even mounted a sea blockade off the coast of neighbouring Mozambique. The last British territory to declare independence unilaterally had been the United States two centuries earlier.

Rhodesia was left with only two friends in the world: Portugal (the colonial power in neighbouring Mozambique), and the one that really mattered, South Africa, its neighbour to the south. Without the help of South Africa UDI would have collapsed within months if not weeks. And the Rhodesian government faced a much bigger threat within its own borders: the vast majority of the population who had inhabited the land for centuries before Cecil Rhodes and his white adventurers had even set foot on its soil. They'd had enough of being treated with contempt by the white bosses and the white farmers who had, they believed, stolen their land while their colonial masters had stolen their country. They wanted it back. They wanted black majority rule. And Smith had no intention of allowing it to happen.

Out in the bush, beyond the calm, well-kept streets of Salisbury, two guerrilla organisations – one led by Robert Mugabe, the other by Joshua Nkomo – had already begun to arm themselves with the help of their black neighbours. Rhodesia, for so long one of the most peaceful and prosperous countries on the continent of Africa, was about to go to war with itself and there could be only one outcome.

The Rhodesian military was small but highly professional and had the support of South Africa. But that support waned as the years went by and the war became increasingly vicious. It began with a few landmines planted in the dirt roads but escalated until the guerrillas (or 'terrs' as the white Rhodesians called them) were shooting down unarmed civilian aircraft with heat-seeking missiles and the Rhodesian forces were resorting to chemical warfare – poisoning the water supplies used by the enemy.

Every white man up to the age of sixty-five was likely to be called up in a massive programme of subscription. Travel outside Salisbury and the other main towns was highly dangerous. Apart from helicopters, which were in precious short supply, the only safe way to travel any distance was in convoys escorted by the military. You could identify by sight the regular military drivers on the Salisbury-to-Johannesburg convoy. Their left arm would be pale, the right burned dark brown – because they would drive south in the morning and back north in the afternoon with their arm resting on the sill of the open window.

My cameraman Francois and I decided foolishly to take a break from the war when our families came to visit us from Joburg. We wanted to see one of the greatest sights Africa has to offer: the Victoria Falls. When we'd phoned the magnificent Victoria Falls Hotel to book rooms, the receptionist had seemed a little surprised. We understood why when we got there. Apart from one other individual we were the only guests. We had the breath-taking spectacle of the falls to ourselves – and what a spectacle it was. No wonder Livingstone called it 'the most wonderful sight I have witnessed in Africa' when he first set eyes on it in 1855. The native Lozi people call it 'Mosi-oa-Tunya' – the Smoke that Thunders. You can see from miles away the spray that rises high into the sky like a great cloud from the billion gallons of water crashing over the edge every minute. And no wonder that in pre-war days this had been one of the most popular tourist desti-nations on the continent. The fact that we were just about the only guests in the hotel bore powerful testimony to the effect the war was having on this extraordinary country. Surely Ian Smith would have to acknowledge the inevitable. It came sooner than many had expected.

Two years later at the end of 1979 I was back in London to report on the Lancaster House conference, which had been called by the British government and was to be attended by all the warring parties in an attempt to bring peace to Rhodesia – or 'Zimbabwe Rhodesia' as it was known by then. I agreed with my old friend John Simpson, who was reporting for radio news, that the conference was doomed to fail and we'd be back home in Joburg before the week was out. It seemed inevitable. Ian Smith had conceded defeat in the guerrilla war, but how could the three warring parties – Smith, Mugabe and Nkomo – ever agree to a peaceful settlement? To John and me and many other observers, it was inconceivable. We could not have been more wrong. The conference lasted for the best part of three months and ended in a peace agreement.

I was to make one more journey into the Rhodesian bush some months later, this time with a squad of British commandos whose job it was to help keep the peace while Rhodesians prepared to vote. All Rhodesians. Black and white. The commandos dug a deep pit, lit a fire in it and kept throwing in wood until there was a great pile of red-hot ashes in the bottom. Then they heaved the carcase of a sheep into the pit, filled it with soil and forgot about it for twenty-four hours. It was easily the best meat I have ever eaten. The next day the voting began and two days later Robert Mugabe and his ZANU party emerged victorious. It was my last election in Africa.

Here is one small footnote which demonstrates wonderfully how the BBC has changed in the decades since I reported on that bloody guerrilla war. In a rather pathetic and totally unsuccessful attempt to win some sympathy for myself I had mentioned to my editor how dangerous it was out in the Rhodesian bush. Today reporters are usually 'embedded' with soldiers if they are to report a war. The commissars of Health and Safety will settle for nothing less. But there were no sympathetic soldiers to guard us in Rhodesia, and although our Land Rover had a piece of tin welded to the bottom to protect us against land mines (fat chance) there was no protection from the guerrillas who would come hunting when they heard the bang. And those desperate men did not discriminate. If we were white, we were the enemy.

'No problem,' said my entirely unimpressed boss, who just happened to be a colonel in Britain's Territorial Army in his spare time. 'You need a couple of sub-machine guns. Loose off a few rounds and that'll scare the buggers off.'

'What? I've never fired a gun in anger in my life. Never fired a gun at all, for that matter.'

'No problem,' he said again. 'The Rhodesian army will be happy to teach you. A few hours should do it. After all, if you do manage to shoot a couple of terrs you'll be doing their job for them.'

I tried one last objection. 'Who's going to pay? I can't just nip out to the nearest arms dealer, buy a couple of sub-machine guns and put them on my expenses!'

'Why not?' he said.

So I did and, to this day, I have a copy of my expenses form with all the usual – hotel bills, car hire, meals, etc. – and at the bottom: 'Purchase of sub-machine guns (2)'. Try to imagine getting that one past the modern BBC bureaucrat. Mercifully, neither my cameraman nor I ever made use of the guns on our reckless drive through the bush to the Victoria Falls. Indeed, after a half-day training course we never even got to fire them – which is stating the obvious because if we had, given my ability on the firing range, I would not be writing these words now.

So, unlike many, I survived to see the end of the war and stand in a Harare stadium watching the flag of the new Zimbabwe being raised for the first time. Today we look back to that ceremony as the beginning of a long nightmare for the suffering people of what had once been a peaceful and relatively prosperous British colony – albeit a great deal more prosperous for the whites than the blacks. Today we know that Robert Mugabe was to become a ruthless monster who murdered his opponents by the thousand, destroyed his country's economy and condemned millions to despair and starvation while he and his wife lived like Roman emperors.

But hindsight is a gift granted to none of us, and on that beautiful spring evening in 1980 even we cynical journalists wanted to believe the promise held out by a man who had impressed so many of us when we interviewed him during the years of struggle. The promise of a new beginning that would, in a very short time, be so savagely betrayed.

One conversation sticks in my mind. It was with a teacher who lived in what were then called the Tribal Trust Lands and we were talking about the promise of democracy. She told me: 'Yes, I want to be able to vote. But if I ever have to choose between having the vote and having enough food for my children I know what I will choose.'

How tragic that she was to be denied both. Her vote was effectively meaningless in one rigged election after another, and precious few Zimbabweans have escaped the horror of hunger.

Sunday Times

22 June 2003

Mugabe should be turfed out of power by force if necessary and his whole rotten crew with him. That is an easy sentence to write. Yet any half-competent diplomat can come up with a string of reasons why it cannot be accomplished. Let me list some of them.

For a white, former colonial power to depose a black leader would be unthinkable. It would risk rallying the entire black population against the attackers. There might be riots on the streets — not just of Zimbabwe but of South Africa and other black African nations. The neighbouring states just would not wear it. It would create turmoil in a region that has quite enough problems already. Who knows what terrorism might be inspired by such action? There would be real military problems in mounting an attack. Zimbabwe is landlocked and South Africa and Zambia would never allow their territory to be used to stage an invasion. And anyway you can't invade another nation just because you don't like the nature of its ruler. But why not?

… The last elections were blatantly rigged, as even the South Africans and Nigerians now acknowledge. When the people try to use their democratic right to protest in the streets or stay away from work, as they did earlier this month, they are terrorised by Mugabe's bully boys.

The list of objections is beginning to look a bit thin. Take the colonial point. If Britain were to intervene it could not possibly be seen as an attempt to recolonise. We would be in and out faster than Mugabe's ministers can steal another farm. Iraq has no history of democracy. Zimbabwe does. There is even a reasonable party structure with a viable opposition.

Riots in the streets? To anyone who knows Zimbabwe at all, that idea is simply risible. Nor is there the slightest risk that military action would increase any potential terrorist threat. By toppling Mugabe we would simply be restoring democracy. Not even the most fanciful could interpret that as a crusade against a religion or an ideology. South Africa could probably end Mugabe's rule simply by cutting off his energy supplies. It won't do it because President Mbeki does not want to be seen to be turning on his old comrade-in-arms and having to take the moral responsibility for his actions.

He would tut-tut a little if someone else did the deed but would secretly be relieved to be rid of his troublesome neighbour. Mbeki's own brother has told me he wants to see him thrown out. Mugabe's rule costs him more than political embarrassment. A vast number of penniless Zimbabweans have fled across the border to seek sanctuary in South Africa. The collapse of Zimbabwe's economy has caused enormous disruption in the region and, according to the Zimbabwe Research Institute, cost the area $2.5 billion (£1.5 billion). That's a lot of money for a poor region.

As for creating turmoil in the region, the opposite would happen. The economic regeneration of Zimbabwe would be the key to unlocking much greater Western investment in the region, especially from the United States. Would intervention create military problems? Hardly. Mugabe's army makes Saddam's look like a Nazi panzer division. Many of his senior officers are already said to be near revolt. It could be just the opportunity they want to throw him out.

So we come to the legal situation. Certainly there would be outrage at the UN. So what? There was outrage over Iraq and it was brushed aside. Nor was there a UN mandate for the action taken by Nato over Kosovo. It was justified on humanitarian grounds. The suffering inflicted by Mugabe on Zimbabwe is worse than anything Slobodan Milosevic managed in Kosovo. The latest reason offered by ministers to justify the war on Iraq is the mass graves uncovered since the invasion. Doesn't it count if the graves are dug in the brown earth of Africa? No, if there were a will to intervene it could be done. But there is not. It may simply be a question of double standards. To put it brutally, for all our talk of the brotherhood of man and the scar of Africa on our conscience, we simply do not care as much when black people kill each other. That's what they're always doing, isn't it? And it's not as if we are watching the suffering of Zimbabwe on our television screens every night. Mugabe has seen to that by the simple expedient of keeping out the cameras and reporters.

Or it might be that the whole humanitarian thing is a bit of a cover story. What matters are strategic and 'security' interests. The sad thing for the people of Zimbabwe is that Mugabe has not been mad enough to set up a few laboratories and manufacture the odd drum of ricin. Not to mention the absence of oil. Or a neighbour like Israel.

But this is all academic. There will be no intervention. The people of Zimbabwe will be left to their fate. Excellent organisations such as Save the Children will do what they can to feed the hungry – to 'stabilise' them, in the jargon. Britain and others will fork out a few million here and there to ship in some aid while Mugabe's henchmen steal what little grain is still being harvested to get even richer and use it as a political weapon to hold onto power.

Mugabe's wife will pop over to Paris occasionally with her husband to do a little shopping. And the West will sigh deeply and do nothing.

Enjoy your lunch.

6

A job that requires
no talent

The farmer and I stood in the front yard of his farmhouse in
Dorset looking south-west, small fields rolling away towards
the horizon, mostly green with tall grass waiting to be turned into
silage, some soft gold with ripening corn, others the harsh yellow
of rape. Here and there a copse of trees and a glint of river and, if
you stood on tiptoes, the distant blue of the English Channel.

'What a view!' I said to the farmer.

'Maybe,' he grunted, 'but you can't pay the bills with the
bloody view.'

Welcome to the romantic world of farming.

This, or so I thought at the time, was to be my new life. The
farmer's approach was the sensible one. I knew nothing about
farming – except that it would be very, very different from the life
I was leaving behind. I wanted tranquillity instead of excitement
and I'd always dreamed of owning a patch of land I could call my
own – ever since I was thirteen and spent a week in Somerset at
harvest time at a farm my cousin worked on. They'd let me drive
the tractor slowly around and around the field while they slung
bales of straw on the big trailer and then got me drunk on cider
in the evening. The hangover went eventually, but the appeal
remained.

And here I was, twenty-five years later, with almost enough
money in the bank to make it happen. That's because of the
extraordinary generosity of the BBC in those years towards foreign
correspondents who lived abroad. The salary was relatively modest

but you paid no tax, your home was provided and anyway you were away so much you lived on very generous expenses. If you chose to leave your children in Britain (we didn't) the BBC paid to send them to private schools and also paid to send them to you for holidays three times a year. It meant you could basically bank your salary and even rent out your home in the UK to add to the pot. One or two of my colleagues wanted even more. Infamously, a radio correspondent charged the BBC for a lawnmower as part of his 'living expenses' allowance. It might have been acceptable if he'd had a large lawn – but he lived in a flat on top of a skyscraper. It cost him his job. Things have changed since then.

I did not end up buying the lovely view in Dorset. I went home to Wales instead and bought Fronlas: 134 acres of dairy farm, lock, stock and barrel. It had been so neglected over the years there wasn't a gate left swinging, a fence left standing or a cow that seemed to realise her job was to stand quietly while she delivered gallons of nice creamy milk. Most were rejects from other herds that the farmer had bought cheaply: savage beasts, some of them, who wanted to kick your head in when you tried to wash their warty teats or too old and weary to bother. Too old and weary to deliver much more than a cupful of milk, too. I didn't spot any of that at the time, of course. I was a novice and failed to notice the way the farmer's eyes lit up when it dawned on him. He knew a mug when he spotted one.

On the day we took over I was on one of my last foreign trips, which happened to be in China. I phoned Eddie, my enthusiastic young farm manager.

'How's it going?'

There was a slight pause and then: 'Well … we've got sixty starving cows plus all the young stock, not a bale of hay or a pound of silage to feed them with and it's just coming to the end of winter so there's not a blade of grass in the fields either. Apart from that everything's fine.'

Luckily, what we did have were generous and immensely helpful neighbours, who bailed us out. Literally. But I learned over the next few weeks the economic reality of small dairy farming. You can survive (just) if you meet a few basic conditions:

- the only labour you employ is your unpaid wife and children;
- you are prepared to work seven days a week;
- you actively dislike taking holidays and your idea of luxury is a new pair of wellington boots when the old ones spring a leak;
- you are highly skilled in animal husbandry, mechanics, soil management, weather forecasting and everything else that normal people pay experts to do for them;
- you actually like cows even when you know they do not like you.

The desperately sad truth – and things have got infinitely worse since I bought Fronlas in 1971 – is that those farmers who create the countryside that we all love so much are vanishing. I mean those small farms with lots of hedges and soil that has not been so plastered with chemicals that worms and other insects and birds have no reasonable chance of surviving.

It is different for those farmers (or farming companies) with a few thousand acres of good flat land in East Anglia, for instance. They have done away with the hedges, so their enormous machines (usually, owned by contractors who roll like an invading army from farm to farm) have nothing in their way as they plough and harvest and spray. And how they spray. The effect was that pretty much the only thing left living in those endless prairies was the wheat or the barley or the oilseed rape. The farmer made a fat profit in the short term, but the soil suffered terribly – and is still suffering.

Some small farmers do manage to make a reasonable living and many of them are those who took the gamble of spurning chemicals and converting to organic farming. I met two of them after I'd been at Fronlas for only a few weeks. They appeared at the bottom of my drive one Saturday morning, welcomed me to Wales and asked what the hell I was doing using chemicals. They were Peter Segger and Patrick Holden, two of the most remarkable people I have ever met. We became close friends and remain so to this day. The organic revolution would not have happened without them and a few other brave and reckless souls in west Wales in the 1960s.

They farmed land near me and both were regarded as completely barmy by just about every other farmer in their county. The rules for profitable farming were straightforward and everyone knew them. You spread tons of nitrogen on the grass in the spring or you'd never grow enough to feed the cows or any other crops; you stuffed the cows full of antibiotics every time they sneezed or they'd curl up and die; you killed off every weed and insect with poisonous sprays or they'd eat you out of house and home. Wasn't that what everyone had been doing since the dawn of the age of intensive agriculture which had revolutionised farming soon after the war?

Peter and Patrick did none of that. They found other ways to crop crops and they very nearly went bankrupt trying to prove it, but they survived. And so did their farms – and their message. Organic farming improves, rather than degrades, the soil, enhances the environment and produces food that is better and, in reality, cheaper. Don't look only at the price we pay in the supermarket; look at all the other costs. Who picked up the £4 billion bill for BSE, just for starters? And what price can we put on the environmental vandalism of industrial agriculture?

Not that I can claim credit for my own organic achievements, alas. I had neither the knowledge nor the aptitude nor the determination nor the ambition. Peter and Patrick wanted to save the world. I wanted to save my marriage. They also needed to prove it was possible for a small farmer to make a perfectly decent living from their modest acreage. I had another job.

I could earn a lot more in a couple of days sitting in a nice warm studio reading a few lines from an autocue than I could in a freezing milking parlour in the middle of winter before the sun has risen waiting for a beast weighing a third of a ton to try kicking me to death.

You might think they are gentle doe-eyed beasts, and so they are when they are dealing with experienced dairymen who know and like them. But I tell you, they can smell fear. And I learned that the first time I ended up flat on my back in a pile of steaming dung with a bruise the size of a very large hoof on my hip, barely able to stand and knowing that I had another fifty cows to milk before the tanker arrived. I learned a couple of other things too: things that should have been obvious to me several years ago. I was not born to be a farmer and Fronlas was not, perhaps, the rural idyll I had created in my dreams. So I sold up in the early 1980s and settled for being a newsreader instead. Not that my path to newsreading had been quite as smooth as Alan Protheroe had promised after that dinner in Stellenbosch.

When I managed finally to get back to London from South Africa many months later, having heard barely a cheep from Alan in the meantime, I reported for duty and asked him when I was to start newsreading. He looked slightly puzzled and, in truth, more than a little shifty. The meeting in Stellenbosch might as well never have happened.

'What? Newsreader? You don't want to be a newsreader, bloody good reporter like you, sitting behind a desk like some stuffed dummy reading an autocue …'

'But Alan, you clearly promised …'

'Nonsense! What we need is an experienced foreign correspondent like you who won't be wasted in Joburg or Washington … you'll live here in London and your patch will be the whole world! If a really big story breaks somewhere you'll be the man to do it. Best reporting job on the planet eh *bach*? And you're just the man for it.' Great. I felt like the waiter taking Alan's order for dinner. Or maybe the piece of steak. This was exactly the job I did not want. I knew what it would mean and I was right. For the next year I barely saw Britain – or my family. I was out of the country for almost nine months.

And then a new editor took over BBC Television News and he delivered on the Protheroe promise. I tore up my passport, burned my suitcase and swore the next foreign trip I made would be across the River Styx or wherever old hacks go when they finally cast off this mortal coil.

Actually I was a little more cautious than that. I suspected I might be called on to do the odd bit of reporting or presenting the *Nine O'Clock News* from foreign parts occasionally but, even so, my life was transformed. I would leave my home in Henley-on-Thames mid-morning, drive to Television Centre and drive back again about twelve hours later. I had a routine. Bliss.

For roughly half the population, I suspect, newsreading is considered a dream job. You get paid a small fortune for sitting in front of a camera for a few minutes and you become famous into the bargain – assuming you measure fame partly by the number of people who catch your eye in the street, do a double take, and sometimes say: 'Don't I know you from somewhere?'

The problem with this, as I discovered fairly early on, is that you can never be completely sure whether you have really met them or not. There is always the danger that you dismiss them with a slightly patronising smile and mutter something like: 'Oh, you've probably seen me on the telly …' And then you remember after they've left, looking seriously puzzled, that you'd actually sat next to them at dinner six months ago and they had no idea you were supposedly famous. No wonder they hurried off, understandably thinking you were a bit of a prat.

Apart from assuming a convincing degree of false modesty the only real skill required by a newsreader is being able to read fluently from an autocue under the pressure of the studio lights, knowing that several million people are watching you do it. My old friend Michael Buerk once described it as 'the only job that actually requires no talent at all'. Just in case we hadn't got the point he added: 'There are some real lamebrains doing it.' For the record, Michael was brilliant at it.

In the early days of the autocue – or 'teleprompter' as it was then known – the words were typed onto what looked like a wide toilet roll positioned just above the camera lens. The effect was to make the reader look either shifty or snooty because you were always staring slightly above the viewer's eyeline. The other problem was that you had to control it yourself with a pedal. The harder you pressed the faster it went. It made for a pretty jerky performance if, like me in my early days, you were desperately nervous and your foot kept jiggling up and down.

It's much easier these days when the autocue screen is positioned in front of the lens and operated by a professional. Most people can manage it perfectly well with a bit of practice – though some need more than others. It was often said that Ronald Reagan – not perhaps the sharpest brain ever to occupy the Oval Office – required two autocue screens when he was addressing a conference. One screen would have 'Good …' on it and the other, when he swivelled his head to take in the rest of the audience, would have '… morning.' Possibly unfair on a much-underrated president but, with the best will in the world, you'd be hard-pressed to describe sitting in front of a camera and reading from an autocue as demanding.

When I joined the BBC, newsreaders were not journalists. They were almost all continuity announcers or, in some cases, actors who hadn't quite made the grade. They were required to have a pleasant voice, an unthreatening appearance, a degree of authority and a certain amount of charm. Silvery grey hair was not exactly compulsory but it was definitely an asset. So was being a man.

I worked briefly as a subeditor in the television newsroom in the days when Robert Dougall was one of the best known and most loved (yes, the audience loved newsreaders in those far-off days) in the business. I was simultaneously intrigued and baffled by the way he dealt with the scripts as they were presented to him by us newsroom hacks who'd written them. The notion of a news-reader writing his own script had yet to be born.

Robert would sit erect in his chair, as though the cameras were pointing at him, and read the lines aloud. Then he would read them again and this time, with a heavy pencil, would underline the word in each sentence that he thought most worthy of empha-sis. Then he would do it again. And again. By the time he'd moved on to the next script almost every word in every story would be underlined and almost every word emphasised. Often the story made almost no sense but it didn't matter: he was Robert Dougall. I truly believe that if Robert had chosen to deliver the news in Aramaic standing on his head, at least half the audience would have assumed there had to be a very good reason for it and they'd have loved him even more.

Many years after he'd retired I asked him whether he was miss-ing the public adulation. 'Not in the slightest old boy,' he told me, 'I was in Regent's Park only yesterday and a couple of elderly ladies approached me to say how much they enjoyed the news when I was delivering it. I told them I'd stopped years ago. "No no, of course you haven't," one of them said as the other nodded, "I saw you only the other night and you were wearing that lovely blue tie. You must never retire!"'

I admit I was slightly sceptical of the tale at the time, but no longer. I still get elderly strangers approaching to ask me what I'm doing these days because they haven't seen me reading the news recently. Unsurprising really, given that I had last presented the *Nine O'Clock News* more than thirty years ago.

The original plan had been for me to present five days a week, which would have been pretty daunting, but the bosses relented. I would do three days and the other presenter would be my old friend John Simpson. Even better. John is a brilliant journalist, one of the kindest and most decent men I have ever known and we share the same, seriously warped sense of humour. And, boy, did we need it over the coming months. The audience did not like us – which is a bit like saying the snake isn't terribly fond of the mongoose. Except that with the mongoose it isn't personal. With the audience of the new revamped *Nine* it seemed very personal. They hated us – partly because we had ousted Richard Baker.

Many felt, with some justification, that Dickie had been treated pretty shabbily by BBC News. He was an institution in the very best sense of the word. He was the first person ever to read the news on television way back in 1954 and he'd been doing it ever since. He was also a consummate professional: always in total control, never flustered. Above all, the audience both liked and trusted him. He was an old friend in every living room in the land.

He was also a very nice man. On the day of my first outing on the *Nine O'Clock* Dickie had been demoted to reading the *Six O'Clock News* and I was doing my best to avoid bumping into him. I tried to imagine how I might have reacted if I'd been in his position – unseated after nearly thirty years of immaculate service by a callow youth who'd never read a news bulletin in his life. I should not have worried. When I went into the newsreaders' make-up room half an hour before we went on air there was a message scrawled across the mirror in lipstick. It read: 'Break a leg John! You can do it! Dickie.'

I can't tell you what my first *Nine* was like because I can't remember. And I can't remember because I was frozen with fear. All I could think about was that 10 million people out there beyond the studio lights were watching me and waiting for me to make a fool of myself. Ten million people. Each of them (with the possible exception of my nearest and dearest and the BBC management) willing me to fail – if only because I wasn't Dickie Baker. But of course I did what I had to do. I read the words on the autocue as they appeared and I suppose I must have been conscious of the director talking into my earpiece from time to time. But only just.

If the autocue had stopped working or a large rat had leaped onto my chest and started nibbling at my nose I would have kept sitting there and kept reading. My brain simply was not functioning. People talk about being on autopilot but it was much worse than that. I was in a state of suspended animation. When it was all over the editor came into the studio and told me I had been brilliant. Obviously I hadn't but what else could he say? 'Sorry old boy, this newsreading lark obviously isn't for you. Maybe you'd be better off going back on the road – or possibly retraining as a messenger!'

The way I was feeling, anything would be preferable to subjecting myself to that twenty-five minutes of torture again the next night … and the next … and the next. It was like looking down a very long tunnel with a torture chamber at the end except that instead of the water slowly dripping off its dank walls there was a bank of very bright lights with all those people on the other side of them – 10 million people who, I was about to learn, hated me and, when he started his stint in front of the cameras, hated John too.

Mercifully those were the days before instant communication. If we'd had email and the ludicrous Twitter mob back then I suspect the bosses would have pulled us off the air immediately, crawled to Dickie to beg his forgiveness and asked him to come back. But it took a few days for the letters to start arriving in the post and another few for the television critics to have their say. And then it began.

I often think that if I had not been sharing an office with John at the time I might very well have taken the lift to the top floor of TV Centre, climbed out onto the roof and jumped off. The word mortifying is nowhere near strong enough. Embarrassing? Certainly. Crushing? Without a doubt. Humiliating? Oh yes! It was John who saved me for two reasons. The first was that the audience seemed to hate us equally so we shared the pain. The second was that John had a brilliant idea.

When the BBC is criticised by the audience its instinctive response is to say sorry. John took the opposite view. He suggested that instead of handing all the letters to the department responsible for complaints we should deal with them ourselves. Every single one of them. And instead of grovelling and promising to try harder in future and be a bit more like Dickie, we would fight fire with fire. The more abusive the letter, the more abusive our reply. And we awarded each other scores for who could write the most creative abuse. John always won.

I almost felt sorry for the poor viewer who had written to tell him that he was the newsreading equivalent of a particularly inarticulate talking dog, or some such. To this day I wish I had been there when he opened John's reply to find himself accused of being lower than a camel's crotch and far more smelly. They didn't have to be clever, you understand, just rude.

And here's the extraordinary thing. We had expected retribution to be visited upon us by our bosses who would, obviously, be overwhelmed by complaints from the recipients of our bile. Exactly the opposite happened. The more vicious our abuse, the more cringing their apology when they wrote back to us as, invariably, they did. They almost always began with something like: 'I'm so sorry if I've offended you by describing you as the worst newsreader in the history of broadcasting ...' I've never been able to figure it out. But eventually the flood of letters reduced to a trickle and then pretty much dried up when the poor old audience realised they were never going to get their beloved Dickie back in his rightful place.

The newspaper and magazine critics were more difficult to deal with. No point in sending them abusive letters: they'd be delighted to know their barbs had gone home. Richard Ingrams, then the editor of *Private Eye* and a *Spectator* columnist, was probably the most vicious. John and I spent happy hours discussing ways we might kill him, or at least cause him the maximum inconvenience. I think it was John who suggested we should find out where he parked his car and pour pee into his petrol tank. I don't suppose we were serious about it, but the childish plotting helped a little.

From the bosses there was an ominous silence until the day I was called into the editor's office. It was a Wednesday and he told me I would need to come in the next day to read the news. I reminded him that John was on the rota. Not any longer, he said. He's on a plane on his way to Uruguay. I've never been able to verify this, but I gather the director general, no less, had decided enough was enough and one of us had to be sacrificed to appease the audience. Why John and not me, I have no idea. I thought he was much better: far more authoritative and convincing than I had ever been. But the decision had been taken and that was the end of John's days as a newsreader.

And what a sensible decision it turned out to be. John was free to do what he has always done superlatively: travel to foreign places and produce reports that tell us what we need to know. That, of course, is the minimum requirement for a foreign correspondent but John has always gone so much further. He is immensely resourceful, a brilliant writer and one of the bravest reporters it has ever been my privilege to work with. We have talked often about the day he got the push from the *Nine*. He has always been immensely grateful to the DG for sacking him.

As for me, I was left to soldier on for another five years. Inevitably I got over my first-day nerves but it's one of the oldest clichés in the slim volume of *How To Do Live Broadcasting* that the day you stop feeling at least a wee bit nervous is probably the day you should stop. In the end (having been asked to present five days a week instead of three) I fell victim to the America Rule: whatever American broadcasters do, the British must eventually copy.

In this case the America Rule dictated that one newsreader may be good but two is better. And, in the perfect world, one will be a grizzled male and the other a rather beautiful younger female. I've never quite understood why, and, even after all these years, I am still embarrassed when I watch one presenter staring raptly at the other reading from the autocue. In a typical half-hour news bulletin there will be four or five minutes of copy to be read. Does it really take two people to do that? But I eventually fell victim to the Rule myself. I was told by my clearly discomfited boss that in future the *Nine* would have two presenters and the other would be Julia Somerville. Then he waited for me to ask the obvious question. It was the only one that mattered: 'Who will read the headlines?'

He looked down at his shoes and mumbled 'Umm ... Julia ...'

And that's when I decided my time as a newsreader was up. I could perfectly well see their reasoning – or at least I tried to pretend I could. Julia was a terrific journalist and broadcaster and (I think we can all agree on this) rather better-looking than me. In fact, she was beautiful and it would be foolish to pretend that good looks don't play a part in a hugely competitive business. And why shouldn't they? Television (the clue is in the word) is a visual medium.

So, one way and another, when the call came from the *Today* programme on that October night, I was ready for it.

PART 2

Today
and
Today

7

A very strange time to be at work

Daily Mail

1 July 2005

'So you like a good argument do you, Mr Humphrys?'

That was the first question I faced when I appeared this week as a witness before a House of Lords committee set up to look into the renewal of the BBC's charter. I probably shouldn't admit it, but it threw me.

How can anyone with a spark of life in his soul and an IQ in double figures not like a good argument?

Lord Fowler, committee chairman and former chairman of the Conservative Party, might as well have asked me if I liked eating and drinking and taking in the odd lungful of air.

Life without argument is winter without a trace of frost, summer with no hint of a blue sky, Christmas without the smile of an excited child.

Without argument, life would be as bland as a plate of fish and chips without salt and vinegar. The food would keep you alive sure enough, but what would be the point?

Sensible people take their time when they are faced with making a decision that will change their lives. I took roughly ten seconds. It was close to midnight on an autumn night in 1986 and I had just returned home from Television Centre. I presented both the *Nine O'Clock News* on BBC1 and the late bulletin as well. The call was from the deputy editor of the *Today* programme and he wanted to know if I would be interested in taking over from John Timpson when he retired at the end of the year after presenting the programme for two decades. I said yes.

I asked no questions. Not how much money I would be paid: it turned out to be not very much in those far-off days. Nor how many days a week I would have to work. Nor even what time I would have to pitch up in the morning. Now that really was very stupid. I might, just possibly, have had second thoughts if I'd known that the answer would be something along these lines: 'What d'you mean ... in the *morning*? If you present *Today* you do *not* arrive in the morning! You arrive in the middle of the night before the dawn chorus has even begun clearing its throat and when most people are either snuggling deeper into the duvet for another three or four hours' sleep or preparing to die.' Nurses will tell you that 4 a.m. is the most common time for departing this vale of tears – not for pitching up in the office.

But, no, I asked nothing. Not even the most crucial question: why do you think I might be remotely capable of doing the job? I would, after all, be taking over from one of the most experienced, talented and respected radio broadcasters of his time on the most important programme the BBC broadcasts. And my own experience of live radio was precisely zero. It's true that television news is live, too, but there's a very big difference. Virtually every word I delivered on the *Nine* was written on an autocue and all I had to do was read it aloud.

Today was different. *Today* was three hours of live radio and I would be doing rather more than reading from a script I had written hours earlier. I would be conducting interviews – lots of them – and often there would be no time to prepare. Added to which, *Today* was not just any old news programme. It was, by a mile, the most important news programme on the BBC. It was also the most controversial, the most loved, the most loathed and, by a country mile, the most demanding,

Apart from having to go to bed before a typical seven-year-old to handle a 6 a.m. start – even earlier than it had been before I joined – it would also mean being forced to read every newspaper every day, being prepared at the drop of a hat to interview the prime minister or to master a complicated subject about which you know precisely nothing and being happy to face national ridicule and/or abuse when you make a fool of yourself. Which would, if I'd paused to think about it, be worryingly often in my own case.

And, of course, it was radio. Boring old steam radio. Everyone knew that radio was on its way out didn't they? How could it possibly compete with appearing every night on television?

Why did it take me all of ten seconds to abandon one of the most cushy jobs in the known universe and commit myself to what would turn out to be thirty-three years in one of the most unforgiving? I suppose the simple answer is that there was no other programme like it. It reigned supreme over the nation's breakfast tables – if only because it had almost no competition. Breakfast television and commercial radio were struggling to make much impact and Radio 5 Live had yet to be born, so if middle Britain wanted serious news in the morning it turned to *Today*.

So let me take you back to 1987 – my first day as a presenter on *Today*. It was a very cold January morning and I had set the alarm for 3 a.m. – even earlier than strictly necessary for obvious reasons, the main one being that I was scared stiff. For a start, I was afraid the alarm might not go off and that meant I couldn't get to sleep. It's one of those nasty tricks the unconscious mind plays on us. It nags away, forcing us to keep checking the time until the last moment, that moment when you have finally slipped away into blissful unconsciousness. And that, of course, is when the alarm bell rings. Is there any more hateful sound in the known universe? You want to scream NO! But there is no appeal against the judgement of an alarm clock.

And, my God, it's cold at that hour of the morning in January. Correction: that hour of the night. How can 3 a.m. be morning? It was so cold that when I turned on the bedside light my breath became a frosty vapour. It was even colder in the bathroom. Why the hell hadn't I showered the night before? That was one lesson I learned very quickly.

I struggled into my clothes, my body pleading for a hot cup of tea or a hot bowl of porridge. Neither was possible. I couldn't use the kitchen downstairs because I was renting the lower floor of the house I had just bought to a couple of lodgers and didn't want to risk waking them up. I'd divorced a year before and the house in Henley-on-Thames went to my wife. It had taken us roughly an hour to agree on a divorce settlement. A neighbour, who happened to be a lawyer, did a quick draft of the agreement in our kitchen and that was that. God knows she had earned it over the years she'd been married to me.

So there I was … sitting on the floor of the bedroom in the middle of a winter's night wrapped in an eiderdown against the bitter cold but still shivering from my shower, eating a bowl of cold porridge, trying not to remind myself that in my old job I wouldn't have even been thinking about getting out of bed until *Today* had finished. I was trying very hard to remember why I had agreed to do this for what would almost certainly be the rest of my career.

In fact if there was one consolation it was that it would never be quite this bad again. Within a few weeks I had established a routine that meant I could be out of bed, dressed, teeth brushed and into the waiting car in ten minutes flat. It meant showering and shaving the night before to get that precious extra ten minutes in bed, finding a supplier of blackout curtains and having not one, not two, but three alarm clocks, always at least one of them a clockwork job in case the batteries on the others run out. I tried, in the early days, leaving my phone plugged in (remember land-lines?) so that the office could call me if I failed to show. But I abandoned that after the first few times I was woken up at strange hours by pizza delivery men phoning to check that this was the right address or drunks who'd misdialled. It has always driven the overnight producers mad that they can't contact me if something very important happens at, say, midnight – but better that than getting no sleep.

One slightly trickier problem was that mine was a terrace house with thin walls and my neighbour went to bed at about midnight. That would not have mattered had he stayed single – he was the perfect neighbour who made scarcely a sound – but he did not. It was, I learned very soon after his new partner had moved in, a passionate relationship – and it regularly reached its climax after I'd been asleep for about three hours. End of sleep. What to do? Banging on the wall was unthinkable and anyway I very much doubt they'd have heard me.

So I sat at my front downstairs window one morning after a particularly torrid encounter the night before and ambushed him when he emerged. I greeted him with a cheery 'Hello Phillip,' (names have been changed to protect the innocent), 'how are things?'

'Fine thanks,' he said, 'and you?'

'Well, feeling a bit tired to be honest. You know how early I have to get up and I keep being woken these days by a curious wailing sound at pretty much the same time every night. God knows what it is. Maybe one of those urban foxes or a couple of cats in the throes of passion ... don't suppose you've been hearing it have you?'

He looked embarrassed and mumbled something that I couldn't quite catch. Not a very subtle tactic, I grant you, but it did the trick.

The subject of sleep is never far from a *Today* presenter's thoughts and we all seem to cope with it in our different ways.

The great Sue MacGregor simply refused to acknowledge it was a problem and was always first to arrive, perfectly made-up looking as though she had just left her favourite beauty salon. I made a tentative comment about it once. She gave me one of those looks. 'Wouldn't dream of coming in without my face on!' she snapped. Jim Naughtie's appearance rather depended on what he'd been doing the night before. If, for instance, it had been a spot of painting and decorating he might well appear in trousers that looked like an artist's palette.

Both Jim and Brian Redhead refused to allow the early start to affect their social lives. Jim regarded an invitation to a political reception as a royal command. It meant he was always on top of the latest political gossip, but sometimes needed to catch up on a little sleep during the weather forecast or a particularly boring interview. Brian would sleep for two hours in the afternoon and spend the evening drinking whisky at his much-loved Garrick Club. I took my cue from him and decided that my social life wasn't going to change much either. I learned the hard way how stupid that was.

I had been feeling no pain at all when I fell into bed at about midnight after a pretty heavy evening in my first few weeks in the job. Nor when I pitched up in the office a few hours later. I was probably still drunk. The hangover hit me at about 7.30 a.m. just after I'd started interviewing a very senior politician – a party leader no less. I realised, as he was answering the first question, that I couldn't think of a second one. The brain froze. That was bad – but not half as bad as realising a fraction of a second later that I couldn't even remember his name.

That was when I swore my self-denying ordinance and I've stuck to it rigidly ever since. It means that I never go out the night before the programme and stay in reading a book for an hour or two before bedtime, possibly with half a pint of weak beer or a very small glass of wine. So much for the glamorous life of a national broadcaster.

There is a cruel irony in the fact that because you present a radio programme with a vast audience you receive endless invitations to parties, dinners, film premieres, theatre first nights and so on. But because you have to get up so early for said programme you have to turn them down. Something else I realised pretty early on was that you can't even enjoy a lie-in on the mornings you're not on duty. Your body clock is set.

Most people assume the early start must be especially hideous in the middle of winter. Not so. They forget that if you are to get up at 3.30 a.m. you must go to bed very early the night before – in my case 8.30 p.m. In winter it can be rather pleasant to snuggle down into a warm duvet when others are having to venture out into the sleet or snow, not to mention always having the perfect excuse for not going to all the dreary receptions and book launches and events you didn't want to go to anyway. But in summer not so much.

I happen to live in a London square with a tennis court in the middle. Very quickly you get to hate all those sporty, happy young people bashing balls and screaming with pleasure when you're trying to doze off. You want to open the window and shout: 'Can't you make less noise! D'you know what time it is!' But of course what they're doing is normal. It's what you are doing that is not.

The ridiculous sleep regime even affected my choice of house. I realised I'd have to move when I discovered that, at the great age of fifty-seven, I was going to become a father again and my partner ruled that a baby needed a garden. True, but the baby's father had needs too: the main one being not to be woken up by a bawling baby. That was what dictated our choice of house and the strategy we employed to find the right one.

When we found something that looked vaguely right my partner would go into one bedroom and I would go into the room that was furthest away. We would close the doors and she would scream. If I could hear the scream we would cross the house off our list and try the next one. Lord knows what the owner or the estate agent made of the screaming, but eventually we found a house that met our needs. In fact the whole bizarre exercise turned out to have been totally (and expensively) unnecessary. We never did need a soundproof bedroom after all. The baby was one of those gifts from the gods who went to sleep at seven and woke up twelve hours later. Without fail.

Getting up in the middle of the night does take its toll.

That's an obvious thing to say, but it really struck home with me only after I'd been presenting for more than thirty years. That's not because I looked in the mirror – something I try to avoid as much as possible – but because I looked at Sarah Montague.

Sarah joined the programme in 2002 and we've been good friends ever since – though it might not have seemed that way to onlookers. She'll probably deny this, but she was always giving me a hard time – turning the studio heating up when I turned it down, berating me for reading the *Daily Mail*, calling me old-fashioned because I refused to have anything to do with social media and so on. But I like and admire her enormously. She was not just brilliant at presenting *Today*, she did it while she was producing and bringing up a family. Now that's a real achievement. She had three children during her years at *Today*. Three daughters in the space of six years and one older stepdaughter. She loved *Today* but she loved her children more and as they grew older she accepted that the two simply did not go together. So she left the programme in April 2018 to present *The World at One*. The next time I saw her – a few weeks later – she had been transformed. It was as though she'd had a massive injection of whatever serum is needed to knock fifteen years off your biological age. And the reason was simple. She no longer had to get up in the middle of the night.

It's not only the weird hours that make *Today* such a demanding programme. It's the shortage of time to prepare for the interviews. Often there is no time. I sometimes reflect on another political programme called *On the Record* which I presented for nine years. It went out on BBC1 at lunchtime on Sundays and lasted for an hour. It usually consisted of a package by a reporter (one of whom was a youngster called Michael Gove, but that's another story) and a couple of live interviews.

Often there was only one interview and we usually knew who it would be at least a few days in advance. I would pitch up at the Westminster office after I'd finished presenting *Today* on Saturday mornings and spend as long as we needed discussing the interview with the editor and his team and planning the shape the interview would follow. If the politician answered the question by saying 'X', I would follow up with one question. If he said 'Y', I would follow up with something else. And so on. I would be fully briefed on all possibilities and able to close his every escape route no matter how much ducking and diving or even (heaven forfend) dissembling there was. At least that was the theory. And I had two brains to rely on – both of them infinitely more politically acute than my own. One belonged to the programme's editor David Jordan. One of his jobs was to talk into my earpiece throughout the interviews and if I went astray he would haul me back onto the right track.

David probably knew more about politics than anyone I have ever worked with and had an opinion on everything. A very strong opinion. In the thirty years I have known him I don't believe I have ever heard him say the equivalent of 'Hmm ... I'm not sure about that ...' He was always sure – and *almost* always right. But he never let his personal opinions colour his journalism. Eventually he became a senior figure in BBC management – director of editorial policy – one of those rare bosses who infuriated those above him and those below him in almost equal measure. He and I had some glorious rows but managed to stay friends.

My other 'brain' was John Wakefield, who had been the editor of *Weekend World* in its glory days when it was presented by the late, great Brian Walden. John is not just one of the cleverest men I have ever met but unique in the world of broadcasting – at least in my experience. When London Weekend closed down in 1992 he could have taken his pick of any number of choice jobs. He took none of them. He enjoyed working in television and writing, but he enjoyed other things more: the company of his partner, walking the hills, playing his piano, reading, lunching and dining with friends. He had enough money to clear his mortgage (the pay-offs from LWT had been pretty generous) and knew he could always earn a bit more if he needed it from the odd freelance engagement such as *On the Record* and he could see no reason why he should surrender his independence by handing over his life to some mighty corporation. So, in his early forties and at the peak of his ability, he 'retired' to enjoy his life. Which is exactly what he has done.

On Sunday mornings I would report to Television Centre a few hours before we went on air and the three of us would go over the programme yet again. A great deal of time and effort involving several experienced journalists and sometimes a Westminster insider went into delivering the one or two interviews in *On the Record*. It was, for the most part, time well spent. I regret enormously that long-form political interviews have effectively disappeared from the BBC. The audiences were never massive, nor did we expect them to be, but they allowed an insight into how the political world works that you simply cannot get from a programme like *Today*. Not that all our preparation absolutely guaranteed a brilliant interview. That depended on who you were interviewing. As the Americans like to say, you can put lipstick on a pig but it's still a pig. Or a boor in this case.

I remember with painful clarity a programme when Gordon Brown was the Chancellor of the Exchequer and the big political controversy of the day was how to deal with the public sector borrowing requirement (PSBR). Mr Brown had agreed to appear and David decided that because the PSBR was such a complicated and important issue we would spend the entire programme dealing with it. We knew the risks were high. I'm not sure that we knew how high.

The first factor, inevitably, was Mr Brown's light touch. He didn't have one. He might have had a brain the size of Parliament

Square, but he was never going to challenge Peter Ustinov for his wit. And the PSBR might have been crucial to the economic well-being of the country, but only an economist could have found it anything other than impenetrably boring. Even so, we thought, we would be able to break through the boring barrier, test Mr Brown's resolve and hold the attention of an audience desperate to learn more. Wishful thinking.

After the first ten minutes I was beginning to have my doubts. After twenty minutes I was starting to grow desperate. After thirty minutes I was sure I could hear David groaning into my earpiece – though it might have been snoring. And after forty minutes I was tempted to rip off my microphone, leap out of the window of Gordon Brown's office in Downing Street, find a guardsman in Horse Guards Parade and invite him to run me through with his ceremonial sword. Drastic maybe, but at least I'd be spared any more PSBR. But I stuck it out and so did some of our viewers. Probably about twelve and all of them economists.

The point is that I would not have been able to contemplate even attempting such an interview on such a complex issue with a politician of Gordon Brown's calibre had I not been briefed up to my eyeballs over the previous two days. On *Today* it's rather different.

On *Today* we do not get a couple of days to plan our political interviews – for the very good reason that we usually don't have the first idea who we will be interviewing until the night before. And sometimes not until we are actually on air. There are one or two exceptions. We'll usually get at least a day's warning of an interview with the prime minister. Note the 'usually'. I still recall with a slight shudder what happened on a quiet spring morning in 1987. It was 6.40 a.m. and I was about to start reading the newspaper review. The voice of the editor came into my headphones: 'Thatcher's on the phone ... asking for you!'

I couldn't reply because the studio was live, so I flicked him a V-sign through the studio window to indicate that I was not amused by his silly joke. Yeah, sure, the prime minister has phoned up and 'asked for me'? As if! The next thing I heard was that unmistakeable voice: 'Mr Humphrys? Good morning.'

I learned later that she had been making toast in the kitchen of Number 10, listening to her radio as was her wont, and heard me interviewing a senior Soviet spokesman about a natural disaster that had struck what was then the USSR. I'd made some reference to the visit she was scheduled to make to Moscow in a few weeks' time and she wanted to correct a slightly misleading impression that she thought had been given. So she ordered the Downing Street switchboard to put her through to the *Today* office.

To this day I give thanks that the producer who answered the phone had not followed his usual night-shift routine of a few pints in the pub for his supper break followed by half a bottle of Scotch back in the office. He was, mercifully, sober. So when the phone rang and the voice familiar to the entire nation announced 'It's Margaret Thatcher here. Please put me through to Mr Humphrys,' he did not reply: 'Sure and I'm the queen of Sheba! Bugger off!'

And so I found myself conducting an interview with the most powerful and most scary woman in the world with approximately two seconds' notice. When we'd finished with the Soviet stuff I suggested to her that, since she happened to be on the line, we might as well have a chat about a few other things as well. She agreed. I interviewed her for about fifteen minutes and we broadcast the interview again at 8.10. Years later I was talking to her formidable press spokesman Sir Bernard Ingham about it. He told me that not only had she not consulted him before calling *Today*, the first he knew about it was when he was driving into work and heard it happen.

'I was so shocked I nearly drove off the fooking road!' he said.

That was the first time I'd been called by a prime minister while I was at work. And, sadly, the last.

Four o'clock in the morning is, believe me, a very strange time to be reporting for work. There are two good things about it. One is that the streets of London are blissfully free of traffic, so the journey from my home to Broadcasting House, which might take forty minutes or more during the day, takes ten. I recall one that was even quicker. That's because the minicab driver chose not to stop at red lights. I pointed this out to him after he'd jumped three lights in a row. He turned to me in the back seat, his foot still on the throttle, grinning broadly and admonished me: 'Chill man … great ganja last night … great ganja …!' The BBC uses a different taxi firm these days.

The other good thing about arriving so early is that you get to leave early too … just as everybody else is arriving. There is something rather satisfying about walking past crowds of people waiting at the lifts as you head for the exit.

The radio newsroom is a strange sight when you arrive. It is how the director of a Hollywood apocalypse movie with limited imagination might imagine the headquarters of a mighty international news operation minutes after the warning had been given to all citizens to head for the bunkers. There are just two tiny huddles of dead-eyed people in a vast space of empty desks and blank computer screens. One is the *Today* team, the other the World Service people who are broadcasting to different time zones around the world.

Did I say the *Today* 'team'? I exaggerate a little. I should say the *Today* 'couple'. There are only two producers, who have spent a long and lonely night worrying about how they will fill three hours of airtime in a way that will satisfy millions of listeners. They face a formidable challenge. They must tell the audience what has been happening in the world since they went to bed and follow up and analyse the most important stories from yesterday. They must fulfil the Reithian remit of informing, educating and entertaining the audience. And they must do it without getting something horribly wrong or offending the director general's best friend or upsetting any one of the myriad self-important pressure groups out there who think the job of *Today* is to reflect their own views faithfully and never call them into question however tendentious or barking mad they may be. And there are just two people to deliver all that.

One of them is the night editor, who will sit in the control room at 6 a.m. knowing that the next three hours will be the most testing three hours of any young broadcasting journalist's career. And also knowing that decisions made during the long and lonely night may well determine his or her fate. The other is a more junior producer who will handle pre-recorded interviews, bash the phones if a new story develops and either try to set up new interviews or cancel existing interviews that might have been set up the day before but are no longer needed. It can be a pretty thankless task. Most people tend not to be too happy when they have set their alarm for 5.30 a.m. and are phoned at 5 a.m. to be told they won't be appearing on *Today* after all.

When the night team reports for duty the evening before, the night editor will have a brief meeting with the day editor and be handed a version of the running order that has been put together by the day team. With a bit of luck every slot will have been filled but there are often gaps and, more often than not, a touch of desperation about some of the offerings. So they will have to spend the night scouring the newspapers and websites in search of new stories that might yield an interview or two – not just to fill any gaps but to try to improve what's on offer.

Do we really want yet another interview with that former Cabinet minister who says exactly the same thing every time he appears, which mostly comes down to a veiled attack on the prime minister for being foolish enough to have sacked him all those years ago? Should we really subject our long-suffering listeners to yet another plea for more taxpayers' money from that well-meaning but terribly dull organisation that could solve all the problems facing young people today if only they had another million quid a week to spend on counsellors?

Do we really care about the latest survey telling us we could all live to be a hundred if only we ate a diet consisting entirely of mung beans and quinoa – especially when it's been funded by a company that flogs them? Is anyone outside its borders really interested in that very small West African country electing a new president?

Do we really need yet another 8.10 interview that might, just possibly, produce a little more detail about the immense complications of the Brexit process but add not a jot to anyone's understanding of it? Is there anything that will actually interest the listeners, that is relevant to their daily lives, rather than just reflect the obsessions of the big bosses who are far more interested in impressing their political masters and making sure the BBC cannot be accused of underplaying an obscure political development?

Is there ANYTHING in this programme that will bring a smile to the lips of the average listener or, at the very least, surprise them a little?

Is there anything to keep listeners listening?

It is a very tall order. Night editing the *Today* programme is a critically important job and easily the most challenging.

Now at this point I would love to report that when we presenters arrive we put aside any petty rivalries and recognise that the editor is in need of a little encouragement, if not a little TLC. In this kinder, better world of my imagination we sit down with the running order and examine it minutely, offering a word of praise here and perhaps sounding a note of caution there – but always positive, always putting ourselves in the shoes of this unfortunate soul who's been doing his damndest all night to turn a cow's ear into a silk purse or, at the very least, something resembling a programme that will engage millions of radio listeners. We are brimful of new ideas and helpful suggestions. In short, we share the editor's burden and provide the boost he will need before facing three testing hours in the control room of a live studio when all he wants to do is sleep. I wish.

It's not that we don't share the same ambition as the editor. We all want to deliver a brilliant programme. Where our paths diverge is that we may have different ideas as to how to make that happen.

The brutal truth is that each presenter wants to play the starring role. We each want to do the big political interview, chair the most interesting discussion and chat with the most famous and amusing guest. So what we are actually doing when we peruse the running order is looking for our own names to make sure we haven't been short-changed.

That may be selfish. It is also inevitable. Journalism is a hugely competitive business and broadcast journalism especially so. On a newspaper, it's true, there is only one front-page headline story and of course every reporter dreams of seeing their own byline against it. But at least there are a dozen ways of making your presence felt in the other sixty or eighty pages. Not so on *Today*. What every presenter wants is the 8.10 slot. And there is only one 8.10 slot.

I came to *Today* from television news and my then boss had thought it would make sense for me to get some experience of editing the *Nine* before I started presenting it. He was right, and I learned a lot. I learned that trying to order the formidable Kate Adie to go and stand in Downing Street for hours in the hope that we might snatch a quick interview with some important minister or other was not a wise thing to do. She fixed me with one of those looks, informed me: 'I am a senior foreign correspondent. I do NOT do Downing Street doorsteps!' and stalked off.

I also learned, much more importantly, that the *Nine* shared its producers with the *Six O'Clock News* and when the *Six* came off the air they took their supper break and went off to the canteen. At least, some of them did. Those were the days when almost all BBC premises had rather pleasant bars. God knows why the bosses thought it was a good idea to give staff the opportunity to get smashed on duty at heavily subsidised prices, but that's the way it was and there were plenty who took full advantage of it. By the time the producers came back to the newsroom to work on putting the *Nine* on the air they were about as much use to the editor as a toddler in the cockpit of a jumbo jet.

So, one way and another, I learned a lot about the difficulties an editor faces as the clock ticks down towards that moment when you have to go on air – whether you're ready or not, whether you have the programme you really want or not. With the benefit of hindsight I believe all presenters of *Today* should be forced to spend some time editing overnight. Then, perhaps we'd be a bit more sympathetic to the night editor and possibly – just possibly – a bit less concerned with our own self-importance.

What keeps the editors awake at night (literally) is the fear that something big is happening out there and they won't find out about it until it's too late. Either that or they simply can't find anyone to stand up the story or dismiss it as a load of rubbish. This is often where they really need more than one junior producer, but that battle was fought and lost a long time ago. Radio is the poor relation. Of course television is more expensive to deliver and gets much bigger audiences in the evening. But not early in the morning. *Today*'s audience is several times the size of any morning television programme and its influence is far greater. There was a time when there was one extra producer and an overnight reporter, but these days the accountants rule. Fair enough on one level – it's licence payers' money as we all know – but it's the unpredictability of 'events' that can make life very difficult for a night editor and too often the programme suffers because of the shortage of staff.

So our young (sometimes very young) night editor and a junior producer settle down in front of the computers and phones at about 10 p.m. to study the running order they have been bequeathed and wait for the phone to ring or the screen to start flashing.

In spite of all the turmoil it will create, ours is probably the only trade where we positively want the unexpected to happen. And the stories most likely to grab the listeners' attention will invariably be about something that has gone very badly wrong. Cynical, maybe, but the idea that our readers and listeners want their papers and news bulletins to be packed with good news stories is patently nonsense. Think of it on a local level. Someone tells you the headmaster at your child's school has been awarded an MBE. You nod approvingly and move on. Someone says he's been caught in flagrante with the maths teacher and you want to hear more. It's just the way we are. No one wants a terrible disaster to happen, but when it does they want to know about it.

Another old cliché is that when thousands of people are fleeing from a country because of the death and destruction created by an earthquake or a revolution we journalists are the people trying to get in. Similarly, we presenters want to be working on that morning when the carefully prepared plans are thrown overboard. At 6 a.m. when we say 'Good morning ... this is *Today*' we want the surge of adrenaline that comes from knowing that the next three hours are going to be the equivalent of navigating a minefield without a map. We want to be forced to throw away our carefully crafted scripts and pre-planned interviews and fly by the seats of our pants. A programme that is unchanged from the running order that was handed over by the day team eight hours earlier is regarded as pretty boring at best, a failure at worst.

Mostly, the changes are relatively minor and forced on us by boring logistical problems: the contributor's taxi getting stuck in traffic or technical problems with the line – though these days we will tolerate much dodgier communications than was the case years ago.

It's tempting to think the programme sounded much better in the days when the engineers had a veto over what was transmitted. If they ruled that the quality of the sound did not pass their very exacting standards the interview did not go out on the BBC airwaves. End of story. They would have had no truck with the vagaries and often weird sound quality of Skype or the unreliability of FaceTime. Now we tolerate pretty much anything, just so long as we can vaguely hear what the contributor has to say. It's a gamble and sometimes it pays off. There is nothing to match the urgency of a reporter on a mobile phone describing a dramatic rescue operation as it happens.

Equally, it's a complete pain if it's a routine interview and it sounds as if the interviewee is at the bottom of a swimming pool or on the far side of the moon. There is no excuse for forcing the listener to have to struggle to make out what they are hearing. We have become far too tolerant of poor sound quality. Not that we didn't have technical problems in the good old/bad old days.

I once introduced an 8.10 interview I had recorded with Tony Benn when he was at the height of his fame. It was a truly extraordinary interview but, sadly, not because of what he said. Someone had pressed the wrong button and instead of the Rt Hon. Anthony Benn MP we heard the voice of a Mongolian throat singer practising his art. You have to hear it to appreciate it. Tony was not amused. It took a while to persuade him that it was not deliberate sabotage by the BBC, which was never far enough to the left for his taste.

Sometimes the running order has to be rewritten because one of the contributors has dropped out at the last minute. It might have been a government minister reported to be on the point of resigning who'd changed their mind in the cold light of dawn. Maybe the prime minister had talked them out of it. Maybe their friends had told them to hold their fire. Maybe they just lost their nerve. Whatever the reason, there's a big gap in the programme because they rather fancied having a crack at the leadership themself. Not that they'd have put it like that, of course.

There are endless reasons why the carefully crafted running order might have to be jettisoned because so much has happened since it was prepared that it's about as helpful to the presenters as an ancient scroll discovered beneath the Parthenon. I still shudder a little when I recall an interview that was set up with the late, great Denis Healey – he of the fierce eyebrows and even fiercer temper. He had been booked for the 8.10. He could always be relied on to do a good turn. He was never a speak-your-weight robot politician. Quite the opposite.

There was one particularly colourful interview when he was Chancellor of the Exchequer and we were, I think, in Washington for a meeting of the International Monetary Fund. He decided he would go a little off-piste – probably because he was bored – and regaled me with the story of an encounter with a very senior IMF official who had displeased him in some way. The anecdote ended thus: 'So I told him he could stick the bloody parrot up his arse!' Sadly it was a pre-recorded interview and the parrot never made the final edit.

By the late 1980s Labour was in opposition and Healey was the shadow defence secretary. But earlier in the morning something happened that made the interview rather more enticing. Healey was appearing on breakfast television and the interviewer happened to refer to his wife, Edna. She was in hospital for some relatively minor procedure. So far, so unremarkable. Then the interviewer asked if it was true that the hospital was a private one, rather than NHS. Healey was very cross at what he regarded as an unwarranted intrusion into his wife's privacy, but he did not deny it. Throughout his career he'd had trouble with the left wing of the Labour Party and he knew that this disclosure would prove seriously embarrassing. A senior Labour politician who preached the virtue of the NHS using a private hospital: phony shock horror all round!

Within minutes of his appearance the story was being reported by all the news agencies. I had mixed feelings about it. Obviously the tabloid hack in me was delighted that I'd have something pretty juicy to ask him when he showed up ... but what if he didn't show up? What if he went into hiding?

Normally the 8.10 interviewee arrives in plenty of time for a bit of gossip and maybe a cup of coffee. But when I left the studio just after eight to greet him in the green room there was no sight nor sound of him. Five minutes went by ... still no Healey. What the hell would we do if he didn't show up? More minutes ticked by and at 8.07 precisely I heard footsteps in the corridor. Thank God for that! The door burst open and there he was. But he didn't come in. He poked his head around the door and snapped: 'You going to ask me about Edna?'

'I'm afraid I'm going to have to …' I stuttered, 'it's running on all the news wires and—'

I got no further.

'Right! Well I'm fucking off!' And so he did – slamming the door behind him.

Oh my God. What now? No Denis, no 8.10 interview.

I held my nerve (or maybe I was just paralysed with fear at the prospect of having to ad lib for ten minutes) and heard his steps receding down the corridor … then stopping … then returning. The door opened … the Healey head poking around it again.

'How much are you going to ask me about her?'

'The bare minimum. It's not as if—'

I got no further.

'Well come on then … let's bloody well do it!'

So we did.

It's the political interviews that stay in the memory – usually because they tend to be the most heated. But not always. Tracey Emin got pretty heated when I interviewed her from her home in London in 1999 about her famous *Unmade Bed*. It was one of the shortlisted works for the Turner Prize and easily the most controversial entry. We got off on the wrong foot from the start when I suggested that artists like her and Damien Hirst had become so successful at least in part because they went out of their way to attract publicity.

She thought that was absolute rubbish: 'I worked for ten years absolutely without a penny. It's only in the last five years. I'm thirty-seven now and I'm old enough to be successful and be respected for what I do … Damien's publicity comes from the work that he does, first of all, and that's the same with me: it's the work that I make that leads on the publicity, not – not *me*.'

Well maybe … and it was hard to argue with her next point: 'After all,' she said, 'you wanted to interview me this morning. I didn't ring you and ask you about it.'

Fair enough. But then I touched a really raw nerve. I wondered what it was that made her bed – with its used condoms and soiled sheets – a work of art instead of any other unmade bed that happened to be in a bedroom rather than an art gallery.

'Because,' she said, 'their bed isn't in the Tate Gallery demanding the attention that mine is and it's not put into a critical position where they make a judgement over it. I decided to make a judgement over this object in my life … I looked at the bed and I decided that it wasn't just the bed, it was something else: it represented something else in my life.'

So did that mean, I asked her, that anybody can claim that a certain object which means something special to them – their child's potty maybe – is a work of art purely because they believe it to be one? And, if so, where does all this end? Hardly an original argument, I know, but not everyone buys into the concept of 'found art'.

No, said Emin, it doesn't work like that. She, after all, had gone to art school. Therefore she was an artist.

'It didn't just come, you know – I'm not lucky. I work incredibly hard.'

So it's fair to say there was no meeting of minds. But the listeners never got to hear the liveliest bit. I finished the interview with the routine: 'Tracey Emin … many thanks.' Her response was not exactly routine. There was the briefest pause while the studio engineer waited for the 'Thank *you*' to come back down the line before cutting her off. Instead there was a brief pause and she – clearly under the impression that she was no longer on the air – exploded. What I heard in my headphones was: 'Who was that fucking c**t!' Mercifully the studio manager was extremely quick off the mark. On the first 'f' of a word that we have never knowingly broadcast on the *Today* programme he grabbed the fader, cut the sound to the mic and all the listeners heard was 'Who was—' Thank God for sound engineers with lightning reflexes.

My next encounter with Emin was in the lift at LWT. I had been invited to appear on *Have I Got News for You* and so, I discovered, had she. She gave me a pretty frosty look but saved her broadside until we were on air. Angus Deayton started to introduce me at the start of the show and she chipped in. All the audience needed to know, she announced, was that I was 'the rudest man in Britain'. And that was probably the high point of the show. It was all downhill from there.

A few years later I was presenting a show on Radio 4 called *On the Ropes*. Unkind critics called it half an hour of bear-baiting and sometimes, I suppose, it did sound a bit like that. But it was a genuine attempt to have a serious conversation with people whose lives had gone horribly wrong at some stage and allow them to reflect on it. One of my guests was Neil Kinnock, soon after his hopes of becoming prime minister had been trampled into the dust by John Major. He gave me some of the reasons why he thought he'd been beaten so badly.

One was the infamous Labour Party rally when Kinnock appeared from the back of the hall as he was announced and marched down the aisle to the stage, arms aloft and hollering: 'We're alRIGHT! We're alRIGHT!' He told me it had all been a great mistake. He was meant to appear, with the minimum of fuss, from backstage and not from the back of the hall. But the organisers got it wrong and he got a bit carried away. And when television viewers saw him taking their votes for granted, they reacted accordingly.

The other reason, he reckoned, was more an accident of birth than human error.

'I've got ginger hair right?' he asked me.

Yup ... no doubt about that. So what ...?

'So when people look at the voting slip in the polling station and see my name they automatically think "pubic hair" and it put them off voting for me.'

Hair colour aside, Tracey Emin had been coming in for a fair amount of criticism for her art and her lifestyle and my producer thought she would make a good subject for the programme. Maybe. But she would also make mincemeat of yours truly. So I pointed out to him that she was about as likely to subject herself to half an hour of being battered by the rudest man in Britain as I was to put in a bid for her unmade bed. He ignored me, put in a bid for *On the Ropes* and she accepted. And that was the start of a beautiful friendship.

She turned out to be a joy to interview: engaging, amusing, hugely knowledgeable about art and even self-deprecating. And the next time we met it was at one of her shows on the South Bank. I'd like to finish this little tale by admitting that I became a convert to her art. Well ... not quite. I'd still prefer to have J. M. W. Turner hanging on my walls than a half-naked Tracey Emin shovelling bank notes into her crotch – but she's done a lot to help young artists and British art and I rather wish I could go back a couple of decades and do that interview all over again.

'Hey Mike. Guess what? John Humphrys of the BBC wants
to interview you ... Mike?'

8

Why do you interrupt so much?

I have interviewed every prime minister since Alec Douglas-Home who occupied 10 Downing Street for a year from October 1963. That's more than half a century's worth. It's almost possible to chart the recent political history of the country through those encounters:

- the 'white heat of technology' promised by a young Harold Wilson;
- Ted Heath's success in taking us into Europe;
- the winter of discontent under Jim Callaghan;
- Margaret Thatcher's mission to tame the trade union bosses;
- John Major's mission to slay the Eurosceptic 'bastards' in his own party;
- the dawn of 'New' Labour under Tony Blair which made him so many friends outside the Labour Party and his decision to take us to war in Iraq which lost him those friends;
- Gordon Brown's mistaken insistence that Britain had ended the 'boom and bust' economic cycle;
- David Cameron's humiliating failure to persuade our European partners to cut Britain some slack so he could persuade the country we should stay in Europe – and then, when they sent him home with a flea in his ear, his decision to call a referendum;

- Theresa May's failure to persuade Parliament that she had the right plan for Britain's departure from the European Union.

If there is a single common factor among those nine prime ministers I suppose it's that they all started out with much of the nation reposing at least a modicum of hope and trust in them and most ended up with the nation wondering why. That tends to support Enoch Powell's view that all political careers end in failure – though he might have been more accurate if he had said all prime ministerial careers end in failure. We'll probably all remember Thatcher for her disastrous poll tax and Blair for his infinitely more disastrous Iraq adventure rather than for the fact that they were each the most successful leaders of their parties in electoral terms since the Second World War.

But in spite of that – or, more realistically, because of it – the interview with the prime minister is invariably the one that all current-affairs programmes hanker after. No matter how often prime ministers are interviewed on *Today* it's always regarded as something of an event – and so it should be. It's a pretty scary event for the presenter. If you make a mess of an interview with a junior minister there is always the consolation of knowing you'll be doing another one tomorrow and you can make amends then and anyway nobody really notices. If it's the prime minister, everyone notices. There's something about the office of prime minister that makes it pretty daunting even if you've been doing it for as long as I did. And it is still a pretty rare event. For every one interview that was granted we probably bid for another dozen.

Mostly we shrugged our shoulders when Number 10 said no and took the view that it was worth a try. We knew the bid would almost certainly fail to get past whoever happens to be the Downing Street spin doctor, let alone end up on the boss's desk. If prime ministers accepted every interview bid they'd barely have time to brush their teeth in the morning, let alone actually run the country.

Even so, we often got cross when our bid was turned down. The *Today* programme is not overburdened with modesty. It sees itself as far and away the most important current-affairs programme in the country and assumes that everybody who is anybody in public life takes the same view.

Sadly prime ministers – or at least their spin doctors – tend to see the downside as well as the upside and, sadly, we don't have the power of subpoena. With politicians further down the greasy pole it's easy: they need us more than we need them. But the opposite tends to be true of their bosses. If the health secretary is making an announcement that waiting lists have fallen by 0.01 per cent and his spin doctor offers us an interview – preferably at 8.10 – we will probably say thanks but no thanks. If, on the other hand, waiting lists have increased by ten per cent and the health service is (once again) 'in crisis' we shall be hammering on their door. And they will almost certainly say the health secretary's diary is crammed full for the foreseeable future. That applies whoever is in power.

What does change is that programmes like *Today* fall in and out of favour with different party leaders. Until relatively recently, for instance, all the party leaders were happy to give us an interview at some point during the party conference. That was until Jeremy Corbyn took over the Labour Party. He – doubtless encouraged by his director of communications Seumas Milne – regarded us with profound suspicion and gave us a wide berth. In the five years after he became leader I interviewed Corbyn precisely once. That may be because he made a bit of a mess of the interview, which he did, and Milne calculated he was much safer talking to the party faithful or soaking up the 'Oh Jeremy Corbyn!' chants at the Glastonbury festival. Which he was.

But generally opposition leaders are far more willing – eager, even – than prime ministers to appear on *Today* and the same goes for the shadow Cabinet members. There's an obvious reason for that. When politicians are in power they do things. They have no choice. And when some of those things go wrong, sooner or later they have to face the music.

The difference with opposition politicians is that they cannot do things: they can only talk about doing things. So there is not the same imperative. Power changes the equation. It's different when we are approaching an election and they have to publish their manifestos. Then the interviewer can, for instance, demand to know how they intend to keep their promises of building more hospitals, making the trains run on time and providing a nice new semi for every young couple while simultaneously cutting taxes. It's also important to allow them a platform to criticise the government – which is the one thing oppositions can do.

We are inevitably attacked by each side for going soft on the other. That's part of the job. Sometimes the criticism is justified but when we got it wrong it was, at least in my experience, unintentional. We tried hard to keep a balance. By 'we' I mean my colleagues on the *Today* programme. There is a much bigger question over whether the BBC as an institution is truly impartial and I want to address that later in this book. Whether we succeeded on the *Today* programme is more straightforward.

Mostly it's a matter of judgement by the editor, and editors need to be made of pretty stern stuff. They get it in the neck from all quarters: whingeing presenters, the big BBC bosses and politicians. Above all politicians – because if they upset them too much they upset the bosses too. When Greg Dyke was the director general during the Blair government years he gave evidence to the Lords for the BBC Charter Review on 6 April 2005. This is part of what he said: 'If you are the news department and Alastair Campbell writes in … two or three letters a week for month after month – I can remember the head of news saying to me at one stage "I have had another letter from Alastair" (and they were rants, at times: you could not always work out what the complaint was) – it inevitably conditions how you respond.'

'Let's stop now, John. They've been grilled enough.'

The chairman of the BBC Gavyn Davies said at the same hearing: 'We heard frequently from Alastair Campbell at different levels of the BBC, and it became an almost incessant drumbeat of complaint. We emphatically felt that we were put – not just the two of us but the BBC as an organisation – under pressure to cover the [Iraq] conflict in a way we did not think was fair.'

The pressure is at its greatest during general elections. Once an election has been called, the BBC is required by law to ensure that the political parties are covered proportionately during the course of the campaign. It keeps a log of who has been interviewed, and for how long, and checks the figures on the database once or twice a week. The appropriate amount of coverage for each party is largely determined by how it performed at the last two elections.

At the same time, normal news judgements apply and any kind of appearance can count towards the running total. On this basis, we could, I suppose, interview a Tory politician for six minutes about allegations that he used public money to take his beautiful young assistant to the Caribbean for a long weekend and then interview a Labour politician for exactly the same time about how she rescued a drowning toddler from a lake, and the same figure would be added to the total for each party. For the purposes of the database, it perhaps means that there really is no such thing as bad publicity, though in this case I rather doubt the Conservatives would agree. The fact is that 'balance' – or 'due impartiality' as we are meant to think of it – is in the eye of the beholder.

Once again 8.10 is the high-status slot and some will refuse to appear unless they get it. Often it's granted on the basis of seniority. The higher up the Westminster pecking order, the greater your chances. Fair enough if you are the Foreign Secretary or the Chancellor of the Exchequer and you have something interesting to say. But if you haven't? There may be a few listeners who want to hear an interview with the chancellor just because he is the chancellor, but I doubt there are many.

Another mistake we've made over the years has been to favour politicians. Again why? Fair enough if there's a strong political story leading the news or if something big is happening somewhere that demands a reaction from the government, but it's too often a knee-jerk response on our part. In the early days of computing the old saying went: 'Nobody ever got fired for buying IBM.' On *Today* it has become: 'Nobody ever got fired for giving the 8.10 to a politician.' Well maybe they should have been. Or maybe the presenter should get fired for doing a boring interview.

Why Do You Interrupt So Much?

Politicians are sometimes wary of the 8.10 for the same reason that they are sometimes so keen to be offered it: they get lots of airtime. It is invariably the longest interview on the programme. There is something all politicians have in common: they love the sound of their own voice. But, to be fair, they also like the extra time because if they really do have something important to say they can say it without being hurried along too much. The downside is that the interviewer has more time to challenge them – which means they need to do their homework and if they are trying to pull a fast one there is a much better chance they will be found out. Either way politicians generally find it more difficult to turn down a request for an interview on *Today* if they are offered the top slot.

I recall only one exception: a senior politician who regularly found an excuse not to appear in the studio at 8.10 but would offer himself for the 7.50 instead – the slot immediately after 'Thought for the Day'. He was Sir Geoffrey Howe, Chancellor of the Exchequer at the time and, if I'm being entirely honest, not a serious contender for the title of most entertaining performer in the great Palace of Westminster. Not for nothing did Denis Healey (himself a brilliant performer) suggest that being attacked by Howe was like 'being savaged by a dead sheep'. He was, almost without exception, an extremely boring interviewee. He delivered his thoughts with all the verve and panache of a priest delivering the last rites. But something curious happened during his 7.50 *Today* interviews.

For the first five or six minutes he would drone on in his usual way, giving a passable imitation of a man who'd just been told his dog had died, and then he would look up at the clock on the wall opposite him and behave as though he'd had half a pint of adrenaline injected into his plump arm. It might be a passionate denunciation of something he was supposed to approve of or the announcement of a policy shift he knew would provoke some heated debate. And when he had finished he would look back up to the clock, give what passed in Geoffrey's case for a small smile, and stop. At last something meaty for the presenter to get his teeth into. Something to challenge him on. Except that you couldn't because there was no time left.

Some years later, when he had long since stopped running the nation's finances, Geoffrey confessed all. He preferred the 7.50 slot, he told me, because he knew exactly when the interview would end. That's because it was followed, of course, by the weather forecast and if there was one thing in those days before smartphones that the listener would not tolerate it was being denied the weather forecast. I often think that's the only thing half our audience really listened to. And clever old Geoffrey knew that. Let others enjoy the limelight of the 8.10: he knew exactly what he was doing. And it worked.

When he retired and wrote his memoirs Robin Day gave the book the title *Grand Inquisitor*. He had earned it. An obituary written by a politician, Dick Taverne, said he had been 'the most outstanding television journalist of his generation. He transformed the television interview, changed the relationship between politicians and television, and strove to assert balance and rationality into the medium's treatment of current affairs.' Things were very different before Robin and his contemporary, the formidable Alastair Burnet of ITN, came along. An interview with the Labour leader Clement Attlee began with this killer question: 'Can you tell us something of how you view the election prospects?'

Short of actually polishing politicians' boots, or maybe even licking them, we could scarcely have been more deferential. When the *Today* programme began in 1957 there was no problem with political interviews because we simply didn't do them. It was Robin himself who had originally suggested the idea of a current-affairs programme at breakfast time on what was then the Home Service. It started life as two twenty-minute segments of 'topical talks' and for years it never quite shook off its fondness for the lighter side of life. John Timpson, who presented the programme from 1970 to 1976 and again from 1978 to 1986, was fond of making jokes about the news – 'Insulation – Britain lags behind' or 'Crash course for learner drivers'.

But largely thanks to Robin, we moved from the days of 'Is there anything else you'd like to add, sir?' to the no-holds-barred, 'they don't like it up 'em' approach. Early in his career, during the 1964 general election, he set the ground rules for us all in an interview with Labour's deputy leader George Brown about the potential nationalisation of the steel industry by the newly elected government.

> *RD:* Would you care to comment?
> *GB:* I have already done it. My good gracious me, Robin, you don't seem to listen—
> *RD:* I do listen Mr Brown.
> *GB:* Well then I don't know why you repeat the question.
> *RD:* I didn't ask you that question before.
> *GB:* Yes but I—
> *RD:* You may be a member of the new administration, Mr Brown, but I'm still entitled to ask you whatever questions I like that are reasonable.

A generation later we had the great Brian Redhead carrying the torch on *Today*. I had the pleasure of sitting alongside him when he launched into the monetary policies of the then Chancellor of the Exchequer Nigel Lawson. Lawson had made the mistake of chiding Brian for his political bias. A lesser interviewer might have tried to ignore what was a serious charge from a senior politician. Brian did not miss a beat.

'Do you think we should now have a two-minute silence in this interview Mr Lawson? One for you daring to suggest you know how I vote and secondly perhaps in memory of your policy of monetarism which you have now discarded.' Lawson made no real attempt to defend himself. He knew he was beaten.

There's nothing wrong with a bit of theatrical knock-about even on a programme with such a strong political agenda as

Today. And every interviewer has a favourite interviewee – somebody who would often prefer a bit of a punch-up rather than revert to speak-your-weight mode. I (almost) always enjoyed interviewing Ken Clarke, for one. How could you not warm to a Chancellor of the Exchequer who admitted that he was unable to answer a particular question on the vitally important Maastricht Treaty, the most important EU document of the time, because he hadn't actually got around to reading it?

Michael Heseltine was another favourite. We became such a regular feature on *Today* when he was deputy prime minister that the *Guardian* ran a leader column making the case for an end-of-pier show: *The Humph 'n' Hezza Show*. John Prescott was another – even though it wasn't always possible to follow his every word. It was said of Enoch Powell that he never began a sentence without knowing exactly how it would end. With Prescott it was the exact opposite. He once rescued the Labour Party leadership from a serious defeat at a party conference with a brilliant, unscheduled last-minute speech. As it happened I'd arranged to have breakfast with him the following morning. When he arrived I told him what a great speech it had been.

'Yeah, I know …' he growled, 'but what did I say?'

I'm pretty sure he wasn't joking. Nor was he when he was the environment secretary and I asked him about some serious problems he was having over his approach to preserving (or failing to preserve) the green belt. He was having none of it.

'The green belt is a great achievement,' he expostulated, 'and this government is going to build on it!' Everyone knew what he meant – even if the words didn't quite work.

The point about all three of them is that they engaged with the interviewer and thus with the audience. There is almost nothing that annoys the listener more than the politician who ignores the question and simply repeats what he told you thirty seconds ago. I use the word 'almost' because there may be one thing the audience finds even more irritating: the interviewer who interrupts so much the politician has no opportunity to make his point.

Clearly there's a balance of interests here. We need the politicians to fill our programmes; they need us to promote their careers, appeal to the voters, or simply because, as elected figures in a functioning democracy, they feel it's their duty to appear. One senior Cabinet minister once opined that if he'd had a bad day as a minister and the press were on his tail, he would volunteer to go on *Newsnight* to deliver his message in the hope of catching the final editions of the papers. If he'd had a good day, the thought of travelling across London late at night to be skewered by Jeremy Paxman held rather less appeal.

The former Labour Foreign Secretary Robin Cook was one of that rare breed of politician who chose to resign on principle rather than cling on to power and all its trappings. For him the breaking point was Tony Blair's decision to go to war against Iraq in 2003 but he and I had many lively exchanges on *Today*. Robin was a brilliant man – many said that in his prime he was easily the best debater in the House of Commons and I approached every interview with him with more trepidation than confidence. So I was astonished (and, yes, a bit flattered) when he wrote in his memoirs years later that the only thing that kept him awake at night was the prospect of being interviewed by me on *Today*.

For such a successful politician Robin had remarkably little self-confidence. He phoned me at home one Sunday afternoon because, he said, he'd heard I was friendly with Rory Bremner, arguably the greatest political impressionist we've ever had. I told him that, yes, I considered him a friend. And the conversation went something like this:

'Why is he so horrible to me on his television show?'

'Because you're the Foreign Secretary and he's a satirist and that's what he does.'

'But he makes it sound as if he really doesn't like me …'

How extraordinary that one of the cleverest and most powerful ministers in the government should worry about a bit of mickey-taking on a show designed to do just that. I tried to console him but I don't think I succeeded. I'd had a taste of Robin's insecurity when John Smith, the leader of the Labour Party, died suddenly of a heart attack in May 1994. He was one of the three being tipped as a possible successor.

A few weeks before the date for nominations closed I found myself in the gents' toilet in Broadcasting House with Robin. I asked him if he was in the running. He said emphatically not. So, obviously, I asked him why. We were washing our hands at the time in front of large mirrors.

'Look in the mirror!' he told me.

'Yes … so what?'

'I'm too ugly. This is the television age.'

It's true Robin would never have been mistaken for George Clooney – there was a certain gnomish quality to him, but I repeat: so what? It's an immensely sad reflection on all of us if a politician of his quality has to rule himself out of the leadership because he's 'too ugly'.

As for our approach to interviewing politicians, I fear that we may have travelled too far from the days of deference to an era of open combat. I would not presume to claim the title 'Grand Inquisitor' – that will always belong to Robin Day – but I have had the rather more dubious honour of being dubbed a Rottweiler or Welsh terrier for what many have seen as my overly aggressive interviewing. Mostly the BBC have shrugged it off and simply pointed out that I was only doing my job – if occasionally rather too enthusiastically. But there were times when the complaints came from sources that could not be lightly dismissed. One of the most potentially dangerous came soon after Labour had taken power in 1997. I became an official 'problem'.

It happened after an interview I had done on lone parents' benefit with Harriet Harman, who was the new secretary of state for social security. Within hours of the interview being broadcast the Labour Party's director of communications, David Hill, wrote to my editor and said: 'The John Humphrys problem has assumed new proportions. We have had a council of war and we are

It's 1945. The war has ended and half of Cardiff was queuing up to go somewhere – anywhere! – by train. I'm the blond toddler in my mother's arms.

An excursion with the Trinity Youth Club. Please note my natty cravat (I'm second from the left on the front row) – and the girls all wearing dresses. Jeans were yet to arrive.

I had just joined the *Merthyr Express*. And if this picture is any guide I wasn't too happy about it …

One of my many reports on the Liverpool dock strikes. The dock workers fought the arrival of containers – and lost.

These kids on a street in Cardiff were far more impressed with the camera than with me.

I'd been the first television reporter at Aberfan. I was twenty-three. Even the picture below gives only a hint of the destruction. Decades later I still cannot comprehend how those brave people were able to cope with such tragedy.

Interviewing a British soldier on the streets of Belfast at the height of the Troubles in Northern Ireland. More than 3,500 people were to die.

Waiting outside the White House for Richard Nixon to make his last appearance as president …

… and covering the convention that had given him the job two years earlier.

Making the most of a snowy
American winter.

The great PG
Wodehouse, still
writing in his eighties
when I interviewed
him. He wasn't happy
with what he'd just
written, but I rescued
it from the bin and
he signed it for me.
A great honour!

Joshua Nkomo, a rebel leader fighting to become the first president of the new, independent Zimbabwe. Mugabe beat him to it.

Protests on the streets of London always attracted the cameras.

Celebrating my departure from BBC TV News with Sue Lawley looking the worse for wear – or just dodging the spray …

The BBC newscasting team in 1981.

seriously considering whether, as a party, we will suspend co-operation when you make bids through us for government ministers.'

This of course was a real threat. What sin had I committed? You may not be surprised to hear that I had apparently interrupted Harriet too much. Mr Hill called it a 'ridiculous exchange' and said that because of the repeated interruptions no one would have been any the wiser as to Harriet's explanation of government policy. She made no complaint herself and my editor, Jon Barton, came to my defence: 'I felt this morning that I was listening to a rigorous, fair-minded interview which illuminated an important policy issue.'

It may say something about my lack of self-awareness that after I'd finished the interview I had not given it a single thought. Yes, it was fairly lively, but no more so than a hundred others I'd done in the past weeks and months. So I was astonished by the reaction from 10 Downing Street. I had not been aware that there was thought to be a 'John Humphrys problem'. On the contrary, it was only a few months earlier that the Labour Party had been praising me for my robust approach in trying to hold the Conservative government to account. Was it really possible to have undergone such a dramatic transformation in such a short period of time from staunch defender of democracy to the 'John Humphrys problem'? From hero to villain in the time it took for the nation to put a cross on a ballot paper.

The obvious answer, or so I told myself, was that it wasn't me who had changed. It was the Labour Party. After so long in the political wilderness they were now in power. That transition can do mighty strange things. Instead of attacking the government's policies, as they had been doing for eighteen years, they had to defend their own. And of course it wasn't just the opposition doing the attacking. It was the media as well. Not because people like me had a particular axe to grind but, as I suggested earlier, it is governments and not oppositions who make policies and therefore become our natural target. In other words, it's all about holding power to account.

The Harman row foreshadowed the start of a much more confrontational relationship between Downing Street and the media and at the top of their hit list was the BBC. Alastair Campbell recognised that in one important sense its reporting mattered more than newspapers. Most *Daily Mail* readers had already made up their minds which way they would vote and so had most *Guardian* readers. The chances of changing their minds were slim to non-existent.

The BBC is trusted by most people to be impartial in a way that the papers are not. We have no choice in the matter. Nor should we. So in terms of winning hearts and minds, there was everything to play for. Thus the logic went. And the Harman row was but a light breeze compared with the hurricane that was to follow over our coverage of the way Blair handled the Iraq War in 2003.

But things were already growing tense as we approached the election of 2001. Labour simply withdrew co-operation from us. It got so bad at one stage that I was asked to explain to the listeners that the reason we might appear to be struggling to give a balanced picture was because the government kept turning down our requests to interview ministers. My editor Rod Liddle blamed the 'paranoia of the press officers in Millbank'.

If nothing else it proved, yet again, the hypocrisy of politicians who love to extol the vital function of a free press. What many of them mean by 'free' is the freedom to praise their own party and rubbish the opposition.

After Rod had left the programme for a brilliant career as a columnist he wrote: 'Our government really, really hates the man [Humphrys] and it is being aided in its campaign by one or two sycophantic News International journalists and one or two naive or envious souls from within the BBC itself ... Labour does not like the relentless and forensic manner in which Humphrys (and, for that matter, Paxman) conducts interviews with government ministers; the refusal to sanction obfuscation and – you have to say – on occasion downright lying.'

But I can't pretend that it was only politicians who complained about my style of interviewing. Whenever I met listeners out there in the real world the same two questions were inescapable.

Why do you interrupt so much?

Why do you give politicians such a hard time?

My answers to both were always much the same. I interrupt when we are short of time (which we often are) and when politicians fail even to try giving a straight answer to a reasonable question. When that happens the interviewer is entitled, even obliged, to press for an answer. If that means sometimes interrupting them when they are in full flow, so be it. It beats yet another party political broadcast. But I'll have more to say about that later.

It's relatively rare to get a call from one of the bosses at home. It's almost never good news. By 'bosses' I mean those people who don't actually make programmes but whose job is usually to make life difficult for those who do. There are rather a lot of them in the BBC. The call I got on the evening of 24 March 1995 was about as bad as it gets.

It came from Steve Mitchell, the head of radio news programmes, a decent man who became a good friend over the years. His mild, almost apologetic manner concealed a sharp brain and a tough character. We'd had a few run-ins over the years but nothing too serious. What he was about to tell me was, for the BBC, very serious. For me it was perhaps even the end of my short career on the *Today* programme.

Steve had just been told about a speech that was being made that evening by a Conservative Cabinet minister, Jonathan Aitken. Aitken was a colourful character who had made his name in journalism and as a television presenter before he went into politics. He was a risk-taker: a debonair Old Etonian who had been acquitted at the Old Bailey of breaching the Official Secrets Act, triggered the wrath of Margaret Thatcher by capturing the heart of her daughter and renouncing her for another woman, and making an enemy of the formidable Anna Ford. He had been instrumental in relaunching *TV-AM* and firing its presenters. Anna was one of them. She repaid him by throwing a glass of red wine over his head at a cocktail party. Now Mr Aitken had me in his sights – and he fired both barrels.

In Aitken's eyes I had committed two great offences. The first was to chair a meeting in Westminster of teachers opposed to the Conservative government's pay policies. I'd been assured when I agreed to do it that both sides of the argument would be represented on the platform, but they weren't: just Labour and the Liberal Democrats and no Conservatives. I was completely impartial in my questioning, but my very presence on the platform gave Aitken the ammunition he needed. I had 'embraced open partisanship', he claimed. It had been a 'bizarre breach of the normal convention that political journalists stay out of partisan politics', he thundered. It wasn't true but it might possibly have looked that way to anyone who wasn't actually present at the meeting.

His second charge was ludicrous. I was 'poisoning the well of democratic debate' with what he called my 'ego-trip interviewing'. This was Aitken at his rhetorical best and his irrational worst. For a BBC presenter it is hard to imagine a more damaging allegation. So what was his evidence?

It was an interview I had done with Ken Clarke, then Chancellor of the Exchequer, some weeks earlier. Aitken accused me of having interrupted Clarke no fewer than thirty-two times in a fairly short 8.10 interview. In the narrowest possible sense he might just have been right. There were certainly plenty of interjections – but it rather depends on what you mean by 'interrupt'. I have always thought an interview should be as close to a conversation as it's possible to get.

In the very early days of current-affairs programmes on the Home Service it was rather different. The BBC man (always a man) would have all his questions written down and ask each in order. He would wait for the answer to be completed and then, regardless of what his interviewee had said, would ask the next one. No follow-up, no challenging of any dubious claims, no expression of scepticism. It's quite a long time since we took that approach and I rather doubt that even Mr Aitken would want to return to it. But perhaps I'm wrong. The obvious point here is that there is a real difference between interrupting for the sake of it and interjecting to try to keep the interviewee to the point if he has wandered off. And there is an even more important principle at stake.

Let's be clear about why we ask politicians onto the programme – apart from the fact that they come free. It is categorically not so that they can deliver a party political broadcast, which is what we'd get if we never interrupted them. It is our job – our duty – to try to hold power to account. And if we ask them the questions we believe our audience wants answered we are entitled to persist. That's our job. You might argue that it's often their job to duck the questions and I would agree. If I ask the chancellor a month before the Budget whether he intends to put up income tax he's absolutely entitled to tell me to clear off. MPs are the first to be told – although so much leaking goes on these days that one sometimes wonders whether there's any point in bothering with the formal announcements on Budget day. But that's another matter.

What I don't believe politicians should be allowed to get away with is refusing to answer a perfectly reasonable question. Not that they ever 'refuse' as such. They have a dozen different formulas for not answering without ever actually saying: 'I'm not going to answer that question.' You might recognise a few of these old favourites:

'I really don't think that's what your listeners are concerned about ...'

'What your audience really wants to know ...'

'This government is on record as having said ...'

'We are absolutely clear that ...'

And so on ad infinitum.

Even more annoying is when you ask them why their party is making such a mess of whatever it happens to be and they insist on telling you, over and over again, why the other party is even worse. The other dreary old tactic is to pretend they have answered the question when they patently have not. Yet another is simply to repeat what they have already said, knowing that the interviewer will have to give up eventually either because there's no time left or because he has simply lost the will to live. It goes something like this:

'Minister, why is the government cutting benefits to people who are struggling desperately to make ends meet?'

'This government has always believed that the vast majority of people in this country want decent jobs that pay a decent income.'

'Indeed ... but some people are forced to rely on benefits and they are now facing real poverty.'

'We are proud of our record, unlike the last government, of building an economy in which there is work available for everyone who wants to do it.'

'My question is about welfare benefits.'

'And I am trying to make the point that there are many, many hard-working people out there who have benefited enormously from the opportunity to earn a decent living which means that they do not have to rely on benefits.'

'And I'm trying to ask you about the cuts to the benefit system ...'

'Let me repeat ... the ordinary, decent, hard-working people in this country take pride in their work and we want to make it possible for them to do that work by ensuring that the economy is robust and works for everyone, not just the few ...'

And so it goes. You will have heard a version of that interview a thousand times. I would suggest that when we interviewers are faced with that sort of non-answer we are entitled to interrupt. But Jonathan Aitken was doing more than attacking me for interrupting. He said: 'Mr Humphrys was conducting the interview not as an objective journalist seeking information, but as a partisan pugilist trying to strike blows.' Now this is a potentially lethal accusation.

Why Do You Interrupt So Much?

There is nothing wrong with partisan journalism or campaigning journalism or investigative journalism. On the contrary, all three are vital in a thriving democracy. Every newspaper worth its salt has opinions and makes them clear every day in their leader columns. If we don't like them we don't have to buy the paper.

Investigative journalists do more than express opinions. They suspect corruption or grotesque incompetence on the part of the authorities and they set about collecting the evidence to prove it. The history of journalism is replete with examples of courageous reporters who have exposed scandals and freed innocent people from prison or sent guilty people there. Many courageous editors have risked jail because they have taken a stand on something they believed needed to be exposed.

One of the most famous examples in recent years was the *Daily Mail* front page in 1997 accusing five young men of having murdered the black teenager Stephen Lawrence. Beneath the headline 'Murderers' and a picture of each man ran this line: 'The *Mail* accuses these men of killing. If we are wrong, let them sue us.' They never did. The *Mail* has won much praise for its coverage of the Lawrence murder over the years and rightly so. If the editor, Paul Dacre, had been sued and his accusers had proved criminal libel he could have gone to jail.

Several years later, when the only story in town was Brexit, Dacre ran a headline that won him not praise but condemnation. It brought the wrath of half the nation down on his head. This time the pictures were of three judges, resplendent in robes and wigs, who had ruled that the government would need the consent of Parliament before it could enforce Article 50. Dacre did not approve. The headline ran: 'Enemies of the People'. The Press Complaints Commission received more than a thousand complaints and many fully paid-up members of the Great and the Good demanded Dacre's head. How dare he treat our great independent judiciary with such contempt? The answer is perfectly simple and it's summed up in two words: free speech.

Democracy cannot survive, let alone thrive, without it. One of the Founding Fathers of the United States, Thomas Jefferson, wrote: 'Were it left to me to decide whether we should have a government without newspapers, or newspapers without a government, I should not hesitate a moment to prefer the latter.' A free press is essential to free speech and free speech must include the freedom to offend – and even to cause outrage. If Dacre had broken the law he should have been charged with doing so. If his readers were outraged by what he had done they were free to stop buying his newspaper.

But the BBC does not enjoy the same freedom as a newspaper. Nor should it. It has a unique status as our national, not state, broadcaster: unique privileges and unique obligations. It has a guaranteed income. If you don't pay the licence fee you can go to jail. It operates under a royal charter which guarantees its independence. But implicit in that guarantee is that its journalists are required to be impartial.

When everything else is stripped away the overriding duty of the BBC is to enable democratic debate. If we fail to do that we should be stripped of our licence to broadcast and someone else should be given the job. And any BBC journalist who allows his ego to override it should be slung out pronto.

Had Jonathan Aitken been able to prove that I was partisan – specifically that I was in league with the Labour Party – that would have ended my career as a news presenter at the BBC. And quite right too. Let's be clear about this. I have views about pretty much every subject under the sun. I know the best way to cook chips and the worst way to peel an orange and the best way to run the country. Or at least I think I do. Don't we all? In my years at the BBC I was happy to disclose the first two but not the third.

Many years ago, when he was a promising backbencher, Tony Blair told me I should give up journalism and become a barrister. Put aside the obvious flaw in the theory (I'd never pass the exams) he was right in one respect. There is a clear link between a barrister entering a courtroom to defend his client whom he strongly suspects is as guilty as hell and a presenter entering the studio who firmly believes the politician he is about to interview is a knave and a charlatan with policies that would probably bankrupt the nation in ten seconds flat if he had his way. The link is this: both barrister and presenter leave their views at the door of the courtroom or the studio.

I mentioned that one of my oldest and closest friends is Patrick Holden, an organic farmer and one of the tiny group of men and women who helped bring about the organic revolution which I believe has done so much to improve the way we farm in this country. Patrick has always complained to me that he gets a rougher ride if he is being interviewed by me on *Today* than if he's facing any of the other presenters. It probably helps that, as a former dairy farmer, I'm reasonably well informed about the subject. But what really drove me was my concern to avoid any accusation of failing to be impartial.

I am acting as a devil's advocate – and so should we all. I suppose if all that makes me sound too much of a goody two-shoes I'll admit that there is another factor. I love arguing – and I don't necessarily mean the sort of arguments I imagine eminent dons engaging in when they are sitting at their high table in one of our great universities after a few glasses of decent claret. I mean just arguing. It really doesn't much matter what the subject is. My mother used to say 'John could argue with the Virgin Mary herself' and she was probably right.

Had Aitken succeeded in proving that I had betrayed that trust I would have been forced to resign. In fact, the bar for him to clear was set even lower. All he had to do was convince his ministerial colleagues – especially those in the Cabinet – that his attack was warranted. So the weekend of that phone call from Steve Mitchell was probably the scariest of my career. I knew – and, more importantly, so did Steve – that if Aitken's colleagues shared his views and refused to be interviewed by me or even threatened to boycott the programme, I was toast.

The Saturday newspapers went big on the story. This, remember, was the era before social media and the BBC relied almost entirely on the verdict delivered by the papers. Some were broadly sympathetic to me, some were inclined to believe Aitken. Some never miss a chance to take a pop at the BBC, which they believe is too big for its boots and too often intrudes onto their territory. It was much the same for the Sunday newspapers. But everyone was waiting to see what would happen on Monday when the *Today* programme was back on the air. How would the top Tories, Aitken's colleagues and friends, react?

I feared the worst. They might well see this as a chance to boot me up the backside. All it would take was a couple of the most respected colleagues to side with Aitken. I spent much of that Sunday discussing with my family how our lives would change if the BBC chose to bid me farewell. I seem to remember my youngest child volunteering that if we found ourselves on the streets having to beg for scraps she would leave school and take a job freelancing on a film set – preferably somewhere like Hollywood. Selfless to a fault.

It was late on Sunday night that the call came. It was the overnight editor on *Today* who took it and the caller was Douglas Hurd. Mr Hurd was the Foreign Secretary, one of the most respected politicians in Westminster. He had been booked to appear on the programme before the Aitken storm broke. He made no reference to Aitken but he had called, he said, to confirm that he would indeed be turning up for the scheduled interview. Oh and by the way, he added, 'If Mr Humphrys is on duty, naturally I'd be happy to have him interviewing me.'

Normally we don't give politicians any say over who interviews them but this was different. The threat may not have quite vanished, but the storm clouds had at least parted. Twelve hours later they vanished. Ken Clarke was on *The World at One* doing an interview about some economic matter and was, obviously, asked what he thought of Aitken's comments. A lot of nonsense, he said. And that was all it took.

A few days later Ken came in to be interviewed by me on *Today*. I met him in the green room beforehand and handed him a calculator.

'What the hell is this for?' he asked.

'Well,' I said, 'I thought it would help you keep track of the number of times I interrupt you and if I exceed thirty-two you can shout "Bingo!" or something.'

Ken looked at the calculator.

'D'you know something? I've never really figured out how to make one of these things work!'

He was, as I say, Her Majesty's Chancellor of the Exchequer at the time. I think he was joking.

There is a postscript to the Aitken story and I shall do my best to tell it without displaying obvious pleasure. *Schadenfreude* is, after all, not an attractive trait whatever the temptation. Four years after his attack on me Jonathan Aitken was no longer enjoying his life of privilege. He was in jail: sentenced to eighteen months for perverting the course of justice and perjury. Nothing to do with me, I hasten to add. Aitken had announced that he intended to sue the *Guardian* and Granada Television for defamation because they had accused him of taking bribes from Saudi Arabia. Just as he did when he had attacked me, he made the announcement with a great rhetorical flourish: 'If it falls to me to start a fight to cut out the cancer of bent and twisted journalism in our country with the simple sword of truth and the trusty shield of British fair play, so be it. I am ready for the fight. The fight against falsehood and those who peddle it. My fight begins today. Thank you and good afternoon.'

That fight ended in a courtroom and a devastating defeat for Mr Aitken. The court chose to believe 'those who peddle falsehood' and he ended up serving seven months at Her Majesty's pleasure. When he came out I asked him if he would appear on my *On the Ropes* programme. To my great surprise he agreed and to my even greater surprise he turned out to be a changed man: modest, repentant, all traces of the old arrogance gone. He had discovered God in prison and he ended up being ordained in the Church of England. He said at the time he did not want to become a vicar because he 'wouldn't want to give dog collars a bad name' but he changed his mind and has since been ordained as a deacon with the intention of becoming an (unpaid) prison chaplain. As for me, I lived to fight another day.

9

'Come on, unleash hell!'

Most people do not trust most journalists. Even fewer trust politicians. At the top of the Ipsos MORI 'Veracity Index' are nurses. When I last checked, they were trusted by ninety-seven per cent, closely followed by doctors and teachers. Journalists tie with estate agents and score a miserable twenty-seven per cent. Professional footballers are even lower but still rank above government ministers who manage only seventeen per cent. And at the very bottom? Yes ... rank-and-file politicians.

So who's to blame? In the United States, President Johnson once complained: 'If one morning I walked on top of the water across the Potomac River, the headline that afternoon would read: "PRESIDENT CAN'T SWIM!"' He had a point. I wish we had managed to find a better way of doing political interviews. One that might engage the audience more. One that acknowledges that most of the big issues facing politicians today are fiendishly complicated, rarely black and white but more often an unexciting shade of grey. And, in return, perhaps the politicians might be encouraged to confess that they are not infallible. I think too many interviews are seen – both by us, and the papers that report them – as a gladiator sport.

Politicians are humans too: the good, the bad and the ugly. Most of them are neither more nor less self-centred or cynical than the people they represent. Are we in effect helping to de-humanise them?

Clearly politics is a minority sport: 'show business for ugly people' as an American journalist once put it. Most people go about their everyday lives and worry about paying the gas bill or how they're going to get to work because the trains are up the spout, or what they're going to have for supper, rather than thinking about the small print of the government's latest White Paper. So if you're a journalist whose job it is to run the rule over their policies, you too are engaged in the minority sport. And, if you're not careful, very soon the conversation between politician and broadcaster can become an arcane activity that is of interest only to political nerds. When that happens the whole process, political and journalistic, can become further and further removed from the concerns of the poor bloody voter.

In 1995 a similar point was made by the director general of the BBC, John Birt. He made a speech in which he said 'Journalists must beware of hyping the artificial. A politician hints at a policy difference with colleagues … a crisis blows out of nowhere, like a tornado.' He spoke of 'overbearing interviewers who sneer disdainfully at their interviewees' and reminded us that 'individual MPs and parties have stood before the public and been elected by them, which [journalists] have not'. Birt was worried about 'courtesy' to ministers. He complained specifically about 'the disorienting open question – the rabbit punch – designed to knock off balance'.

The press of course saw this as a direct criticism of Paxman and me. So did I. It turned out that I was wrong. A few days later Birt sent me what he called a 'billet-doux' – a personal letter in which he said that 'whatever the papers may have said' I was the last person on his mind. I don't know whether Jeremy got a similar letter. Either way, he stuck with the 'rabbit punch' opening. He once delivered a humdinger to David Cameron, who was then the leader of Her Majesty's Opposition.

'Mr Cameron,' he asked him, 'do you know what a pink pussy is?' For the avoidance of any doubt, I should explain that a pink pussy is – or was at the time – a popular cocktail recipe based on vodka. Cameron had held a non-executive directorship for a chain of bars and nightclubs. It may not have raised the tone of the political debate, but I bet nobody switched off. And let's not pretend that that's not important. No listeners or viewers means no point in doing the interview.

The Birt analysis of sneering interviewers had a fairly mixed reception in the press. Mark Lawson, writing in the *Independent*, was not impressed:

> The first important consideration is that, in the short history of broadcasting, the demeanour of interviewers has been a reflection of national manners. When journalists wore morning dress and asked the prime minister 'What subject you would like to address tonight', this was merely an extension of accepted social deference towards politicians. The high theatre of a Jeremy Paxman interview on *Newsnight* – the voice and body language veering between boredom and disbelief – is just as logically a product of an age of anti-institutionalism and questioning of authority. What most astonished BBC current affairs producers about their leader's speech last week was that their own postbags and polling indicate a desire for the barbecue rather than the sun-lounger to be laid on for ministerial visits. Any complaints which the director general may have been acknowledging are likely to be coming from politicians rather than the public.

Lawson may have had a point. I say 'may' because presenters like me get mixed messages when we confront the listeners directly. Over the years I've appeared before many people in theatres or lecture halls who want to question the questioner. The number of people who attack me for giving politicians a rough ride are outnumbered hugely by those who say I let them get away with murder.

After the Birt speech the BBC commissioned rather more scientific audience research. It showed that most listeners thought giving politicians a serious grilling was necessary to arrive at the truth. A former controller of Radio 4, Mark Damazer, wrote that *Today*'s 'gravitational pull is through interviews with important people making important decisions, and them being questioned firmly on behalf of the audience. You need some sense of intellectual tension to get that, and vigour.'

By and large the politicians who can handle themselves are the least likely to complain, as Ken Clarke demonstrated when I handed him that calculator.

You don't set out to have a row but if a row develops, you don't necessarily want to back off. Sometimes it can be illuminating – but not always. Often it just gets in the way of the argument and irritates the listener. Then again, if the politicians get cross, it can tell you something about them, about their personality and how they react when they are put under a bit of pressure. So a heated exchange is not necessarily a bad thing. The idea that all the public ever wants to hear are reasoned discussions is nonsense and we should not be afraid to stand up to those in power. But there is a difference between being fearless and showing off.

Jeremy Paxman is well known for suggesting that he went into interviews thinking 'why is this lying bastard lying to me?' In fact he was quoting the words of the old *Times* correspondent Louis Heren: 'When a politician tells you something in confidence, always ask yourself why is this lying bastard lying to me.' And Jeremy went on to make a more subtle point: 'Do I think that everybody you talk to is lying? No I do not. Only a moron would think that. But do I think you should approach any spokesman for a vested interest with a degree of scepticism, asking "why are they saying this?" and "is it likely to be true?" Yes of course I do.'

There is a fairly clearly defined balance of power between politician and interviewer.

'Come On, Unleash Hell!'

Our advantages:

- We have less to lose. If we screw up it's possible no one will notice or, indeed, care too much. If you've been around as long as I have you might get the benefit of the doubt. It's even possible – God forbid – that once you've established a bit of a reputation, your colleagues and even your critics might be slightly reluctant to attack you.
- We get the chance to make amends with the next interview – either later in the programme or in days to come.
- The stakes are much higher for the politician. If they say something daft it will be quoted everywhere and they may pay a price. We knew that Mrs Thatcher listened to *Today* and if she heard one of her ministers making a mess of an interview she put a black mark against his name.
- We set the agenda. We know what the first question is. They don't. Interestingly, it's vanishingly rare for a politician to ask how you're going to start.
- We can interrupt – though this is a double-edged sword.
- We can research (or have a producer research) the areas we want to pursue.
- We're in charge of the timing.
- We can set the tone: deadly serious; mildly patronising; positively incredulous, etc., etc.
- We are on our home turf. They are often in a radio car or at the end of a dodgy technical set-up.

Their advantages:

- We might be dealing with half a dozen subjects in the course of a programme. They are concerned only with their own.
- They have a team of bright people briefing them to the eyeballs day in, day out. They will always know more than us.

167

- Yes, we choose the questions but they choose the answers – or not, as the case may be. If they avoid the question and choose to answer a different one our options are limited. We can interrupt – but only up to a point.
- They get media training.

Ah yes, media training. How pervasive it has become. The phrase 'spin doctor' crossed the Atlantic from the United States in the 1980s and within a decade it came to dominate the relationship between our own politicians and the media. In October 1982, before spin had been turned into an art form by the political parties, I remember the Conservative minister John Nott walking out of an interview with Robin Day about his role during the Falklands War:

Nott: My task is to maintain a balance between all three services, and most expert opinion is of the view that we've probably got the balance about right.

Day: But why should the public, on this issue, as regards the future of the Royal Navy, believe you, a transient, here-today and, if I may say so, gone-tomorrow politician, rather than a senior officer of many years?

Nott: I'm sorry, I'm fed up with this interview. Really, it's ridiculous. [Exit the Secretary of State for Defence, microphone still attached.]

Day: Thank you, Mr Nott.

From all his many years of public service, it was the one event for which Nott would be remembered. Twenty years later he gave his autobiography the title *Here Today Gone Tomorrow*. He wrote 'The irony is that I shall be remembered only for a media event, when I was – for a senior politician – almost uniquely unskilled at such things, and, indeed, rather contemptuous of the whole media charade.'

How quickly things changed. With the advent of the spin doctors, the political parties may still have been contemptuous of the 'media charade', but they were determined to take charge of it. Labour rebranded itself with the red rose, the Tories with an oak tree. The idea was to distil their 'product' into an appealing logo. In fact, the tree started off with green leaves, but the Tories decided to include a Union Jack when they realised that they were losing votes to UKIP. The other parties followed suit. Politics became a business like any other, and voters became customers. Identity branding, in the world of marketing and advertorial development, refers to the way that 'your complete corporate image can be perceived emotionally by your target audience. In other words, your logo, and the colours that you use in your branding, help to decide the kind of personality or background your customers, or voters, use to describe your party.'

Ye gods. So that's what we are meant to be thinking as we stand in the polling booth with the stubby pencil in our hand and the black boxes waiting for our cross in front of us. Maybe John Nott had a point.

And there are other factors at work. Today, politics has become a career of first choice, rather than a possible avenue for would-be politicians to explore after they have had some experience of the real world. When the Smith Institute analysed the 2015 Parliament in its study *Who Governs Britain?* it found that some forty per cent of Conservative MPs had previously worked in politics, public affairs or the media. For Labour it was forty-five per cent with another fifteen per cent who had been trade union officials.

So politics has become a profession as opposed to a vocation. Maybe that's a good thing. Maybe not. I spent the early years of my journalistic career reporting on local councils: endless hours, usually in the evenings because the councillors had jobs to do in the day, wishing I was in the pub rather than hearing them droning on. They were the polar opposite of today's professional. If you'd talked to them about 'branding' they'd have pictured a cowboy lassoing a steer. What they really did know about was the state of the toilets in the run-down primary school or whether the council houses needed a new lick of paint or the library needed more books. And, to be fair, they weren't always boring – even to a teenage reporter.

I cherish the memory of the councillors in Merthyr discussing how to make the local castle a bit more attractive to visitors. One suggested digging a moat around it. Another approved and proposed they should put a gondola in the moat. Another, not the brightest of the bunch, offered: 'Bloody good idea, Dai. Let's get two so they can breed eh?'

Today's councillors are a different species altogether – and so are their officials. The clerk has gone – to be replaced by a chief executive who probably earns at least as much as the prime minister. And many of the councillors themselves see the job as a stepping stone to Westminster.

Given that political careers can be nasty, brutish and mostly short, it's hardly surprising that the parties are obsessed with presentation and marketing and how they are perceived by the voter. We're not talking policies or track records here so much as impressions. One illustration: it is drilled into every young wannabe politician that something the voter will not tolerate is evidence of disunity in the party. They must all sing from the same song sheet.

There is plenty of evidence for that in the history of a warring Labour Party in the 1980s and 90s, let alone the ghastly years following the Brexit referendum. From 1979 to 1997 Labour watched the Tories triumph over and over again. And one of the lessons they learned was the need to get their messages across through sound bites that distilled party policy into phrases that were short enough to catch the attention of the editors of television news bulletins.

A perfect example of that was crime and policing – always a part of the battleground totally dominated by the Tories. Labour came nowhere. Until Blair delivered this: 'Tough on crime, tough on the causes of crime.'

Crime and policing was Tory policy – always had been, always would be – yet Blair stole it from them with one highly effective slogan. Another had just one word in it – used three times. 'Education, education, education.' That worked brilliantly too, as did the phrase that was coined on the sad day the Princess of Wales died in a car crash in a Paris tunnel. She had been, a sombre Blair informed us, 'the people's princess'. A year later Blair or, rather, his spin doctor Alastair Campbell, outdid himself with a sound bite delivered on 7 April 1998. He was in Belfast to sign the Good Friday Agreement. Here's what he said: 'A day like today is not a day for sound bites, we can leave those at home, but I feel the hand of history upon our shoulder with respect to this, I really do.'

How brilliant was that? And how crass. It was a sound bite that was a warning against the use of sound bites at one and the same time.

Tony Blair might have been the best political communicator since Harold Macmillan, but the first prime minister of the television age was Harold Wilson more than thirty years earlier. It was his great good fortune when he led the Labour Party in the 1964 general election to have as his opponent a Tory leader, Sir Alec Douglas-Home, who was about as posh as it gets. Wilson made the most of it. He created an entirely phony image of himself as the working-class lad from 'oop north' who loved nothing more than his pipe and a pint. (He didn't. He much preferred a decent cigar and a good claret.)

His election broadcast showed that he was never happier than when he was kicking a football around the back streets of Liverpool with a gang of scruffy urchins. Poor old Sir Alec was so naive he allowed the cameras to film him shooting grouse. Tweed jacket, plus fours and all. Wilson, the grammar-school boy, won.

The Tories learned many lessons from the Douglas-Home debacle. There was not to be another 'posh' Tory prime minister until David Cameron (Old Etonian) two generations later. Edward Heath had been a working-class boy and Margaret Thatcher the daughter of a grocer. Tony Blair might have been

Labour (or New Labour as he would have it) but he was pretty posh too – public school and Oxbridge – though he concealed it well.

Wilson had recognised the political importance of television but Blair and Campbell took it a step further. With the Labour Party scarred by so much of the media's hostility to Neil Kinnock, New Labour was determined to show they were controlling the narrative. They made it clear from the start that they would be pulling the media's strings and the malevolent puppet-master was the 'Prince of Darkness' himself, Peter Mandelson, a former LWT current-affairs producer. We had a sense of his enormous influence from a joke that was doing the rounds in the early days of New Labour:

A bloke wearing earphones goes into a barber shop for a trim. The barber thinks he recognises him. The customer tells him he was elected last month as the local Labour MP. The barber congratulates him and asks him to take off his headphones so he can make a decent job of his haircut. He seems reluctant and asks the barber to snip around them, which he does. After a few minutes he falls asleep and the barber, wanting to do his best for his new client, slips them off his ears. More minutes pass and he notices, with great alarm, that his client has stopped breathing. He dials 999 and, while he's waiting for the ambulance, listens to what's coming out of the headphones. It is the voice of Peter Mandelson: 'Breathe in, breathe out, breathe in ...'

Blair and New Labour took political marketing to a new level. In opposition, Alastair Campbell ran the party's press operation and, working with Mandelson, turned it into a fearsome machine. The party stayed on message – or else. Policy launches were co-ordinated and an instant rebuttal system readied for war. Campbell once told me he had wanted to alter fundamentally the way the party dealt with the media. He wanted to change the terms of the trade. There was no doubt in his mind that the press had been setting the political agenda in a way that was damaging to Labour. Under his regime nothing could be said against the party, no criticism voiced, no story run, without attracting an instant and frequently bruising response.

In office, Campbell continued in the same vein, creating a strategic communications unit at Number 10 to co-ordinate all government activity. The rapid rebuttal unit was still in place, and covering politics became a hostile activity for the journalists concerned. Campbell was far more than a spin doctor. He controlled the entire government information machine in a way his predecessors could only have dreamed of. Not just Downing Street but every department. If he disapproved of the press officer in the department for waste-paper disposal, the poor chap soon found himself looking for another job. Campbell was master of all he surveyed.

One lobby correspondent – a member of that elite group of journalists whose job is to tell the world what is happening behind the shutters that politicians try to erect to guard their reputations – told me what it was like to become a target for Campbell. 'You'd be sitting at your desk in the press room putting the finishing touches to your latest scoop and Campbell would wander by, perch on the edge of your desk, and say something like: "Got yourself a so-called story I hear? Not too helpful to Tony apparently? Hmm … Everything OK at home? Still paying off that big mortgage are you? Wouldn't want anything to damage your prospects here would we …?"' And off he'd wander.

A bit exaggerated maybe, but Campbell took no prisoners. He and I were reasonably friendly when he was a newspaper hack. He even suggested I take over a column he was writing at the time. I liked him and still do in a funny sort of way. But Campbell's greatest weakness – and perhaps his greatest strength too – has always been his unswerving loyalty to the leader. You were either with him or against him. Sometimes that could be pretty scary, sometimes a bit silly.

I remember an interview at the Labour Party conference in Brighton with Blair when he was prime minister. Campbell wanted to do it in Blair's hotel suite rather than come to the

BBC's conference studio. Blair sat on a sofa and I sat on a chair facing him. Campbell sat at the end of the sofa, a fat pile of newspapers between him and his boss. It was a live interview at 8.10.

The moment I started, Campbell picked up one of the newspapers, flipping the papers noisily and when he'd finished dropped it to the floor and picked up another. And then another. When we finished the interview Blair turned to Campbell: 'What the hell were you doing with the papers?'

Campbell: 'Trying to put that bugger off.'

Blair: 'Well you weren't – you were putting me off!'

All pretty innocent stuff, no doubt, but our relationship got steadily worse and reached its climax during the Hutton crisis, which was to bring down both the chairman and the director general and threaten the very existence of BBC News. More on that later. My abiding memory of Campbell was a letter about me he wrote to *The Times* after I'd said or done something disobliging. John Humphrys, he informed *Times* readers, 'is not the Queen Mother'. So at least he got some things right.

'Mr Humphrys. We've been sent by the Labour Party. Congratulations you're just about to qualify for disabled benefits …'

'Come On, Unleash Hell!'

The brilliant writer Armando Iannucci set out to create a clone of Campbell in his BBC political satire *The Thick of It*. He succeeded magnificently. His loud-mouthed spin doctor, Malcolm Tucker, was a dead ringer for Campbell: 'Stats, percentages, international comparison, information! Email them fucking WADS of information! And tell them they'd better get their heads around it before they put pen to paper, or I'll be up their arses like a fucking Biafran ferret, right? COME ON, UNLEASH HELL!'

Interviewing Margaret Thatcher was seldom less than terrifying – partly because she was fiercely clever and entirely unpredictable but also because she did not believe in taking prisoners. What she never did – at least not with me – was complain afterwards. Ever. But of course she had a team of PR advisers as well and she relied heavily on her clever marketing guru Sir Tim Bell. Their job was to make her a little more user-friendly. They told her she needed to lower the pitch of her rather shrill voice and they chose 'photo opportunities' for her that would make her seem, if not warm and cuddly, a little less like the Iron Lady with no heart. The picture of her holding a calf on a Suffolk farm during the 1979 general-election campaign was a classic. She did her best to smile for the cameras, but the look she gave the calf suggested she would have preferred to be tucking into a nice dish of veal cutlets.

Sadly for them, the spin doctors could not control her when she was in a live interview. She said what she thought. Imagine a modern politician describing people who campaigned on behalf of the worst off in society 'drooling and drivelling'. They'd be ripped apart. But that's pretty much what she said in an election campaign interview with David Dimbleby. Here's how it went:

MT: High unemployment … has been falling. There would have been far higher unemployment had we not pursued our policies because company after company would have failed to be competitive and we should have gone into a much bigger recession and we should have gone into much bigger unemployment. Now we have manufacturing industries, service industries that are fit, which are competing the world over, and that has been achieved alongside a reform of trade union law which was sorely needed. And a higher standard of living for everyone.

DD: [tries to interrupt] But—

MT: Please. If people just drool and drivel that they care, I turn round and say 'Right. I also look to see what you actually do.'

DD: Why do you use the words 'drool and drivel that they care'? Is that what you think saying that you care about people's plight amounts to?

MT: No, I don't. [Pause.] I'm sorry I used those words. But I think some people talk a great deal about caring, but the policies which they pursue – and I'm sorry I used those words – the policies which they pursue do not amount to what they say.

Clearly she realised the moment Dimbleby picked her up on those words that she was handing a loaded revolver to her opponents, but in the end she got away with it. The difference between then and now is that a mistake like that is virtually inconceivable. Senior politicians are given media training to within an inch of their lives. Virtually every ounce of spontaneity is pounced on and extinguished. They stick to their scripts and it's the devil's own job for the interviewer to shift them from it. Interviewing Thatcher was like riding a big dipper: moments of sheer exhilaration and moments of pure terror. But it was never boring.

The first time I interviewed her was on the lawn of the White House. She was visiting Washington in her capacity as education secretary. The most newsworthy thing she did during those years was to stop schoolchildren getting free milk, which meant that wherever she went thereafter she was greeted with: 'Thatcher, Thatcher! Milk snatcher!' The only memorable thing about that interview was a curious squirrel which, unnoticed by the cameraman or Mrs Thatcher, appeared on the branch of a tree hanging a few feet behind her just as she began answering my first question. It seemed to contemplate leaping onto her beautifully coiffured head: advancing … backing off … advancing … backing off. The audience at home must have loved it. I imagined a few million viewers (especially the free-milk victims) urging the little creature on: 'Go for it! Jump!' Sadly, it chickened out.

I have always wondered how she would have coped if a little furry bundle with sharp claws had landed on her head as the nation looked on. Would she have ignored it, brushed it away, carried on regardless? I thought about Jimmy Carter. He foolishly recounted the story when he was president of the United States of the day he had been fishing from a small boat in a Georgia swamp and had been approached by a large rabbit swimming towards him. The way he told the story it seemed he was almost relieved to have survived. It was for ever dubbed the 'incident of the killer rabbit' and Carter's dignity never quite recovered from it.

A few years later, after Mrs Thatcher became prime minister, I was the new boy on *Today*, trying desperately to prove to myself what I didn't really believe: that I could handle even the toughest interview without batting an eyelid. Thatcher was the toughest of them all and I had to interview her during the 1987 election campaign. She had been prime minister for eight years and, like any other right-thinking human being, I was terrified of her. She had built a formidable reputation and would have no trouble dealing with a gauche young man who was trying to get the hang of his new job. So what could I do to rattle her – if only a little?

I toyed with reminding her right from the start that the economy was in terrible trouble and millions were out of work because of her policies. I would demand to know what she was going to do about it. But she'd have had no trouble with that. She dealt with it every day of her life. So I opted for a different approach. I recalled that on the day she moved into Number 10 she had made a little speech in which she quoted St Francis: 'Where there is discord may we bring harmony.' So my brilliant opening question would remind her of her Christianity and demand to know how she defined its essence. She would be taken aback and would almost certainly say (wouldn't we all?) something like 'love' or 'charity'. I would then remind her that millions of people were suffering because of her heartless policies and demand to know how she could call herself a Christian? She would be devastated, resign on the spot and I would become the hero of a grateful nation. At the very least she would be severely rattled. Or so I thought. She did not hesitate for a millisecond. She snapped back a one-word answer: 'Choice!'

One of us was struck dumb and it wasn't her. Much, much later I grasped what she meant, but it was far too late by then. I never again tried anything clever with Margaret Thatcher.

10

A pretty straight sort of guy?

On 2 May 1997 a fresh-faced Tony Blair, hand in hand with his beaming wife Cherie, entered 10 Downing Street. Not for this prime minister the armour-plated Jaguar sweeping up to the door of the most famous address in the country. He and Cherie arrived on foot, cheered every inch of the way by the adoring crowds. The message could not have been clearer: this was to be a prime minister of the people, the like of whom we had never seen before. In the words of the pop song that would be played relentlessly at every Labour Party event for months to come: 'Things can only get better!' Better or not, things would certainly be different.

Blair would go on to win the next election and the one after that. In electoral terms he would prove to be the most successful leader in the history of his party. He entered Number 10 with a massive majority in the House of Commons, the unchallenged leader not of the 'old' Labour Party but New Labour. He had the country at his feet – including the BBC. It was almost as though we had signed up to the New Labour religion with its three tenets:

- the old adversarial politics had gone;
- there would be a different approach;
- this was the era of new politics.

None of it was true – and even it had been the BBC had no right to reach such a judgement. We were to learn very swiftly that the new politics would come to look very much like the old and there was one word that bridged the gap: sleaze.

Blair had demolished John Major in the election campaign by painting him as the ineffectual leader of a government riddled with sleaze. Blair's own government, he declaimed passionately over and over again, would be whiter than white and 'purer than pure'. But, only six months after that triumphant walk up Downing Street, Blair would find himself sitting opposite me in the prime minister's country home, Chequers, begging the country to accept that he was 'a pretty straight sort of guy'.

His government, just like John Major's, had been overwhelmed by a tsunami of sleaze and was struggling to keep its head above the water. His words, in the closing minute of a live *On the Record* interview that had lasted for nearly an hour, were to haunt him for the rest of his time in Number 10.

The story of Labour sleaze had been dominating the news headlines for weeks. It came to a climax with what became known as the Ecclestone Affair. Bernie Ecclestone, the billionaire boss of Formula 1, was fighting to exempt the sport from a ban prohibiting their racing cars from displaying tobacco advertisements. It was a hugely lucrative source of funds. Ecclestone made a donation to the Labour Party of £1 million. A few months later he had a meeting with Tony Blair at Number 10. Within hours of that meeting Blair gave orders for F1 to be exempted from the ban. Blair and his ministers insisted that there was no connection between the two events but his opponents and almost the entire media took another view. He and his government were besieged on every front. It made the various 'sleaze' charges against John Major seem relatively small beer. There were even calls for Blair to resign. His fall from grace was spectacular: from hero to zero in a matter of months.

By the middle of November 1997 the scandal had reached hurricane force. It was the dominant political story for every news outlet in the country. But there was a problem facing the journalists trying to report it. Senior politicians were terrified of speaking about it – at least on the record. Serious *Labour* politicians, that is. The Tories were, of course, hammering down the doors of every radio and television studio in the land. Here was their tormentor, the man who had almost single-handedly brought them down after eighteen years in power, now impaled on the very weapon he had wielded so effectively to attack them. Sleaze.

Politicians are seldom generous when they scent blood – especially if the wounded animal happens to be the very man who deprived them of power. They were merciless and all too ready to tell interviewers like me why their opponent should do the decent thing: come clean and resign. But what we all wanted to know was what Blair's own party made of it – above all his most senior colleagues in the Cabinet.

Clearly it was inconceivable that any of them would be brave enough or foolish enough to desert their leader in his hour of greatest need. If Blair survived the crisis and they were deemed to have been disloyal (perhaps the gravest charge in the world of politics) they could bid farewell to the red boxes and ministerial car and return to the back benches whence they had come. There was no shortage of party figures prepared to speak to journalists off the record. There seldom is. But that was no use to a programme like *On the Record*. There's a clue in its title.

Would Blair be forced to resign only six months after he had become prime minister? On one level it seemed inconceivable but the question was out there and we had to have a credible Labour figure sitting in the studio at 1 p.m. on 16 November 1997 to deal with it. God knows how many politicians we tried. The producers and researchers and correspondents phoned every contact in their books, begging, pleading, cajoling and even threatening – or at least they would have threatened if they'd had anything to threaten with. But nothing. They had started at the top with the members of the Cabinet and worked their way down the ranks. In normal times a junior minister – let alone a backbench MP – would have sacrificed his firstborn for half an hour on a prestigious programme like *On the Record*, but these were not normal times. They knew the risks and they said no. All of them.

I recall endless occasions over my decades presenting when I have watched colleagues trying to find an interviewee who just might agree to come on the programme, but never anything like that Saturday afternoon in the editor's office. They had tried everyone and they had failed. We had the biggest political story we could remember and a vast, gaping hole in the programme where the interview should be. Someone suggested mass resignation. Someone else suggested mass suicide. That was when the phone rang. It was Alastair Campbell.

'I suppose you fuckers want to interview the prime minister tomorrow?'

If we'd had a larger office I would have run around it yelling triumphantly and punching the air. Instead I kicked the wall. My foot went through it. The hole remained until the programme was taken off the air some five years later. In fact, it may still be there for all I know.

Those unfamiliar with Alastair Campbell might be a little taken aback at his graceless telephone style but by his standards that was par for the course. He once said he did not have power: just influence. That, surely, is a distinction without a difference. When you have unrestricted access to the most powerful man in the land, when you control every aspect of the message delivered not just by Downing Street but by every other department in government, when you attend every crucial meeting and you are feared by every minister on the payroll, that is power. The only place where Campbell's writ did not run was the house next door to Number 10: Number 11, the home of the chancellor Gordon Brown. That was a rival empire.

I remember once sitting in the prime minister's office in the House of Commons having a coffee and a chat with Blair. Just the two of us. The door burst open and Campbell appeared with a jacket in his hand. He didn't so much as nod at me but threw the jacket across the room to Blair, snarled 'For fuck's sake Tony, you've got a meeting!' and left. Blair threw me one of those 'What can you do?' hapless shrugs and left too.

I'll return to my own relationship with him later, but if the pope had appeared right then and there in the *OTR* office and announced he needed to find someone to elevate to sainthood we would unanimously have nominated Alastair Campbell. He had just given us a prize beyond the wildest dreams of any political programme. One minor snag: the interview was to take place at Chequers. So all we had to do now was arrange for an outside broadcast crew to get there, set up the cameras and everything else for a programme that always came from a fully equipped studio in Television Centre and be up and running within a matter of hours. Normally the outside-broadcast department would expect at least a week's notice. Oh … and there was the small matter of thinking up some questions for Tony Blair and planning an interview which, one way or another, would determine the course of his premiership for the foreseeable future. Just a minor detail.

We worked late into the evening on the interview and when we set off for Chequers the following morning we were reasonably confident that we had a pretty strong case. Confidence matters – at least it does to me. I've lost track of the number of interviews I've done that should have been pretty straightforward but have been a complete dog's breakfast because of the nasty little doubt in the back of my brain that told me I hadn't really done my homework or wasn't properly briefed or I simply didn't fully grasp the point of the interview. Not this time though. I reckoned that I had done all I could realistically have done – and anyway I had a brilliant editor talking into my ear to keep me on track and alert me to any dangers.

And so, at 12.55 p.m. on Sunday when I took my seat in front of the lights in our improvised studio in Chequers, I was feeling pretty good – if a little nervous – about the coming hour. My only slight, niggling, worry was that none of us had actually set eyes on Tony Blair himself. It's not that I'd expected a great welcoming party when we arrived at the mansion, but we had thought Blair or Campbell would pop by for a moment, if only to say hello. But when the sound technician clipped my microphone onto my jacket there was no sign of him. And when the clock struck one and the signature tune for *OTR* rang out there was still no sign of him. Nor did he appear during the four minutes when we cut away to the newsreader in London for the news bulletin. It was a very long four minutes and when London handed back to me I was hearing an awful lot of cursing in my earpiece along the lines of 'Where the fuck is he?' and 'You don't think Campbell's pulled him at the last minute!' I was still staring at an empty chair when I began my introduction to what would be the biggest interview of my career. I was steeling myself to say something like: 'Well, I had expected the prime minister to be with me but …'

And that's when he appeared. Whether Campbell had delayed him deliberately to get me rattled I suppose I shall never know, but if he did, it worked.

In one sense, though, this was a doddle of an interview. Unlike most interviews with prime ministers we had not had to spend many hours agonising over what subjects to focus on, where he might be most vulnerable and what questions the audience most wanted answered. There was only one subject. Campbell had decided that Blair should do it to persuade the people of Britain that he was, to use that memorable phrase with which he would end the interview, 'a pretty straight sort of guy'.

I suggested to Blair that at the very least a little warning light should have come on in his head when Ecclestone asked for a meeting with him after he had handed over £1 million with the suggestion that more might be forthcoming. Here's how it continued:

JH: Shouldn't that little warning light have said: hang on a minute, should I be seeing him under these circumstances? Should I not say: no, I won't see you. You go and see somebody else. Or, alternatively, perhaps, I'll give the money back before I see him?

TB: John, at the time, on the sixteenth of October, it hadn't been decided that we should exempt Formula 1.

JH: No, no, that isn't the point.

TB: No—

JH: You knew that he was going to ask you to do that.

TB: No. He didn't ask us to do that …

JH: He wanted something from you and he had given you a million pounds.

TB: Yes, but the point is that as at the sixteenth of October there'd been no decision to exempt Formula 1. We never discussed an exemption of Formula 1. What would be odd, frankly – particularly after he'd seen other heads of government, including Chancellor Kohl and Prime Minister Padraig – is that because he'd been a donor to the Labour Party, you refused to see him and passed him on to somebody else in the Labour Party.

And this is how it ended:

JH: You've been in power for six months and a bit now and you've had a quite extraordinary period in office. I mean you have been the most popular prime minister since ever. Now the papers are saying that the issue surrounding you is one of trust. Do you believe that as a result of what has happened in this past week or so you have lost the trust of the British people?

TB: No, I don't believe that. And I hope that people know me well enough and realise the type of person I am, to realise that I would never do anything either to harm the country or anything improper. I never have. I think most people who have dealt with me, think I'm a pretty straight sort of guy and I am …

JH: But you've been tarnished.

TB: I don't believe I've been tarnished – no. I think that mistakes have been made but I think in the end the country's got to look at me. It's got to in a sense, got to decide whether the person that they believed in is the same person they've got now and it is.

I had a quick coffee with Blair, Campbell and Cherie after the interview. Campbell was his usual friendly self: 'Didn't lay a finger on him!' was his opening growl at me. Blair looked a little less certain and so did Cherie. Unsurprising, really, given what we now know about that unedifying episode. In the end, as history records, Blair survived. It was to be another two years before the country was to be shown the smoking gun. The *Sunday Telegraph* published documents released to them after a long Freedom of Information battle showing that the request for the policy on F1 tobacco advertisements to be changed had indeed come directly from Blair himself. He had personally intervened within hours of his meeting with Ecclestone. Even his own civil servants thought his denials were 'disingenuous'.

It's always interesting to contrast what a spin doctor says in public when a crisis is raging and what he confides to his diary in the privacy of his bedroom. We know what Campbell thought because he published his diary ten years later. The 'nightmare', as he described it, 'was entirely of our own making and we had badly handled virtually every move to get out of it'. He quoted Derry Irvine, the head of the legal chambers where a young Blair had once been a pupil barrister and was now, as Lord Chancellor, still guiding Blair. Or trying to. Campbell records that Lord Irvine told him Blair believed his own propaganda and 'thinks he's invincible'. He added: 'It happened to Thatcher after ten years. It's happened to Tony after six months.' Campbell himself wrote that Irvine 'could not believe how badly we had fucked it up'.

But I made no attempt to argue with Campbell in that rather awkward little chat in the drawing room of Chequers. What would have been the point?

Perhaps the most illuminating thing to come out of it was Cherie's attitude to Humphrey the Downing Street cat. I won't suggest he rivalled Ecclestone for column inches, but he was definitely big news. He had disappeared some days before and the word was that Cherie, who was allegedly not a cat person, might have had something to do with it. If I couldn't get Blair to admit to the charges against him, maybe I could get a confession from Cherie. So I put it to her straight. Was she behind Humphrey's disappearance? She said nothing, just pointed down at her feet and a sly little smile crossed her face. She was wearing slippers. Very furry slippers. I'll never be able to prove anything, but let's just say that the fur bore a definite resemblance to that of the late Humphrey.

As for Blair, he not only survived but went on to fight and win another two elections. But my own relationship with him was to come to a fairly abrupt end – and all because of one interview.

Blair gave his first interview at the start of the 2001 election campaign to the *Today* programme. When I prepared for it I reflected on how short political memories can be. It was four years since Blair's landslide victory against a Tory party fractured over Europe and mired in allegations of sleaze – allegations that Labour had ruthlessly exploited. In the Cheshire constituency of Tatton, Labour and the Liberal Democrats had even stepped aside to allow 'the man in the white suit', my colleague Martin Bell, to stand as an independent candidate against the sitting Conservative, Neil Hamilton, who had been caught up in the 'cash for questions' affair. In the 1997 Labour manifesto, Blair had promised the brave new world of 'a new politics':

The reason for having created new Labour is to meet the
challenges of a different world. The millennium symbolises a
new era opening up for Britain. I am confident about our
future prosperity, even optimistic, if we have the courage to
change and use it to build a better Britain. To accomplish this

means more than just a change of government. Our aim is no less than to set British political life on a new course for the future. People are cynical about politics and distrustful of political promises. That is hardly surprising. There have been few more gross breaches of faith than when the Conservatives under Mr Major promised, before the election of 1992, that they would not raise taxes, but would cut them every year; and then went on to raise them by the largest amount in peacetime history starting in the first Budget after the election.

I felt it was important to remind the audience of one of the key promises Blair had made in fashioning his landslide victory (he had won in 1997 with a majority of 179 seats). In 1995 he had accused Major of bowing to the 'squalid monetary interests of the Conservative Party' and insisted that once in office Labour would be 'purer than pure'. Had it been? Almost immediately Blair had been discomfited by the Formula 1 revelations. That phrase he had used with me – that he was a 'pretty straight sort of guy' – had stuck with the nation. The problem for him was that it was inevitably followed with: 'Oh really?'

There had been other difficult moments for his government also related to 'sleaze'. In 1998, it had been badly shaken by the resignation of two of its senior ministers. Peter Mandelson, one of the prime minister's closest advisers, had resigned as trade and industry secretary after it emerged that he had borrowed £373,000 from a fellow minister, the Paymaster General Geoffrey Robinson, a multimillionaire, to buy a house when the pair were in opposition. Robinson resigned hours later, making it the first time that two ministers had resigned on the same day since 1982.

In February 2000, the parliamentary standards watchdog Elizabeth Filkin had begun an investigation into allegations that the Foreign Office minister Keith Vaz had accepted several thousand pounds from a solicitor which he had failed to declare. He was censured for failing to register two payments worth a total of £4,500 but he had also been accused of blocking Filkin's investigation into the allegations. A year later, in March 2001, a new inquiry was ordered into his links to the wealthy Hinduja brothers who ran an Indian business conglomerate and had been pressing for British citizenship. In June, Vaz admitted that he had made representations on their behalf while he was a backbench MP.

Mandelson had made a political comeback as Northern Ireland secretary. But he too was forced out by the Hinduja affair. A subsequent independent report into the so-called 'cash for passports' affair by Sir Anthony Hammond QC found in Mandelson's favour, concluding that neither he, nor anyone else, had done anything improper. But the question remained. Was this what 'purer than pure' meant? Or had we simply seen politics as usual over the last four years? By focusing on that question, I thought we could test the mettle both of Tony Blair and the government itself.

So I decided to return to sleaze for my opening question and reminded him that in the last election campaign he had promised the British public he would be 'purer than pure'. My question was: 'Have you been?' This was what John Birt used to call a 'rabbit punch' question. Blair made no serious attempt to answer it and tried to divert the interview onto his own agenda.

> Well I think where we haven't been, where people have fallen down then action's been taken against them, but I think on the overall record of the government in terms of economical stability, investment and public services, the measures we've taken to make this country fairer and stronger, then I think that even though there is a very great deal more to do, we can be proud of what we have done.

It's worth analysing the subsequent interview in a little detail. Blair simply refused to be drawn on 'purer than pure' and tried to derail my line of questioning by going on the attack. The purity of his government was not important to voters – I should be asking about things that concern them. It was a masterclass in how a skilled operator can turn the tables on the interviewer by appealing directly to the listeners.

> *JH:* You said you wanted to be purer than pure. On that basis, all these questions should have been addressed – I'm suggesting to you – more directly, and more firmly, because it isn't only Keith Vaz, there's the case of Geoffrey Robinson as well, against whom many charges were found to be proven.
>
> *TB:* Well hang on a minute. In respect of Geoffrey Robinson the committee has given him time to respond, and in respect of Geoffrey Robinson I may remind you he left government. But when you talk about trust in government …
>
> *JH:* He did, but other allegations had been raised against him and proven before he left government.
>
> *TB:* No hang on a minute, the allegations raised against him were not proven, there are a fresh set of allegations and he's been given time to respond, but he is actually a backbench Member of Parliament. But when you raise the issue of trust in government surely the most important aspect of trust in government is whether we deliver on the promises that we set out, on the issues that really concern people, on the issues that I'm sure your listeners would like to hear about.
>
> *JH:* It's all sorts of things surely?
>
> *TB:* No hang on John, let me just finish this …

Now Blair defends his government's record not just by pointing to its success in policy areas but by implying that I am asking the wrong questions …

> *TB:* … because when you talk about trust in government, I think questions of course have to be asked from the politicians, maybe some questions should be asked from people like yourself as well.

… and that gives him the opportunity to answer at length questions I haven't asked but which he is effectively asking himself. He can stress his government's achievements while at the same time criticising me for not asking about them. It's a quite brilliant tactic, reinforced by his use of repetition.

> *TB:* Surely the question of whether we delivered economic
> stability in the way that we promised, we said we would be a
> different Labour government from previous Labour
> governments matters. Surely the issue of whether we've
> delivered on the pledges that we set out in schools and
> hospitals and crime matter. Surely the pledge as to whether we
> could lift a quarter of a million young people off benefit and
> into work which we've actually done. Surely that question and
> whether it's been delivered upon is also of relevance to trust in
> government, so when you talk about trust in government, of
> course you guys, because this is your agenda, want to focus on
> the individual conduct of individual people, but I think for the
> country far more important is whether the government is
> pursuing the big aims and objectives that determine the future
> of this country …

So by now it's even more important that I should remind listeners of the great play Blair, as opposition leader, made of 'sleaze' in the Major government and what people think of politicians now. Blair's government had never successfully shaken off the suspicion that it had itself promoted such cynicism because of its devotion to, and undoubted skill at, the dark arts of spin and public relations.

> *JH:* The point I'm making to you is that trust in politics is about
> more than competence, is about more than managing affairs.
> *TB:* Well of course it's about more than competence …

This time it's a direct appeal to me – effectively, oh come off it John!

> *TB:* … but surely the big questions in this election – I mean John, really – the big questions …
> *JH:* There are many big questions are there not?
> *TB:* Yeah, but well let's – we've dealt with one that you say is the big questions – let's deal with some more, let's deal with schools and hospitals and crime.
> *JH:* Well let me leave that one, let me just be absolutely clear …
> […]
> *JH:* … so for the rest of this campaign can we see a bit less of the stage management that we have seen thus far?
> *TB:* Well, I think it would be a good idea if people concentrated occasionally on the substance of what I say rather than all the trimmings and trappings …

It was a classic of its kind. There wasn't even an acknowledgement of the part he had played in the Ecclestone Affair, let alone all the other scandals. Action had been taken against 'people who had fallen down'. Action that excluded, of course, the man at the top. There was barely half a sentence on sleaze and then a swift swerve to the sunlit economic uplands he had created. Vintage stuff. And that's pretty much how the rest of the interview progressed. And the more he refused, the more I persisted. But I got nowhere. It was two ships passing in the night.

It showed the limitations of even a lengthy broadcast interview when you're pitted against someone like Blair. In the end, if they're sufficiently resourceful, politicians can move any question onto the ground on which they're most comfortable. Of course, they have to be plausible and it helps if you have enough facts at your fingertips. Blair was able to summon up the fine print of his manifesto from four years ago, and question the use of economic statistics entirely fluently, without hesitation or deviation, but maybe with some repetition. Alastair Campbell once said of his boss admiringly 'he doesn't make mistakes'. He was pretty much a bombproof interviewee. Sometimes, as a professional broadcaster, you just had to admire his skill.

Was it a waste of time? Possibly. It's certainly true that we learned nothing new. But surely the great British public choose their leaders not just on the basis of competence, but of character too. We want to know whether we can trust them. And who would argue today that trust – or the lack of it – became the defining characteristic of the Blair years.

The interview achieved something else – though not a result I had aimed for. It was conducted 'down the line' with me in the *Today* studio and Blair in his constituency home in Sedgefield. Alastair Campbell was, of course, sitting at the table with him. John Cary, the *Today* producer who was also there, told me afterwards that when the interview ended Campbell ripped off his headphones, threw them across the table and uttered just one word: 'Wanker!'

John paused and added: 'To be honest, I wasn't quite sure who he had in mind ...'

Inevitably, though, Campbell had the last laugh. I was not allowed to conduct another interview with Blair until the election of 2005, four years later. By then Campbell had left Number 10. Maybe a coincidence, but I doubt it.

11

Management are deeply unimpressed

I suspect most broadcasters harbour the secret fear that when they finally meet their professional doom it will happen live on air with millions of people listening or watching. You begin the interview knowing that you are hopelessly unprepared and that your interviewee is one of those politicians who drowns kittens for a hobby. You remember that he harbours a powerful grudge against you for once having made him look rather foolish and that if he believes in anything at all it is the old saying that revenge is a dish best served cold. And if you (just about) survive the interview you don't quietly celebrate, you say to yourself something like: 'Phew! Got away with it that time but sooner or later …'

I was *not* expecting to meet my doom as I settled into the chair for a chat with Jon Sopel, our North America editor, at 4 a.m. on a bleak Monday in January 2018 to record a quick interview with him for use later on *Today*. Jon is an old friend and colleague. I've known him for close on thirty years and we invariably exchange a little banter before we start recording – usually a bit of mutual mickey-taking. On this particular morning there was a lot to banter about.

The night before I had been phoned at home by the boss to be told something quite extraordinary about the following morning's programme. My fellow presenter was to be our China editor, Carrie Gracie. Nothing extraordinary about that. She was one of several correspondents who stood in occasionally when we ran out of regular presenters. She was good at it: confident, composed, quick-witted and, given her thirty years as a BBC journalist, well informed. Especially on China, obviously. So I was looking forward to presenting with her. At least, I was until the boss told me what she had just done.

A few hours earlier she had published an open letter announcing that she had resigned from her China job. The reason she gave was to light the fuse on an explosion that would cause enormous damage to the BBC. It would cost it a fortune in salary increases but, far more importantly, it would present the BBC to the world as a duplicitous, double-dealing, dishonest, deceitful, disloyal organisation that had treated her and hundreds more like her with contempt. Her claim was that she and her colleagues were being punished for the sin of being the wrong gender. They were women and, for year after year, they had been paid less than men.

Here's part of what she said in her letter: 'The BBC belongs to you, the licence-fee payer. I believe you have a right to know that the BBC is breaking equality law and resisting pressure for a fair and transparent pay structure ... It is not living up to its stated values of trust, honesty and accountability.'

By any standards, these were extremely grave charges to bring against any organisation. And the BBC is not just any organisation. It is uniquely privileged. It has a right to broadcast and a guaranteed income to pay for it. As Carrie rightly said, it is owned by its licence payers. It is not answerable to a group of shareholders or a small collection of wealthy individuals but to every one of its viewers and listeners. And they, in turn, have a right to expect the highest standards from an organisation that so often had claimed to occupy the high moral ground.

When Carrie challenged its commitment to its values of trust, honesty and accountability, she was striking at the very heart of the BBC. If BBC News itself was not to be trusted how could it presume to hold others to account? And for that charge to come not from a disgruntled ex-employee nursing a grudge but from one of its most senior and respected journalists, was infinitely more damaging.

So when my boss told me about the letter I came to what I assumed was the only possible conclusion. Carrie Gracie should certainly appear on *Today* the following morning – but not as a presenter. She should appear as an interviewee. The reason was obvious. This was clearly a big story. It would generate headlines for days if not weeks or even months to come. It would have enormous implications for the BBC. *Today* had to report it just as it would report any other big story. Gracie was at the heart of it so clearly she would have to be replaced and another presenter hauled in. And then equally obviously, we would invite her to be interviewed in just the same way as we would interview anyone else at the heart of a big story. I said as much to my boss.

There was the sound of some throat-clearing at the other end of the line and then: 'Umm ... no ... It's been decided that she'll still be presenting.'

What! How could that possibly be allowed? It would make us a national laughing stock. An Exocet had been fired at the BBC with huge consequences and the person who'd fired it would be sitting beside me for three hours presenting the most prestigious news programme on Radio 4 without even a reference to it. I tried to find some consolation in the ridiculous situation ...

'Well at least I'll be able to grill her about her claims ... should make a bloody good interview.'

There was the throat-clearing again. 'I'm afraid not. That's been ruled out. You won't be allowed to talk to her about it.'

Once again ... What!

This wasn't just poor news management. It was the worst sort of cack-handed news management handed down from on high. It made the Kremlin *circa* 1950 look sophisticated. I tried to imagine the programme. The story would have to be given a pretty prominent slot in the news bulletins. If not it would seem (reasonably enough) that the BBC was censoring stories it might find embarrassing. So the newsreader would read out the story while the source of the story sat a few feet away in the same studio. It would also, inevitably, have to appear in one of the three paper reviews which are read out by, yes you've guessed it, the presenters. So we might have the excruciating spectacle of Carrie Gracie reading out a story from *The Times* about Carrie Gracie without offering any comment. The alternative – just as excruciating – would be the other presenter (me) reading out the story about Carrie Gracie while Carrie Gracie sat next to me.

I made it fairly clear to my boss in pretty robust language what I thought about that and in the end we reached a compromise. A ridiculous compromise, but it was either resign in protest or settle for it – which is what I did. With the benefit of hindsight, I realised there had been another option. I could have come down with a terrible stomach bug and called in sick. Then someone else would have had to be found to do the dirty work. It would have saved me embarrassment on two fronts: one inflicted by the BBC bosses and the other entirely of my own making. But I'd never pulled out of a programme before and, to my eternal regret, I stuck with it.

Here is what the listeners heard me say in the papers review at 6.40 a.m. I tried to suggest by my tone of voice that I found it as bonkers as they would find it, but I'm not sure I succeeded:

JH: And a big story in all the papers pretty much – the resignation of somebody called Carrie Gracie as the BBC's China editor. It's the main story in *The Times*, on the front page of the *Telegraph*, the *I*, the *Sun* and so on. *The Times* says her decision reflects the depth of anger felt across the corporation over pay inequality between men and women. It says 134 female employees at the BBC have issued a statement expressing whole-hearted support for her and the revolt represents one of the biggest crises to hit the BBC since Lord Hall took over as director general in 2013. The BuzzFeed news website which was the first to publish her open letter to licence-fee payers describes it as explosive and a bombshell ... And ... [slight sigh] at this point [slight laugh] ... given that Carrie is sitting ...

CG: [laughs] What's happening next John? Where do we go from here?

JH: Well indeed, given that you are sitting next to me in the studio perhaps listeners would expect me to do a really tough interview with you about that bombshell letter but the BBC has rules on impartiality which mean that presenters can't suddenly turn into interviewees on the programmes they are presenting. However [she interrupts off mic], however, however [more interruption]. Well, maybe, anyway, you are going to be doing an interview on *Woman's Hour* on Radio 4 at ten o'clock but just a very quick thought. You're not allowed, well you know the rules ...

CG: ... We're not doing an interview ...

JH: You are not doing an interview ...

CG: ... you're going to ask me one question.

JH: Well ... just about the reaction. It's been quite a big one hasn't it?

CG: It has. It's been very moving actually, and the two things that have struck me most about it and moved me most – and one is, I think the scale of feeling, not just among BBC women but also just more widely across the country and also internationally, the support that I've had in the last few hours over this, I think it does speak to the depth of hunger for an equal fair and transparent pay system and the other thing I'd like to say is that what is lovely for me is that people are mentioning my China work because I would not wish to be remembered forever as the person who, the woman who complained about money, you know, I want to be remembered—

JH: Too late. Too late!

And that was that. An utterly pointless and rather embarrassing exchange. Carrie had the opportunity to make her case, which was fine, but I was banned from asking her any questions about it, which was not. So the BBC had managed to shoot itself in the foot not once but twice. First by allowing somebody who was at the centre of a hugely controversial story concerning the BBC to present a programme like *Today*. Secondly by preventing the other presenter (me) from conducting a standard rigorous interview with her about very serious allegations. That, after all, is what *Today* is for.

And as if all that was not enough I had managed to shoot myself in my own foot even before the programme went on the air – though I was blissfully unaware of it at the time. Which takes me back to that 4 a.m. chat with Jon Sopel.

Because of the five hours' time difference between London and Washington it's standard practice to pre-record interviews with correspondents like Jon as early in the morning as possible, which means they can get to bed before midnight rather than in the small hours of the morning. It's the sensible thing to do even if it's not ideal for the presenter. We will have literally only just arrived in the office. We'll have had ten minutes to scan the newspapers in the back of the car en route to New Broadcasting House, but we won't know much (if anything) about the story that has led to the interview. That doesn't really matter with old hands like Jon. They know what they want to say and it's our job to give them the chance to say it.

I've always made a habit of trying to have a very quick chat with the correspondent – sometimes to put them at their ease if they're fairly new in the job, sometimes to make sure they know what I want to talk about and sometimes, in the case of someone like Jon, to catch up on a bit of gossip and even engage in a bit of mickey-taking. To my eternal regret that is what I did on that fateful morning. I knew Jon would have heard about the Gracie affair and would have been as baffled as me at the way the BBC was handling it and so, before we began the recording, I indulged in a bit of banter. Big mistake.

I pretended that the subject of our interview had been changed and instead of talking to him about Donald Trump I wanted to discuss the Carrie Gracie affair in the context of his own salary and how much higher it was than hers. I suggested to him that he might consider sacrificing some of his own pay to help even things out. He pointed out that my salary was even higher so if anyone should take a cut it was me. I replied (admittedly using some colourful language and with just a touch of exaggeration) that I'd already given up more in voluntary pay cuts than he actually earned. Jon, rather more worldly-wise than me, suggested we draw the chat to a close. So we did. The whole jokey exchange took no more than a minute and I forgot all about it.

And then, two days later, one of the bosses phoned. Somebody had leaked it. It was inevitable that it would find its way onto social media and could lead to a bit of embarrassment for all concerned. He also said that he had listened to it himself, agreed that it was obviously meant to be a joke and didn't think much would come of it. He was wrong. Within twenty-four hours it was everywhere – all over the Internet and the newspapers – and I had apparently joined the ranks of the world's great misogynists. I was right up there with Donald Trump and, on the other side of the intellectual scale, Aristotle, who was credited with claiming that a proper wife should be 'as obedient as a slave'. It was manna from heaven for those militant feminists who already regarded men as the natural enemy. They had a new villain in their sights.

I had no idea how to react. How do you prove that you are not a misogynist? I was invited by every other paper in Fleet Street to write a piece or do an interview defending myself, but what could I have said? It was a joke OK? A pretty silly joke admittedly, but it was 4 a.m. and I was talking to an old mate and we were winding each other up as we had done a hundred times before. The difference this time was that some cowardly sleazebag had seen fit to leak it for their own shabby reasons.

I suppose I could have pointed out a few inconvenient truths to my accusers. I have always believed men and women should receive equal pay for equal work. I have been on the record for several years making the case that the next director general of the BBC should be a woman because it is outrageous that in its ninety-seven years (and counting) the BBC has never had a woman in charge. I could even point out that when I lined up with a group of *Today* women for a photograph on the morning we celebrated the programme's sixtieth birthday I was praised by them for my attitude to the women on the programme. I know that's hardly the equivalent of hailing me as the saviour of womankind, but in the age of Me Too it was nice to hear. And I had many private emails from women sympathising with me over the whole Sopel affair.

But so what? The obvious response would have been: 'Well, he would say that, wouldn't he?' And anyway there's something both undignified and unseemly about bleating: 'I'm a good boy ... honest I am!'

The fact is, I had been stupid and naive. It had not occurred to me for a second that my idiotic private conversation would have been relayed to the world. So in the end, it was nobody's fault but my own. Even so I was disappointed by the BBC's reaction. Yes, of course they should have given me a bollocking: something along the lines of 'How could you have been so stupid?' But they might also have made the point that it was obviously a silly joke and my fifty years' service at the BBC showed that to accuse me of misogyny on the basis of one bit of 'private' banter lasting a minute was risible. Fat chance. Instead they came up with the typically pompous comment: 'This was an ill-advised off-air conversation which the presenter regrets.' And off the record a 'source' told the *Guardian* that 'management are deeply unimpressed'. What a pity they hadn't had the nerve to say it to my face. Once again I toyed with the idea of resigning but it would have been seen as an acceptance of guilt for some terrible crime I had not committed.

At the close of that horrible week I was listening, as usual, to *PM* on Radio 4. I heard Eddie Mair introduce what purported to be an item about women's pay. He said:

Some well-known voices on the BBC have been stopped from conducting on-air interviews about equal pay. Among the people the BBC has prohibited, the Radio 4 *Woman's Hour* presenter Jane Garvey and Winifred Robinson from Radio 4's *You and Yours* who both commented on the resignation of the BBC's China editor Carrie Gracie. She stepped down because she said she could not 'collude' in a policy she described as 'unlawful pay discrimination'. The BBC justified its decision to silence some presenters on the grounds of impartiality.

That, I thought, was a curious verb to use: 'to *silence* some present-ers …' The BBC did no such thing. You could hardly switch on a news programme or a social media site without hearing their views. Quite right too. They were entitled to express outrage at the BBC deliberately discriminating against women. What they were told they would not be allowed to do 'on the grounds of impartiality' was conduct interviews. Here's how the BBC put it:

> One of the tests of the independence of BBC News is that, as well as being independent of political, commercial or personal interests, News should also be independent of BBC corporate interests. BBC News should be able to report on the BBC without fear or favour. And it does. But disagreements within the BBC do create particular challenges for those who present and report the news: they are required to be impartial and not to take sides in disputes lest it jeopardise one of the BBC's most important values, its commitment to impartial news and current affairs. In general this means that BBC presenters and reporters do not reveal their personal views of public controversies.

For once I agreed with every word the BBC said. No presenter should be allowed to conduct interviews if they have publicly expressed their views on the subject. I have been a victim of that basic rule myself – albeit a willing victim.

Like most people, I happen to feel very strongly about many things. Close to the top of my list is the way we add to the suffering of people who are facing a hideous death from incurable illnesses such as motor neurone disease. I believe that they should be helped to die if they have made it clear that they cannot face the slow death by suffocation that inevitably awaits them. As the law stands it is unlawful to assist suicide even though the act of suicide itself is lawful. I wanted to write a book making the case for it. I told the BBC and they made no attempt to stop me – it was, after all, a matter of conscience – but warned me that I would no longer be allowed to conduct interviews on the subject. I agreed. I could not be seen to be biased on the subject.

After Mair had informed his listeners that the women were being 'silenced', he asked, in the solemn tones he usually reserved for moments of national crisis: 'So what should the BBC do about John Humphrys, who presents Radio 4's *Today*?'

Then he read out a transcript of my entire conversation with Jon Sopel, his voice growing ever more sombre. Listeners might have thought I had been caught plotting some deadly campaign to destabilise democracy, or at the very least been discovered at dead of night, armed with an AK-47, trying to scale the perimeter wall of Buckingham Palace. At no point did he even suggest something he obviously knew to be the case: it had been a silly joke between two old friends who invariably engaged in a bit of banter in the small hours of the morning before getting down to business.

At the end of his performance he introduced his interviewee, a former editor of *Today*, Phil Harding. When Phil rather timidly suggested that the transcript made it pretty clear that it had been a bit of banter Mair was having none of it. Here's how it went:

EM: But there are plenty of people who have the impression that the boys are allowed to talk about this and the girls aren't.

PH: [blows out his breath] Um. Well. If you're talking specifically about the John Humphrys comments clearly they weren't on

air and they weren't intended to be on air, and they weren't
intended to be public.

EM: But they are in the public domain.

PH: Well they are but you've also got to ask yourself were they
intended to be taken seriously. I will leave that for others to
judge when they read the transcript. Clearly some people have
taken them as serious comment …

EM: [incredulous] But you don't?

PH: … others have taken them as a joke. It's a judgement. I think
they were joshing around, they were unwise comments to
make, they were, er, ill-judged to use that phrase, er, but I
don't think they were meant to be taken that seriously.

I went ballistic and did something I'd never done before. I
phoned the control room of *PM* when they were live on air and
demanded to speak to the editor, Roger Sawyer. Why was an
idiotic little bit of private banter being treated as a matter of
national significance? Why hadn't I been given the basic courtesy
of being asked to take part in this travesty to defend myself or
even, at the very least, been warned that it was being planned? If
PM regarded this as a significant news story why did they not do
what every news programme and every competent journalist
does and try to speak to the person at the centre of the story? Me.
It would not have been difficult. Our desks are in the same office.
It would have taken a few seconds to walk across the room or
even pick up a phone. Had he informed the big bosses that a
BBC programme was about to stitch up a BBC presenter without
even giving him the opportunity to defend himself? If not, why
not?

There was much more of that sort of thing from me and much
inarticulate stammering from the other end. I told Roger that I
expected a right of reply to my public defenestration. If Mair had
really wanted to know whether I was making a 'serious comment'
he had only to ask me. But of course he didn't. There's an old joke
trotted out by world-weary hacks that says never let the facts get

in the way of a good story. In this case if I had been interviewed it would have ruined Mair's 'story'. So I wasn't.

There were still twenty minutes left of the programme. I awaited Roger's call. Ten minutes went by and my phone remained silent. So I called him again. He told me that he could not allow me on his programme. I don't think I've ever heard an editor sound so discomfited. I threatened dire retribution, told him (rather childishly) that he'd better keep out of my way in future, and hung up.

When I finally simmered down I felt sorry for Roger. I knew why he couldn't answer any of my questions and why he 'could not have me on the programme'. Eddie Mair had said no. Roger Sawyer was the editor of *PM* but the real boss had come to be seen over the years as Mair. One acting editor, a first-rate journalist with a brilliant track record, told me that in the months she edited *PM* he had addressed scarcely a word to her. She was deeply hurt by her experience and celebrated when her attachment to the programme came to an end. So I was hardly alone in being chosen as a Mair target.

Let's make one thing clear. Eddie Mair is a brilliant broadcaster. In his early years at the BBC the possibility of his coming to *Today* was often discussed. But all those who had some experience of working with him said it would be unthinkable for a two-presenter programme. Mair was not a team player.

When he joined *PM* in 2003 it was a straightforward news-based programme doing much the same job as *Today*, *The World at One* and *The World Tonight*. By the time he left it had become, for me at any rate, a vehicle for his ego. Even as I write this I can picture the reaction of his fans, many of whom doubtless listened to *PM* purely for Mair. He was different from the other presenters, they will protest. He showed an empathy in a way few other presenters did. And all of that is true. His interviews with Steve Hewlett, the Radio 4 *Media Show* presenter who was dying of cancer, had been both moving and revealing.

But he perhaps suffered from the affliction that threatens so many of us in my business. He saw himself as being bigger than the story and bigger than the programme. And we're not. None of us is. With the possible exception of David Attenborough.

And one final word in my own defence. When I learned how much more money I was being paid than my colleagues – especially Sarah Montague and Justin Webb – I offered to cut my own pay. I had already agreed to one cut when I rejoined the staff of the BBC after nearly forty years as a freelance. When the Gracie row broke I volunteered two more cuts – reducing my income from *Today* by almost half. It was not exactly a massive sacrifice. I was still earning far more money than most people in this country can imagine. But I was a little surprised to read Jane Garvey in the *Guardian* saying that the row 'had never been about men taking pay cuts' and then dismissing what I and others had done as 'diversionary tactics'. How very strange. There was me thinking the whole row had been about the disparity between the pay of men and women.

The Sopel saga may have been the most ludicrous of my brushes with the BBC bosses but there were many others. One of the choicest, which made many front pages, was the shocking and completely fabricated accusation that I was not impartial on the subject of Brexit because I was a very close friend of the man who was then the Brexit secretary, David Davis. Indeed we were so close – shock horror! – that we even went on holiday together. What made it just about credible was that it was being tweeted by a man who had been one of Davis's most senior advisers. What made it a little less credible was that I had known Davis for close on thirty years (just as I had known scores of other MPs) and in that time we had had lunch together twice. The story was pure fiction.

The sad truth behind it was that the poor chap who tweeted it had been having problems and was apparently in the middle of some sort of nervous breakdown. But, yet again, the BBC's immediate instinct was to go into apology mode – when all they'd needed to do was make a two-minute phone call to me to establish the facts.

Far more serious was a 'story' that emerged in June 2005.

I was sitting in the back of a taxi on the way to a literary festival and skimming the newspapers. I got as far as *The Times* and stopped skimming when I reached a story with my name in the headline. It was spread across two pages and it read: 'Humphrys says all Labour ministers are liars.' This was dynamite. You can't be a *Today* presenter if you believe such nonsense and say so publicly. Apart from anything else, it would be impossible to do the job. Imagine trying to interview a Labour minister. It wouldn't matter what the first question was, the answer would be something like: 'What's the point of me even trying to answer your question, John, given that you already think I and all my colleagues in government are liars?' Clean bowled. Slow and shameful walk back to the pavilion. End of promising career.

And then, as I was reading the story for the second time, my phone rang. It was Steve Mitchell, my boss. A very sombre Steve. All hell was breaking loose, he told me. The chairman of the BBC himself, Lord Grade, had been on the phone to the director general Mark Thompson, who had been on the phone to Steve. Grade wanted me sacked. There would be an inquiry, of course, and I would be allowed to defend myself but there hardly seemed any point. It was all there in one of the most respected newspapers in the land. The full account of a speech I had made to company directors on a cruise liner berthed at Southampton docks. They had a recording of my speech and I was bang to rights.

But there were a few problems with the story. One was that I had not been making a speech: I had been answering questions. The second, rather more crucial, was that I had never said it. The third was that it was a Labour Party stitch-up from start to finish. But how could I prove it? By definition I had no copy of the 'speech' – not even the most cursory notes. I seldom do on these occasions.

When I started out on the so-called after-dinner circuit some thirty-odd years ago I was so terrified of drying up that I scripted every line and read it out from start to finish. God, it must have been boring. Eventually I gained enough confidence to rely on a few carefully prepared notes, but I always knew exactly what I wanted to say. And then it occurred to me that, rather than tell my audiences what I thought they wanted to hear about the *Today* programme or the BBC or whatever was going on in the world, I should let them ask me questions and tell them what they wanted to know.

The appeal of that approach was obvious. The audience knew they weren't getting the same old rehearsed guff because no two audiences asked the same questions and I was forced to think on my feet. That meant there was a danger in it too. There are some rules about what a BBC hack should and should not say in public and I might get carried away and say something I shouldn't. Was that what I had done on that fateful evening in Southampton? After all, given the public's scepticism about our politicians, it is a question I'm often asked.

I toyed with that thought for no more than a few seconds. I knew the answer had to be no – and for a very good reason. I did not and do not think that all government ministers – whether Labour or Conservative or any other party – are liars. So it follows that I would not have said it. What I did say was I think MPs fall into three rough groups.

The first is made up of those who are pretty much incapable of lying. Maybe that's out of fear of being caught out but maybe it's because they'd actually prefer to tell the truth, the whole truth and nothing but the truth. Members of this group tend not to get too far up the ministerial ladder because their potential for embarrassing their ministerial colleagues and incurring the wrath of the whips is too high.

The second group would prefer not to lie but occasionally accept that political expediency demands they be a little economical with the truth. Just like most of us, in fact. In this group there will, inevitably, be some who don't much care whether they lie or not. Just as there are in society at large.

The third group are those who manage to rise to the giddy heights of the Cabinet. They are then subject to what is called collective Cabinet responsibility. If they are asked in the *Today* studio, for instance, whether they approve of the prime minister's policy to deal with the housing crisis by slaughtering all first-borns they must either find an elegant way of fudging their reply or they must offer their approval or they must resign. Mostly they fudge but sometimes they lie. That is what I said in Southampton. And I would say the same if I were asked that question today. Indeed, I often am.

So how and why did *The Times* come to print such a grossly misleading version of what I had said? This is where the political stitch-up comes in. Unbeknown to me, the team organising the event had made a recording of what was meant to be a so-called 'Chatham House Rule' evening. In other words, everything said is strictly off the record. That recording had found its way into the hands of one of Labour's former spin doctors, Tim Allan, an unappealing character who served as Alastair Campbell's right-hand man until he left politics (theoretically) to go into PR. It seems Allan had telephoned the event company and asked them if they had a tape of the meeting so that he could check what I had said. With an apparently persuasive account of why he wanted it and what he planned to do with it, he convinced the company to supply the tape.

Allan handed the tape to another practitioner of the dark arts, Tom Baldwin. Baldwin went by the title of deputy political editor of *The Times*. He had delivered some decent stories as a journalist but he was notorious at that time among those who knew him for his two other enthusiasms: cocaine and the Labour Party.

His cocaine habit had been well known to most of those who worked with him and he was once publicly accused by Lord Ashcroft, a former treasurer of the Conservative Party, for his liberal use of the drug. He never challenged Ashcroft. His contempt for the Tories was even more widely known. He was more propagandist than journalist. Allan knew what Baldwin would do with the tape and he was not to be disappointed. The story he delivered was a travesty of the facts and he must have known it because the truth lay in the recording.

Predictably, the BBC's immediate reaction was to take it at face value and set up an 'inquiry'. The deputy director general Mark Byford, the most senior figure in BBC News at the time, was in charge of it. He phoned and asked me to attend. I told him, almost politely, to go to hell. As far as I was concerned there was nothing to inquire into. All they had to do was listen to the tape or read the transcript of what I said – as opposed to what Baldwin claimed I had said. It would take roughly an hour. But that is not the way the BBC proceeds. As I suggested earlier, the managerial instinct is the pre-emptive regret.

The next day I had a call from Byford. The inquiry had been called off. It would seem that I was in the clear. And that morning *The Times* printed an editorial, more in sorrow than in anger, conceding that I had not said all Labour ministers are liars. And that was that.

As for Baldwin, he continued to lend a hand to his friends in the Labour government. Baldwin was, of course, a close friend of Alastair Campbell. It was Baldwin who was later to identify Dr David Kelly, the highly respected scientist who had given an explosive briefing to Andrew Gilligan on the so-called 'sexed up' Iraq dossier affair – on which more later. When Baldwin appeared subsequently at the Hutton Inquiry he refused to disclose the source of his information. He would say only that it had been 'Whitehall sources'. When Campbell himself gave evidence to the inquiry he was sent on his way with a warm hug in public from his good friend Tom Baldwin. Within weeks of being identified, David Kelly committed suicide.

In 2011 Baldwin finally got the job for which he had worked so hard. He was appointed Labour's chief spin doctor. It was he who advised Ed Miliband throughout the 2015 election campaign. Labour were defeated.

The production company tricked by Tim Allan into handing over the recording of my chat agreed to pay £10,000 in compensation to the Kitchen Table Charities Trust, a charity I had founded a few years before to help mostly dirt-poor children and their mothers in sub-Saharan Africa.

So, in the end, some good came of what had been a pretty unedifying episode.

12

Hamstrung by a
fundamental niceness

Queen Mary famously said when she died that the word
'Calais' would be found engraved on her heart. It was on
her watch in 1557 that more than 200 years of English rule were
brought to an end by the French. When the BBC ultimately
meets its maker it too will bear the scars of an eviction from
Europe. A rather different set of circumstances I grant you. Mary's
staunch yeomen were driven from the Continent by French
soldiers. The people of the United Kingdom decided to leave of
their own free will in 2016. Not that all our listeners would agree
with that.

The referendum may have resulted in a majority voting to leave
the European Union, but I bear many scars inflicted by angry
listeners for having said so more than once. Was I, they demanded,
so stupid and/or so biased in favour of Brexit that I missed the
crucial point? It was only a majority of those who actually voted.
It was NOT a majority of the population. Well … umm … yes
… that was indeed the case. In other words the referendum
followed precisely the same process that this nation and every
other democratic nation on the planet has followed for every election or referendum ever held. But those who felt cheated by the
result were not about to let a simple fact or two stem their righteous anger. And, by God, there was an awful lot of it. A great deal
of it was directed at the BBC.

Most of our listeners were gracious enough to concede that we
had covered the referendum campaign itself reasonably

impartially. They were not so impressed with what followed. According to the Brexiteers we were disgracefully biased in favour of Remain and always had been. According to Remain the exact opposite was true. And those positions became more entrenched in the years of vicious political infighting that were to follow.

It would be nice to claim that the BBC was not, and never has been, biased for or against the EU. But it wouldn't be true. I mentioned earlier in this book that my late, great colleague Charles Wheeler had been pulled out of Washington at the height of Watergate – the biggest scandal ever to rock the United States and for a long time simply the biggest story in the world – even though there was no foreign correspondent on the planet better qualified to report on it than Charles. And yet he was sent to Brussels.

It was like pulling Usain Bolt out of the Olympic Games and sending him to compete in the local primary-school sports day. It made no sense at all – unless you believed that the BBC's director general, Charles Curran, had been put under pressure by 10 Downing Street. The prime minister at the time was Ted Heath, the man who had fought for so long to take us into Europe. I doubt he would have had to apply too much pressure on Curran to persuade him that it would be in the nation's interest to give the EEC a much higher profile. The BBC believed in Europe and Britain's place in it and that was that.

Long before the UK referendum, Eurosceptics had been protesting loudly that their views were not being properly reflected by the BBC. They believed this country was being harmed by the over-mighty bureaucrats of Brussels and a lack of genuine democracy. And they were scared that there was much worse to come. Brussels would not rest until the flag of the United States of Europe flew in every capital city and there was a European Army to keep us safe in our beds.

Their central point was that the EU was not the organisation Britain had joined in 1973. That was demonstrably true. We had joined the European Economic Community (the EEC). It did not become the EU until after the Maastricht Treaty was approved nearly twenty years later and, as the sceptics pointed out, it was a very different beast from the organisation it replaced. It had become far more than an economic community. Brussels now had the ability to develop a common foreign and security policy and 'enhanced co-operation' in the domestic affairs of its member states. Or, in the language of the sceptics, the power to meddle in our own domestic business.

The next step on the march towards greater integration was the birth of the euro in January 1999. For the first time the EU had not only its own flag and anthem, but its own currency. For some countries, above all Germany, the euro was to prove hugely beneficial. For others – notably Greece – it has been disastrous.

The charge levelled against Brussels was not merely that Greece should never have been allowed to join the eurozone because its economy failed to pass the tests, but that Brussels had known perfectly well that it was not qualified. Goldman Sachs, the mighty bank that stepped in to give the Greek economy the once-over, converted the country's debt to give the appearance of healthier finances. Greece was allowed in. To this day millions upon millions of ordinary Greek citizens are paying the price. They have seen their country's economy destroyed.

One of my own sons (Christopher) has lived in Greece since the 1990s. Until the euro fraud was perpetrated on the country he and his family, like other middle-class Greeks, had lived a comfortable life. Since then the middle class has been effectively wiped out. Greece has become an economic basket case. Germany has grown richer from the euro.

The sceptics also point to the alarming growth of populist movements in EU countries from Hungary to Italy. While Brussels has grown ever mightier, they say, the individual member countries have seen their own sovereignty diminished. For many Eurosceptics the Maastricht Treaty had been the last straw: a deliberate attempt to create a European state which would effectively end British sovereignty. So, one way and another BBC's coverage of Europe was under close scrutiny even before Brexit came along and put a bomb under it.

For years one of the most serious allegations against the BBC had been that it was not impartial in its coverage of the EU. The response of the governors in 2004 was to set up a review. A former Cabinet secretary, Lord Wilson, was appointed to chair what was described as an independent panel – a pretty meaningless phrase if ever there was one. Independent from whom precisely? Anyway, the panel went to work and when it delivered its report it did not mince its words. It found that there was 'a widespread perception that the BBC suffers from certain forms of cultural and unintentional bias' and 'the BBC's coverage of EU news needs to be improved and to be made more demonstrably impartial'. Lord Wilson called it bias by omission.

The panel had commissioned polling to find out what audiences thought of coverage. It's not often that you find pollsters stumped for an answer but in this case they discovered that most people knew so little about how the EU functioned and what it was supposed to do that it 'severely limits their ability to make a judgement on the impartiality of the BBC's coverage'. That lack of understanding, it said, translated into 'low interest and limited consumption'. In other words, the nation simply switched off, either unconsciously or literally. That meant most people were in no position to compare the BBC's EU coverage with what other broadcasters were doing. With some neat footwork – and possibly in order to avoid the report proving to have been a complete waste of time – they concluded that 'we therefore view the issue of accessibility to be the cornerstone of this report'.

BBC management, of course, took the report to heart, which is to say it made sure it put in place enough structural changes and professed loudly enough the importance of its commitment to persuade the governors that it had taken the issue seriously. In future, the BBC solemnly pledged, we would offer our audiences

clear, accurate and accessible information about the way EU institutions worked and their impact on UK laws and life. We would
ensure impartiality by reflecting the widest possible range of
voices and viewpoints about EU issues and we would test those
viewpoints by using evidence-based argument or informed opinion. We would demonstrate the relationships between the different member states and the European Union; and we would reveal
and explain to our audiences areas of contentious fact and
disputed principle.

All highly commendable – except that the phrase motherhood
and apple pie comes to mind. If the BBC had not been doing all
that stuff in the thirty-odd years the UK had been in Europe,
what in God's name had it been doing?

Inevitably, though, the regulatory spotlight moved on to other
matters. So did the BBC. Did that mean the whole exercise had
been a waste of time? If you were a concerned outsider looking in,
most certainly. If you were an insider – a very important insider
– it did the job. A review had been set up, an inquiry held, a
conclusion published and senior figures were able to appear in
front of the microphones looking very solemn and saying important lessons had been learned.

In the case of the BBC's impartiality, the review process was
deemed such a success that the governors, and the BBC Trust
which took over from them in 2007, ordered one every year. In
the satirical conclusion of one somewhat disillusioned senior
manager, it became an annual exercise in damaging the BBC
brand. In 2006 there was a review of the coverage of the Israeli–
Palestinian conflict; in 2007 a review of the BBC's business coverage; in 2008 the network's coverage of the four UK nations. And
so it went on, each year, until 2014 when coverage of rural affairs
came under the spotlight. By then trust in the Trust was evapo-
rating swifter than a puddle in the summer sun. A few years later
the government saw fit to put it out of its misery and hand the
regulation of the BBC to Ofcom, since when a measure of sanity
has prevailed.

It's not that reviews are inevitably a waste of time – sometimes lessons really can be learned – but it depends on who is asking the questions and why. It was always something of a mystery that the BBC itself, in the shape of its own regulator, was the body that chose which subjects to review and, by implication, criticise in a very public way. But then you cannot easily be both cheerleader and regulator – as the governors were to find out to their cost in the wake of Lord Hutton's inquiry into the BBC's Iraq coverage.

In the case of the review into coverage of the European Union there were, in fact, one or two significant changes. Most important was the appointment, for the first time, of a Europe editor based in Brussels to focus on the politics, policy and economics of Europe and the European Union 'so as to give our audiences an authoritative overview of significant EU stories'. How strange to think, looking back on it, that there was a time when the BBC did not have a Europe editor.

The other big change was that programme editors had to keep a record of their European coverage in a central database. The intention was entirely honourable, given that the BBC is sworn to report on any subject with 'due impartiality' to be demonstrated over time. How could it judge whether it was impartial if it did not keep a record of its output and review it not just daily (as it does in news meetings) but over, say, a month or a year? In fact the database turned out to be a form of madness. It became more the product of a mass-observation society than a useful editorial tool.

Take just one example.

Let's say that in November 2012, it showed that there had been a total of 279 guest appearances in coverage of the EU on the *Daily Politics* show. This may have provided an answer, but what was the *question*? If there were fifteen 'broadly anti-EU appearances' was that the right number? Should other views, over and above the positions represented in the database, have been aired? What other views were being put forward on these subjects? What political support did they attract? What was the status of the people putting them forward? Which views were simply interesting, irrespective of these considerations? What platform on the BBC, if any, did they deserve?

None of this, in any case, was enough to appease the critics. The 'Newswatch' survey of *Today* became an annual rite of passage, endured by a succession of weary editors. The review had been sponsored by the staunch Eurosceptic Lord Pearson of Rannoch. He was a Conservative peer who turned his back on his party and, in 2014, called for voters to back the UK Independence Party. Along with three other peers, he was then expelled by the Tories and backed his words with deeds by joining UKIP. The survey had the *Today* programme in its sights at first but it was eventually expanded to other areas of BBC output and in 2007 it formed the basis of a complaint to the BBC Trust. To get an idea of the sort of complaints that come in from those who have skin in the game, it's worth looking at this one in some detail.

The survey had monitored the *Today* programme's coverage between September and December 2006 and calculated that 275 minutes were devoted to EU-related coverage. That was only 2.9 per cent of the airtime available, they said, and of that only sixty-nine minutes had focused on the structural plans of the EU, as opposed to the day-to-day proposals, legislation and rulings. This was, apparently, only 0.7 per cent of the available feature airtime.

Still with me? Sorry, but there's more.

The survey continued: 'European Union news was often presented in sections of *Today* with the fewest listeners – between 6 a.m. and 7 a.m., suggesting an editorial mindset that the EU affairs were of secondary importance.'

Fascinating I'm sure you will agree, but does anyone really believe you can judge a programme's journalism, let alone its editorial integrity, by the stopwatch alone?

The authors were adamant that none of our coverage delivered what the director general Mark Thompson had promised, which was to 'explore the views of UKIP and other shades of Eurosceptic opinion more regularly and thoroughly'. They said only four pro-withdrawal speakers had appeared on *Today* in this period, and only one of these contributions had focused on calls for substantial change within the EU. Of the seventeen politicians who appeared in interview sequences – usually the more substantial and prominent items – only two had been Eurosceptics. No government minister had been asked directly about EU structural policies, and the Conservative attitude towards the EU – which had appeared to change significantly on 3 October 2006 when party leader David Cameron had said that 'banging on about Europe' had not worked – was examined 'only cursorily'.

The BBC Trust's Editorial Standards Committee rejected the complaint. It concluded that *Today had* provided appropriate coverage of Europe; that the choice of news stories was an editorial judgement based on the assessment of the day's news agenda; that stories concerning the EU were important but they were not guaranteed a slot on a busy morning news programme; that the BBC was not mandated to cover certain issues or provide a set percentage of time to coverage of a specific area of news; that during the survey period news about the EU had not been of particular significance and, as a result, would not figure as often or as prominently in news programmes; that the report had provided no evidence to suggest the use of neutral or factual views had been to the detriment of the coverage of the EU; and that impartiality did not require that a Eurosceptic voice was included in every discussion on Europe, nor was it appropriate to do so.

It was a rarity for a whole survey to be treated as a complaint, as opposed to an individual item of coverage, and there had been some discussion in the BBC as to whether it should have wasted its time on it. But the Trust was (surprise surprise) a cautious and bureaucratic body in thrall to its lawyers' advice, so the hearing went ahead. From then on, though, management could neatly avoid replying in any detail to any of the specific complaints that landed on their desks, which is exactly what they did, year in year out without fail.

But Lord Pearson and his team did not give up. They fired off letter after letter to the BBC chairman, the director general, the director of editorial policy and anyone else who they reckoned were denying them a fair hearing. They demanded meetings and they got them, usually attended by a couple of MPs of similar Eurosceptic persuasion. On and on it went, with Pearson and his colleagues arguing that the BBC had not delivered on its promise to explain to the British people how the EU actually worked, and to give Eurosceptics enough airtime to put their case. God knows how many hours, days, weeks of management time were occupied by all those meetings. Still, as one rather disillusioned junior boss told me, it wasn't all bad or, as he put it: 'Gives them something to do, doesn't it?'

The BBC responded by delivering many more hours of coverage of the goings-on in Brussels – though not exactly in prime-time slots on BBC1. It included *Democracy Live* on BBC News Online, which covered the European Parliament: all of its plenary sessions in full and a wide range of committee hearings. *Inside Europe* – also online – had guides to the way the EU worked, including the European Parliament. There were blogs by the BBC's Europe editor and many lesser mortals. In one year alone, BBC Parliament provided 190 hours of coverage of the work of the European institutions. I think it's fair to say the audience figures posed no great challenge to the ratings for *Strictly Come Dancing*.

There was also, obviously, a fair amount of coverage on the mainstream channels but in spite of everything I'm not sure the BBC as a whole ever quite had a real grasp of what was going on in Europe or of what people in this country thought about it. The truth is that politics rarely makes exciting television even when we're reporting on our own affairs. How much more of a switch-off is the politics of an organisation that involves twenty-eight different countries, a mighty bureaucracy in the shape of the commission, another body made up the individual nation's leaders, and a court of justice on top of it all.

So there has always been a certain reluctance among some news programme editors to carry European stories unless there was a sense of crisis attached to them. And the trouble with covering a crisis is that it can paint a false picture of reality. John Birt had had a similar concern with the way the BBC covered crime stories. When someone is murdered it's a big story. It creates headlines if only because murders are mercifully rare. But unless you add some context – perhaps to show that the murder rate is actually falling – the audience's fear of the crime might far outstrip the facts.

There was another problem. News judgements are always relative. Editors must always judge the significance of a development in one area against the strength of other events on any given day. But the significance of European stories was harder to judge given the EU's very different political processes. Try this for size from the BBC's own website:

> The main aim of co-decision is to give an equal say to the
> European Parliament, representing citizens, and the Council of
> Ministers, representing governments. The European
> Parliament's Strasbourg seat is where the main sessions are
> held. Complex rules can dominate proceedings. If, after a
> maximum of two readings of the proposal in both institutions,
> no agreement can be reached, a Conciliation Committee made
> up of representatives from the Council and the Parliament is
> formed to try to find a common position. If this still fails to
> reach agreement, the commission proposal falls. The
> co-decision procedure is used in most of the 'day-to-day' policy
> areas that the Parliament has to deal with, such as
> employment, immigration, workers' rights, internal market,
> free movement of workers, culture, agriculture and fisheries.

Simple, eh?

We did our best to demonstrate how the EU system worked and the impact of its legislation on UK life. Some of the scare stories were fairly easy to deal with: bendy bananas for instance. Rather disappointingly the commission never did want them banned. What EC Commission Regulation No 2257/94 stated was that all bananas must be 'free of abnormal curvature' and at least fourteen centimetres in length. So all it does is set industry grading rules to help importers know exactly what they are getting when they order a box of bananas. Not exactly a cause to get the revolutionaries storming the barricades. The big stuff proved infinitely more difficult.

In pre-referendum days Nigel Farage told us that the EU was making seventy-five per cent of the UK's laws. An utter disgrace, many listeners said: proof if any were needed that we were no longer a sovereign state. Total rubbish said many others: Farage was making it up, deliberately confusing regulations with laws.

Our own research suggested that his claim was based on a German government statement. So we asked the BBC's Europe editor, who told us the last time they had tried to establish an accurate figure they found the whole thing too 'jelly-like' to nail down. One problem centred on 'categorisation', where laws might have been passed by the British government before EU rules had come into place, sometimes by several years. So that's sorted then.

In spite of all that – or perhaps because of it – the audience figures suggested people still didn't seem to be terribly interested in the EU. A BBC survey in December 2011 found fewer than one in five UK adults followed the coverage reasonably closely. Two years later the Trust ran the rule over it yet again by commissioning a 'Breadth of Opinion' impartiality report. By now, it had dispensed with panels and it turned to one man: the former ITV executive Stuart Prebble. His report was what the Trust described, possibly with an arched eyebrow, as an 'engaging' read. They might also have described it as a trial by anecdote. Here's a flavour of how it began:

In common with a great many men of my age and disposition, I am a serial insomniac. As such, I am a frequent sampler of a very wide range of stories from around the globe, courtesy of the BBC World Service. Some years ago, I remember my tortured small-hours imaginings being further persecuted by the long-running account of two tribes in Africa, whose enduring conflicts involved raids on neighbouring villages in which the young men of the village would be rounded up, and their hands would be chopped off with machetes ...

You get the drift.

But when Prebble dealt with the various charges against the BBC he was pretty blunt. He found that the news coverage had been 'slow to give appropriate prominence to the growing weight of opinion opposing UK membership of the EU'.

There was no single point in history when Euroscepticism became mainstream establishment thinking, but as the political pressure grew at Westminster David Cameron lit the touch paper for a referendum on our membership of the EU if he won the 2015 general election. He was determined to see off the threat from UKIP and some members of his own party. And so, a year later, on 23 June, it happened. I could say the rest is history but that would be, at the very least, misleading. The effects of that referendum will reverberate through Westminster and the nation at large for generations to come. And the consequences for our journalism are profound.

First, the referendum campaign itself. At times of a national vote the BBC is under the microscope even more than it is on a daily basis. Every word, every report, every interview is scrutinised by each side. The problem for the BBC is not just that it is the most important platform at a time of national debate: it is that the politicians tend to regard it as 'their' organisation, to be pushed and harried and even bullied in a way that no newspaper would stomach. There was another difficulty for the BBC during the referendum. In its day-to-day reporting the BBC is required to show due impartiality, and that word 'due' is important. The BBC's Editorial Guidelines define it thus: 'Impartiality must be adequate and appropriate to the output, taking account of the subject and nature of the content, the likely audience expectation and any signposting that may influence that expectation. Due impartiality is often more than a simple matter of "balance" between opposing viewpoints.'

But during a general election, or a referendum, the system has to change. 'Due impartiality' is still important but we also have to provide an appropriate level of coverage of each side of the debate. In an election, the relative coverage of political parties has to be kept in line with both the BBC's Election Guidelines and the Ofcom Code, by assessing 'past and current electoral support' – effectively then, over two electoral cycles. In the 2017 general election we would get complaints that we were favouring UKIP over the Greens because our critics were not aware of the 'two cycles' rule. In the referendum, however, there were just two sides – yes and no – with no previous referendum results to fall back on. So it was right that each side should get a half-share of our news coverage. Crucially, however, the BBC's Editorial Guidelines say: 'news judgements continue to drive editorial decision-making in news-based programmes'. And that's where I think we had a problem.

If a report contained unremittingly bad news for one side or for a political party, it would still count towards the share of coverage. In other words, it was the *amount* of coverage that was important under the rules, not the *type*. But there was, I think, an inherent tension in some editors' minds. They knew they were required to share the amount of coverage equally between the two sides but it was easy to interpret this as an instruction to produce 'on the one hand but on the other hand' type of coverage and to lose sight of the instruction that normal news judgements should apply. Our guidelines made clear that due impartiality meant that we must achieve 'broad balance' between the arguments on each side. But this did not mean that every 'fact' or opinion from one side had to be balanced by a contradictory fact or opinion from the other side. Our obligation was, rather, to ensure the two sides could set out their political arguments for our audiences and then, crucially, to scrutinise the claims they might make.

In fact, during the campaign itself there were very few complaints from either side. It was afterwards that it was seen in a different light, as if the Remainers were blaming the BBC for the result. The Royal Economic Society was particularly unhappy. It said, long after the event, that it was concerned about the way in which studies and assessments of the likely economic outcome of the UK leaving the EU had been presented in our output. Its point was that an overwhelming majority of economists had taken the view that leaving the EU would be economically damaging but we had not reflected this in our coverage. It was true that the institutional weight of the country was behind Remain – from the Bank of England downwards – but the BBC's point was that there were some reputable economists who had taken a different view. And for BBC News to have reported the 'institutional' views without referring at all to such alternative viewpoints would have breached the requirement for due impartiality.

But at the same time I'm not sure the BBC was clear enough, often enough, where the weight of the argument lay. Of course, it could point to examples of its virtue. The BBC is so big it broadcasts four or five hours of output for every hour of the day. What that means is that there will always be some coverage somewhere that it can point to, as it did with the previous complaints about its EU reporting, to enable it to show that it had fulfilled its public service duty. But in pursuing the entirely correct aim of providing an equal amount of airtime to each side in the referendum, I'm not convinced that we scrutinised the claims made by each side with sufficient rigour. And that was a key editorial obligation. Part of the problem lay in the nature of the referendum itself. True, it was a device to get David Cameron off a political hook, but it required the great British public to vote 'yes or no' to an issue of incredible complexity. The debate ranged from the political to the constitutional, legal and economic, and it was beyond the bounds of any one person to know which claims were justified and which were, frankly, rubbish.

Maybe we needed to be guided by St Isidore, known as the last scholar of the ancient world, who tried to record everything ever known. Instead we had a 'Reality Check' team. This did a lot of invaluable work. One example: it debunked the claim written in huge letters on the side of the Leave campaign bus that the UK would take back £350 million a week once it had left the EU and the money could go to the NHS. That was not just misleading: it was simply wrong. In the first place the figure did not take into account the money the UK gets back from the EU after paying into the budget, the rebate that was negotiated by Margaret Thatcher way back in 1984. And anyway much of the money would find its way back to the UK in, for instance, regional aid. In other words, we'd be getting our own money back.

BBC Reality Check pointed out the problem with the figure and the UK Statistics Authority has since ruled this was a 'clear misuse of official statistics'. On the day after the Brexit referendum result, Nigel Farage disowned the claim. He said it was one of the mistakes that had been made by the Leave side. But a poll by Ipsos MORI published in June 2016 found that nearly half the British public believed it, and for Remainers the claim came to symbolise everything that was wrong with the referendum campaign.

On the other hand, the chancellor George Osborne had said if we voted to leave we would need an emergency Budget the next day to restore stability to public finances – and that was spectacularly wrong. He also claimed, in front of a poster advertising the point, that the cost of Brexit would be £4,300 for every British family. The Reality Check team showed that a fall in GDP (which was predicted) did not equate directly to the cost to each family, as the Treasury had implied. This was complicated stuff. There were simply too many unknowns; as Anthony Reuben, the BBC fact checker, wrote in his book about statistics we did not know what sort of trade deals the UK would manage to do after leaving, how long they would take to negotiate, how much of the UK's contribution to the EU budget would be saved, what that saved money would be spent on, whether the regulations that the UK government devised to replace the EU ones would be better than the EU ones and what effect all that would have on the economy. We also didn't know whether Brexit would create some sort of feel-good factor in the UK economy, or the opposite.

But what made it particularly hard was that models are built based on what particular events have done to economies in the past. We know that joining free-trade areas tends to increase trade and economic growth, but we don't know what effect leaving free-trade areas has because it hardly ever happens. Economists trying to model this looked as far back as the break-up of great empires in history to work out this effect. In the end, most of the models around the referendum were based on the idea that if joining free-trade areas was good for trade and growth then leaving them was likely to be the opposite. There was much more of the same. It was, in short, a comprehensive demolition of the Osborne claims.

Predictably enough, the biggest battering the BBC took after the result came from the losing side, the Remainers. But as the months rolled on the BBC's coverage became dominated by the hugely complicated process of reaching an agreement for leaving the EU and its consequences. And many Leavers took exception to what they were hearing. Increasingly they saw it as unduly negative.

It's safe to say the BBC devotes more effort to checking claim and counterclaim in the new, post-Brexit world than it ever did before. Some of that is to do with the way the referendum was conducted by each side and some of it is to do with the new 'fake news' era in which we live. One illustration was an interview I did in

November 2018 with Peter Lilley, the former Tory Cabinet minister and now a member of the House of Lords and a leading Brexiteer.

He had come onto *Today* to promote a new report from the European Research Group which we were promised would 'explode the myths of leaving the Customs Union'. It ended up in a pretty angry ding-dong with Chris Morris, the Reality Check correspondent for BBC News.

Chris is one of our best correspondents: incredibly hard-working, utterly dedicated to his job, a first-rate broadcaster and reporter and very bright. Exactly the right man to have in such a tricky job. My problem is that I'm not convinced there should be such a job. The creation of a Reality Check correspondent seems to me to contain an internal contradiction. That's partly because of the wording. What do we mean by 'reality'? It's like 'truth' and raises the same question: whose truth?

So let's substitute 'fact' for reality. The BBC has a programme on Radio 4 called *More or Less* devoted entirely to checking claims made on a seemingly endless range of subjects by all sorts of organisations, most of them entirely reputable, and the way those findings are reported in the media. It almost always concludes that either the 'facts' were dubious in the first place or the way they were presented (often on other Radio 4 programmes) was hugely misleading. I speak from personal experience. Like most of my colleagues, I've been bang to rights.

But let's assume that we call Chris our 'Fact Check' correspondent. Wouldn't work would it? Because much of the time we are asking him to check assumptions as much as 'facts' and, as I have tried to demonstrate, the assumptions about this or that claim on the effects of Brexit can be highly contentious. And what message are we delivering to the listener? Are we telling them that Chris can be believed in a way that no other contributor can be? And if so, why do we choose one set of 'facts' or one 'reality' over another? If we are effectively telling the listener that anything which has not had to be given the once-over by Chris can be trusted without question, what does that say about the various claims that he has not been taking the trouble of 'checking'?

For all those reasons and more I was often uneasy at the way we made use of Chris and the Lilley encounter added to my unease. My brief was to interview Lilley and then get Chris to run the rule over what he had said. But that, obviously, meant Chris having the last word. I would be closing the interview with Lilley and then effectively saying to the audience: 'OK ... that's what Lord Lilley thinks. Is he right or is he pulling a fast one? Let's ask our reality correspondent.'

You may argue that we often turn to a correspondent after we have interviewed a politician and ask them for their views. I've done it more times than I can remember with our estimable political editor Laura Kuenssberg. But that's different. What Laura delivers is her analysis of what the politician has just said. Typically, I would ask whether the minister had said anything that changed whatever crisis we happened to be talking about and she'd give me her view. Invariably a well-informed view, but that's not the point. What I don't ask her is: 'Was the minister telling the truth?' But that's exactly what I was expected to ask Chris, while Lilley himself was expected to sit alongside him in silence. Lord Lilley had other plans in mind. When Chris started taking apart what he had just said Lilley exploded: 'I think it's wonderful how you've cross-checked me in this way, I would love to see the same degree of rigour applied to those putting forward arguments for the Remain side ...'

At that point I broke the rules. What I should have done was override Lilley, point out that he had had his say and now it was Chris's turn. But that seemed to me patently unfair. Chris would have had the last word and the audience would have been left believing his version of the 'facts' rather than Lilley's. So I left them to it, giving them just the occasional nudge. Here's a tiny flavour of their exchange:

Chris: ... Lord Lilley's basic point in his report – many of the problems ascribed to leaving the customs union are imaginary and most of the rest are exaggerated – I think it is fair to say the vast majority of trade experts and freight companies certainly that I have talked to would disagree with much of that fairly robustly.

Lilley: And would the people, would firms in the European Economic Area disagree? Are they agitating?

[...]

Lilley: You are supposed to be a reality check, not an arguer for Remain!

Chris: Well, I was just trying to make some points but you kept interrupting.

As the *New European* reported it later: 'The pair appeared to descend into an argument, with the fact-checker asking the Brexiteer not to interrupt him as Lilley insisted the reporter was "getting it wrong". Humphrys was forced to intervene, telling the pair: "Please calm down – it's usually people saying that to me!"'

What the *New European* did not know was that the two continued their argument outside the studio long after I had called time inside – and it got pretty heated. In fact, I wish we'd been able to broadcast the whole thing.

Three years after the referendum the BBC's audience research suggested that audiences were still struggling to understand the key facts about Brexit. I'm not surprised. The BBC was playing a risky game when it presented poor old Chris as the ultimate arbiter of what was right and what was wrong. But perhaps, rather than beating up the messenger, we should go back to the root of the difficulty. We elect our politicians to take these decisions for us. Was holding a referendum on an issue as complex as this ever going to produce anything resembling peace and harmony? That's what is known in the trade as a rhetorical question.

And just one final observation on those tricky questions about the BBC's impartiality. I have already written about the lengths to which presenters will go to make sure they are presenting on the morning of a really big story. Who does not want that fabled 'ringside seat at history'? But bosses are the same. The really top executives seldom appear at the coalface. They might make the occasional state visit to the grubby newsroom when they first get their jobs, but it doesn't take long for them to discover that it's much more important that they spend their time talking to other executives in their plush office suites with their teams of PAs and secretaries positioned outside to repel any attempted invasion by the lower orders.

They do, however, appear on the mornings after, say, general elections – possibly because they've been up all night celebrating or drowning their sorrows with all the VIPs and politicians who pass through the television studios. Then, with a few nods and smiles to the poor bloody infantry who have been slaving over their computer screens all night, they will offer the odd encouraging remark, perhaps a thoughtful observation on the mood of the nation, and go on their way trailing in their wake that almost imperceptible scent of power.

The morning of 24 June 2016 was different. By about 3.45 a.m. we knew that Leave had won. This was not what the BBC had expected. Nor what it wanted. No nods and smiles when the big bosses appeared. No attempt to pretend that this was anything other than a disaster. Their expressions were as grim as the look on the face of a football supporter when his team's star player misses the penalty that would have won them the cup. A few days later I happened to be doing an interview for the *Radio Times* and they asked me how it had been in the newsroom on that momentous morning. So I told them and thought nothing more of it.

A few days later when the story appeared my phone pinged and a message from one of the big bosses appeared. Thanks a lot, it said with all the sarcasm it's possible to manage in a short text, I thought you were supposed to be on the BBC's side.

I refrained from making the obvious point.

The Brexit crisis had exposed in different ways a fundamental flaw in the culture of the BBC. Its bosses, almost to a man and woman, could simply not grasp how anyone could have put a cross in the 'Leave' box on the referendum ballot paper. That might explain why, when Stuart Prebble produced his report on impartiality, he found that the news coverage had been 'slow to give appropriate prominence to the growing weight of opinion opposing UK membership of the EU'.

On one level I understand that. I was one of those who voted to stay – partly because I feared the economic consequences of leaving but mostly because of something far bigger. I was born in the closing years of the war. In my childhood I played with friends on the ruins of neighbours' houses that had been bombed by the Luftwaffe who'd been attacking the docks or the steelworks and missed. At some level I understood that my neighbours and their children had been blown to bits. I think I remember – though it was probably hearing my older brother talk about it later – being carried in a box to the neighbouring chemist's shop when the bombers were overhead. They had a cellar to shelter and sleep in. Hence the box.

Rationing was much easier for a hungry child to remember – I was constantly told that, no, there were no more eggs or meat let alone chocolate or bananas. Obesity was not a problem. Years later I talked to relatives who had suffered terribly on the battle-field and I heard, over and over again, the refrain that my parents themselves had heard so often after the First World War: never again.

So when France and Germany talked about forming a union and when even Winston Churchill had used the phrase 'a United States of Europe' it made a mighty impact on my adolescent brain. How could *anyone* be against something that might bring a lasting peace to this war-torn continent? Surely, however incompetent and bureaucratic and expansionist the Burghers of Brussels turned out to be, a united Europe was infinitely to be preferred to a divided one. I understand how naive that will sound sixty years on, but the fact remains: it is simply impossible today to imagine Germany waging war against a European country and there is no greater prize than peace.

But that was then and this is now – and peace in Europe is taken for granted. It was questions about sovereignty and the economy that dominated the referendum campaign and, as Prebble pointed out, one hugely important issue. The BBC 'had not caught up with public opinion on one area that was to prove critically important'.

That area was immigration.

The report concluded that the BBC was hamstrung by a 'fundamental niceness' and reluctance to give offence. It was 'slow to reflect the weight of concern in the wider community about issues arising from immigration'.

Prebble was not alone in his criticism. The late Steve Hewlett – who had been a terrific editor of *Panorama* and later presented the *Media Show* on Radio 4 – shared those misgivings. He suggested that there was a 'general corporate sensitivity ... which might even lead to a sort of collective blindness'.

Even the woman in charge of BBC News at the time, its director Helen Boaden, agreed there was a problem. She went further. She was aware, she said, of 'a deep liberal bias' in the way that the BBC approached the topic. She might have added: '... and in the way that the BBC approached many other topics'.

Robin Aitken has made something of a name for himself over the years for his view on what he sees as the BBC's political stance. I worked with him when he was a senior journalist at the BBC and he declared that 'being a Tory in the BBC is the loneliest job in Britain'. He took the extraordinary – and undeniably courageous – step of putting together a dossier of examples from broadcasts which, he said, proved that the BBC followed a left-wing agenda: 'Throughout the 1980s, the 1990s and well into the new century the BBC was, in contravention of its commitment to impartiality, wholeheartedly and unashamedly pro-EU,' he said. Then he sent it to the director general and every single governor and waited for a response. He knew he was putting his head on the block and expected a roar of outrage – or possibly a detailed rebuttal of his claims. Instead he was virtually ignored – until the day when, as he put it, 'someone came along and just told me to fuck off … which I did'. He was fifty and he's written a couple of books since then, returning to the charge.

In his latest he recalls an argument with a senior BBC editor in which, he writes, 'I asserted that the sceptics' argument was about democratic legitimacy. Eurosceptics, he told me, were xenophobes and Little Englanders, actually clinically mad in his view.' He called his book *The Noble Liar.*

Well, it's a view and Aitken has a point when he says it's lonely being a Tory at the BBC. But that's not the same as saying there is some grand conspiracy orchestrated by a group of sinister lefties. I don't believe that for a moment. And even if that is what the top management wanted I doubt they'd have had the first idea how to go about it. As the former director general Greg Dyke once put it, trying to organise journalists was like trying to herd cats. That's probably true – though the very notion of organising them should have been an anathema to him. You don't 'organise' journalists as though they are soldiers in an invading army. You tell them to try to find out what's going on out there and report it fairly and if they're no good at doing it you suggest they find another job.

More bizarre was Dyke's suggestion that BBC journalists should stop reading the *Daily Mail.* As far as he was concerned – and he wasn't exactly alone – the *Mail* was the enemy. You can see why. It seldom missed a chance to hurl a grenade over the walls of Broadcasting House. It's attacked the corporation over the years for being bureaucratic, politically correct, spoon-fed, profligate with public money, high-handed, overly ambitious, lefty, liberal, greedy, incompetent, badly managed … you name it. Some of the attacks have been fair, some not. And sometimes it has actually come to the defence of the BBC – a few times in its hour of greatest need, such as during the Hutton crisis. But either way it was silly to suggest we shouldn't read it. What Dyke himself should have read was the ancient Chinese philosopher and military strategist Sun Tzu: 'Know your enemy and you shall win a hundred battles without loss.'

That there is a form of institutional liberal bias I have no doubt. And a big factor – perhaps the biggest – is the corporation's recruitment process. As a potential employer the BBC has a status most other organisations would die for. It can pick and choose between the cream of the arts graduates from the top universities. And it's a racing certainty that there won't be more than a handful of Tories among them if only because most will have spent three years being taught by academics on the political left. According to a survey in 2017 they make up eight out of ten in the leading universities. And overwhelmingly most recruits are from the middle class. For many of them – perhaps most – the BBC is regarded as a continuation of institutional life by any other means.

I was one of the vanishingly rare exceptions. No degree, no middle-class credentials. For much of my career I have felt rather like the junior butler trying to blag a seat at His Lordship's dining table in *Downton Abbey*. But that may be down to the deep insecurity suffered by me and so many of my presenter colleagues even though we pretend to be lords of all we survey. As for my own politics: I'm damned if I know.

As I wrote earlier, my parents were both staunch working-class Tories so naturally, when I was a youngster, I rebelled and claimed to be a Labour supporter. I agreed with my father on two things though: the monarchy was a waste of space and all authority was to be distrusted. Quite how he reconciled that with his support for the Conservative Party was always a bit of a mystery. As for me, I have never joined a political party and, at some time or another, have voted for most of them – though never for the far right or the far left. I am pitifully middle-of-the-road and vote for the party that promises to put three aims at the top of their agenda: a strong economy from which everyone can benefit; a serious programme to reduce carbon emissions; a foreign policy that says every child in the world should be able to go to bed on a full stomach and have a decent education – and believes that that's a more practical route to world peace than ever more powerful armed forces.

Lord knows precisely where that puts me on the political spectrum. I neither know nor care. If a lifetime of reporting on politics and interviewing politicians has taught me anything it is that I know I'd make a lousy politician. Plus the realisation that if a politician looks and sounds too good to be true that's probably because he is.

There has been another factor at play over the years that might help explain the liberal bias and it's a bit more tricky to evaluate. One of our best programme editors told me he thinks of BBC News as a huge body with a small brain. There is seldom, if ever, any thought given to how all the different organs in the body – the individual programme editors – are interacting. True, there is a priesthood of sorts with the job of developing and trying to enforce editorial policy. It has the power to rap knuckles if an editor delivers a programme that disregards the BBC guidelines on, say, a tricky Israeli–Palestinian issue or if there is a breach of election rules. But it is not meant to be the 'brain', let alone the conscience, of the BBC. The many programme editors operate pretty much independently of each other.

On one level that might seem a good thing. Let a thousand flowers bloom and all that. But if you ask any editor – or indeed any big boss – who they believe is responsible for the face the BBC presents to the world they will look at you blankly. Again, you might say that's as it should be. Obviously the BBC must not have a political viewpoint. It must not cleave to any ideology. And that, surely, means there is no need for such a figure.

Well, clearly not if we're thinking of some sort of Wizard of Oz character hiding behind a curtain and orchestrating everything. But if you believe – as I do – that there is a groupthink mentality in the BBC it matters enormously to ask who is behind the curtain pulling the levers even if the answer is that there isn't one.

Of course the editors themselves have many meetings with their own programme teams and there's a big meeting of the editors every weekday morning chaired by whoever happens to be the most senior boss in the building at the time. But, again, that is mostly about the day's news agenda. The more thoughtful of the editors I've spoken to would welcome the chance to air their misgivings with the big bosses, discuss the broader picture, perhaps even get some guidance as to whether the 'brain' has noticed any bias colouring the overall coverage. These are some of the questions they might raise:

Would a reasonable viewer or listener have an opinion as to whether the BBC holds a particular ideology, a collection of beliefs and values which it seeks to spread? If the answer is yes, what might that ideology be based on?

Is it 'progressive' or conservative?

Is it in favour of social reform or does it hold traditional values?

Is it broadly left-wing or right-wing?

Is it libertarian or interventionist?

Lord Reith once said the BBC is not impartial as between good and evil. How do we decide what qualifies as evil?

And what qualifies as good?

I suspect many would regard these questions as hopelessly recondite and perhaps even inappropriate – but not if we accept that the BBC has an enormous influence on how the nation thinks. I am not, God forbid, suggesting that there should be a new department set up to monitor this process, nor even a regular weekly meeting to discuss what to do about it. But I am suggesting that editors should be more conscious of the fact that their decisions are almost all reached within the same shared editorial framework. There is an overall, if implicit, BBC attitude to what makes news. And there is very little digression from that shared view. In an organisation like the BBC nobody wins a prize for straying too far outside the framework.

It's interesting to compare the way the BBC operates with a large national newspaper. The paper's editor wants to know where his more senior writers stand politically. That's not because he will sack anyone who doesn't toe the party line supported by the paper – a good editor knows his readers want to hear both sides of the argument – but he wants to exercise control over the message his paper is delivering.

BBC editors should also have a sense of where their producers stand politically – but for the opposite reason. Their programmes must not deliver a message but that doesn't mean the editors should be totally indifferent to their producers' views. There are two ways for a news operation to deliver a message. One is the newspaper's way with a blazing editorial, and the other is through the way the stories are selected and treated. That's why it would be useful – or even essential – for the editor to know the political leanings of their staff. If, say, ninety per cent of their producers refused to allow the *Daily Mail* in their homes lest their children be contaminated, that might give the editor pause for thought. The same would apply if they regarded the *Guardian* with derision. This is not about control. It's about being aware.

When the BBC does respond to accusations of bias it points out that it gets attacked with equal venom from both sides so how can it be biased? It must mean it's somewhere in the middle. I can't pretend I haven't used that defence myself when listeners have attacked me – often over the same interview – for being both a fascist pig and a commie dupe. But it's a mistake to argue that if we're getting hammered by both sides we must be doing something right. It could simply be the case that we have been *doubly* wrong. And this raises the question: when do noises off become part of the mainstream? At what point should the BBC begin to take note of views we might have instinctively regarded as eccentric or simply mischievous? Politics evolves, and so does public opinion – especially on social policy.

The BBC has to reflect a changing society and few would argue otherwise. More difficult is the extent to which it connives in that change. Or encourages it. This is a problem for the BBC. Even if it is not institutionally biased there is a uniformity of news judgements that are made within the confines of the 'machine'. A large news-production operation in London may not be sufficiently sensitive to the undercurrents of the news, to be able to gauge what is going on at the grass roots.

In this respect, the 2007 impartiality report on *Safeguarding impartiality in the 21st century* was remarkably prescient. It noted: 'Recent history is littered with examples of where the mainstream has moved away from the prevailing consensus. Monetarism was regarded in the mid-1970s as the eccentric, impractical love child of right-wing economists. Today it is a central feature of every British government's economic policy. Euroscepticism was once belittled as a small-minded, blinkered view of extremists on both left and right: today it is a powerful and influential force which has put pro-Europeans under unaccustomed pressure.'

It also had something to say about multiculturalism which, for years, had been seen by many in Britain as the only respectable policy for managing the problems posed by immigration. How could any decent citizen deny to others the right to practise their own culture and speak their own language? For them the very word 'integration' was offensive. That all changed the closer we moved to the EU referendum and it became clear that immigration would become a central issue – if not the defining issue.

The report concluded: 'Programme-makers need to treat areas of consensus with proper scepticism and rigour.'

13

A meeting with 'C'

The graveyard slot on *Today* is the one just before the business news at about 6.10. Each presenter has a couple of minutes to interview someone – almost always a correspondent – about a story that's considered just about worthy of squeezing into the programme when the audience is at its smallest. Usually it's something the overnight editor feels obliged to give a couple of minutes to – if only so that he can deny ignoring it altogether. It is seldom memorable. Sometimes it is a taster for a report that a correspondent has spent some time working on and will be broadcast in full at 7.30 or 8.10.

The interview I did at 6.07 on 29 May 2003 was expected to be not much more than that. A taster. Nobody had expected it to create a fuss or indeed make the news. We were wrong. Spectacularly wrong. If news stories can be rated as earthquakes, this would be off the Richter scale altogether. It would lead to the suicide of a decent man, the destruction of what remained of Tony Blair's reputation after Iraq, the downfall of the two most powerful figures in the BBC, and indeed threaten the very existence of BBC News.

My interviewee was Andrew Gilligan, one of those troublesome journalists who reckon that the job of a reporter is finding out stuff the people in power do not want us to know and pay scant regard to whatever embarrassment they may cause to their employers in the process. The then editor Rod Liddle had ruffled a few feathers in senior management ranks by appointing him as

Today's defence and diplomatic correspondent and he'd been breaking stories and causing trouble ever since. The subject of our very brief chat was a dossier that the government had published back in September 2002, six months before the war.

The purpose of that dossier had been to persuade the British people and MPs that we should join the United States in invading Iraq. As we were to learn much later, Tony Blair had already promised President Bush privately that we would do just that. The nation was deeply hostile to it and so were most MPs. Nobody doubted that the Iraqi leader Saddam Hussein was a psychotic mass murderer and the Middle East would be better off without him. But the overwhelming view – from the lofty heights of the United Nations down to the marchers who came out in vast numbers to protest on the streets – was that regime change was not a legal justification for war. And anyway, this was not our fight. It was not as if we were being threatened by Saddam after all. Or were we?

Blair recalled Parliament early after its summer break determined to quash those misgivings. He presented MPs with the dossier which, in his view, made the case for war unanswerable. In its preface it said: 'Saddam's military planning allows for some WMDs to be ready within forty-five minutes of an order to deploy them.'

This, on the face of it, changed everything. Saddam was not only a threat to his own people but to the region as a whole – even, in theory, to Britain's own forces in Cyprus. And the first his victims would know about these terrible weapons of mass destruction would be when they were en route to their targets. Blair had desperately needed a justification to take Britain to war and fulfil his promise to Bush. This dossier provided it. And we could trust its conclusions because the information came from intelligence sources. If our own spies and arms experts believed that terrifying forty-five-minutes warning, how could we possibly doubt it? Surely it was inconceivable that we were being misled. Gilligan told me that was exactly what was happening.

He'd had a secret meeting at the Charing Cross Hotel in London with a man he described as 'one of the senior officials in charge of drawing up that dossier'. I didn't ask Gilligan who he was because I knew he wouldn't tell me. Journalists do not identify their sources for the obvious moral reason that it would be a gross betrayal of the promise of anonymity and for the more practical reason that the journalist would never be trusted again. This is part of what he said he'd been told by his source:

> The government probably knew that that forty-five-minute figure was wrong even before it decided to put it in. What this person says is that a week before the publication date of the dossier it was actually rather … erm … a bland production. It didn't … the draft prepared for Mr Blair by the intelligence agencies … actually didn't say very much more than was public knowledge already and … erm … Downing Street, our source says, ordered a week before publication … ordered it to be sexed up, to be made more exciting and ordered more facts to be … erm … to be discovered.

We were talking, remember, six weeks after Baghdad had fallen and Saddam had been defeated. So the occupying forces – the Americans and the British – had had over two months to find the 'weapons of mass destruction'. They did not find them for the very good reason that they did not exist. So the notion that they could be deployed within forty-five minutes was patently nonsense. And now here was a senior official involved in the preparation of the intelligence material apparently telling Gilligan not only that Downing Street knew that, but had sent the dossier back so that it could be made more 'exciting' and ordering more 'facts' to be discovered. In his memorable phrase so that the dossier could be 'sexed up'.

That was a sensational allegation to make. But perhaps there was a plausible explanation for it. After all, collecting hugely sensitive information in a hostile country expecting to be invaded

242

by foreign forces is a difficult and dangerous enterprise. Confusion abounds. Maybe the intelligence agencies had simply got it wrong or perhaps they had inadvertently misled Number 10. Mistakes happen. But this, according to Gilligan's senior official, was not a mistake. Here's what Gilligan said: 'What I have been told is that the government knew that claim was questionable even before the war, even before they wrote it in their dossier.'

And later he went on to say something that would ultimately change the whole course of the debate about the rights and wrongs of going to war in Iraq with such devastating consequences. He claimed the official told him: 'That information was not in the original draft. It was included in the dossier against our wishes, because it wasn't reliable. Most things in the dossier were double-source, but that was single-source, and we believe that the source was wrong.'

This really was dynamite: an accusation from a 'senior official' that someone in government had taken a report that was supposedly based on reliable intelligence sources and 'made it sexier'. In other words they had deliberately altered it to make it appear that Saddam was a far greater threat than we had believed. So great a threat that it justified sending British men and women to war, knowing that some of them would never return. A war that was to achieve pretty speedily the overthrow of Saddam Hussein – but was to turn Iraq into a hell on earth. The invasion might have gone according to plan – Saddam's forces were hopelessly mismatched against the might of the United States even without the help of Britain – but the occupation that followed was shamefully mishandled. Saddam's reign of terror was followed by something even worse: year upon year of murderous anarchy and civil war. Millions lost their homes or fled the country. Nobody can put an accurate estimate on the number who lost their lives but a study three years after the war estimated there had been half a million 'excess deaths'.

The effect on the wider Middle East was, if possible, infinitely more catastrophic. It was to lead to the destruction of the delicate balance of power between the two mighty branches of Islam – Sunni and Shia – that had prevailed for perhaps a thousand years. The consequences were to prove cataclysmic. It would influence the rise of the barbaric ISIS; the wars in Syria, Libya and Yemen; the prospect of all-out war between Iran and Israel.

It is impossible to put a figure on the numbers who have died as a result but it is safe to say that we have seen some of the greatest humanitarian crises since the world went to war in 1939. And all that without even taking into account the trillions of dollars poured into financing those wars; the vast hordes of penniless refugees who have fled their homelands in search of a new life in Europe; the destruction of ancient towns and cities with all their great treasures that had survived since the days Jesus walked the earth.

All of this for what? For the overthrow of one man to satisfy the vanity of a foolish American president desperate to show his people that the horror of 9/11 would be avenged. Even though the terrorists behind 9/11 had nothing to do with Saddam. Their paymasters were Saudi Arabian extremists. And, yes, one brutal dictator was overthrown. But many more have risen in his place in the chaos and carnage that followed.

It was inevitable that Downing Street would react quickly to Gilligan's disclosures and they did. When the *Today* editor Kevin Marsh arrived in the office half an hour later he already had smoke coming out of his ears because of what Gilligan had said. If a correspondent has managed to get hold of a story that's likely to cause trouble, the editor wants to know about it before it's broadcast – if only on the basis that forewarned is forearmed – and this one was most definitely going to cause trouble. So Gilligan had already briefed Marsh the day before on what he would say in his quick chat with me at 6.07 and sent him the transcript of his longer report to be broadcast at 7.30. But it's fair to say that Gilligan was never at his best at the crack of dawn and he had gone more than a little off-script with me. Marsh had a more immediate problem to worry about though.

One of the young assistant editors, Gavin Allen (ultimately to be promoted to be controller of all news output), had the phone clamped to his ear. As Marsh recalls in his book *Stumbling Over Truth* Allen pointed to the handset and mouthed the words 'Downing Street'. When he finally hung up after a long and largely one-sided conversation he told Marsh that Downing Street were claiming that Gilligan's story was one hundred per cent untrue. They demanded that we broadcast a denial in the next news bulletin.

We shall never know for sure what would have happened if Marsh had caved in to that demand, effectively disowned the Gilligan interview with me and decided not to broadcast the report that was scheduled to run in only twenty minutes or so. It would have been the safe thing to do and it is likely that one of the greatest crises ever to face BBC News would have been averted.

Along with every editor in the BBC – and probably every other national news organisation for that matter – Marsh was familiar with the Downing Street bully-boy tactics under the leadership of Alastair Campbell. They were in a different league from their predecessors. Getting complaints from politicians through their spin doctors and often from the politician directly has always been routine for a programme like *Today* and, inevitably, sometimes they are justified. But usually not. Sometimes it's pretty half-hearted. Mostly we know when they're just trying it on and they know we know, so they just register their protest and leave it at that. But not under Campbell. It was seldom just a light skirmish – more like a blitzkrieg.

As Marsh put it, what they were always trying to do was 'fixing the headlines and punishing those, like me, who refused to take their dictation: flinging handfuls of grit into the machine just like they had in opposition'.

But the consequences of the decision he faced on that May morning were way beyond anything he could have imagined based on what had gone before. There was simply no precedent for it. The message the nation would take from it was, quite simply, that we had been taken into a disastrous war on a lie. A senior minister (who used to work as a BBC reporter) told me on air the following week it was 'the most serious accusation that I can ever remember being levelled against a government in my lifetime'.

Later Gilligan was to concede that he had gone further in his live two-way than he should have done. He had not scripted it ahead of time, as correspondents often do if they are dealing with a difficult or sensitive subject. He should not have made the suggestion that the government 'probably knew' the forty-five-minute figure was wrong. In an earlier, scripted, report for Radio 2 he had not made that point. And having made the allegation at 6.07 the BBC never made it again. At 7.40, Gilligan was stressing that the intelligence services, not the government, thought the claim was wrong. By ten that evening, BBC TV news was simply saying that 'parts of the report overstated the threat'.

But that fateful morning Number 10 was doing much more than raising a relatively mild objection to a particular aspect of Gilligan's interview. They were claiming that it was completely untrue. The whole lot. And they wanted us to admit it. Marsh had absolutely no intention of doing so.

As he recalls:

Shortly after seven, Downing Street called again. Allen took the call and soon became exasperated. Again and again he asked: 'what exactly are you saying is wrong?' They kept saying 'Everything!' In the meantime Humphrys had wandered out of the studio and into the office while the news bulletin was on air. It was one of the few chances I ever got to speak directly to the presenters during the programme and usually we'd talk quickly about the items in the next hour of the programme. This time, though, all we could do was stand by Allen as he explained to Downing Street that we were not going to put on air a 'denial' that we knew was untrue and misleading. He kept asking what it was about Gilligan's story they were saying wasn't true. Were they saying the document had not been

At the *Today* papers desk with Sue MacGregor and Roger Mosey, the editor, 1993.

On air with Brian Redhead, 1991.

On air with Sue MacGregor.

Shooting the breeze with John Cleese,
in a very nineties picture.

Trying to show Jim Naughtie
who was boss outside the old
Broadcasting House.

Our production office at
Broadcasting House on the day
we moved to Television Centre
in White City in 1998.

Interviewing John Major.

David Cameron. Ties were no longer required for prime ministers.

Jimmy Carter – still going strong in his nineties.

Tony Blair and me on the set of the late, lamented *On the Record*.

The Tony Blair interview on *Today*, as seen from the control room.

John MacGregor, one of Thatcher's cabinet ministers, tasked with removing my head. His accomplice was Terry Wogan. They failed.

With British forces at their military base in Basra in 2003. The war in Iraq had ended, but the fighting would continue for years to come.

transformed by Number 10 in the week before it was published, for example? They said they would not discuss 'processology'.

I tried to talk to John through the next few items but his attention was on the Downing Street call. He was amused. He had more of a taste for these early morning scraps than I did but by the time he had to go back into the studio we still hadn't resolved anything.

And then Downing Street phoned again, this time with a statement that had almost certainly been dictated by Alastair Campbell himself. It was a bizarre piece of writing. It began: 'These allegations are untrue. Not one word of the dossier was not entirely the work of the intelligence agencies.' An interesting use of the double negative you might think. But it went on to say: 'The suggestion that any pressure was put on the intelligence services by Number 10 or anyone else to change the document are entirely false.'

This presented Marsh with a real dilemma. Even if he were minded to broadcast a denial (which he wasn't) he could hardly deny this – for the excellent reason that Gilligan had not said it. Neither had his source. The forty-five-minute claim had been made in the preface of the dossier, which Blair had read out to MPs. Gilligan had not said pressure had been put on the intelligence sources to change the document. But, as Campbell well knew, the BBC had to respond. When Downing Street issues a statement after the BBC has broadcast such a serious allegation we cannot simply ignore it. And the clock was ticking down to the next act in this drama.

I was back in the studio doing interviews about all the other stuff going on in the world and Marsh and Allen were out in the office desperately trying to decide how to react to Number 10. They didn't have long. Gilligan's report, which had been the subject of his 6.07 interview with me, was scheduled to go to air within a very few minutes.

They rushed into the control room, still going over the shorthand notes that Allen had made of his Downing Street conversations and Marsh made his decision. The only way we could use the statement, he decided, was for me to read it out but then make it clear immediately that it was denying something no one had said … and then, as he put it, 'hope that somewhere in the forest of double negatives the audience would find something comprehensible'.

It would have been a tricky enough problem if it were being addressed by a group of BBC senior managers calmly discussing it with all the time in the world in the oak-panelled boardroom over a cup of decent coffee. The control room of a news programme when it is live on air is marginally less conducive to calm, measured reflection. Especially when, as in this case, the editor has literally two or three minutes and can't even speak to the presenter because the presenter is speaking to the nation.

For the presenter himself it's even worse.

Obviously I had a rough idea of what was going on, but I'd been live on air when the Downing Street statement arrived and had not seen sight nor sound of it. Nor did I know what Marsh's thinking was. Were we going to cave in or take it to the wire? Would Marsh risk his career on a judgement taken not just in the heat of battle, but with the shells whistling in over his head from one of the most powerful figures in the land? And if he got it wrong, would he take me with him? As he said, you can't stop a programme to sort out a problem and there is no golden thread attached to the words uttered on air to pull them back once they're out there. And when it's a live programme, not everything that gets out there is exactly what you want. Here's how he described what happened next:

Allen started to speak to Humphrys through his headphones. I was shouting at the studio producer to get Gilligan's line up so I could speak to him. (He was at home and not, sadly, in the studio.) Humphrys meanwhile was gesticulating. He couldn't say anything because the sport report was going out and was in the middle of a live item. He ripped the headphones off and stormed through to the cubicle.

'I can't read this rubbish!' he told me.

'You have to!' I told him.

We were now seconds away from hour zero. No time for arguing. Here's Marsh again:

Humphrys was back in the studio. The green light went on telling him that his mic was live. In a fraction of a second he had to fashion in his head a new introduction to Gilligan from the script he had in front of him, which was now outdated, and from the tortured English of the Downing Street statement. And he had to turn it all into a question to which Gilligan could give the answer: 'That's not the allegation.'

I fear I let my editor down. He thought I had 'overcooked it' because I described the dossier as 'cobbled together' at the last minute with some unconfirmed material that had not been approved by the security services. He had a point and I dare say that if I'd had a few minutes to think about it I would have been more precise. But I didn't and I suspect the audience got the gist of it. And anyway, I had the chance to make amends half an hour later.

By happy coincidence the 8.10 interview happened to be with a minister who was well placed to deal with the 'sexed up' allegations: the defence minister Adam Ingram. He had agreed to come on the programme to deal with some difficult questions raised in a report about the way British forces had used cluster bombs in Iraq close to civilian targets. Obviously all bombs are designed to cause death and destruction, but cluster bombs are particularly hideous because they scatter small 'bomblets', many of which do not explode and are abandoned, to be picked up and played with by children weeks or months later. The children are either killed or suffer horrific injuries. Not an easy subject for a minister to address – but Ingram knew that it was not the only thing I would want to talk to him about.

Marsh thought of Ingram as 'one of those New Labour ministers who enjoyed fighting with Humphrys' and could slug it out while keeping to his brief. What I had no way of knowing was how closely he had been briefed on the substance of Gilligan's allegations and what his defence might be.

I began by reminding him of the language Blair had used when he described to MPs the threat from Saddam's so-called weapons of mass destruction. He had said: 'It is active, detailed and growing … It is up and running now and it could be activated within forty-five minutes.' I emphasised the 'forty-five minutes' and then I said:

'It is now forty-five or more days since the war ended. Not one WMD has been found.'

Downing Street would claim later that this had been an 'ambush' – a favourite word if an interviewer asks ministers questions they are not expecting. That was ridiculous on so many fronts it's hard to know where to begin and, in fairness to Ingram, he did not try to duck the question. Indeed, it was obvious that he had been briefed (almost certainly by Campbell) as to how to deal with me. Which made what he said next all the more surprising.

He effectively confirmed one of the most damaging allegations. The official who had spoken to Gilligan had told him the reason why the intelligence agencies were so shocked by his forty-five-minute claim was that it had been made by a single source – a source that, as it was to transpire, was completely untrustworthy. It is a golden rule in the intelligence services that you do not trust information from a single source unless it is someone who has earned that trust over the years. That was not the case here. Yet this is what Ingram told me: 'Well that was said on the basis of a security source information single source. It was not corroborated.'

I tried not to show it, but I was stunned and I wanted him to repeat what he had said lest there be any doubt.

'Single-sourced …? So you concede that?'

Ingram must surely have realised the significance of what he had said as soon as the words had left his lips so he tried to down-play it: 'I think that has already been conceded.'

The giveaway in that escape attempt was the phrase 'I think'. A minister as clever and well briefed as Ingram would have known that it could not have been 'conceded' for one very simple reason. The allegation had not been made until a few hours ago and Downing Street had dismissed everything Gilligan had said. 'Everything' they had said, 'was wrong'. Now here was a minister actually accepting live on air that one of the central allegations was not only true but had been 'conceded'.

This was vitally important. Not only had a defence minister unwittingly blown a hole through Number 10's denials, but he had bolstered the credibility of Andrew Gilligan's source – the mysterious 'senior official'.

If Number 10 had hoped to kill the story before it took off they were to be sorely disappointed. That 6.07 interview ignited a media firestorm. Blair himself, we know from Campbell's diary, saw it as an attack on his own integrity. The spin machine went into overdrive and, not for the first time, they were aided by my old nemesis Tom Baldwin of *The Times*. On 4 June he wrote a bizarre story which claimed that 'rogue elements with the intelligence services are using the row over weapons of mass destruction to undermine the government'. Senior Cabinet ministers, he wrote, believed the government was the victim of 'skulduggery'. According to Baldwin they wanted to 'settle scores' with Blair and Campbell. My next big interview was with one of those senior Cabinet ministers who had contributed to Baldwin's story, Dr John Reid.

Reid was a classic example of Old Labour turned New Labour. He had fought his way (sometimes literally) from the back streets of working-class Glasgow to a seat among the most powerful in the land. He was a bruiser and he was not known for taking prisoners. The *Guardian* told the story of how he once arrived drunk at the House of Commons and, when an attendant tried to stop him getting onto the floor to vote, he threw a punch at him. So I was looking forward to the interview. My editor wasn't.

He wrote: 'I never looked forward to Humphrys' tussles with the New Labour bruisers. They created headlines, maybe the odd mis-speak or gaffe, but rarely any genuine enlightenment. When I was at my grumpiest I saw them as a bout between a couple of ageing, bare-knuckle prize fighters, groggily shuffling around an imaginary ring, jabbing and weaving, looking for the killer punch that both knew would never come.'

I'm not sure I agree with every word of that. Ageing? I was a mere stripling of fifty-nine. Nor was he right that the 'killer punch' never comes. It depends, I suppose, on what you mean by a killer punch.

I knew that Reid would pour scorn on Gilligan's allegation that the government probably knew the forty-five-minute figure was wrong even before it decided to put it in the dossier – and that's exactly what he did. He described it as Gilligan's 'final untruth'. I pointed out that there was not a single shred of evidence to prove that the forty-five-minute claim had been true.

He replied: 'We were accused of forcing the security services to produce information in a public document in an attempt to dupe the people by putting in false information.'

Yet again a government minister was denying something that nobody had accused them of and I pointed that out. 'Forced them? Forced the security forces to provide information to dupe the people of this country? I don't remember me saying that and I don't remember Andrew Gilligan saying it.' I also said I had spoken to one or two senior people in the intelligence services who had suggested to me that what the government had indeed done was exaggerate the threat from Saddam. At that point I could have delivered a killer punch. But I didn't – and to this day I wonder whether it had been a mistake to hold back.

A Meeting with 'C'

Some weeks earlier I'd had a call in the *Today* office a few minutes after coming off air from a rather posh-sounding man who said he would like to invite me to lunch with a certain Very Senior Person. There was a condition attached. I was not to reveal anything that was said at the lunch and he would not reveal the name of the VSP if I did not agree to the conditions. I would have to accept that the lunch had never happened. Would I agree? I replied as you would expect: 'How can I agree to have lunch with someone if I don't know who he is?' So he told me. He was Sir Richard Dearlove, the head of the British Secret Intelligence Service (MI6). (Within the service all heads of MI6 are known as 'C', and are the real-life equivalents of Ian Fleming's character 'M', the boss of James Bond.) He was the most powerful spy in the land.

It was not the first time this had happened. I'd had a similar invitation in exactly the same cloak-and-dagger circumstances many years ago so I knew roughly what to expect. One difference was that on that occasion when I'd asked for the address I was told I wouldn't need it. They would send a car to pick me up. They didn't want me giving the address to taxi drivers. After all, who knew what they might do with it? It struck me as somewhat para-noid. It seemed unlikely that there were too many taxi drivers in London who did not know the headquarters of MI6 – or, indeed, too many Russian spies for that matter. I accepted and imposed my own condition. I wanted to take my editor with me. He agreed.

It was a tantalising prospect. The last invitation had been soon after the Berlin Wall came down and the Cold War had come to an end. It became pretty obvious early on why I had been invited. MI6 were worried that now the old enemy had run up the white flag there would be less demand for their services. So 'C' wanted to deliver the message that there were still plenty of enemies out there and it would be madness to cut back on the number of spies and, therefore, his budget.

Interestingly, when I asked him what the nation should fear most now the red terror had been dealt with, he said Middle East terrorism and cyber-attacks. As it turns out he wasn't far wrong.

But what message did Sir Richard Dearlove want to send me away with? I assumed there was only one possible subject. Iraq. I was right.

There were two other top spooks at the lunch – his deputy Nigel Inkster and another senior officer Nigel Backhouse – and there was the usual small talk for a while. I made the obligatory request for an interview with Dearlove and he did what I knew he would do and graciously declined. Then I mentioned that he must have been seeing rather a lot of Blair recently and he said indeed he had. He had been popping into Number 10 most mornings to give him the latest intelligence briefings in the run-up to the war. Now, of course, the war was over and Saddam had fallen and the search for the WMDs had begun.

We recalled Blair's dark warnings about the threat the WMDs had posed. I thought it was worth asking Dearlove whether Blair had been entirely accurate about that and specifically the forty-five-minute warning but I couched it in slightly more diplomatic language. Where, I wondered, did Dearlove place Iraq in the list of countries posing a danger to our security? His answer was simultaneously Delphic and immensely revealing: 'On any Cartesian analysis,' he said, 'I'm not sure we would regard them as being at the top of our list.' Indeed, he went further and suggested they were very far from the top and certainly below Syria and Iran. But what about those WMDs, I wondered. Where were they and why hadn't they been found yet and when were they going to be found? Instead of answering directly, the question was turned on Marsh and me.

What if they were never found, we were asked? What if Saddam had ordered, as the allied troops were closing in on Baghdad and his defeat was inevitable, that the WMDs should be destroyed? How did we think the media would react to such an announcement from the British government?

There was only one answer to that. The first response would be total incredulity and the second would be hilarity. We would reach the obvious conclusion in about ten seconds flat that, in spite of everything we had been told, the fabled WMDs had not been found for the very simple reason that they had never existed. I think it's fair to say it was the answer our hosts had been expecting.

Now here I was, several weeks after that lunch, facing a senior Cabinet minister live across the *Today* programme microphones, knowing that if I told him about that conversation it would be impossible for him to deny it – short of calling me a liar who'd made the whole thing up. And he couldn't do that even if he'd been minded to because I had witnesses. It really would have been a 'killer punch'. I knew that Tony Blair had exaggerated the threat from WMDs and that they had posed no serious threat to our security because the most senior intelligence figure in the land had told me so. I also knew that I could not say so because I would be breaking a promise, betraying a source to whom I had promised anonymity. So I did my best to convey the information without breaking pretty much the only rule that is respected by all journalists.

'Well let me tell you,' I said to Reid, 'I myself have spoken to one or two senior people in the intelligence services who said things that suggest the government exaggerated the threat from Saddam and his weapons of mass destruction.' This was not, as he and some of his colleagues had claimed, 'something that's been got up by a few disaffected spooks'.

I was not surprised when I came off the air to be told there was a call awaiting me. Even less surprised that it was from MI6. They had listened to the interview with some interest, said my caller, and wondered whether, when I used the phrase 'senior people', it had been a coded reference to my lunch with the chief. I had visions of my name being entered in whatever little black book the spooks use to list those who have incurred their displeasure and what punishment they might deem fitting in my case. But I protested my innocence, reminded him that I had named no names and, anyway, pointed out that the chief was not the only senior spook who did a little private briefing when it seemed expedient. I could have been referring to almost anyone, couldn't I? He seemed happy enough with that, so I tried to get a sense of how MI6 were reacting to the Gilligan disclosures. Did they think there had been a certain amount of cherry-picking with the intelligence in the dossier?

He replied: 'Inevitably.'

I kept my promise not to reveal any details of the secret lunch but as it turned out I might as well have written an open letter about it to every newspaper in the land. A few weeks after the Reid interview the *Observer* splashed it all over its front page. They got some details wrong but the important stuff, including the details of my exchange with Dearlove over the threat posed by Saddam, was accurately reported. So someone had leaked it and to this day I don't know who. All I know is there were five people there and it wasn't me.

One effect of the leak was that it strengthened the resolve of senior figures at the BBC – above all the director general Greg Dyke – to stand firm behind the Gilligan disclosures. But BBC management did not focus on the gap between what Gilligan had meant to say at 6.07, and what he had actually said. This would come back to haunt us. In that same edition of the *Observer* there was an interview with Tony Blair in which he said the allegations amounted to 'about as serious an attack on my integrity as there could possibly be'.

So the stage was set for an almighty battle that would ultimately inflict terrible harm on Blair's reputation but claim many more victims too – including the men at the very top of the BBC. What we had seen so far were barely the opening skirmishes because something was about to happen that would take it to another dimension altogether. At its heart was another case of a journalist refusing to reveal his sources – but this was to have far greater consequences than my own so-called 'secret' lunch with the spooks. The source in this case was the whistle-blower who had given Andrew Gilligan the information that had lit the fuse for this crisis back in May.

He had done so, of course, on condition that his identity would never be revealed. Gilligan had agreed and was true to his promise. But the hunt was on to identify him and it was led by 10 Downing Street. Not just to identify him. For Blair's reputation to survive, the source's credibility had to be destroyed.

The first stage of that campaign was farcical and, if the stakes had not been so high, would have provided perfect material for a BBC2 late-night satire. It involved not just Tony Blair and Alastair Campbell but also the defence secretary Geoff Hoon, BBC bosses, assorted spooks, their respective teams and a seemingly endless and increasingly frenetic stream of emails, letters and phone calls with everybody blaming everybody else and most of them either denying that they knew or making it clear that actually they did know perfectly well who it was but were damned if they were going to say so in case they got the blame. It proved relatively simple to identify him – there were, after all, very few senior officials who had been UN weapons inspectors with personal knowledge of Saddam's Iraq – but from Campbell's perspective it was important not to be seen as the man behind the leak. To this day he has denied being implicated. So perhaps it was just a coincidence that the newspaper that eventually named the whistle-blower on 10 July 2003 was *The Times* and the name attached to the story none other than Tom Baldwin, Campbell's old friend. For most of the characters in this dark drama what had been at stake so far was their reputation. The consequences of this latest revelation were to prove tragic.

The name of the 'senior official' who had sat with Andrew Gilligan in the Charing Cross Hotel on 22 May and told him – on a strictly unattributable basis – why the nation should not believe Tony Blair's interpretation of the notorious dossier was Dr David Kelly. He was a mild-mannered, highly respected scientist. He was an expert in biological warfare employed by the Ministry of Defence and he had been a United Nations weapons inspector in Iraq. If anyone could claim to know from first-hand experience over many years the state of Saddam Hussein's arsenal of weapons it was David Kelly.

A few weeks after his identity was unveiled, on 15 July 2003 Dr Kelly was summoned to appear before the Foreign Affairs Committee of the House of Commons to be questioned about what he had told Gilligan. He appeared to be under severe stress and spoke so softly his answers were almost inaudible. The air conditioners had to be turned off even though it was one of the hottest days of the year.

Two days later he was at his home in Oxfordshire. In the afternoon he was called by his superior officer at the Ministry of Defence, Wing Commander Clark, and they spoke for six or seven minutes. When Clark phoned back some twenty minutes later Dr Kelly's wife told him he had gone for his usual afternoon walk in the nearby woods. He did not return. Early the following morning he was found dead. There were knife wounds to his left wrist and nearby a bottle of painkiller tablets. He had swallowed as many as twenty-nine of them.

As I write these words we still cannot say with absolute certainty how Dr Kelly met his end. The official verdict was, unsurprisingly given the circumstances, suicide. But that verdict was delivered not by a coroner's court as a victim's family are entitled to expect under English law, but by a judge conducting an inquiry at the request of a politician. An inquest had indeed been opened four days after his body was discovered but three weeks later the then Lord Chancellor Lord Falconer, who happened to be an old flatmate of Tony Blair, ordered it to be adjourned indefinitely. It was revealed later that on the morning Kelly's body was discovered Falconer had two telephone conversations with Blair, who was on an aeroplane from Washington to Tokyo. That same morning it was announced that he had asked Lord Hutton to chair an inquiry into the circumstances surrounding Kelly's death. The questions to be answered were whether the government bore any responsibility and the part played in it by the BBC.

Our coverage of the 'sexed up' dossier and our treatment of

Kelly's whistle-blowing were of critical importance. It was, perhaps, the biggest challenge to the BBC's integrity and professionalism we had ever faced. Every one of the BBC's 7,000 journalists knew that the findings of the Hutton Inquiry would influence, if not determine, the future of BBC News. If the Hutton Inquiry were to report that the BBC's journalism had been flawed in some details but essentially sound we would be able to hold our heads up high. If it were to condemn us, a reputation built up over the past eighty years as the world's most respected news organisation might be destroyed. It was as serious as that.

The BBC was not optimistic. There were grave misgivings about the suitability of Hutton for the job. That was partly because he did not have the skills and experience of a practised coroner. He did not even call as a witness the police officer heading the investigation into Dr Kelly's death, Chief Inspector Alan Young. But also because he was seen by many as a 'tame judge' – far too friendly to the political establishment. Those misgivings were to be borne out by the events that followed.

The inquiry opened in August 2003 and its findings were delivered nearly six months later.

When a big story is breaking, a newsroom is an exciting place to be. Breaking news is what we are about. It's in the DNA of every journalist who operates to a daily news deadline. We want to be there when it happens – which is why I broke the habit of a lifetime and went back into the newsroom on that January afternoon even though I had presented the programme in the morning. Hutton had reached his verdict and would be delivering it any minute now. But there was no excitement, no anticipatory thrill. I have never known the atmosphere in that place to be so resigned, so depressed.

Perhaps it was because we knew what to expect. There had been so many leaks from the Hutton team and the conduct of the inquiry had struck us as so weighted against the BBC that we feared the worst. Some of us might even have felt we deserved it. We had been pummelled for so long by the government and its spin doctors and supporters I suspect many of us were beginning to doubt our own professionalism and even our integrity. Our big bosses seemed to have lost confidence in their own ability to control the organisation and some of them were coming under attack from their own senior colleagues – prepared to wound but afraid to strike.

It was true that we had made mistakes. Gilligan had publicly admitted he'd got some things wrong and done things he should not have done and his judgement had been found wanting. So had the judgement of some of the most senior figures in the BBC. But surely, after six months of investigations, Hutton would see the wider picture. Gilligan had broken a story that had to be told. Blair had – for whatever reason – misled the nation and we had gone to war on a false prospectus. And a decent man had died because he felt the nation should know.

One of the oldest jokes in the BBC is that whenever you ask a member of staff about morale they will shake their head ruefully and mutter: 'Bad … never been as low as this.' This time it was not a joke. We were, I suspect, resigned to our fate as we sat slumped in the newsroom or leaned against our desks in small groups waiting for Hutton to appear in front of the cameras.

He did not disappoint those of us who feared the worst. His report might as well have been written by Alastair Campbell himself. He exonerated the government of pretty much every charge levelled against it. Nobody, he said, could have anticipated that Dr Kelly would take his life. There was no 'underhand government strategy' to name him as the source of the BBC's accusations. Gilligan's accusations were unfounded and the BBC's editorial and management processes were 'defective'. Oh … and the dossier had not been 'sexed up'. In short, the claims made by Gilligan had been false. The BBC's chain of management should not have defended his story and the governors should have recognised that the allegations against the government's integrity were unfounded.

Within minutes of Hutton leaving the stage Tony Blair made his appearance in the House of Commons. Blair has almost always been a consummate judge of the public mood with an instinct for the right tone to adopt. There must have been a temptation to exult, to crow over the corpse of the BBC's lost journalistic integrity. He did neither. His words were measured and delivered in sorrow more than anger. His tone was almost regretful. But he left his audience in no doubt that he and the words he had spoken from that very same spot before he took the nation to war had been vindicated.

When Alastair Campbell appeared in front of the cameras soon afterwards his approach could not have been in greater contrast. He was no longer a public figure – he had left Number 10 after having resigned the previous August during the Hutton Inquiry – but the setting he chose would have done credit to a South American dictator intent on demonstrating his dignity and gravity to his adoring people. He appeared to the waiting cameras at the foot of what must surely be one of the grandest stairways in one of the grandest houses with one of the grandest addresses in London: Carlton House Terrace. The house, now home to the Foreign Press Association, had once been the residence of William Gladstone. All that was missing was the presence of a corps of trumpeters sounding a ceremonial salute as Campbell descended the carpeted stairs, his left hand resting lightly on the sword with which he was about to smite his enemies. He was angry and, unlike his former master, he wanted the world to know it.

The BBC, he declaimed, had waged a vicious campaign to paint him and Tony Blair as liars. He went on: 'The prime minister told the truth, the government told the truth, I told the truth. The BBC, from the chairman on down, did not.' Apart from the chairman, Gavyn Davies, the other liars he listed were the director general Greg Dyke, the director of News Richard Sambrook, Andrew Gilligan, and my own editor Kevin Marsh.

Whether Campbell believed that rubbish I have no way of knowing, but I suspect he did. I got to know him reasonably well when he was a journalist before his Downing Street days and both liked and respected him. He was a decent man and loyal to a fault. His weakness was that he demanded the same unquestioning belief in his leader – whether it was Neil Kinnock or Tony Blair – from everyone. Even from journalists who, as he well knew, had an absolute duty to report dispassionately. As I've mentioned earlier, for Campbell it was simple: you were either for Blair or you were against him. And if he had you marked down as a threat, however limited, he would do his damndest to destroy you. And on that bleak day in January 2004 it seemed that he had succeeded. The next day the chairman resigned. He was followed by the director general and then by Andrew Gilligan. The BBC had been decapitated. It seemed in those dark days it would never again occupy the same journalistic high ground.

But that was not the end of the story. Another chapter would be written. The final chapter. Another inquiry – infinitely more detailed, thorough and impartial – would be conducted. But it would not even be set up until long after Tony Blair had left Number 10 and Gordon Brown had moved in, and it would take more than seven years to complete. It was called the Chilcot Inquiry.

Lord Hutton had barely ended his press conference before the criticism of his inquiry began: both the way he had handled it and its conclusions. The following morning the front page of the *Independent* newspaper had but one word splashed across it: 'WHITEWASH?' That pretty much summed up the opinion of a large section of the public and the political world – large and growing larger almost by the day as Iraq and the Middle East descended ever deeper into violence. A powerful committee of privy councillors had been pressing for a proper inquiry into Britain's involvement in Iraq, the run-up to the invasion, the conduct of the war and the horrendous aftermath. The Blair government blocked it at every turn, but in 2009 Gordon Brown announced that it would happen. It proved to be everything that the Hutton Inquiry had failed to be.

Its chairman, Sir John Chilcot, was no 'tame judge': he was a highly respected career diplomat. And he did not sit alone.

Alongside him were four other equally respected figures, each expert in their own fields. They were not merely thorough. They were relentless: forensic and detailed to the point of mind-numbing boredom for all those of us who just wanted them to get on with it. But the conclusions, when they came after a seemingly endless seven years, were more than worth the effort. The final report ran to a daunting million words.

In spare and precise language it blew apart the conclusions of the Hutton Report and the claims made by Tony Blair in that sexed-up dossier thirteen years earlier. Saddam Hussein did not pose an 'urgent threat' to British interests. The intelligence regarding weapons of mass destruction had indeed, as Dr Kelly told Andrew Gilligan, been presented with 'unwarranted certainty'. The peaceful alternatives to war had not been exhausted. The United Kingdom and the United States had undermined the authority of the United Nations Security Council. The process of identifying the legal basis for war was 'far from satisfactory'.

I have often tried to imagine how Tony Blair must have felt when he first had sight of that report. There has never been a prime minister who has not feared the verdict of history. When the door of Number 10 closes behind them for the last time the ambition that has driven them for so much of their lives closes with it. The past matters more than the future. And surely Blair must have known that Chilcot had destroyed what remained of his dream to be the prime minister who had led the nation to victory in a just war. The morning after the report was published Blair came into the studio and gave me his first interview. It was different from any I had ever done with him. Not because he made any great admission of guilt or grievous error – he did not and never has – but his tone and his manner were different. He seemed more subdued, less defiant. But I suspect what many listeners wanted was at least an acknowledgement that the invasion of Iraq had stoked a series of blazes that were to consume great swathes of the Middle East. They wanted a touch of repentance. They were disappointed.

I have known Blair since he was a young, eager backbench MP who wanted to achieve great things – as indeed he did. In electoral terms he was the most successful leader the Labour Party has ever had. 'Blairism' became the creed of 'New' Labour and Blair was seen as the party's saviour. By the turn of the century he seemed all set to enter the history books as one of the great post-war prime ministers. But after Iraq he became one of the most reviled.

I have interviewed him many times since the war and tried to wring from him at least a recognition that its awful consequences must have given him some second thoughts. But he has never, for a moment, strayed from his mantra that the world is a better place without Saddam. That was the purpose of the war and it was achieved. But though his words tell one story I have often sensed his eyes telling another: the eyes of a deeply conflicted man. But perhaps I see only what I am looking for.

I remember one interview with particular clarity for one specific phrase. It was the longest interview I had ever conducted on *Today*. Blair resigned as prime minister on 27 June 2007 – almost exactly ten years since he had entered Number 10 – and, of course, every news programme wanted his final interview. It was assumed that, showman as he was, he would choose television over radio but he didn't. He gave me not one but two live interviews. It was agreed that one would cover domestic matters and the other foreign affairs. I took that to mean Iraq.

Rather than come into our studio Blair chose to do the interview in Number 10. It was a rather intimidating set-up: a large reception room with Blair and me plonked in the middle facing each other and his most senior aides sitting in a row behind me. It meant I could not see them but he could and his gaze would often switch from me to them – as though he were seeking approval for what he was saying.

Normally even the most important 8.10 interview must give way to sport. *Today* has its structure and listeners tend to get cross when we override it, which means we seldom exceed eighteen minutes. This interview lasted for a record-breaking twenty-seven minutes. By far the most revealing exchange was when I pressed him on his reason for going to war in Iraq and made what I thought was the obvious point. His justification was the threat posed by Saddam's weapons of mass destruction but those weapons did not exist and he must have known it. It was a long and heated exchange and he ended it with a phrase that I remember vividly to this day: 'I only know what I believe.'

That struck me as the most extraordinary thing to say. I tried pointing out that surely it was a prime minister's duty faced with such an awesome decision to act only on what he knew, not what he 'believed'. And the only way to 'know' was to interrogate the intelligence reports relentlessly. If they supported his case, well and good. If they did not, the fighter jets would have to stay in their hangars and the troops in their barracks. But Blair had promised Bush we would go to war alongside him and that is what happened. Because Blair believed it was the right thing to do.

14

The director general: my part in his downfall

The dream *Today* programme sometimes turns into a present-er's nightmare. Here's a typical scenario. There's a big story dominating the news and you waltz in at 4 a.m. and say to the overnight editor: 'Great story eh? Obviously we've got the prime minister/movie star/disgraced banker coming in for a live at ten past eight?' What you are actually doing (rather childishly) is winding up the editor because you know there's not a cat's chance in hell that the PM or whoever happens to be making the big headline news will willingly put his head in the *Today* noose on this of all mornings.

That means you will probably have to settle for an obscure backbench MP or your own correspondent who will tell you what they think the person at the centre of the story might have said if they had actually been prepared to risk it.

Thus it was on the morning of 11 November 2012. The big story was the BBC. Its new director general George Entwistle was facing enormous pressure over a catastrophically shoddy piece of reporting which had led to a distinguished Conservative member of the House of Lords being accused of child abuse when he was entirely innocent. And that had come hot on the heels of another piece of lamentable journalism: the BBC's failure to identify a man who really was guilty of it. Forty years of it. Hundreds of children abused – many of them while they were sick in hospital, yet more of them while they were in BBC dressing rooms. He was, of course, Jimmy Savile. The BBC had a lot to answer for and an awful lot of explaining to do.

So when I arrived in the office I greeted the editor with the entirely predictable: 'I suppose we've got the director general coming in this morning then?' There was only the slightest of pauses.

'As a matter of fact … yes. Entwistle will be here in the flesh.'

What! For as long as I've worked for the BBC the big bosses have had a tried and trusted way of dealing with crises – especially potentially career-threatening crises like this one. They order 'comms' (the communications people charged with spreading the gospel according to the BBC) to prepare a statement and then programmes like *Today* are meant to read it out. When you dispense with all the management-speak it invariably says something like: 'Dunno what they're talking about: it's all got up by the tabloids' or 'Please God let it all go away!' What the big bosses do not do is volunteer to appear live on the programme and answer the questions that are begging to be answered. And that's because they know they will have no control over those questions. Statements are much safer. They are not alone in that. It happens all the time when powerful people find themselves in big trouble.

You will be familiar with the formula. We report at some length on a story that is enormously embarrassing to the government minister or the company boss or the police chief or whoever happens to be the subject of the attack and at the end you will hear the presenter say something along these lines: 'No minister was available but the department issued this statement …'

This is nonsense. I decided many years ago that I would no longer play the 'statement' game.

Take that phrase 'No minister was available'. All the main government departments have five or six ministers, at least one or two of whom are required to be on duty at all hours of the day or night in case of emergencies of one kind or another. Mostly they are not dealing with emergencies. They are either engaged in the routine business of government or simply getting on with their private lives. But there is *always* someone who is on call. That's how big organisations work. And yet, when it comes to a potentially embarrassing interview, we are asked to believe that there is no one 'available'. It's not as if, in these hi-tech days, they have to come into the studio to be interviewed. They can do it from the comfort of their own homes. They can do it from their beds, for heaven's sake. And yet there is no one who can spare the few minutes it would take to answer our questions. Do we really believe that? Of course we don't – or, at least, we shouldn't.

The spin doctor who has to deliver the message to the producer knows it is nonsense. The producer knows it is nonsense. And yet, time after time, you will hear presenters dutifully inform the listeners: 'No minister was available.' I reckon there are two ways of dealing with that. One is to say 'The department tells us no minister is available' – with a very heavy emphasis on 'tells' and possibly a slight sneer in the voice, leaving the listeners to draw their own conclusion. The other is the simple: 'The minister didn't want to do an interview.' At least it has the merit of being true.

The statement ruse is worse. The typical scenario is that one of our correspondents will have reported on something pretty scandalous that's been happening in, say, a government department or public body. It will almost invariably have been a well-researched piece of journalism but the one thing lacking is an interview with whoever is responsible for the scandal. At the end of it you will hear the presenter saying something like: 'The ministry/company/whatever has issued a statement in which they deny absolutely everything and insist they are doing an utterly magnificent job and the taxpayers/customers should have no concerns whatsoever. Oh … and those people claiming otherwise are lying through their teeth.' I exaggerate a little, but that's the message they want to leave the listener with. And that's why we should not indulge them.

In reality there are two explanations for a powerful figure ducking an interview when serious charges have been made publicly.

One is that they are bang to rights and the other is that they are not prepared to face the music. We know it and they know it. So why should we indulge them by allowing them to make a statement which is the last word the audience hears and which cannot, by definition, be challenged by the presenter? Even as we read it out we know it's probably rubbish, yet read it we do. Very occasionally there might be some tricky legal complications in the story and the BBC lawyers might advise us to read the statement in order to guard our backs, but they are few and far between. And anyway I've always thought we give in too easily to the lawyers.

All large news organisations employ them but the difference between the BBC and a typical national newspaper is that the paper uses its lawyers to get tricky stuff published – assuming, of course, it's in the public interest – whereas we often seem to use ours to do the opposite. At least that's the impression you get as a humble presenter on a daily news programme when you are always up against the clock. It's different for an investigative programme like *Panorama* when their legal advisers may well be going into battle with the lawyers from the other side. But on *Today* it's frustrating to be told a script has been 'legalled' and therefore must not be changed. Too often a cautionary word from a lawyer is enough to make too many producers and editors run for cover and take the easy way out. They seem to regard the word of a lawyer as the law. It's not. It's advice. No more and no less. It is there to be accepted or rejected and it is the responsibility of the editor to make the decision.

If I had my way I'd order the famous words of the duke of Wellington from 1824 to be printed on little plaques and placed on the desk of every news editor in the BBC. The duke had been told by his lawyers that a lady of uncertain virtue was about to publish a book in which she planned to reveal details of the relationship they had once enjoyed. She was prepared to remove the details from the book to save the duke from embarrassment in return for a pretty large financial consideration. In simple language: she was blackmailing him. His lawyers suggested to the duke that it would be wise to pay up. His response: 'Publish and be damned.'

Sadly, the BBC's response when it's facing a difficult decision tends to be the exact opposite: 'Least said … soonest mended.'

Given that background you will understand why I thought my editor must have been winding me up when he told me we had Entwistle on the programme. The dream interview. Or was it a nightmare?

Yes, it was beyond our wildest dreams to have the man at the very top of the organisation prepared to face the fire. Had there been a stray bottle of champagne lying around I'd have cracked it open. But hang on a moment. I'm going to be the poor sap sitting across the table from him doing my damndest to expose his failings – and he's my boss. Not just my boss but my editor's boss too. In fact he's everybody's boss. And it will be my job to do everything in my power to prove that he is guilty of some very serious charges. Is it him putting his head in the noose, or is it me?

What if I blow it?

What if I get something horribly wrong or lose my nerve?

My reputation, such as it is, would never survive it. I've done plenty of dreadful interviews over the years, but never with the director general of the BBC.

Alternatively what if I don't blow it? What if I succeed in making him look like either a fool or a knave – somebody unfit to be running the BBC? That's not something he's likely to forget in a hurry. It's one thing to nail prime ministers – all they can do is complain – but it's another thing to nail your boss. He can sack you – or at least make your life so difficult you might wish he had. So, yes, I was just a wee bit apprehensive. But here's an interesting thing about interviews when there is so much riding on them: everything else disappears from your brain.

I have known George Entwistle ever since he was a young assistant producer for my old programme, *On the Record*. I had watched him rocket up the BBC management ladder with a touch of admiration and respect. He's a very clever man and a rather nice man too. I liked him. But the moment he arrived in the studio he might as well have been a total stranger.

Maybe it's a defence mechanism – the part of your brain kicking in that says he is the interviewee and you are the interviewer and that's all that matters. I'm not suggesting that news presenters are paragons of virtue and nor, God forbid, that they should be devoid of humanity. Obviously if you are interviewing someone who's had something bad happen you will react with sympathy. If they are almost paralysed with nerves, you will help reassure them. And sometimes, let's be honest, you come up against someone you know is a thoroughly bad lot and you really want to nail him. In other words – and in spite of rumours to the contrary – presenters are human too. Sometimes anyway. It's just that if you are going to survive in this job you probably have to be wired a bit differently.

That's why, when I looked across the table at George I did not see my boss, the most powerful figure in British broadcasting. I saw a slightly nervous human being who had some extremely difficult questions to answer – and it was my job to put them to him. At the heart of them was child abuse.

Entwistle took over the BBC in September 2012. A year earlier on 29 October 2011, Jimmy Savile had died and within two weeks BBC Television, with Entwistle then in charge, had broadcast its first programme in tribute to him. At Christmas, another tribute programme *Jimmy Savile at the BBC: How's About That Then?* was shown, two days after a BBC1 revival of *Jim'll Fix It*, fronted by Shane Richie. These programmes were, we now know, a monumental misjudgement because it soon became clear that Savile had been a monster who had been getting away with child abuse for decades.

Virtually everyone who'd had any dealings with him used the same word to describe him: creepy. He was one of our earlier guests on *Celebrity Mastermind* in 2004. I winced when they told me he had been invited and had accepted. I had interviewed him a few times over the years and, like almost everyone else, had heard worrying rumours about him. But nothing had been proved and if the BBC deemed him a fit and proper person, why should rumour disqualify him? He was, after all, a big star by any standards and it wasn't always easy attracting big names to *Celebrity Mastermind*. All they get is a donation to their chosen charity and the very real opportunity to make an idiot of themselves.

As it happens, the show went off without incident but after Savile had left and we'd finished the last recording I asked the *Mastermind* team what they had thought of him. Everyone had much the same reaction: a brilliant performer on camera but a bit … umm … weird? The young women who have the job of looking after our guests and making sure they're comfortable thought he was a bit more than weird. They grimaced. Then one of them volunteered that when they'd greeted him in reception they'd had a quick conflab among themselves. 'We agreed we didn't want to be alone with him,' she said, 'so there were always two of us and we did *not* take him into his dressing room … just opened the door for him and handed him the key!'

That's hardly a shock revelation I know, but if those three young people formed that impression of him instinctively, knowing nothing of his reputation, then it is odd – to say the least – that down the years the BBC seems not to have recognised, or dealt with, the issue.

Two days after Savile died a *Newsnight* producer, Meirion Jones, had approached his editor Peter Rippon and told him he wanted to investigate Savile. He also approached the editor of *Panorama*, Tom Giles. Like many other experienced investigative journalists, Jones was convinced that Savile was a predatory paedophile and that he could prove it. Rippon, who was relatively new to the job and had little experience of television investigations, gave him the go-ahead and a few days later Jones started work. His reporter was Liz MacKean and his researcher Hannah Livingston.

A week later they heard that the BBC was planning a Christmas tribute programme to honour Savile. They were appalled. The BBC paying tribute to a man they were convinced had been preying on children for most of his adult life? A man who, they were trying to prove, had been abusing his fame and his reputation as a dedicated charity fundraiser and volunteer to gain access to children. In their minds it raised some alarming questions. What if they completed their investigation and their story was cleared for broadcast before the tribute was due to be aired?

The idea that the BBC could portray Savile as a monster on, say, 16 December and then as a saint a fortnight later was obviously preposterous. But equally, what if the tribute were broadcast as scheduled and then, a week or two later, the Jones investigation was ready for broadcast?

The *Newsnight* journalists could see the problem clearly enough but further up the organisation the two parts of the BBC's 'brain' were not talking to each other. It had failed to realise the existence or import of two programmes with such diametrically opposite remits.

Here we had a TV star whose behaviour over the years had been at the very least questionable. So much so that at least one police force was known to have sent a report about him to the Director of Public Prosecutions and who escaped justice because the DPP said they could not find sufficient evidence against him. A man whose behaviour had caused many of those who had worked with him over the years to recoil in disgust. But a man who had almost godlike status among the many fans who saw only the public face and not the dark side.

It is a central principle – I almost wrote 'sacred' principle – of the BBC that its journalism takes precedence over all that it does. If you strip away everything else, that is the reason for its existence. And it must be independent. The only possible qualification is in time of war when the very survival of the nation is at stake. Then – and only then – has the BBC allowed itself to deliver a message that strays towards propaganda. But even then it has put up a fight. The Savile affair hardly came into that category, but the principle of unprejudiced journalism is sacrosanct.

If the BBC had good reason to believe – or even strongly suspect – that the man they were proposing to praise was a paedophile, the tribute programme should not have been broadcast by BBC Television and I've no doubt it would have been dumped. But the wider BBC had simply failed to understand the significance of the Meirion Jones investigation, not least because BBC News dropped it.

It was not until a year later, when an inquiry set up by the BBC finally reported, that we had a clear picture of what had become perhaps the greatest scandal ever to hit BBC News. The inquiry's findings set out in painful detail the sequence of events that led to a catastrophically damaging decision at the very top of the organisation.

Meirion Jones had been given the go-ahead in November 2011 to conduct his investigation. By the end of the month, confident that he had enough material to support his allegations, Jones sent his editor, Peter Rippon, and the BBC lawyer a very rough script.

Rippon appeared to be enthusiastic but, a couple of days later, told Jones he was not confident that he had enough to justify the continuing investigation and he was cancelling the editing facilities that had already been booked for him to start putting the programme together. He might well have been right about insufficient evidence at that stage, but what he should have done was continue to pursue the investigation until there *was* enough or hand it to a programme that had much more experience of this sort of investigation such as *Panorama*. Killing it stone dead at that point meant the wider BBC was largely unaware of it and its consequences for the tribute programmes.

Jones, convinced that the BBC was beginning to run scared, was so appalled he took the slightly bizarre step of sending himself an email warning of the possible consequences for BBC News if his story was dumped and the tribute was aired. He called it his 'red flag' email. Bizarre but, as events were to unfold, a wise thing to do.

The next day, 2 December 2011, the most senior person in BBC News, the director Helen Boaden, happened to bump into George Entwistle at an awards lunch in London and mentioned the Savile investigation in passing. She told him that if it went ahead it might have an impact on the Savile tribute and, therefore, the BBC TV schedules.

Three days later Surrey Police confirmed that they had investigated a historical allegation of child abuse by Savile at a children's home and had referred it to the Crown Prosecution Service. Two days later the CPS told Jones they were not prosecuting because there was not enough evidence. Rippon told Jones to drop the story. The tribute to Savile was then broadcast as planned on BBC2 on 28 December, two days after the new edition of *Jim'll Fix It*.

Within a week stories began to appear in the papers.

The investigative reporter Miles Goslett had already got wind of the fact that the *Newsnight* investigation had been pulled and was asking the BBC for confirmation. By February he was also reporting that some of the children abused by Savile had been on BBC premises – in studios and dressing rooms. He went further. He said the BBC had information about Savile that the police did not have and that the director general Mark Thompson knew of it. The next day Rippon asked Jones if he had that information. Jones said he did. By now the *Sunday Mirror*, the *Daily Telegraph* and the *Daily Mail* were all piling in.

Over the next eight months almost every senior figure in BBC News became embroiled in the affair. For those of us watching, appalled, from the sidelines it seemed like some hideous game of 'pass the parcel'. And eventually heads began to roll. The first to be moved was Rippon himself. And then the two most senior people in the News division, Helen Boaden and her deputy Steve Mitchell, were effectively cut off at the knees. They were 'recused' from having any more contact with the Savile investigation or any analogous stories which, given that Savile had come to dominate virtually everything the BBC said and did, was the equivalent of sending them off on gardening leave. I knew Steve well. We had become good friends over the years. He had given his professional life to the BBC and felt he had been betrayed by the organisation he had loved. Both he and Helen were required to find lawyers and faced a long-running quasi-legal inquiry that cost £2.5 million, their reputations unfairly shredded even before its conclusions were known.

On 22 October 2012, a year after *Newsnight* had begun its inquiries into Savile, an investigative programme was finally broadcast. But not by *Newsnight*. It was an investigation by *Panorama* into what the BBC had known about Savile and why it had dropped its own investigation. What could have been an example of BBC investigative journalism at its best had come to be seen as a shocking demonstration of corporate cowardice and buck-passing – on the face of it, a betrayal of everything that BBC journalism could and should have stood for.

There was though, another, more accurate, explanation. The management of the different parts of the BBC was so contained within its own silos that the right hand didn't really have a clue what the left hand was doing at any given time.

The official inquiry, run by the former head of Sky News, Nick Pollard, eventually concluded that the decision to drop the *Newsnight* investigation was flawed, but had not been driven by the desire to avoid a clash with the tribute programme. That was the key charge, but BBC managers had then showed a 'complete inability' to deal with the fallout. It was also revealed that George Entwistle had been sent an email two years earlier warning him about Savile's 'darker side' but had failed to read it.

The one certainty is that never in the history of the BBC has there been such a damaging fallout from a programme that the viewers never even got to see. But with senior management side-lined, as the Savile affair unwound, the BBC soon had to face up to the consequences of running a story that *was* wrong.

Once again, the villain of the piece was a suspected paedophile. The difference was that with Savile we'd got the right man and failed to report it. In this case we'd got the wrong man and we did report it. The innocent victim was Lord McAlpine, a senior political figure with an unblemished reputation who had once been the treasurer of the Conservative Party. He was not named by *Newsnight* but it was clear it was referring to him because he had been identified even before the programme was broadcast.

In allowing the item to go ahead, the BBC's senior management, or rather those who were left holding the reins in the absence of the News leadership that had been sidelined over Savile, appeared desperately out of their depth. It had to achieve two objectives: to show that the BBC was still capable of serious investigative journalism in the public interest and also that it had not been scared off by the Savile debacle. Like Odysseus it was caught between Scylla and Charybdis but, unlike him, there was no goddess to look to for guidance.

The genesis of this crisis was a statement made in the House of Commons by the Labour MP Tom Watson as the Savile crisis was reaching its climax about a different scandal involving child abuse. He suggested that there had been a cover-up of a paedophile ring and this one was linked, not to showbiz stars, but to Parliament. Angus Stickler, a former *Today* reporter then working for the Bureau of Investigative Journalism, listened to Watson with some interest. He had won awards for his investigative work, including a powerful documentary he had made twelve years earlier for Radio 5 Live about sexual abuse of children at care homes in North Wales.

One of the victims he had interviewed was a man named Steve Messham, who had told Stickler the police had shown him a photograph of a man he identified as his abuser. That man, he said, was Lord McAlpine.

Stickler wanted to revisit the story – not with the intention of naming McAlpine but to investigate failings by the police and a previous inquiry into child abuse in the homes. He contacted *Newsnight*. The acting editor Liz Gibbons, who had taken over from Peter Rippon, commissioned the piece. What she did not know was that the previous inquiry had found Messham to be severely damaged psychologically: a man who 'presents himself as an unreliable witness by the standards that an ordinary member of a jury is likely to apply'.

That was not the only weakness in the story. Some pretty basic fact-checking of material that had been on the public record for ten years would have sounded a few warning bells with even the most reckless editor. One irony was that the man who might have alerted Gibbons to its weaknesses was himself occupied with other matters at the time. He was Meirion Jones. And he was busy preparing his own witness statement for the inquiry that was looking into the BBC's failure to broadcast his report on Savile. A report that would have proved to be entirely accurate.

But those warning bells did not sound and in one sense it's just about possible to understand why. The greatest risk for any investigative journalist lies in making charges against a specific individual or organisation and getting it wrong. He might well get away with claiming that a government has been behaving corruptly. Accusations like that are commonplace and if he fails to provide hard evidence, so be it. He might get a lot of stick from politicians and commentators but m'learned friends will show no interest. But if he says the chancellor himself has been fiddling his expenses or even, infinitely worse, abusing children, that's a different matter altogether. Governments can't sue. Individuals can – and do. And then the journalist and the organisation publishing the allegations have to satisfy a court of law that there is enough evidence to prove the allegations are true. If they fail, the damages (not to mention the legal costs) can be spectacular and the more high-profile the victim, the higher the costs.

In this case *Newsnight* might have been able, if things turned nasty, to fall back on the defence that they were not actually naming any specific individual. But it wasn't quite that simple. McAlpine's name was being bandied about to such an extent that it might as well have been printed on banners ten feet high and hung over the entrance to Television Centre.

The night before the programme was due for transmission the Oxford Union staged a debate with the motion 'British politics is in the hands of the media'. As David Leigh of the *Observer* wrote a few days later, Iain Overton from the Bureau of Investigative Journalism was there and boasted that the following evening's *Newsnight* was going to report that a top Tory had abused teenage boys at a North Wales care home.

Michael Crick, ex-*Newsnight* and then the political correspondent of *Channel 4 News*, was also there. He asked Overton: 'Do you mean McAlpine?' Overton replied: 'Well you said it.' By the next day, twelve hours before *Newsnight* was about to hit the airwaves, the story was everywhere. It was given another nudge when Overton tweeted: 'If all goes well we've got a *Newsnight* out tonight about a very senior political figure who is a paedophile.'

While he was tweeting merrily away, Crick was doing something that you might have thought one or two other journalists should have been doing – possibly one or two journalists working for *Newsnight*. He tracked down McAlpine to his home in Italy, told him what the BBC was going to allege that evening and asked for a comment. He said later that McAlpine didn't seem particularly angry and suggested the story was based on rumours that had been dismissed years ago but he added: 'They'll get a writ with the breakfast toast.'

It's hard to imagine how BBC bosses would have reacted when they saw Crick's tweet later that morning. And there was more to come from him. Three hours before *Newsnight* was due to go on air he went onto *Channel 4 News* to report that a victim of abuse in a North Wales care home had said he had been raped by 'a former senior Conservative official from the Thatcher era'.

That increased enormously the chances of McAlpine being identified. The temptation for the BBC to run for cover and drop the story must have been intense. But how could they do that when they were still trying to regain some respect after the Savile disaster? The newspaper headline that would have followed that little announcement wrote itself: 'BBC bottles it again!'

The columnists and leader writers would have torn us apart. Not only had BBC News been forced to drop what would have been a frighteningly accurate portrayal of a predatory paedophile in favour of a snivelling tribute that was an offence to his many victims, but here was another investigation into a powerful figure that had also been dropped. And in this case the man was still alive and, therefore, still a potential danger to children. So the temptation to publish and be damned was powerful.

But what if, unlike the Savile investigation, *Newsnight* was indeed allowed to broadcast that investigation and its conclusion turned out to be wrong? Not just a bit wrong, but sensationally so. What if there was not an ounce of truth in it? They could hardly hide behind the defence that they had not named the abuser. It might have been literally true – they had not actually used his name – but there could be no possible doubt over the identity of the 'former senior Conservative official from the Thatcher era'. Obviously Crick already knew who it was and the Twittersphere was buzzing with rumours.

Nor was there any question that McAlpine would take legal action. And what a case that would prove to be. It's hard to think of a more serious libel than to identify a blameless public figure as a contemptible child abuser.

If ever there was a story that cried out to be adjudicated on by the most powerful figure in the BBC it was this one – all the more so because half the most senior news bosses had either been removed from their posts or sacked over the Savile affair or were fully engaged in trying to contain the damage. The man in charge now was George Entwistle. He was director general and editor-in-chief. Yet nobody contacted him or briefed him.

The final draft of the *Newsnight* script was signed off just seventy-five minutes before the programme went on air by the lawyer, Roger Law, and the new 'shadow' News management that included the controller of Radio 5 Live Adrian van Klaveren, who had been a deputy director of the News division. And this is how the programme began: 'Good evening,' said Gavin Esler, the presenter. 'A *Newsnight* investigation into the abuse of boys at children's homes in Wales can reveal that two victims say they suffered sexual abuse at the hands of a leading Conservative politician from the Thatcher years.'

By Monday morning some prominent figures were going on Twitter relishing the downfall of a 'senior Conservative figure' and making no attempt to hide their belief that it was McAlpine. They were to pay dearly for that in the months that followed. By the following Wednesday senior figures at the BBC were beginning to realise that a terrible blunder had been made. The *Guardian* suggested it might have been a case of mistaken identity. And then on Friday, a week after the broadcast, McAlpine himself went public.

In a long statement, he said that Messham was mistaken. He had only ever been to Wrexham, the town where the children's home was based, once in his life and the allegations, he said, were 'wholly false and seriously defamatory'. Even worse was to come.

The story had been based on the evidence of that one man: Steve Messham. He phoned Angus Stickler to tell him that Lord McAlpine had not abused him. Now that he had seen a picture of him he realised that it had been another man. Stickler had not shown him the picture. It was, it turned out, a crucial mistake.

And so, just one week after *Newsnight* had broadcast its investigation, it was forced to return to the subject. This time to deliver a cringing apology. At the beginning of the programme the presenter, Eddie Mair, said: 'A new crisis for *Newsnight*. Tonight, this programme apologises.' Shortly afterwards, Messham appeared and said: 'Humble apologies to Lord McAlpine. That certainly is not the man that abused me.'

Unlike the Savile affair, however, there would be no multi-million-pound inquiry into what had gone wrong: just a quick internal review by a senior executive. It was a curious case of how the consequences of *not* broadcasting a story could be more damaging for the editors and executives involved, than broadcasting one that was terribly wrong.

Ten hours after *Newsnight's* confession, George Entwistle faced me across the *Today* programme microphones. We had no chance for even a brief chat before my first question because the studio was live, but we both knew that this interview would decide his future as the boss of the most powerful broadcaster in the land. There was one question I was longing to ask him but, for obvious reasons, could not: why on earth have you decided to do this interview now?

He had ordered a report into the whole fiasco and that was due to be published in two days, so he could have claimed – entirely justifiably – that he needed to wait to study the report's findings. Or he could have followed decades of BBC tradition, ducked the interview and left it to the report's author. Or he could simply have played for time and waited for the heat to die down. It almost always does.

Or perhaps there was another explanation for this bizarre and seemingly suicidal timing. Perhaps he knew something that I didn't, that he would produce a few killer facts and I would be left floundering. But his appearance suggested otherwise. He looked drawn, utterly exhausted and more like a convicted man facing his executioner than someone about to prove his innocence and win a last-minute reprieve. And so it proved from his answer to my very first question:

GE: We made a film that relied upon a witness who yesterday
came out and said he had made a mistaken identification. That
mistaken identification meant that the film we had broadcast
was wrong and we apologised for it, because we should not
have put out a film that was so fundamentally wrong. What
happened here is completely unacceptable; in my view the film
should not have gone out. I've taken clear and decisive action

to start to find out what happened and put things right. I've commissioned a report from one of my senior editorial leaders, director of BBC Scotland [Ken MacQuarrie], which I've asked to have on my desk by Sunday and further action will follow from that, disciplinary if necessary ...

JH: And once again we are shutting the stable door after the horse has bolted. Why didn't you ask those questions before the film went out?

GE: Well, not every film and not every piece of journalism made inside the BBC is referred to the editor-in-chief.

JH: Was this *just* another film, just another piece of journalism?

GE: No, it's an important piece of journalism and obviously I've asked Ken MacQuarrie to get to the bottom of exactly what happened and I want to be careful about prejudging what he says. But from the inquiries I've been able to make so far this was a piece of journalism referred to senior figures within News, referred up to the level of the management board and had appropriate attention from the lawyers. Now the question is: in spite of all that why did it go wrong? And there's no stepping away from that. Something definitely and clearly and unambiguously went wrong here and we now have to be clear, we have to find out exactly what happened.

JH: When did you know that this film was being broadcast and when was it drawn to your attention that it was going to make extraordinarily serious allegations about a man whose identity would inevitably be uncovered – wrongly as we now know?

GE: The film was not drawn to my attention before transmission.

JH: At all? Nobody said to you – at all – in the BBC?

GE: No John, I need to explain that there are an awful lot of pieces of journalism going on around the BBC which do not get referred to the editor-in-chief.

JH: Of course there are.

GE: Not everything gets to the editor-in-chief. The key is, is it referred sufficiently far up the chain of command and in this case I think the right referrals were made – but I need, of course it's important to give Ken MacQuarrie the chance to find out exactly what happened.

JH: But you must have known what happened because a tweet was put out twelve hours beforehand, telling the world that something was going to happen on *Newsnight* that night that would reveal extraordinary things about child abuse and that would involve a senior Tory figure from the Thatcher years. You didn't see that tweet?

GE: I didn't see that tweet John, I now understand—

JH: Why not?

GE: I check Twitter sometimes at the end of the day or I don't check it at all.

JH: You have a staff. You have an enormous staff of people who are reporting into you on all sorts of things. *They* didn't see this tweet that was going to set the world on fire?

GE: John, this tweet I'm afraid was not brought to my attention so I found out about this film after it had gone out. Now the …

JH: Can I just be absolutely clear? Nobody said to you at any time, or to anybody on your staff who would then report to you at any time: look we've got this *Newsnight* film going out – '*Newsnight*' should already light a few bulbs with you, surely – but we've got this film going out on *Newsnight* that is going to make massively serious allegations … nobody even mentioned it?

GE: No.

JH: Isn't that extraordinary?

GE: In the light of what's happened here, I wish this had been referred to me but it wasn't and I run the BBC on the basis that the right people are put in the right positions to make the right decisions. Now in this case the piece was not signed off in *Newsnight*, legal advice was involved, it was referred to the right places in News management and further referral upwards was made so in short a serious consideration was given to this but that in my view makes it all the more important that Ken

MacQuarrie gets to the bottom and finds out what's happened here.

JH: So when did you find out? When did you find out?

GE: I found out about the film the following day.

JH: The following day? You didn't see it that night when it was broadcast?

GE: No I was out.

JH: So you heard about it the following day and then what did you do?

GE: I made inquiries as to find out why what had happened on Twitter had happened – because it seemed to me that the events surrounding the film in terms of what happened on Twitter were an important part in understanding how this thing had achieved a scale and created a noise around potentially identification that was clearly surprising. It's important to say, it's no excuse or exoneration in this case, but it is important to say that the film itself did not name, did not make a named allegation.

JH: We know exactly what the background to that is now. You *have* seen the film now I take it?

GE: Yes I have seen the film now.

JH: And your view of it was that it was an abomination journalistically?

GE: My view of it is that if Mr Messham has made a mistake in his identification, then the film cannot stand.

JH: It's no question of *if.* He says so.

GE: No, as he has, but if you had known that prior to transmission of the film, the film could not stand.

JH: Does it not surprise you that nobody actually showed Mr Messham a picture and said 'Erm, was this the man?'

GE: Well John I think there are a number of—

JH: Well does that surprise you? Put aside all the other things, that is so fundamental that it's hard to exaggerate it.

GE: Well can I just cover a number of journalistic questions I have which I hope Ken MacQuarrie will answer for me? Did the journalist carry out basic checks? Did they show Mr Messham the picture? Did they put the allegations to the individual? ... If they did not, why not and did they have any corroboration of any kind? These are the things we need to understand because this film as I say had the legal referral, was referred up the chain, yet it went ahead. There is some complexity here I absolutely need to get to the bottom of.

JH: Precisely when did you understand, learn, that Mr Messham was in this case, in this specific case, an unreliable witness?

GE: Well I think that's a harsh thing to say about Mr Messham ...

JH: But he's already told us he made a mistake, he's apologised profoundly.

GE: In the course of the film Mr Messham tells a number of stories, gives a number of accounts of abuse in the North West care-home system.

JH: Well rephrase it if you like but in this particular case he's an unreliable witness because he said that he got it wrong. When did you learn that?

GE: I became aware that Mr Messham had got this wrong yesterday, when he made his statement.

JH: When did you learn that there were doubts about the testimony, about his testimony?

GE: I only found out yesterday when I saw him make his apology ... that there must be doubts about his testimony.

JH: And you didn't ask any questions during the course of the week? Because questions began to be raised very early on in the week as you know.

GE: No John, I didn't.

JH: Do you not think you should have?

GE: The number of things that there are going on in the BBC mean that when something is referred to me and brought to my attention I engage with it.

JH: So you've no natural curiosity. You wait for somebody to come along to you and say 'Excuse me, Director General, but this is happening and you may be interested.' You don't look for yourself? You don't do what everybody else in the country does: read newspapers, listen to everything that's going on and say 'What's happening here?'

GE: The second this was brought to my attention last night I immediately—

JH: Brought to your attention! Do you not read papers? Do you not look, do you not listen to the output?

GE: I saw this break on the web, John, that's where I saw this, it's not a question of it being in the papers but the second I saw it I started to make inquiries about what had happened.

JH: But it was in the *Guardian* yesterday, did you not read the *Guardian*'s front page yesterday morning?

GE: No John I was giving a speech yesterday morning very early on.

JH: Aren't some things more important than others, do you not have to have a different set of priorities?

GE: You have to prepare for speeches you have to make, John.

JH: The *Guardian* yesterday carried a front-page story, which we now know was right, that cast doubt, serious doubt, on the BBC's *Newsnight* programme, a flagship news programme for the BBC. You didn't know that that had actually happened?

GE: I'm afraid I didn't.

JH: When people ask questions about the role of the BBC and the director general of the BBC, they point out … that he is the editor-in-chief. How do you define the responsibility of the editor-in-chief?

GE: The editor-in-chief has to take complete responsibility for the BBC's journalistic output but that does not mean the editor-in-chief sits and signs off every single piece of it. The organisation is too big, there is too much journalism going on. The way the system works is that things brought to the attention of the editor-in-chief are effectively handed over to him – responsibility is given to him at that moment. If the system is not referring things it should refer to the editor-in-chief then it's not working properly. This is one of the things I need to look at.

JH: We now know that it didn't work properly, don't we? We now know that *Newsnight* failed massively on one programme and it has failed massively on another programme and it's caused the BBC enormous damage. You as editor-in-chief are ultimately responsible. Therefore it leads to the obvious question – you should go, shouldn't you?

GE: No, John I've been appointed the director general. The director general isn't appointed only if things are going to go well – the director general is appointed to deal with things which go well and things which go badly. Now *Newsnight* has had two serious blows and I have reacted in both cases.

JH: No, the *BBC* has had two serious blows—

GE: Yes, I understand the BBC has – but the two serious blows in this case refer to the programme of *Newsnight* and in both cases I've taken the action, the right action, to understand what happened and to start to be able to learn the lessons we need to learn.

JH: But you did it too late, massively too late?

GE: It's very important, John, to recognise that this is about *Newsnight*. Of course that has huge implications for BBC, for trust in the BBC, I absolutely accept that but it would be absolutely wrong to slur by extension the rest of the amazing work that's going on across the rest of BBC News, the reporting from America, from China, the fine work this programme does. Ninety-nine per cent of what the BBC does is going out to the usual excellent standards and to the enormous satisfaction of its audience. I don't say any of that because I am in any sense complacent but I've got to understand what seems to have been going wrong on *Newsnight*. And the latest case – there is no question about it – that film shouldn't have gone out.

JH: Did you want to stop that programme last night, the apology programme last night?

GE: No, I thought it was absolutely vital.

JH: Did you ever think about stopping *Newsnight* last night?

GE: I thought about a number of things, John …

JH: Including that?

GE: I've decided I am going to wait until Ken MacQuarrie reports before I make my mind up. The key thing last night was that *Newsnight* was given the chance to apologise. They made a mistake. It was really important that that apology was put out in their programme.

JH: You've already said that *Newsnight* will carry out no more investigations, for the time being at any rate.

GE: No. What I have said is that all investigative projects on *Newsnight* need to be halted while we check the editorial rigour and supervision.

JH: Have you given any thought at all to shutting down *Newsnight*?

GE: No I haven't, John, *Newsnight* is a thirty-two-year-old programme with an incredibly proud record of excellent award-winning journalism. Two … one … mistake has been made for certain here. We need to allow the Pollard review to determine what happened at this time last year – I think it would be absolutely disproportionate at this stage to talk about closing *Newsnight* down.

JH: How can you have a news programme that is not allowed to do investigative journalism, whatever investigative journalism is, however you define it?

GE: I'm taking the simple prudent step there of ensuring that the quality of investigative journalism going on on *Newsnight* is up to scratch. That is not the same as saying it can't do it. I need to look, I need to check everything it's got under way and we need to make sure no more mistakes of the character of last Friday's are going to be made. That is vital. I'm not saying that *Newsnight* can't investigate in future – it's had a fantastic investigative record – I hope it will go on to do amazing investigations again.

JH: The BBC has – I hardly need to tell you this – a unique position in this country, it has unique privileges and it earns those on the basis of the trust that the people of this country have in the BBC. That trust has been severely damaged … possibly destroyed hasn't it?

GE: I don't believe it's been destroyed. The BBC has had crises of trust before. This is a bad crisis of trust. I admit it. But what you have to do is show your audiences that their trust in you is ready to restore and the way you do that is you are open and clear about finding out what's gone wrong and we are doing that through Savile. We have two reviews, independent reviews, to find out what went wrong there in both cases and to be able to put those facts in front of the audience and show them the lessons we've learned from it. I'm doing the same thing here [with McAlpine]. This is a more contained case. I'm acting decisively and quickly this weekend. I hope to have a report on my desk by Sunday by which point I will, I hope, know exactly what happened and I will know what action to take – including disciplinary action if that is appropriate.

JH: Disciplining other people, but at no point will you say to yourself: 'I George Entwistle should have been much more alert to the dangers in all this. I should have been watching it like a hawk right from the very beginning, everything *Newsnight* did in this area, I should have been on top of. Not editing the programme – down there on the stone, as it were but I, as director general, the editor-in-chief, should have been on top of everything the programme did. I was remiss in that. It's no good me blaming other people because I am the boss.' Do you not see that people will say 'He's talking about disciplining other people – he's not saying "I was remiss."'

GE: John, you are effectively asking me to become the editor of *Newsnight*, I was editor of—

JH: I'm not. I'm absolutely not doing that, it has an editor, he answers to you and therefore you should have said to him what are you up to old boy, or old girl?

GE: I was editor of *Newsnight* [2001–4]. I know what level of attention to detail that takes. That is where that level of scrutiny should take place—

JH: Not with you at all? You are entirely blameless in this?

GE: And I answer to my bosses – I answer to the Trust.

JH: So not unless the Trust says to you: 'Mr Entwistle, we are worried about the way you have been running the BBC in this regard, this vitally important regard over the past few weeks' … not unless they do that will you consider your own position? Is that right?

GE: John, I am a director general who has encountered these problems and is doing everything I can, I believe I am doing the right things. I know there were times when I was thought to be a bit slow over Savile. I could have been a bit quicker to move to announcing the independent inquiries by a few days – I've admitted that – but the truth is I am doing the right things to try and put this stuff straight. I am accountable to the Trust in that endeavour. If they do not feel I am doing the right things then obviously I will be bound by their judgement.

JH: George Entwistle … thank you very much.

Within ten hours he had resigned. He had been with the BBC for twenty-three years and director general for fifty-four days. The manner of his departure was – at least as far as I was personally concerned – gracious.

We'd had no chance for a quick chat before the interview because I was live on air when he arrived and no chance of a chat afterwards because (as we now know) he had a rather important meeting to attend. In fact we couldn't exchange even the briefest of words because after the interview Jim Naughtie and I went straight into the papers review so the microphones were live. But George did something that will stay with me.

After I'd thanked him on air he paused for just a few moments, left his seat and started walking out of the studio. When he was halfway through the doorway he stopped, rather as though he'd forgotten something, turned around and came back in. I was reading whatever it happened to be – probably a story about the crisis at the BBC – and George leaned across my microphone and stuck out his arm. He gave me a rueful smile, shook my hand warmly and left. His car was waiting to take him to that meeting at Broadcasting House: an emergency meeting of the BBC Trust, the men and women who held his fate in their hands. Every one of its members would, of course have heard the interview.

With him in the car was Paul Mylrea, the BBC's director of communications. The chauffeur, an old friend of mine, told me many months later that when they got in his car Mylrea was seething with anger. He spat out my name and added something like: 'What a bastard! He screwed you.' Or words to that effect.

'No he didn't,' said George, 'he was just doing his job.'

15

Turn me into a religious Jew!

Mishal Husain: It's ten to eight and time for 'Thought for the Day'. With us in the studio this morning is our speaker John Humphrys. Good morning John.

JH: Good morning Mishal and good morning Martha and may I say what a great privilege it is to be allowed to fill this hallowed slot after so many years of merely introducing it ...

And that, to the relief of millions of listeners no doubt, is where my 'Thought' would have to end. I would be allowed to go no further. I would be banned, disqualified, forbidden from offering whatever thoughts I might have in this, the most protected three minutes on radio. I do not have the qualifications demanded. Nor do many more who are far better equipped than me to offer the nation their thoughts.

Even so I've always rather fancied doing a 'Thought'. After half a lifetime of asking questions, always demanding to know what other people might think and why, the prospect of playing the wise teacher holds a certain appeal. Even better to be playing the preacher. Perhaps a latter-day Martin Luther King, inspiring my audience to dream great dreams. Perhaps a kinder, gentler version of Savonarola driving out corruption with my fiery rhetoric. Not that I'm much in favour of burning books, and the prospect of ending up being hanged and burned holds little appeal. And anyway I have no idea what I would say.

If I were a Christian I'd have no problem with that aspect of it. I would choose one of the more interesting news developments of the previous few days – preferably something that poses a profound moral dilemma – and tell the audience how Jesus would have dealt with it. I would then exhort my many listeners to behave likewise. Similarly if I were a Muslim or a Buddhist or a Sikh or a Hindu or a member of any other religion. There are an awful lot of gods out there to believe in – the Hindus alone have millions, though only four main ones so that's not too bad. But my problem is that I don't know what any of them would have done because I do not believe in any of them. I am an atheist. And that disqualifies me – and everyone else who happens not to believe in one god or another – from presenting 'Thought for the Day'.

That is absurd. In fact it's worse than absurd. It is – to use the word that causes every right-on boss in the BBC to quake in his shoes – discriminatory. Whoops … let that last sentence be struck from the record! Even as I typed it I could hear the sirens of the Thought Police squad car screaming around the corner into my street, pulling up outside my house, blue light flashing. My crime? I typed 'his' when I know perfectly well that some bosses are men and some are women and some are (probably) trans. In the modern BBC that's probably enough to get me sacked. Fair enough. Discrimination is, after all, a bad thing. So how come the BBC is allowed to discriminate between those who have been blessed with the gift of faith and those who, like me, have had it cruelly snatched away from them?

Let's remind ourselves what it's called. It is 'Thought for the Day'. It is not 'Religious Thought for the Day', let alone 'Sermon for the Day'. It's perfectly reasonable that the *Sunday Worship* programme on Radio 4 should be all about religion. The clue is in the title and if I don't want to join in the worship, which I don't, I can go elsewhere. Equally, the *Sunday* programme, presented by the brilliant Edward Stourton, is based on religion and I often listen to that (I almost said 'listen religiously') because it's thoughtful and raises interesting questions. But, again, it's a stand-alone programme. We know where it's coming from and what informs it.

'Thought for the Day' is not. It is plonked into the middle of a news programme when the audience is at its peak and consists of millions of people who are listening to *Today* because they want to find out what's going on in the world. Not because they want to be preached at.

That's not to say there aren't lots of listeners who welcome a few minutes of calm reflection. As Tony Blair once said in another context, I bear the scars on my back from all those listeners I have upset by sounding off about it.

It was probably twenty-five years after I'd joined *Today* that I first summoned up the courage to go public and suggest that maybe we should have second thoughts about 'Thought'. I might as well have suggested burning all Christians at the stake. I gave up counting the letters of protest – almost always letters rather than emails, incidentally, which may or may not suggest something about its defenders. Either way, there are an awful lot of listeners who would, it seems, willingly go to the stake themselves to retain 'TFTD'.

It is not, though, popular with most presenters, producers and editors. Barring royal deaths and the intervention of big bosses, the editor has the last word over what goes into *Today* and how it is treated. But not when it comes to 'TFTD'. It's the one segment of the programme where the journalists who work on it have no say whatsoever. The editor does not get to decide who presents it nor what subject it addresses, let alone whether the 'thinker' is a reasonably competent broadcaster. All of that is the prerogative of the Religion & Ethics department in Manchester.

If it sometimes sounds more like a party political broadcast than a religious tract, so be it. It matters not a jot whether the editor or producers think it is brilliant or boring, witty or witless, stimulating or soporific. There is nothing they can do about it.

Stranger still is that even the contributors do not always get the last word as to what they say. That right also goes to R&E and they defend it as fiercely as a grizzly bear facing a hunter trying to steal her cub.

Many past *Today* editors have come a cropper when they have tried confronting the Religion department. One of them decided back in the 1990s that, rather than try to appeal over their heads to senior management, he would unearth the evidence to prove that most listeners thought it was a turn-off – literally in many cases. So he commissioned a survey of listeners. The ostensible reason was to find out what they most liked and disliked about the programme, what should be allocated more time and what should get less. The real motive was to amass the ammunition which could be used to blow 'Thought' off the air. It failed miserably.

We had all been convinced that 'TFTD' would be given the thumbs down by the majority of those we surveyed. Instead the message was clear and consistent. Cut back on boring politicians who never answer the questions anyway. Don't bother with company results and most other business news unless it's something to do with the price of electricity. Don't keep speculating about the Budget on Budget day when we will know exactly what's in it in a few hours' time. Even, God forbid, give the racing tips a well-earned rest. But leave 'Thought for the Day' alone – or else! So much for our faith in surveys.

The next editor tried a different tactic. If we can't dump it, he suggested, maybe we could just trim it a little. In those days it ran for four minutes. Why don't we cut it back to three and see if anyone notices? So we did … and they noticed. It's one thing to be brave in the face of adversity; it's quite another – as our editor learned – to place your head in a noose and invite someone to kick away the chair on which you're standing. In other words, the Wiltshire Banana went bonkers. I may need to explain that.

In July 1925 the world's first long-wave transmitting station was opened. It brought the total audience within listening range to ninety-four per cent of the population. The idea of a national broadcaster had become a reality. Seventy years later it was obsolete – defeated by the upstart FM. But there were still a few areas where FM could not penetrate and one of those was in Wiltshire. The area was shaped more or less like a banana and its inhabitants loved Radio 4 – or the Home Service as they probably still called it. When they learned that they were to lose their long-wave signal they decided to protest. They marched on Broadcasting House.

These days the merest whisper of a protest outside the BBC means pretty much total shutdown. The police arrive. The barricades go up. The staff are given instructions as to how to enter and leave the building and what to do if they are captured and held hostage until the protesters' demands have been met. It can only be a matter of time before all staff are issued with flak jackets. It was different when the Wiltshire Banana first staged a protest.

When they arrived at Broadcasting House they were welcomed by the polite receptionist and invited in for a nice cup of tea and a chat with one of the bosses. Then they went home again. Job done. They may not have won a promise that the BBC would spend millions keeping the world's last long-wave transmitter operating so that they could listen to *The Archers* without any irritating squeaks and squawks, but they had made their point. They had proved they were a force to be reckoned with. No sane editor would risk their wrath over 'Thought for the Day'.

I have long been in the dog house with millions of listeners because I do not approve of it. They sum up my views as follows.

'It is invariably boring, sanctimonious, poorly presented by religious zealots out of touch with the real world and is roughly thirty years past its sell-by date. It should be dumped forthwith and more room freed up for pointless political interviews so that preening presenters like me can parade our prejudices before an audience that is yearning for a few minutes' respite: a few minutes of reflection; a few minutes to think more elevated thoughts.'

Some of that may be true, but not all of it and not all the time. What follows is a 'Thought' delivered by the former chief rabbi, Jonathan Sacks, in November 2017:

Good morning.

Coming in to Broadcasting House this morning I saw for the first time the statue, unveiled this week, of George Orwell, with its inscription on the wall behind, 'If liberty means anything at all, it means the right to tell people what they do not want to hear.' How badly we need that truth today.

I've been deeply troubled by what seems to me the assault on free speech taking place in British universities in the name of 'safe space', 'trigger warnings' and 'micro-aggressions', meaning any remark that someone might find offensive even if no offence is meant. So far has this gone that a month ago, students at an Oxford college banned the presence of a representative of the Christian Union on the grounds that some might find their presence alienating and offensive. Luckily the protest that followed led to the ban being swiftly overturned. But still …

I'm sure this entire movement was undertaken for the highest of motives, to protect the feelings of the vulnerable, which I applaud, but you don't achieve that by silencing dissenting views. A safe space is the exact opposite: a place where you give a respectful hearing to views opposed to your own, knowing that your views too will be listened to respectfully. That's academic freedom and it's essential to a free society.

And it's what I learned at university. My doctoral supervisor, the late Sir Bernard Williams, was an atheist. I was a passionate religious believer. But he always listened respectfully to my views, which gave me the confidence to face those who disagree with everything I stand for. Now that's safety in an unsafe world.

And it's at the very heart of my faith, because Judaism is a tradition all of whose canonical texts are anthologies of arguments. In the Bible, Abraham, Moses, Jeremiah and Job argue with God. The rabbinic literature is an almost endless series of Rabbi X says this and Rabbi Y says that, and when one rabbi had the chance of asking God who was right, God replied, they're both right. 'How can they both be right?' asked the rabbi, to which God's apocryphal reply was: 'You're also right.' The rabbis called this 'arguments for the sake of heaven'.

Why does it matter? Because truth emerges from disagreement and debate. Because tolerance means making space for difference. Because justice involves '*audi alteram partem*', listening to the other side. And because, in Orwell's words, liberty means 'the right to tell people what they do not want to hear'.

I wish every listener had been able to sit opposite Jonathan as I did while he was delivering those words. It was like watching a revivalist preacher, but without the histrionics and the nonsense. His passion and his belief are palpable. He frowns with concentration and sometimes with frustration, seemingly directed at the inadequacy of mere words to express what he believes. He clenches his fist – almost in anger at himself because he feels what he is saying is so important and he's not doing it justice. But of course he is. If I were forced to make the case for 'Thought for the Day' in only two words they would be: Jonathan Sacks. And if I had to pick a few of his 'Thoughts' that made the case for it, this would be one of those near the top of my list.

It was everything that 'Thought' should be. Jonathan took a current topic of supreme importance in a democracy – freedom of speech and, specifically, academic freedom – and he argued his case with fluency and wit. He didn't presume to tell us what God thought – he'd be appalled at the notion – but he did tell us how he had reached his own faith. He didn't patronise the listeners or preach at them. He told them what he thought about one of the great issues of our day – and he made us think.

Why would anyone want to get rid of something like that? I know I wouldn't. My problem is that for every Jonathan Sacks out there there's at least one Alan Bennett. I'm thinking, of course, of a very young Alan Bennett and his brilliant sketch in the 1960s *Beyond the Fringe*. Bennett played the well-meaning young vicar struggling with the meaning of life in his weekly sermon:

> You know … life … life … it's rather like opening a tin of sardines. We are all of us looking for the key. Some of us – some of us – think we've found the key, don't we? We roll back the lid of the sardine tin of life, we reveal the sardines, the riches of life, therein and we get them out, we enjoy them. But, you know, there's always a little piece in the corner that you can't get out. I wonder … I wonder, is there a little piece in the corner of your life? I know there is in mine.

Brilliant satire – and naturally I wouldn't suggest for a moment that any of our 'thinkers' has ever been quite so crass or (more's the pity) quite so funny. But too many of them manage to get horribly close to Bennett's young vicar. They seem to feel they must draw both a moral and religious lesson from everyday events. You know the sort of thing. There will be a story in the news about some so-called celebrity who has made a fool of himself with his high-and-mighty behaviour and our thinker will use his example to tell us that Jesus was so humble he washed his disciples' feet before the Passover dinner. So maybe we should all just get out there and start washing people's feet – whether they want us to or not. Very enlightening.

It was that sort of thing I had in mind when I made the great mistake of telling the *Radio Times* as part of a long interview that 'Thought' was 'very very boring'. The wrath of God descended on me. Or at least, the wrath of Dr Giles Fraser, which is pretty much the same thing.

Giles, as it happens, is another one of *Today*'s thinkers worth listening to. He's clever, articulate, often funny and nearly always angry. You tend not to get homilies and promises of salvation with Giles so much as dire warnings of what will happen if we don't change our ways. In the many years I have known and liked him Giles has never been exactly one of those 'turn the other cheek' Christians. Quite the opposite. He belongs to the militant wing – the left-leaning militant wing. He often used the weekly column he once wrote for the *Guardian* to savage those who do not share his views of the way the world should be run – and why not? The world needs people who care and aren't afraid to say so no matter who they might offend or what might be the cost to them. Giles is one of those who puts principle before power – and has paid a price for it.

He held the imposing title of canon chancellor of St Paul's Cathedral in 2011, at a time when anti-capitalist protesting was all the rage. A group of activists calling themselves 'Occupy London' staged a protest in the City calling for an alternative to our 'unjust and undemocratic' system. When they weren't allowed to camp outside the Stock Exchange they pitched their tents just outside St Paul's Cathedral, causing much inconvenience to all and sundry. After ten days Giles's superiors decided they had to be moved – by force if necessary – and he resigned in protest.

As I write he is the parish priest at St Mary's Newington, a rather more downmarket area of London where, I suspect, he's more at home ministering to his flock than he was in the splendour of one of the world's great cathedrals. Both ministering to his flock and taking a pop whenever the opportunity arises at yours truly.

It must be said, he has a nice turn of phrase. When he attacked me over my *Radio Times* interview he said I had delivered my 'Thought' comments 'with all the critical sophistication of a slovenly adolescent squirming his way through morning prayer'. It was, moreover, indicative of my 'assumed superiority … as if there is something about religious belief and religious believers that is not really worthy of his attention or interest'. And, just in case we hadn't got the message, he accused metropolitan liberals (like me apparently) of thinking that religion is 'beneath them' and is not something to be 'taken seriously'.

Now that's the one that really hurt. Because I do. I take religion very seriously indeed. And Giles knows that I do. So seriously that I wrote a book about it in 2012 – which would be a curious thing to do for someone who regarded God as unworthy of attention. And guess who went to considerable time and trouble to help me with it – for no greater reward than a bowl of my (admittedly superior) home-made soup and my sincere thanks in the acknowledgements? Yup. Giles Fraser. We spent many hours in my kitchen arguing about religion and it's partly down to those conversations that the book got its title: *In God We Doubt: Confessions of a Failed Atheist*.

Note that. It was not *For God We Have Contempt: The Final Proof that Atheists are Right*. I used the word 'doubt' because if I believe in anything it is that we do not know and never will know who or what God might be. Assuming, obviously, such an entity exists. We can be pretty sure that the God described in the Old Testament does not – and that if he did he'd be a nasty piece of work. Unless, of course, you happened to be an Israelite in which case he looked after you rather well. Either way, we can be entirely confident that the Genesis version of how the universe came into being is codswallop.

And yes, I know any halfway competent theologian would make mincemeat of my glib objections. Only the most extreme fundamentalist believes the Bible is literally true. But you don't need a theology degree to point out one obvious flaw in the God scenario. Faith is something that cannot be proved. If it could be proved it would be science. And if it could be proved scientifically you would not need faith. You would need only to study the evidence. So faith, by definition, is something that can be acquired or, perhaps, granted – but not proved.

It is also indisputable that there are vast numbers of people who do believe and have held on to that belief. And this is what really puzzles me.

Let's assume that faith is a gift – which is a reasonable assumption because the Church endlessly tells us so. And forgive me if I concentrate here on the Christian faith – partly because this is a reflection on 'Thought for the Day', which has more Christian speakers than others, and also because it is the 'established' religion of this country. Let's also assume that it is in God's power to grant that gift.

Maybe, like St Paul, you are going about your business one minute and then the next minute Jesus appears to you in a divine revelation. You are now a Christian. You have been blessed with faith in Jesus. Or, to use a more topical illustration, perhaps you happen to be listening to 'Thought for the Day' one morning and the speaker says something that ignites the divine spark in your brain and you become a believer. You are a born-again Christian. Who knows? It might well have happened, given how long it's been running.

My question is why some are blessed with the gift of faith and others are not. Obviously you don't have to be good to be blessed. Paul himself did some pretty nasty things to Christians before God showed him the error of his ways. And, rather more recently, we've had far too much evidence that 'devout' Catholic priests were doing evil things when they weren't actually worshipping God. Like abusing children.

So faith clearly cannot be earned. It seems entirely arbitrary. In fact it's much more pernicious than that. Isn't God meant to be fair or, to use a word deployed incessantly by priests, 'just'? If that is so, why are vast numbers of people denied a decent life reasonably free from suffering and, into the bargain, denied the gift of faith? Why are some deemed more worthy than others? Certainly it's true that many people lead exemplary lives and it's fair enough that they should be rewarded by God. But what of those who never had a chance?

What of the child born into squalor who never knew his father and whose mother is a drug addict and does not know the meaning of that most precious of all states: love? How can you express love if you have never experienced it? His only role models are other desperately deprived, unloved youngsters who teach him that the way to lead a good life – or at least a better life – is to arm yourself with a knife, steal what you need and avenge yourself on a society to which you owe nothing. He's probably never been in a church in his life, except maybe to try to steal something.

Is it his fault, when he lies bleeding to death in a gutter after a rival gang caught him on their patch, that he has not been blessed with the gift of faith? At least he might then have found comfort in the knowledge that he could be on his way to heaven? But of course he can't. He does not believe in God. He has no faith. Is that his fault? As I wrote earlier, I once asked Margaret Thatcher how she described the essence of Christianity and she said 'choice'. I wonder what choice that child had. And if God does exist, how unfair to be denied faith in him. How much more fulfilling life must be for those with an unshakeable faith.

It's true that being a devout believer carries with it some obligations – maybe modest stuff like going to church every Sunday morning or helping raise money to mend the church spire. Maybe, at the other end of the scale, giving up all the comforts of a middle-class Western lifestyle and living in some godforsaken corner of sub-Saharan Africa. Or taking their medical skills to a country torn apart by civil war and risking their lives to save injured children. Or maybe slaughtering the infidels who refuse to share their own faith. What they all have in common is the comfort of knowing they will be rewarded in the afterlife.

For lost souls like the boy dying in the gutter there is no such comfort.

My own mother was a good Christian and she took it for granted that her children would grow up in her faith. I did my best. I desperately wanted to believe too. I was enthusiastic about being confirmed in the Church in Wales when I was fourteen and I even wrote my own prayer book as part of my confirmation preparations. Then I decided that I really needed to understand the Bible, so I read it. Every last page of it from cover to cover. What a spectacular waste of time that proved to be. True there is some wonderful, poetic writing (entirely unappreciated by my young self) and some pretty good storytelling. But most of it struck me as pure nonsense with about as much relevance to the modern world as a horse and carriage has for a space traveller.

I did learn (though not from the Bible) that Christianity had bestowed some benefits on my compatriots. On our rare holiday excursions to west Wales, where there were many more sheep than humans, I was told that in the old days human urine was an important part of the process of preparing the raw wool for spinners. Locals were paid a penny a gallon – unless they were Methodists, in which case they were paid twopence. Their urine was deemed purer because they drank no alcohol.

My faith, such as it was, did not last long into adulthood. Every Sunday of my childhood I had been told why I should believe in God. He was all-powerful. He was all-loving. He was all-merciful. He heard us when we prayed to him. He answered our prayers. I was twenty-three when I began to think that we had been sold a false prospectus. My epiphany – a strange word in this context perhaps – dawned in Aberfan.

I have written earlier in this book about that terrible tragedy. It was not the greatest disaster in scale that I have ever witnessed as a journalist. One small school in one small village. I have reported on earthquakes and wars and famines around the world that have killed countless thousands. But if Stalin, one of history's greatest mass murderers, got anything right it was his claim that the death of a million is a statistic; the death of one is a tragedy. At Aberfan only 144 died. Only?

Most of them – 116 – were children. As I wrote earlier, they had been buried alive under that obscene avalanche of mud and rock that had roared down the hillside only a few minutes after they had settled down at their desks. Their fathers were nearly all miners. They had been going about their work deep beneath their school digging out yet more coal, yet more waste to add to the tip that would destroy the school. Destroy their lives. Deep though they were they heard the roar and they knew what it meant and they raced to the surface. Nothing could have prepared them for the horror of what awaited them.

To drive your spade or your pick into that foul mess knowing that it might strike the body of the human being you loved most in the world. To stand motionless holding your breath when someone thought they might have heard a child cry out. You had to wonder how could any human withstand such agony? These men seemed to me to be superhuman.

And how could God have allowed it to happen? Where was that much-vaunted mercy? What love had been shown to those blameless children? To their digging, weeping fathers atop their grave? To their mothers huddled in groups watching that awful tableau? Most were beyond tears. The tears would come later.

These were decent, hard-working, God-fearing, chapel-going people. I had known some of them for years. I could not weep for them – not then and not later when I watched their tiny coffins being carried into the chapel when there was no hope of finding another child alive. After all, I was a journalist. I was doing my job. Journalists are not meant to weep. You have to get on with the job. I hated myself for that. And I hated this God for allowing it to happen. Yet how can anyone hate a god they do not believe exists?

This was a conversation I was to have many times over the years to come with the great and the good, prime ministers and prelates and, much more importantly, with those who had every reason to hate God but did not: the bereaved mothers and fathers of Aberfan. Surely what had happened to their innocent children must have shattered their belief in an all-powerful and merciful God?

For some, it had. But for many others it was their faith that had got them through the agony and despair of their terrible grief. Of course there was anger too. The anger of the grieving fathers, experienced miners who had warned their superiors that the tip was unstable and a danger to their children. But also anger in their village at the arbitrary nature of that disaster.

I talked some years later to one mother who had lost her daughter. She told me that she had been angry with herself. How could that possibly be? In the weeks after the tragedy, she said, she had been unable to leave her house in case she saw a child walking in the village.

'Because it would bring back the memory of the child you had lost?' I asked her.

'No,' she said, 'because of the resentment I would feel towards the child's mother. Why was her daughter spared when mine was taken?'

I am sometimes asked what it is like to have been a foreign correspondent who must, inevitably, witness suffering on a scale that most can only imagine or can view only through the sanitising prism of a television screen. The awful truth is that you become hardened to it. Both hardened and angry.

Why are these men dropping bombs or firing rockets on totally innocent people trying to live decent lives? Why are these earthquake victims, who have lost everything they possess in a few minutes of disbelieving horror, now facing a future of misery, knowing their corrupt rulers will grow even richer stealing so much of the aid sent to help them?

Why are these children starving to death when there is more than enough food on this planet for everyone?

You watch a child being weighed at a medical station in the heart of a famine area. His hair is ginger, his stomach swollen, his arms and legs like sticks. You can count every rib. His mouth is distorted into a rictus grin because the flesh on his face is pulled so tight. It is the face of a very old man. You are told he is four years old and is beyond help. He will die very soon. Probably tonight. So of course you feel anger. Guilt too when you think of your own four-year-old and the life he can expect to enjoy.

You watch the relief planes fly very low over a dirt strip that is too short for them to land so they push the bags of rice out through the loading doors. Some burst, and hordes of children descend on the spilled rice, picking up single grains until they have a handful and then running off with it before the men can chase them away. And you think of the meal you will soon be eating in your hotel that night and how you complained last night because it wasn't exactly what you had ordered.

It is the single isolated incidents that stay with you. I stupidly tried to give a couple of hungry children in Ethiopia some cereal bars I had in my bag and there was an immediate riot. The men waded in, delivering hard smacks to the heads of the dozens more children who had arrived within seconds.

I stopped the car on a dirt road in Sudan on the outskirts of Khartoum to talk to a woman who was walking, very slowly, with her three emaciated children. They had been begging in the city. It was a two-hour walk from her village. Two hours there and two hours back at the end of the day. I asked how much she had raised. She thrust her bony hand into the pocket of her frayed smock and showed me. A few crumpled notes. Perhaps fifty pence. My film crew and I gave her what cash we had and our local guide shook his head in disapproval. 'That will be stolen from her when she gets to her village,' he told us.

Thirty-eight years after Aberfan, when I had long since stopped reporting on the ground and retreated to the comfort of a London studio, a group of heavily armed Islamic terrorists attacked and occupied a school in the Russian town of Beslan. They murdered some of the children and teachers and held the rest hostage. They wanted independence for their homeland of Chechnya. They warned they would kill everyone in the school if their demands were refused. Instead, the Russians sent in the police and the army. We held our breath.

And finally, after a siege lasting three days the army stormed the school. At least 334 people were killed, 186 of them children.

Throughout those three days their mothers held a vigil outside the school gates, begging the terrorists to release their children, praying to God that they would show mercy. On the second day I phoned the archbishop of Canterbury, Rowan Williams, and asked him if he would come onto the *Today* programme to reflect on what was happening. To my huge surprise he said yes.

It was brave of him. He would surely have known what questions awaited him. As one of the most respected theologians of his generation he must have devoted countless hours to those questions over the years. But scholarly examination of a theological conundrum is one thing. This was different. On that Friday morning in 2004 we were not discussing some theoretical concept, some tricky question of theology. We were talking about a group of mothers standing at their school gates as we spoke, each and every one of them suffering simultaneous agonies of hope and despair.

They didn't know whether their child was still alive and, if they were, for how much longer. It was simply not possible to imagine their anguish. So I asked Rowan: 'Where is your merciful God in Beslan?' There was a long pause – the longest pause I have ever experienced on *Today*. Years later Rowan told me he had expected the question but when it came he found he could not answer it. Eventually this brilliant and almost painfully honest man mumbled an answer. God, he suggested quietly, was in the hearts and minds of those brave teachers who had tried so hard to save the children and in the love of the mothers at the school gates. We both knew it was painfully inadequate.

Some years later I returned to the question with Rowan and, once again, I sensed the same uncertainty when I asked him how the mother of a child dying from cancer could find faith in a supposedly merciful God. He told me there was always hope … hope of healing. But how and when, I asked?

'In God's perspective,' he told me. 'In God's time, maybe within this world and maybe not. And part of the difficulty of living with faith is the knowledge which you underlined so powerfully that for some people in our time frame in this world there is not that kind of feeling. It's not there. And that's not easy to face or to live with.'

'But *you* can live with it?'

He hesitated again and then: 'Just … Just.'

I can hardly claim that my questions to Rowan were original. Ever since the Holocaust, Jewish philosophers have argued over the claim that God was put 'on trial' in Auschwitz by some of its inmates. A few years ago the BBC produced a film which imagined what that 'trial' might have been like. It was one of those programmes that justifies the existence of the BBC: immensely powerful, moving and deeply troubling. Of course it produced no answer to the question: where was God in Auschwitz? How could it? Nor did it settle the debate as to whether the trial had actually happened. The two distinguished Jewish scholars who advised the BBC at the time conceded that it was entirely plausible but it could well have been a legend.

And then, soon after the programme was broadcast, one of the great men of the last century made an extraordinary statement at a Holocaust appeal dinner. He was Elie Wiesel. No one spoke with greater moral authority than him. He had survived Auschwitz and gone on to win the Nobel Peace Prize. The Nobel Committee called him a 'messenger to mankind'. It said that through his struggle to come to terms with 'his own personal experience of total humiliation and of the utter contempt for humanity shown in Hitler's death camps' he had delivered a message 'of peace, atonement, and human dignity' to humanity.

This is what he told the *Jewish Chronicle* at that dinner: 'Why should they know what happened? I was the only one there. It happened at night; there were just three people. At the end of the trial, they used the word *chayav*, rather than "guilty". It means "He owes us something". Then we went to pray.'

Perhaps, then, one answer to the question is – as Rowan had suggested when those terrorists were holding their guns to the heads of children – God exists in the hearts of those who want him to exist. In the hearts of the Jews in Auschwitz or the mothers outside the school. My problem is that if he is omnipotent, why does he allow evil? And it won't do simply to repeat what Margaret Thatcher told me all those years ago. Of course we can choose to be evil just as we can choose to be good. But the mothers of Beslan had no choice. The Holocaust victims had no choice.

We know there was evil in the hearts of those who planned and committed those terrible deeds. Unthinkable, unimaginable evil. To murder 6 million Jews in the concentration camps. To hold a gun to the head of just one small child in a school and pull the trigger. There is no hierarchy of evil but much of it is carried out in the name of God. Perhaps most of it. Five hundred years ago Christians were burning other Christians at the stake because they were heretic. Their great sin was that they had different interpretations of the Bible. As I write, Muslims are killing Muslims because of a difference over who should have succeeded the Prophet Muhammad in the year 632.

'Where was God?' may have become a clichéd question but it is no less fundamental for that. The great philosopher David Hume summed up his answer thus: if God is all-powerful he would not allow evil to exist. If he allows evil to exist he cannot truly be all-powerful. So it surely follows that if God is not all-powerful, he is not God – and certainly not in the sense in which he is presented to us by any of the three great Abrahamic religions. Which takes me back to where I began this chapter: 'Thought for the Day'.

I am banned from presenting it not because I would almost certainly do it very badly and would most definitely annoy an awful lot of people, but because I do not believe in God. There are many thousands of potential contributors out there who are serious people with serious things to say about the greatest mysteries of our time – or maybe occasionally with offbeat reflections that might shed a little light on something that's been worrying us. But they lack the essential qualification: they don't believe in God.

Can it really be the case that non-believers have nothing to offer? No valuable experience to impart, no wisdom to share with the audience? No spiritual insights that might offer comfort? If so, that's a pretty bleak judgement on an awful lot of people in this country.

It's true that the last national census showed most of us declared ourselves to be Christians, but pollsters point out that the question was deeply flawed. It asked 'What is your religion?' That makes the assumption that we all have one, even if it's Jedi. So when YouGov did its own poll some months later it asked a different question: 'Are you religious?' This time sixty-five per cent of the respondents said no. And research published in *Church Statistics* in 2018 showed that thirty-five years ago about twelve per cent of the population went to church; now it's down to five per cent and still falling.

And yet. I've presented quite a few programmes for the BBC over the past fifty years and the one that produced the biggest response from the audience – bigger than all my other one-off programmes put together – was *Humphrys in Search of God*.

There were no fancy production gimmicks, no clever sound effects, no whooping audiences. It was just a series of conversation between me and the leaders of the three monotheistic religions in this country: Christianity, Judaism and Islam.

I knew I was taking a bit of a risk with the whole thing – not least the title. Michael Gove, who was writing a column for *The Times* in those days, created a fictional radio series: *God in Search of Humphrys*. There was plenty of that sort of thing, none of it flattering. The obvious difference between the series and my day job was that these were personal conversations, rather than an attempt at news-breaking confrontations. I was inviting the three foremost clerics in the land to convert me live on air. They must have felt a bit like the wannabe comedian in the agent's office being told: 'Go on then … make me laugh!'

And the result? Well … it's pretty clear from everything I have written in this chapter. They failed. I suppose it was obvious they would. What I found striking was the difference between Rowan Williams and Jonathan Sacks. Jonathan was combative, Rowan almost apologetic. But what stayed with me was a brief exchange I'd had with Jonathan when I first suggested to him the idea of the series. He asked me what I hoped to get out of the interview with him.

'Well,' I said, 'it's simple enough. All you've got to do is convert me … turn me into a religious Jew.'

Jonathan laid his hand on my arm and smiled rather forlornly. 'John,' he said, 'I wouldn't dream of it. You've got enough problems already.'

I thought he was joking, but I've never been quite sure.

PART 3

Today
and
Tomorrow

16

The political deal

I joined the BBC in 1967 – probably about forty years too late with the benefit of hindsight. One or two things had already changed since the very early days and not necessarily for the better. Certainly not for the staff. Stuart Hibberd, one of the first announcers, described what life was like when he signed up in the 1920s. In those days the BBC (the British Broadcasting Company as it was) was based at Savoy Hill in one of the swankiest parts of London. Here's his account of a typical day: 'We broadcast only a little in the afternoon, mainly schools and teatime music and no news bulletin was permitted to be broadcast before 7 p.m.' Importantly, Hibberd wrote, the schedule 'allowed the announcers to go across to the Savoy Hotel where we could dance if we wanted to' (having first changed from the dinner jackets worn at work) and 'an excellent supper was provided by Monsieur de Mornys, the Savoy Entertainments Manager in a private room upstairs'.

Hmm ... I'm not sure the basement canteen in New Broadcasting House quite matches the cuisine at the Savoy. Then again, making sure one's bow tie was properly knotted must have been a bit of a pain. I did once wear a dinner jacket to work – I was more than usually bleary-eyed at 3.30 a.m. and mistook it for an old blazer – and wondered why I got a slightly strange look from the security guard in reception. But I think the overnight editor was rather impressed.

In his wonderful memoir *This is London*, Hibberd puts his finger on something that's a tad more relevant to the BBC of the

317

twenty-first century than dancing at the Savoy or even the supper provided by M. de Mornys. He writes that in 1933 the BBC broadcast a report which referred to Poland 'spending thirty per cent of her revenue on armaments'. This was a hugely important story, given that a nervous Europe was struggling to recover from a terrible war that had ended only fifteen years earlier. A hungry, resentful Germany had just been taken over by a megalomaniac intent on restoring her greatness. The implications of the report were all too obvious and the Polish government protested to the BBC about it. The dispute, we are reliably informed, was 'amicably' settled. But that led to a perceptive comment in the highly respected 'Scrutator' column in the *Sunday Times*. The author was worried that the BBC might 'retract what it had reported' and he asked this:

- Should broadcasting be as free to express opinion as the printed word or is it always to be the servant of official policy in international affairs?
- Should it hold the balance between the parties in domestic politics?
- Should its leaning be towards the support of whatever government is in power or should it have a mind of its own?

Those three questions are as relevant for the BBC today as they were almost a century ago.

The BBC's motto – adopted around about the time that Stuart Hibberd was adjusting his bow tie in front of the unseeing microphone – is 'Nation Shall Speak Peace Unto Nation'. An ambitious but hopelessly quixotic aspiration. Perhaps if we were to replace the word 'peace' with 'truth'? Equally quixotic, but perhaps more relevant to the BBC's mission. I wouldn't mind seeing 'fearlessly' in there somewhere too. Again too ambitious I suppose. Individual warriors can perform acts of bravery even at risk of their own lives but that option is not available to organisations. The first and perhaps the only truly inviolable rule for any organisation is its own survival.

Obviously the BBC does not have to worry about customers in any conventional sense because its income is guaranteed through the licence fee. Nor does it have shareholders – although it now has a 'chief customer officer' to develop a 'more personal relationship with consumers, licence-fee payers and those signing in to BBC services'. Her role, she says, is 'putting the customer at the heart of what we do'. I've never understood the difference between 'consumers' and 'customers'. Isn't everyone a 'consumer'? But I'm also deeply puzzled by the notion of putting 'customers at the heart of what we do'. As opposed to what?

So the BBC is a public corporation owned by the licence payers. But clearly they can't exercise direct power over the managers. If they could we'd probably end up with fewer managers attending fewer meetings. The modern BBC does, though, have to pay heed to one supremely powerful body which determines the size of the licence fee and the future of the charter. And if the BBC is doing its job properly it will, sooner or later, find itself in conflict with that body. That body is the government.

According to Winston Churchill the BBC's darkest hour came in 1940. France had fallen to Nazi Germany. The British army had to be rescued by small boats from the beaches of Dunkirk. The threat of invasion was real. And the BBC, according to Churchill, was doing more harm than good to the nation's morale. He described it as 'the enemy at the gate'. It's hard to think of a more serious charge from a man who would ultimately lead the nation to victory. But let's balance that against something said by a man nobody outside the BBC had even heard of. His name was Noel Newsome and his job was news editor of the BBC's European Service. Here's what he told his staff: 'What we have to do … is to establish our credibility. If there is a disaster [for our forces] we broadcast it before the Germans claim it, if we possibly can. And when the tide turns and the victories are ours, we will be believed.'

Newsome was right. Credibility is everything. The real enemy at the gate is news we cannot trust. I recall reporting from Moscow at the height of the Cold War, a time when the Kremlin was relentlessly extolling the achievements of the corrupt and failing communist regime through the columns of *Pravda*. Its title was Russian for 'truth' but its content was pure propaganda. Self-defeating propaganda. When I first arrived I was puzzled by the number of people who carried empty shopping bags everywhere they went. Eventually I was told by my guide (foreign journalists weren't allowed to go anywhere without an official guide) that almost nobody left home without one – just in case they happened to spot a shop that happened to have something on sale that they needed. Such as food.

Day after day I watched shivering Russians standing in endless queues hoping that the shop would not have run out of bread before they got to the counter. Some were holding a copy of *Pravda*, which breathlessly reported that, yet again, the USSR had broken all records for grain production. Small wonder they never believed a word they were told. Newsome understood what Churchill did not – at least seemingly not at that stage in the war. If the people are lied to once they will not believe you the next time when you may be telling the truth. And there is a profound difference between sowing confusion in the minds of the enemy about, say, an imminent invasion and lying to your own people to improve morale. Apart from anything else, it doesn't work.

What did work was Newsome's approach. In 1943, four years into the Second World war, the great British historian G. M. Young said the BBC's news broadcasts had given it 'a standing without rival on the European Continent'. It may seem such an obvious point to make but it bears repeating often and forcefully. If the BBC is not trusted it is nothing.

So the idea of being the 'servant of official policy' in international affairs or anything else for that matter is antithetical to everything the BBC stands for. Yet history tells us that governments do not trust the BBC when its own interests are at stake. There have been endless occasions since its birth when the BBC has been called to account for daring to question government policy in time of crisis or taking a particular stand on foreign affairs. In the 1930s there were questions in the House complaining about our coverage of Spanish politics which led to the devastating civil war and the rise of General Franco. The BBC was accused of 'red bias'.

In the 1950s, during the Suez Crisis the prime minister Anthony Eden accused the BBC of 'giving comfort to the enemy'. When Harold Wilson was fighting the general election in 1970 he repeatedly harangued the director general of the BBC for allowing programmes to present him in an unfavourable light. The programmes included not only the usual suspects like *Panorama* but also *Woman's Hour* and, rather bizarrely, *Sportsnight*.

In the 1980s Norman Tebbit, chairman of the Conservative Party at the time, produced a detailed and unfavourable analysis of the BBC's reporting of the American air-force raids on Libya. In the 1990s John Simpson was fiercely criticised for his supposedly 'biased reports' about the impact of NATO bombing on Belgrade. And this century the BBC came under sustained attack from some of the most senior figures in the Labour government for allegedly acting as 'a friend of Baghdad' in our reporting of the Iraq War.

Richard Sambrook was the director of News at the centre of the row over the BBC's coverage of the Iraq dossier which I wrote about in an earlier chapter. He makes the point that it's the job of the BBC to 'shine light in dark places'. The use of intelligence by the Blair government in the run-up to the war was a very dark place indeed. Long after the crisis was over Sambrook talked about it with Charlotte Higgins of the *Guardian*:

I think the BBC could have done it in a different way and in hindsight I regret that we didn't manage it properly. But if the BBC says to the government that fundamentally there is rot at the core here, that's a big problem. And the BBC has to be very, very careful, because it is in the end dependent on a political deal to exist … You can only do so if you have the courage of your convictions – if you have done your journalism properly – and if you are properly able to weigh up the consequences of your actions. If the BBC is weak, or lacking in confidence, or isn't sure about its editorial judgements and methods, then it runs the risk of being pushed around … of losing independence in all but name.

One of the biggest stories of 2013 had been delivered by a former American CIA man, Edward Snowden. Snowden became a computer programmer for the National Security Agency in the States and had access to a vast databank containing the names and whereabouts of thousands of American spies. He stole the lot. It was the biggest leak of top-secret documents in history. He did it, he says, because he was worried about the extent to which intelligence agencies and Internet companies were spying on countless millions of people around the world. Some called him a hero, some a traitor. But whatever the verdict on him personally, his action had exactly the effect he had hoped for. He handed the computer files to the *Washington Post* and the *Guardian*, both of which gave them massive coverage in the weeks and months to come. Snowden himself went into hiding in Russia and remains there to this day.

But what if he had taken his story to the BBC, to *Newsnight* or *Panorama* perhaps? How would we have dealt with it? Could we have done what the *Guardian* did? That's a question Sambrook has often asked himself and his answer is intriguing:

No. No, they couldn't … They might have been able to do a piece at a meta level, a headline level, but they could not have done what the *Guardian* did with Snowden. I find it uncomfortable to say that, but it's the truth.

So what does that tell us about the BBC? Here's what Sambrook says: 'It tells you that in the end there is a limit to its independence – some would call that public accountability. It is a wonderful news organisation. It does fantastic journalism every day. But there is a limit to it. And I think in the end that was part of a miscalculation in the Kelly story. We thought we were genuinely independent. And we weren't.'

So there is a thread of events here that suggests that the BBC's independence, which it prizes and fights to defend in its daily decision-making, is always potentially under threat – especially when the government of the day is coming under pressure on different fronts.

The struggling Labour government of the 1970s wanted to 'do something' about the BBC and Cabinet records show it considered getting rid of the licence fee and making its financing part of general government expenditure. That would effectively turn it into a state broadcaster.

But even confident governments with a solid majority facing a weak opposition have sometimes felt the urge to take on the BBC. As its official historian Jean Seaton records, the challenge from the Conservative administration elected in 1979 and by a large majority in 1983, was fundamental:

> For the first time, the legitimacy of BBC values as well as their practice was directly contested. The government in the short term calmed licence-fee negotiations by taking the 'permanent revolution' out of them. But it began to articulate a series of arguments: that the licence fee was a state handout inimical to free expression; that funding by advertising and greater 'choice' between channels would be more democratic; that impartial news was a deception and 'responsible national interest' a better value; that to articulate opposing views was biased and sometimes treacherous; that the BBC was part of an establishment that needed to be re-engineered.

History tends to repeat itself. A generation later the question of the licence fee returned to haunt the BBC. It had made what turned out to be a devil's pact with the government. In return for a new licence-fee settlement and charter renewal, which would last until 2027, it agreed to take responsibility from 2020 for free licence fees for people over the age of seventy-five. The bill – roughly £750 million – had been paid out of government funds. In 2019 the BBC announced it could not afford to pay it and the pensioners would have to cough up – or, at least, those who were not receiving pension credit. They might as well have announced that all pensioners should be rounded up, carted off to Dover and shipped out to the Falkland Islands. The country went ballistic.

After months of angry newspaper campaigns led by some of the best-loved (ageing) celebrities in the land, the director general Tony Hall appeared before a select committee of MPs – a pretty heated appearance. Hall raised a few eyebrows when he acknowledged that a great deal might change under the new charter agreement. He raised the possibility of the BBC switching from the licence fee to a voluntary subscription model – something like the Netflix arrangement – and accepted that it would be 'very very different to the sort of BBC you have now because you would be giving subscribers what they want, not the breadth of the population'. As for his own views on that, he said: 'I would argue that that's the wrong model for supporting the BBC.'

He could have gone much further, in my view. He could have said that such an agreement would be the death of the BBC as we understand it today. The licence fee is more than just a funding model. It's entirely possible that subscription would enable the BBC to continue doing much of what it has always done. But not everything. The BBC might very well survive – but it would be a very different BBC.

All newspapers and media organisations strive to be part of the society on which they report. Apart from anything else it's good for business. But the BBC has a problem in this regard. Unlike its commercial competition, it is seen as part of the establishment – a bit like the Church. Every so often the Church will make headlines for a day or two with, say, a controversial report claiming that the government is allowing children to suffer because it cares about the rich more than the poor. Or maybe the latest archbishop will want to prove his peace-loving credentials by criticising the nation's warlike policies. Whatever it is, the government makes either sympathetic or slightly irritated noises and takes not the blindest bit of notice. The relationship with the BBC is rather more complicated and potentially much more problematic.

James Harding discovered that the hard way. For nearly five years he was the editor of *The Times*, the newspaper that had once been at the nexus of power in this country. A century ago there would have been little difference between the august *Times* and the equally stately BBC. Both were run by upper-class gents who'd been educated at the same schools and Oxbridge colleges, dined at the same clubs and were pretty much indistinguishable from each other. They were part of the establishment, even though that word was not yet commonly used to describe the ruling elite. And then Rupert Murdoch – the 'Dirty Digger', the scourge of the old-boy network – arrived on the scene. Murdoch took over the *News of the World*, then the *Sun* and eventually, in 1981, *The Times* and *Sunday Times*.

He knew exactly what relationship should exist between him and the political leaders. He was the boss and he called the shots. He also knew what he wanted from his editors. Harding either could not or would not provide it and, for whatever reason, Murdoch moved against him. As Harding put it at the time: 'If the proprietor has a different view from his editor it's not the proprietor who has to leave.' So Harding got the sack and joined the BBC.

The world he was joining might have dealt in the same commodity as the world he was leaving – news – but it had a very different relationship with the people in power. If a newspaper has a strong proprietor with an ego to match and he broadly approves of what the government is doing, everything is hunky-dory. If the government steps out of line it can expect trouble. In the bad old days of Fleet Street the tale was often told of Kelvin MacKenzie, the editor of the *Sun* at a time when it sold far more copies than any other paper in the land – so many that he didn't care whom he upset. Neither did Murdoch. It was a Tory paper – a huge fan of Margaret Thatcher at her union-bashing best. MacKenzie was not so fond of her successor John Major. He enjoyed telling the story of how Major phoned him the day he decided Britain had to leave the European exchange rate mechanism and asked him how his paper was going to report the story the following day. This, says MacKenzie, was his reply: 'Prime Minister, I have on my desk a very large bucket of shit, which I am about to pour all over you.'

I doubt there are too many BBC editors who have had similar conversations with the leader of Her Majesty's Government over the years.

The relationship between the BBC and the newspaper proprietors has always been tricky. Most of them have long resented what they regard as the overweening ambitions of the BBC. Under Paul Dacre the *Mail* took the view that the BBC was a brilliant organisation – so long as it stuck to a couple of TV channels and Radio 4. There were people in Broadcasting House who quietly agreed with him.

Things got nastier when the digital revolution began to change the world of journalism. Papers like *The Times* and the *Mail* watched with growing frustration as the BBC began setting up its enormously successful websites and, as they saw it, creaming off vast numbers of readers and damaging their commercial interests. They argued that it was using public funds to compete in a commercial market. It was not a level playing field. Again, they had a point. But the real enemy has been the explosion of social media. The circulation of all the newspapers is in a downward spiral and the frightening success or, if you prefer, sheer greed of YouTube, Facebook and the like are largely to blame.

Much of their content consists of material they have taken from newspapers and magazines. The papers have always argued that they should pay to use it. After all, the reporters who provided the stories had to be paid. The likes of Mark Zuckerberg claimed from the start that they should not. They argued that they were mere platforms and not publishers – which is nonsense. Even more damaging has been the effect of social media on newspapers' revenue from advertising, their biggest source of income. They simply cannot compete. YouTube is by far the largest video-sharing platform. By early 2019 more than 400 hours of video were being uploaded to the site every minute. Its target in terms of viewing those clips was set at a billion hours a day. By the time you read these words it may well have passed that target.

When Harding took over BBC News he seemed a bit baffled by the corporate bureaucracy. If you run a newspaper, editorial meetings are a vital part of the day – but the shorter and fewer the better. If you run anything in the BBC (or even if you don't but hope to one day) meetings are an end in themselves.

I once knew the chief executive of one of the early digital technology companies. It did brilliantly for a few years and then sales started dropping sharply. He announced that all meetings were to be cancelled for a month except those directly involving customers. During that month sales bounced back. The problem with doing something similar in the BBC, say the cynics, is that a third of the bosses might have nothing to do so they'd have to be sacked. Harding abhorred the meetings culture.

More important even than that, he had to cope with keeping the politicians sweet almost as much as he worried about giving the audiences what they wanted. There has always been a sense of entitlement on the part of certain senior politicians. Some believe it is perfectly proper that they should try to influence the content of news programmes – even their running orders – and the BBC should listen to what they say. It simply would not occur to them to try the same approach with other media organisations. They wouldn't dare.

There was a blatant example of that in the general-election campaign of 2015. With just over a week to go before polling day David Cameron's director of information, Craig Oliver, wrote to the BBC warning that there would be a 'major complaint' from Number 10 if BBC news bulletins did not make a Conservative promise on taxes their lead political story the following morning. The BBC did not reply. Oliver must have known the inappropriateness of his warning – he had been the editor of the BBC's *Ten O'Clock News* before he went to Number 10. When Cameron resigned he gave him a knighthood.

Mostly the BBC has been pretty robust at dealing with that sort of thing and with the day-to-day political pressure. At an operational level on a programme like *Today* it tends to come from relatively junior figures such as 'SPADs', special advisers to ministers and senior MPs. If they're trying it on they will demand that their boss get the 8.10 interview, insist that there must be no question of taking part in a discussion with the opposition and (if they're very new to the game) even ask for the questions in advance. Not that any self-respecting interviewer has such a list. Usually the next question depends on the previous answer – or at least it should.

Not all politicians rely on assistants to do their dirty work for them. Paddy Ashdown was one of those who liked to fight his own battles. Almost literally on one occasion. I remember one morning when he burst into the *Today* editor's office during the news break, so angry that I thought he was going to rip the editor's head off the way he'd been trained to do when he was in the Special Boat Service in his youth. His language would have made a drunken squaddie blush. It was all rather frightening but he calmed down eventually. Some misunderstanding, apparently, as to whether he'd actually been booked for the slot he thought he'd been booked for. It took the editor a while to recover.

Mostly relations between the poor bloody infantry who man the phones day and night on a programme like *Today* and their Westminster equivalents are reasonably cordial. They have their jobs to do and they get on with it. It's inevitable that there will be clashes. The reason the politician will refuse to do an interview is often because he's in trouble – which is precisely the reason we think he should do it. And often vice versa. He wants to boast when things are going well. We tend to be less impressed. It all becomes more serious when the integrity of the government is being called into question. The invasion of Iraq was easily the gravest example of that during my years at the BBC.

Unlike commercial news operations the BBC has a unique institutional position at the intersection of politics and journalism. If it tries to break free of those bounds, or puts a foot wrong in the process, then the damage can be real and lasting. Such crises have become an inevitable part of the BBC's history. Three out of the last seven directors general have lost their jobs: Alasdair Milne in 1987, after political pressure from the Conservative government, Greg Dyke, and George Entwistle. What history tells us is that when the BBC is under real political pressure or is facing a dangerous clamour in the press, it will put its own survival ahead of any consideration of the impact on its employees, even those at the very top.

If I'd had to put money on the first woman in the BBC's long history to become director general I'd have had not a moment's hesitation: Helen Boaden. She rose through the ranks to become the controller of Radio 4 and then the director of BBC News. She was thoughtful, clever, articulate, charming and ambitious. But she had the fatal misfortune to be running News during the Savile affair and was hung out to dry. She and her colleagues were subjected to the multimillion-pound investigation I mentioned earlier in the full glare of publicity with the chairman of the BBC, Lord Patten, even likening it to the Leveson Inquiry into phone hacking. Of course, as we've seen, the central charge – that the BBC had conspired to drop the investigation into Savile in order to run a tribute programme – was proved to be nonsense. But by then it was too late, or at least it didn't matter. The BBC had survived, at the cost of terrible reputational damage to some of its staff. As she put it in her leaving speech: 'Like all institutions, there is a chip of ice at the BBC's heart.'

Survival is not a dishonourable ambition: the BBC is, after all, a mighty force for good. Our democracy needs it. But the danger is that it survives by making too many cosy compacts with the establishment, the better to ensure its future. Where to strike the balance between 'safe' and edgier journalism? Robert Peston, steeped in the newspaper world, felt strongly after his years as the BBC's economics editor that the BBC was a risk-averse organisation: 'When the BBC wants people who can break stories it has to look to recruit from outside. When the BBC is training young journalists, it starts by telling them about the regulatory restraints: it starts with the rules and says: "Don't you dare break them."'

The BBC's relationship with the royal family is a good example of how it prefers not to challenge certain established institutions. Here's an illustration. In early December 2018, Kensington Palace contacted our 'royal liaison officer' (yes, there really is such a post) about a BBC News Online article that carried artwork from a far-right website depicting Prince Harry with a gun to his head and some highly stylised blood behind him. This sounds alarming and it was: the report was the result of a long investigation by BBC News which led to three men being arrested. The BBC felt it was important for the audience to understand the kind of shocking and violent material that the men had produced. It tried to include the image of the prince in a responsible way, by informing the audience in the top paragraphs of the story about the nature of the content. There was another reference in the story to the men engaging in racism and misogyny and glorifying violence and cruelty. Before readers could see the image of Harry there was a warning that one of the violent images to which the article referred would be shown.

The BBC has a team of editorial policy advisers who had cleared the image for publication, but when the word from the palace reached the director general, who happened to be abroad at the time, he ordered the image to be removed. He hoped, I suppose, that because the BBC had done its bit the row would go away. But it didn't. Instead, Kensington Palace pushed its case and wrote to complain officially about the use of the picture. This presented a peculiar problem for the BBC. The News division stood firmly behind the use of its picture. So did the director of editorial policy. In the end, in an episode redolent of the comedy programme *W1A*, Lord Hall had to agree that BBC News should send a letter explaining that it was right to use the image, even though it had in fact been taken down.

The fact is, the BBC treads very carefully in its relations with the royal family – far too carefully in my (admittedly republican) view. My father could never see the point of the monarchy and, as the proverb goes, the apple never falls far from the tree. So maybe I have him to blame for my reaction to *Today's* triumphal announcement that Prince Harry, no less, was to be one of our 'guest editors' in 2018.

That's fine, I said grumpily, just so long as we get to ask him some proper questions and don't allow him to use the programme as a PR exercise for himself and his family. Nobody took a blind bit of notice of me. He did exactly that, of course, and the programme was a great success. By which I mean that the audience loved it and so did the newspapers. So I was wrong – and I remain grumpy to this day.

There was, at least for me, one minor consolation some months later: a royal bid that failed to strike gold. Sarah Sands was our editor at the time and, in lots of ways, a brilliant one. We happen to share an interest in trees and she was very keen that I should interview Prince Charles about them. At least that was the ostensible reason. She wanted him on the programme because it's good box office. And this was as good a ruse as any. How could he refuse to do an interview about such an important subject that lies so close to his nature-loving heart? Quite easily, as it turned out. He's pretty savvy when it comes to the media and, try as she might, Sarah never did manage to persuade his minders that I would stick strictly to the script. Which I wouldn't have.

Let's state the obvious. The Queen herself does a good job and has done for a very long time and maybe King Charles will too. But that's not the point. The BBC should not treat the whole royal-family apparatus as though it is beyond criticism. We should treat them with respect – but not with kid gloves. It's a relatively small example of the nature of the BBC's relationship with the establishment but, I think, a revealing one.

On any given day, on any given issue, the BBC must decide whether to stand or fight or just give in when it feels it is being challenged by powerful interests. Sometimes it does both. In 2014 the BBC used a helicopter to film a police raid on the home of Sir Cliff Richard. He was not there at the time. He was deeply upset and later won substantial damages from the BBC. The Home Affairs Select Committee questioned the BBC director general Tony Hall about it. One MP suggested it had been 'OTT'. Lord Hall said: 'Looking at the output was it used disproportion-ately? No … It was a proper story for us to cover, in the right matter, proportionately, which I think is what we did. I wasn't surprised the police didn't ask us not to broadcast the story.'

Rightly or wrongly it was a classic example of the man in charge defending his news team. The BBC was standing up for itself.

Four years later, however, he told MPs the coverage had indeed been over the top: 'I think the helicopter was overdoing it … it was something to report but down the bulletin,' he said.

His fleetness of foot went unnoticed by the press, and the later position was almost certainly the right one to adopt. But it shows that to survive at the top of the BBC, and for the BBC itself to survive, the DG has to make editorial judgements within the context of not just the attention of the licence-fee payers, but politicians too. There is governmental machinery that needs oiling simply because it is the BBC that is involved, rather than any other media organisation. This breeds a certain caution.

*   *   *

The BBC was barely out of its nappies when it faced the first real test of its independence. It was 1926 and the general strike was threatening to bring the nation to its knees. The man charged with protecting the economy was the Chancellor of the Exchequer, a certain Winston Churchill. If any politician recognised the importance of connecting with the masses by delivering the right message speedily and directly into the home of the citizen, it was Churchill. He recognised that the fledgling BBC was capable of influencing its audience in a way that newspapers could not – even those few that just about managed to keep printing during the nine days that the strike lasted. When the *Daily Express* thundered its opinions in big, black headlines everyone knew they were the views of its owner Lord Beaverbrook. Almost all the press lords were, like him, rich and powerful men with a vested interest in the outcome of whatever it was they were reporting. The BBC was different.

Churchill had recognised as much when he was Home Secretary. That's why, according to John Reith who was the BBC's managing director, he 'wanted to commandeer the BBC' for the duration of the strike. The prime minister Stanley Baldwin, who could see the value of the BBC being seen to be independent but in truth having Reith on his side, refused.

For the first time in its short history the BBC broadcast its own news bulletins three times a day during the strike and the BBC's official history notes that Reith himself vetted almost all of them. He also dealt with the 'political aspects' of the strike as well. He refused a request by the archbishop of Canterbury to appeal for an end to it but he did allow the reporting of statements from the TUC to be broadcast.

Even more controversially, he helped Baldwin to write a speech to the nation, which was delivered from Baldwin's own home in Westminster. Hardly the action of a truly independent BBC – not least because Reith coached the prime minister in what he should say and how he should say it. And when the leader of the opposition, Ramsay MacDonald, asked for a right to reply Reith referred his request to Baldwin. Baldwin said he did not think it would be a good idea and Reith, apparently reluctantly, refused the request. A curious way for him to demonstrate impartiality, you might think, but it paid off. The day before the strike ended Baldwin ruled that the BBC should remain independent. Churchill summed up his view of that in one word: 'Monstrous.' But when the strike was called off, it was Reith who wrote a homily about it which ended with Blake's poem 'Jerusalem'. As the final words were read an orchestra swelled up in the background.

Later, Reith mused on whether he should have let Churchill get his way and commandeer the BBC but he concluded 'it would have been better for me, worse for the BBC and worse for the country'. He believed that it would destroy the BBC's reputation for independence and impartiality and that his victory would signal to the country that there was a fundamental difference – a clear dividing line – between being the *national* broadcaster and the *state* broadcaster. But Reith was nothing if not a canny operator. In her account of those early days Charlotte Higgins wrote: 'The prime minister, the reassuring, tweed-clad figure of Stanley Baldwin, adopted a subtler position than Churchill, his chancellor. A Cabinet meeting on 11 May, according to Reith's diary, took the view that the government should be able to say "that they did not commandeer [the BBC], but they know that they can trust us not to be really impartial". In other words, it was seen that there were advantages in retaining at least the appearance of an independent BBC.'

And Reith had his critics – even among his own senior staff. Hilda Matheson was the first director of Talks at the BBC. She chose her words carefully: 'It is not suggested that the weight of the BBC was not thrown preponderatingly on the side of authority; the important point, for the social historian, is that a degree of independence and impartiality could be preserved at all.'

More forceful was Rex Lambert, the first editor of the broadcasting periodical the *Listener*: 'I have heard Sir John Reith many times express his pride in the part played by the BBC in supplying the public with "unbiased" news during the strike. But Labour circles received these boasts with scepticism; the only point of general agreement being that the cessation of newspapers during the strike had given broadcasting its first big opportunity of showing what it could do to influence a steady public opinion in a crisis.'

So both Matheson and Lambert, in their different ways, had their doubts about the BBC's ability ever to be truly impartial. They recognised that there was a difference between impartiality and independence. What Reith's approach had done was help pave the way for the BBC's transformation, just months later, from the British Broadcasting Company to a public service corporation – with a mission 'to inform, educate, and entertain'. When the BBC was granted a new royal charter ninety years later it repeated those three obligations but added another promise: 'To act in the public interest, serving all audiences with impartial, high-quality and distinctive media content and services.'

So it's worth returning to those three questions posed in *The Times* in light of how the BBC has evolved in the ninety years since they were first asked.

First, should the BBC 'be as free to express opinion as the printed word or is it always to be the servant of official policy in international affairs?'

There is, as I say, a constant tension with politicians over the BBC's reporting. It's a necessary tension. Neither side should be overly strong or weak in the tug of war between politicians and journalists, which is an essential part of democracy. But if the BBC's independence sometimes falls short of what it might hope for, what about its commitment to impartiality? There is a clear difference between the two. Most journalists can never be entirely independent of their financial backers – whether those backers be the proprietor of their newspaper or the BBC licence payers – but as far as the BBC is concerned its journalism must be entirely impartial. So the answer to the question of whether the BBC should be free to express opinion is obviously no – for the very good reason that the BBC, unlike the 'printed word', does not have its own opinions. How could it? Whose opinions would they be? The view of the individual correspondent on whatever story they happened to be covering, or some corporate view on the world in general handed down from on high? In fact, various editors in radio and television have flirted over the years with the idea of their programme having the equivalent of a newspaper's leading article. We tried it out in the 1980s on the *Nine O'Clock News* with Gerald Priestland.

Gerald was about the last of a dying breed: one of those very distinguished old-school correspondents (Charterhouse in his case) whose appearance and manner were more that of a high-court judge or diocesan bishop than cynical old hack. If Gerald told you something it would not occur to you that he might be exaggerating for the sake of a headline, let alone inventing it to stand up his story. You believed him. So we sent him off around the world to give us his views on everything from the virtues of democracy to the existence of God or the culinary merits of fish and chips. He was never less than interesting but there was some-thing about it that didn't feel right. It became obvious pretty quickly what that was. BBC News is not, cannot be and never should be a vehicle for its journalists to give the audience their opinions. Their analysis: certainly. But not their opinions. That must be left to the people we interview or invite to present authored documentaries or commentaries clearly labelled as personal viewpoints.

The second question raised by *The Times* in 1926 was whether the BBC should 'hold the balance between the parties in domes-tic politics'. And the answer is no. It should not even hold a view as between the parties. Too purist? I don't think so. Many of us in the News division were uneasy at the fuss made over the appear-ance of Nick Griffin, the leader of the British National Party (BNP) on *Question Time* in 2009.

I happen to find Griffin and his views repugnant. I shared the views of the then Home Secretary Alan Johnson that the BNP was a 'foul and despicable' party and so, I'm pretty confident, did the vast majority of BBC staff. So what? There are others who approve of it. The BBC does not hold the balance: it tries to establish where the balance of public opinion lies. A party with a demonstrably large level of support will get more airtime during elections than one with a much smaller level. It really is that simple. Griffin had a right to make his case on *Question Time* and he did. And it backfired on him. Good.

The last *Times* question is the trickiest. It is an 'either/or': should the BBC lean towards the support of the government in power or should it have a mind of its own? That first bit is easy. Of course it should not 'support' the government. There might possibly be an exception if it were, for instance, a government of national unity formed in wartime when the security of the nation was at risk. Even then the BBC would have to be free to broadcast views critical of the government. But 'a mind of its own'? If that means refusing to be dictated to by the government in power, then the question answers itself.

But does the BBC actually have a mind of its own? It is a huge news machine, bigger now than ever. It has an enormous number of different outlets from local radio to the World Service, the *Today* programme to *Newsnight*. Obviously some have vastly bigger budgets than others, but none of them is so well resourced that it can operate independently of the central machine. They must all depend on it to a greater or lesser degree.

By and large editors are allowed to edit – just so long as they realise they are part of the machine. It's a machine that makes decisions influenced, if only subconsciously, by what it has done in the past. It can too often be willing to settle for the status quo, settling into the same lines of thought. This, even more perhaps than the charges of overt liberalism that are laid at the BBC's door, may explain why sometimes it fails so badly to spot a change in the nation's mood in hugely important areas. As we've seen, immigration was one of them. Euroscepticism was another. It's no coincidence that they are closely linked.

Financial Times

26 January 2012

There is a wide streak of sentimentality running through old journalists. They tend to go all misty-eyed when they describe the Linotype machines in the printing room spewing out their slugs of hot metal and the building shuddering slightly when the presses started up. Those were the days, eh? When men were men (women need not apply) and it took real skill and a lifetime's experience to compose a new front page on the stone with the deadline minutes away. Not like these days when any ten-year-old can do it with fifty quid's worth of software and a bog-standard laptop.

What gets lost in the nostalgia fest is that the ten-year-old's effort may actually look rather good and a modern newspaper makes its hot metal counterpart seem as enticing as a spam sandwich. As with newspapers, so with broadcasting.

When I left print journalism to join the BBC in the 1960s, television newsrooms were staffed almost entirely by refugees from newspapers – and how we chortled at the quaint old ways of our colleagues left behind. We were the future. Why would anyone want news that was at least twelve hours old when we could deliver it live? What a contrast between the old printing room where the soles of your shoes stuck to a century of spilled ink on the floor and the surgical spotlessness of the TV studio.

Look at these state-of-the-art cameras you sad old hacks and weep in frustration. Gawp at the BBC's iconic buildings: the majestic prow of Broadcasting House, its statues of Prospero and Ariel created by the great Eric Gill as God and Man. No false modesty here. Or Bush House: marble-pillared and porticoed. Even the unlovely Television Centre, dominating the wastelands of White City and flaunting the technology that we really thought had the papers licked. We were at the cutting edge.

Well … up to a point.

We were wrong when we thought we would kill off the newspapers. They adapted to meet our threat. If they could not beat us on speed of news delivery they could – and did – slaughter us on the features pages and in the opinion columns. They chose a battleground on which the national broadcaster, shackled by guidelines that demanded impartiality and balance over polemic and opinion, could not compete.

The real threat to newspapers turned out to be not television, but the Internet: too much information and opinion too freely available to too many people. With a bit of luck, deep pockets and strong nerves some of the papers will eventually make it work for them, but the Internet threatens broadcasters too.

The danger will come if viewers no longer see any value in television channels. You hear people saying: 'I'm a Radio 4 listener'. You tend not to hear them say: 'I'm a BBC1 viewer'. I asked a group of bright sixth-formers at a school in Birmingham what television they watched and they said they didn't. They watch their computers instead.

The BBC points out that the death of family viewing has been much exaggerated and we still settle down happily enough in the living room to watch Strictly *or* Sherlock *at the weekend. Perhaps, but we probably tend to overestimate the short-term effects of new technology and underestimate the long-term effects. Who knew the iPlayer would become this popular? And who knows what effect IPTV (Internet Protocol TV) will have? At the very least, it will test to the limit the ingenuity of the channel bosses.*

17

Shrivelled clickbait droppings

You might think that a reporter's job spec is pretty simple: it's to find out what is happening and tell the audience in as accurate, straightforward and interesting a way as possible. And, ideally be the first to find out. You would be right about that. That's how it was when the gentleman from *The Times* was despatched to the Crimea to report on the Battle of Balaclava and the Charge of the Light Brigade, and it is still so. Technology may have changed a bit in the intervening century and a half, but the principles remain the same.

The BBC has expanded enormously in my half-century with the organisation. It now has the largest broadcast news operation in the world. It produces hundreds of hours of output every day and provides news and current-affairs programmes to the BBC's five national radio stations in the UK, three of its digital radio stations and its four main television channels (if you include BBC3 which is now online). It has a twenty-four-hour news channel, a global TV news channel, and a vast News Online site. The BBC World Service broadcasts in more than forty languages. The BBC's justification for this enormous expansion is that if it doesn't piece together a big enough audience on all its different platforms it might soon become a legacy broadcaster with a dwindling reach. The licence fee would be doomed.

The BBC, inevitably, has a word for the people they need: replenishers. The days have long gone when it could rely on BBC1 or Radio 4 to bring in the audience. On top of that, it has to meet the needs of those who rely on podcasts and vodcasts and an iPlayer and digital television stations and News Online. And probably news on the fridge as well before long. It has no choice. Even the BBC's sternest critics concede that when times change the BBC must change with it.

I can vividly remember as a child how we huddled around the enormous mahogany wireless with its glowing valves, waiting for the announcer to inform us in his calm and perfectly enunciated Queen's English what was happening in the world. It was from the Home Service in 1956 that my parents and I learned that HMS *Hermes*, one of the mightiest aircraft carriers in the Royal Navy, had set sail for Suez carrying, among others, my older brother, Able Seaman Graham Humphreys. It was a sombre moment for us. We were not to know in those scary days that the Suez crisis would end in an undignified withdrawal rather than all-out war and *Hermes* would return without a shot being fired at her.

When we listened to the BBC news it might have been the Queen herself addressing us for all the respect we accorded it – except, of course, that back then no mere woman could possibly be considered to possess the necessary gravitas for so responsible a task. Such was our blind trust that if it was on the wireless it followed that it must be true. In the calm, measured tones of the BBC bulletins there was an authority that commanded respect. And anyway there was no alternative. The BBC had no competition. ITV had yet to be born and it was to be a few generations later before children could retreat to their bedrooms with their smartphones to choose between endless hardcore pornography and trying to start the Third World War by hacking into the Pentagon's control centre.

In truth, though, the rot had begun to set in before I was out of my teens.

No self-respecting youngster would have admitted to listening to 'Sing Something Simple' on *The Light Programme* once Radio Luxembourg had started offering an alternative – even if it was a pretty crackly one. And then the pirates arrived. In 1964 a scruffy old freighter with an enormous mast hove up off the coast of Essex and started broadcasting songs young people really wanted to listen to with DJs who made BBC announcers and presenters sound as though they still wore dinner jackets and black ties. The new young DJs – Tony Blackburn, John Peel, Kenny Everett and many others – were cool. Within a few years there were a dozen pirate radio stations out there broadcasting to 15 million young people. The BBC had to react. It tried getting the authorities to force the pirates off the air but never stood a chance. Within three years of the first disc being spun on Radio Caroline it acknowledged the old maxim that if you can't beat 'em, join 'em.

We now know, of course, how piffling was the threat from pirate radio compared to what was beginning to stir in the breasts of a handful of technical geniuses and would change the world before the century was out – the digital revolution.

I wrote earlier about the massive benefits of digital technology, but it brought a whole new set of challenges with it. Sure, the BBC can set up a very sophisticated studio in the back of a van when they would have needed half a dozen big trucks only a generation ago, but so can anyone else. In 1964 the pirates needed a ship to broadcast from. Now all anyone needs is a laptop. In the 1970s we needed a satellite to send pictures across the Atlantic. Now we need a smartphone. Then we had three channels. Now we have more than we can count. That's one of the reasons that the BBC has to do an awful lot with the money at its disposal. It can deliver so much output only by sharing material between its different programmes and services. In other words, it is resourced to hit an average. A high average perhaps but an average nonetheless. It means that *Today*, the flagship of the airwaves, has two overnight producers. Two! It is run on a shoestring, and not a very robust one at that. As I write *The World Tonight* team is being 'merged' with *Newshour* on the World Service. *Newsnight*, before it got into near-terminal trouble with the sex-abuse allegation that ended up bringing down the DG, had been starved of resources. That's one of the reasons it had to work with an outside investigations team that ended up getting the story so badly wrong. One editor of the main evening news says he always knew that when he'd had a good day, the opposition BBC News Channel must have had a bad day. And vice versa. In other words, there simply weren't enough resources to go around.

It was probably inevitable that the first victim of all this would be individuality. News – especially television news – has been homogenised. For more than half a century the flagship of BBC TV news output was the *Nine O'Clock News*, later to become the *Ten O'Clock*. It was more than just a bulletin: it was a programme with its own editor and presenters and unique status and style. In 1984 the *Six O'Clock News* was also expanded to a full half-hour and became a rival to the *Nine*, also with its own unique character. Then, in 1997, News 24 was launched. For the first time the BBC had its own television news service broadcasting around the clock. Its viewing figures were dismal. There was much grumbling about the resources devoted to a service that virtually nobody watched and a few brave bosses began to suggest it was time to put it out of its misery. The opposite happened.

In 2005, News 24 (soon to become the News Channel) was put at the centre of the output rather than the *Nine* or the *Six*. The separate editorships of the *One* and the *Six* were abolished, with the *One* going to the controller of the News Channel and the *Six* to the editor of the *Ten*. And then, a year later, *News at Ten* was simulcast on News 24, soon to be followed by the *One* and the *Six*. The homogenisation was complete and pretty soon News Channel presenters began appearing on BBC1, especially at weekends. This was not exactly the seven-days-a-week operation led by the flagship evening news programme that John Birt had envisaged. Soon the coverage was being led by the demands of the 'wheel' and not by the more analytical bulletins of old.

The role of reporters and correspondents has changed out of all recognition too. It's only just possible to remember an era before it was ordained that a television reporter's main function was to pop up in a news bulletin and tell the audience in a 'live feed' what they've already just told them in their report while waving their arms around in a meaningful way.

Which is not to say they are incapable of doing a good job. Quite the opposite. The standard of reporting is as high as it has ever been.

So a lot has happened to television news over a relatively short period – and I suspect we ain't seen nothing yet. It's becoming vanishingly rare to find a teenager who 'consumes' (no escaping that dreadful word I fear) his or her news while they're sitting in the living room watching television. What they do instead is watch snippets or brief reports on YouTube or other social media platforms. And increasingly they are being fed by small, independent outfits rather than the great broadcasting corporations. The captains of broadcast news are well aware of this and it's giving them many sleepless nights.

They still have enormous advantages over the young upstarts: worldwide networks of experienced correspondents and the ability to feed a big breaking story to every corner of the globe within minutes or even seconds. But they need to do more than that. Two basic rules of reporting are: get it first and get it right. But if you're the BBC you have to do more. You have to supply context and background too: all the information the reasonably intelligent listener or viewer needs to make their own judgements.

You have to answer all the most obvious questions:

Is this a story with the lifespan of a mayfly which I can dismiss, or is it something I should pay attention to because it will dominate the news schedules for days or weeks or (in the case of Brexit) decades to come?

Is it something I need to know much more about because it might have real implications for me, my family, my country?

Do I need to form an opinion for myself or can I leave that to others?

Should I make sure the car is full of petrol for a quick getaway or should I be filling the cupboard under the stairs with tins of beans and bottles of water?

I'm talking not about speed of coverage, but depth. And my fear is that the BBC – and other mainstream broadcasters for that matter – have too often sacrificed the depth that we once regarded as our duty. On the hamster wheel of minute-by-minute coverage we may justifiably boast that we never miss a story, but there is the danger that too often we gloss over what it actually means. Is there still a bias against understanding, against which Birt had railed all those years ago?

Today the biggest problem facing the editor back home is no longer how to get a story covered but how to distinguish between the mass of material that appears almost instantly on social media in one form or another.

This goes much further than the instant supply of information. News is also about reporting the opinions of those who watch and listen to the programmes. The BBC cannot report the nation to them if it does not have a grasp on what the nation is thinking. This is where social media comes in. I recoiled when I read an email circulated to *Today* staff in the never-ending battle to improve the quality of briefs handed over to presenters to help them with their interviews.

The recommendation at the top of the document from one of the most senior journalists on the programme was that the first thing the producer should do was scour Twitter to see what, if anything, people were making of the story and brief the present-ers accordingly. Scour Twitter? I know what I'd like to do with Twitter and it does not include bowing reverently before it and treating its tweets as though they represent the views of the nation. They do not. Some are measured and thought-provoking. Many more are banal or asinine rants. And many of them are grossly offensive and intended to be. One simple question: is the world a better/safer place because Donald Trump is able to churn out his childish and often asinine views to his adoring followers whenever it occurs to him? I rest my case.

My concern is that broadcast news generally, fighting in such a crowded market, is so homogeneous that all the big players feel they must rely on showbiz gimmicks to accentuate their appeal. Obviously it would be idiotic to claim that technology has not transformed production values for the better – or, rather, what we must now call the 'viewing experience' – but there is a price to pay for it.

It was terribly exciting when newsreaders like me were able to come out from behind our desks and prove to the audience that we had legs – though it did mean in my case that I had to abandon the jeans I wore with my suit jacket when no one could see below my chest. But the more studio designers strive to appear different from all the others, the more they all end up looking the same. And that's without taking into account the requirement to have two newsreaders doing a job that can perfectly well be done by one. But those are details.

More important is the extent to which the twenty-four-hour news channels – whether they are from China, France, Qatar, or even the UK – are marked by their similarities. All the twenty-four-hour news channels share a similarity of style, of pace, of structure, and even of presenters. And they have caused broadcast journalism to change. Correspondents, locked to the wheel of live coverage, complain that they are too often stuck to the spot for a succession of interviews with different programmes, rather than trying to find out what is actually going on.

So the worry is that BBC News has become a machine-driven operation, running very fast to stand still, without a proper awareness of the world around it. That increases the risk that it can be taken by surprise – perhaps by Euroscepticism or immigration or the rise of Trump and populism. The price we are paying for the explosion in the media, made possible by digital technology, is that broadcasters like the BBC have become news factories. Hundreds upon hundreds of journalists are rooted to their desks back at base, turning the material round. The combined BBC Newsroom is like a scene from Fritz Lang's *Metropolis*, a dystopian vision of journalistic hell. With regional and local newspapers in decline, despite the BBC running a local democracy reporters' scheme to try to support them, there is a danger that journalism and broadcasting in particular have become rootless.

In the course of my career, newspapers have survived radio, and radio has survived television. All have survived online and social media – though not unscarred. I should, of course add two words to that sentence: 'so far'. Today we can cover more news, more speedily. But it does not mean we are covering the news more deeply or more analytically. We may be generating heat. But are we really delivering light?

Towards the end of August 1997, I was taking a short holiday, supping an early morning coffee on the terrace of my hotel in Istanbul when the waiter approached with a message on a tray. Remember those wonderful days before cellphones? If you didn't want to reply to the message you could always claim it had never arrived. It was from the office in London and asked me to phone urgently. I did. They told me Princess Diana had been killed in a car crash in a tunnel in Paris and would I please return to London ASAP. I pretended it was a dodgy line and said I'd call them back. And when I did I said no. They were puzzled and they were right to be. It was a massive story – it totally dominated the news for weeks to come – but I knew I would make a rotten job of reporting it.

My suspicions were confirmed when I eventually returned to London several days later. It was a city – indeed a nation – in mourning. A different city from the one I had left less than a week ago. Or at least, that's what we were told by every news bulletin on radio and television and pretty much every story in every newspaper. But it wasn't.

True, a vast mountain of flowers and cuddly toys had been left at the gates of Kensington Palace and every person vox-popped by television seemed to be mourning. Even the Queen was forced to speak in public of her own grief and flags were lowered to half-mast. The message was clear: a great transformation had overtaken the nation. What I saw with my own eyes told me something else.

I went to Parliament Square where hundreds of people were already camping out to get a decent view of the funeral planned for the weekend – but the atmosphere was not one of mourning. They were there for much the same reason that people camp out to get a good spot for a big royal wedding or any other great national occasion. They were spectators rather than mourners. I went to a concert in the Albert Hall – the first I have ever attended when the audience was instructed not to applaud. It was meant as a mark of respect for the dead princess but the audience seemed baffled.

It was hard to avoid the conclusion that the media – above all the BBC – was not so much reflecting the national mood as creating it. Interestingly, the initial reaction (or so I was told) had been relatively low-key. In fact the audience for a BBC1 special programme broadcast on the evening after the tragedy was surprisingly modest in spite of a day of unrelenting coverage. But as the week wore on and we continued to be bombarded with endless accounts of the nation's 'outpouring of grief' the mood clearly changed.

I have no problem with newspapers setting out to 'create' a mood if they think it will help boost their sales. But I do have a problem with the BBC doing the same. It is not for us to tell the nation what it should be feeling. I'm not even sure the word 'nation' is appropriate in this context. I suspect the vast majority of the population were not, in any real sense, grieving. Of course we all felt the death of Diana was a tragedy. So is the death of any human being in such circumstances. But to invoke a national mood of mourning for a single individual with whom we did not and cannot have had any direct connection is simply wrong – if only because it invites comparisons. In my case and, I suspect, many others, I found it hard not to reflect on the tragedy of Aberfan a generation earlier. Surely the death of 116 children in one small Welsh village was a greater justification for national mourning than the death of three people in a tunnel in Paris. Even if one of them had once been married to the heir to the throne.

Tony Hall, at the time the chief executive of BBC News, commented on its coverage in an article in *The Times* entitled 'The people led. We followed.' I believe it was the other way around. He suggested that something profound had changed in the nation during that week of mourning. I would suggest history says otherwise. Nothing had changed – except, perhaps, even greater cynicism directed towards politicians like Tony Blair with his 'people's princess' sound bite and a sense thereafter that we had, or should, become a more lachrymose society.

Hall wrote that the death of Diana had taught the BBC a 'tough lesson'. We learned, he said, that emotion has its political dimension and that by giving voice on our airways to the thoughts and feelings of 'ordinary individuals' we could get at 'some kind of truth which would otherwise elude us no matter how many facts we assembled'. I have a problem with 'ordinary individuals'. What other sort are there? It may seem strange to quote Shakespeare in this context but his villainous creation Shylock made a singularly wise speech in *The Merchant of Venice*:

> Hath not a Jew eyes? Hath not a Jew hands, organs,
> dimensions, senses, affections, passions; fed with the same
> food, hurt with the same weapons, subject to the same
> diseases, healed by the same means, warmed and cooled by the
> same winter and summer as a Christian is? If you prick us, do
> we not bleed? If you tickle us, do we not laugh? If you poison
> us, do we not die?

Substitute 'human' for 'Jew' and 'Christian' and this is Shylock defining 'ordinary individuals'. He is saying there is no other sort and, of course, he is right. We journalists (also 'ordinary individuals'?) need to tread very carefully when we start putting people into silos and suggesting that they hold some sort of truth that eludes us if we rely on facts alone. No doubt there is something to be said for the wisdom of crowds but that's not what we achieve when a reporter pokes a microphone under someone's nose and asks them what they think. I've always been very sceptical of the editorial value of vox pops.

We ask a dozen people in a given town centre their view on hanging and we may get a dozen in favour. Does that mean the nation wants to restore hanging? Obviously not. So what if we ask another dozen and all of them are opposed? Does that prove the nation is evenly divided between the pros and the antis? Of course it doesn't. Professional pollsters recognise that you need at least 1,000 opinions on most subjects before you can even try to assess the nation's mood and even then there is no guarantee that they will get it right. But, time and again, we invest half a dozen vox pops with an authority they obviously do not have.

Of course it was great fun to hear the way Brenda from Bristol reacted when she was asked by a journalist to react to the news that Theresa May had called an election: 'You're joking! Not another one!' Our hearts warmed to her and to the disgust she was expressing with such genuine indignation. But did it – or the other vox pops we have done over the years and keep doing – tell us anything we did not already know about the nation's mood? I doubt it but we persist in doing it.

As I write I hear a presenter on *The World at One* promising that the programme will be 'finding out what people are thinking about the election results in two different towns …' But of course it won't. It will tell us what precisely four different people think: two from one political standpoint and two from another. Perfectly balanced, utterly meaningless and totally misleading. We should stop doing it.

So what about the notion that by giving them the run of the airwaves we 'reach some kind of truth'? I have another problem with this for the obvious reason that journalists do not deal in 'truth'. We deal in facts – or, rather, that's what we try to do.

I lost count of the number of times I was berated by angry Remainers following the Brexit referendum result for failing to tell our listeners the truth. My answer now is the same as it was then: 'Whose truth do you want? The "truth" that we would be better off economically if we waved farewell to Brussels, or the "truth" stated by the Chancellor of the Exchequer that we'd need an emergency Budget the day after the referendum if we voted Leave?'

The reality is that, with some rare exceptions, journalists should not presume to deliver the 'truth' for the obvious reason that we do not know where it lies. The notion that there is some inalienable truth out there no matter how complex the issue is, I fear, fanciful. Whose truth do you fancy: the politician you've just heard on the radio, or the one you heard on the telly last night, or the expert you've just read in *The Times* or the other expert you've just read in the *Guardian*? They might well have each had a different version of the 'truth' so who do you believe? Journalists must deal in facts. And if the facts are in dispute, we must say so.

Some years ago social scientists identified what they called the hostile-media phenomenon. Most of us who have had to report on Brexit over the years know pretty much what sort of reaction we will get from any given group of listeners or readers, and we know it will depend on how they feel about our membership of the EU. If they are in favour of it, then almost anything we report that contains criticism of Brussels will be regarded as a lie. If our report supports their view they will regard it as the truth. Here's how the brilliant *Times* columnist Daniel Finkelstein put it: 'Everyone is sure that the coverage is biased against them. This phenomenon is partly because everyone thinks they are objective and thus that everything they disagreed with is biased. And partly because everyone thinks they are right.'

Speculation is a different matter, of course. If speculation were closed to us God alone knows how we would fill our acres of airtime. We speculate endlessly about what is likely to be in the Budget right up until the moment the chancellor tells us. We are a bit like the addicted gambler who will wager his last few pennies on which of two raindrops will descend faster down the window.

Worse, we will sometimes ask one of our specialist correspondents what the minister is going to say in the statement he will release later, even as the minister sits in front of our microphone waiting patiently to tell us.

So what 'facts' were the BBC and others relying on to define the national mood in the days after Diana met her untimely death? We knew that a very large number of people had expressed their sadness in a variety of ways and we knew that huge numbers would turn out to watch the funeral procession make its sad way through London. What we did not know and had no conceivable way of knowing was how many of those people were there for the spectacle or simply because they wanted to be part of an extraordinary moment in the nation's life. We did not know how many were grieving. And we never will.

That's one of the reasons why I had no wish to be part of the great team reporting on the death of Diana and the nation's reaction to it, let alone the team reporting on the funeral itself. I would have found it very difficult, if not impossible, to sound as though I were grieving. Like countless millions more I felt sadness at her death – but no more and no less sadness than I have felt at any of the other untimely deaths I have witnessed more times than I wish to remember.

So, no, the nation had not changed. We in the media helped to create a mood by seeing what we wanted to see.

It's impossible to talk about the BBC's news output without reflecting on the people who work for it. Many of its critics blame the BBC's 'liberal intelligentsia' for its approach to journalism. I've argued that the machine is a key factor, but clearly it has to be programmed by somebody.

In truth, for all the years I have spent in the BBC, I've never felt entirely at home there. There was a Wills cigarette-card collection on BBC radio celebrities in the 1930s that said 'unlike the others, Stuart Hibberd cannot be said to be an Oxford man'. Well … good for him. Obviously they didn't have comprehensives back then, but maybe he was a grammar-school boy who fought his way to the top? Not exactly. He could not be said to be 'an Oxford man' because he went to Cambridge. That rather summed things up, and I am not sure a lot has changed since then.

After my decision to leave *Today* was made known my colleague Michael Buerk wrote in the *Radio Times* that I was 'nobody's nob'. He went on:

His departure is not just another oldie shuffling off into the sunset, it's the end of an era when people from ordinary backgrounds could make their way into, and make a big success of, the media ...

When he and I were BBC TV News reporters together in the 70s hardly any of our colleagues had a degree. They were mostly tough men from Fleet Street, belligerent alpha males whose stag-like rivalries were the stuff of legend. They were sharp, if not particularly bright, but they had the smell of the street about them and an empathy with those in the underprivileged sticks from which most had hailed.

When John goes, all four of the *Today* programme's regular presenters will have been privately educated, like a quite remarkable proportion of other people working for the BBC, on both sides of the microphone. The same is true across the media as a whole. Even tabloid newspaper hacks have been to Westminster and Cambridge, these days.

I'm a bit reluctant to go too far down this route for several reasons. Partly because bright people are bright people, irrespective of where they were educated – but also because when David Dimbleby was guest-editing the *Today* programme I had a bit of a run-in with him and came out second best.

Anyone who's ever watched David on television over the decades will know that he is a brilliant presenter of live news and current affairs. In my view, perhaps the best we have ever had. He's always done his homework and has never been less than well informed. His questioning was as sharp as a knife. He's authoritative without being pompous and he is almost never patronising. And he's funny too. He's also a bit posh. At least that's how I've always thought of him. My mistake was to say so aloud. Live on air. In David's presence.

Now I've been around long enough to have learned by heart the first lesson taught to every trainee barrister, which applies equally to interviewers. It's this: never ask a question to which you do not know the answer. It was the great American civil rights lawyer Clarence Darrow who formulated the rule back in the nineteenth century. He liked to take as his example a smart-arse young lawyer who was cross-examining the only witness in a case in which his client was accused of biting off a man's ear in a fight. It went like this:

'Did ya see my client bite off his ear?'

'No sir, I didn't.'

Job done, Darrow told his students. Only one witness and he hadn't seen the alleged assault. The lawyer should have sat down and waited for the acquittal. But he didn't. He wanted to show off.

'If ya didn't see him bite off the ear … how come you know he done it?'

'Well sir, I saw him spit it out.'

Case closed. Lawyer humiliated.

I actually made two mistakes in my interview with David even though it was no more than a few minutes' chat at the end of the programme. As well as breaking the Darrow rule, I had given the interview no thought. It's a simple rule: never take anything for granted. And so, totally unprepared, I mentioned to David that he'd done a great deal of commentating on great state occasions over the years and suggested that he must have become quite close to the royal family. Did it help, I wondered, that he himself was quite posh?

'Sorry John …' he retorted. 'There's a typical sneer in that question. "*You're* quite posh," I'm about as posh as you are. I come from Wales, as you do.'

I was not expecting that. This is how I should have replied: 'No you don't. Your mother was Welsh, it's true, but you were actually born in Surrey and anyway being Welsh doesn't mean you can't be posh. *And* I don't imagine you were brought up in Splott in a tiny terraced house with an outdoor loo *and* you went to one of England's great public schools *and* you were sent off to Paris to learn French and to Perugia to learn Italian *and* you went to one of the most prestigious colleges at Oxford (dare I say one of the poshest?!) *and* ...'

But I said none of that. The best I could manage was: 'Well ... you had a very distinguished father.'

'Ha!' said David, obviously relishing an easy victory in this ridiculous battle. 'That doesn't make me posh! I had a distinguished father ... that's a bizarre question.'

And so it was.

As he pointed out with a chuckle ten seconds after we'd come off the air, all I'd had to do to make my case was use two words: 'Bullingdon Club'.

Of course! Nobody, but nobody, got invited to join the Bullingdon Club at Oxford University unless they were posh. Very posh. That was the whole point of it. And David had been one of its members. But I hadn't done my homework.

The Bullingdon Club has, I'm happy to say, fallen on hard times since David's years at Oxford. It is now regarded as a rather tacky relic of a bygone age. The BBC has changed too. It's had no choice. One of my closest friends and colleagues when I worked in newspapers was desperate to get a job in broadcasting but, like me, he spoke with a pronounced Cardiff accent. He was advised to take elocution lessons, which he did. He got the job, but to my ear he never sounded quite right. Mercifully the days of received pronunciation have long gone. Now a regional accent is probably an advantage. Which is not to say that there are no problems with the BBC's general employment practices. As Michael Buerk put it: 'Many of today's generation are brilliant, *Today*'s presenters particularly so, in my view. But there are serious implications here. The BBC, itself, seems a smaller tent. It is not deliberately biased, in my experience, indeed struggles painfully for impartiality. But its world view is bound to reflect the collective set of assumptions of those who work for it. These are more uniformly middle class, well educated, young, urban and smart, with little experience of – and sometimes little sympathy for – business, industry, the countryside, localness, traditions and politicians.'

Perhaps this, too, is a reason why the BBC machine can seem out of touch.

Today the BBC's whole drive is towards being very much in touch or, more specifically, in touch with young people. The logic is inescapable. If you don't catch them while they're young, they'll never develop the BBC habit. The notion of BBC universality and with it the justification for the licence fee will wither on the vine. In short, young people pose an existential threat to the BBC.

This is one reason why the BBC decided in 2018 to launch BBC Sounds, which mixes streams of the BBC's existing national radio stations with podcasts and other specially commissioned audio material. There were, predictably enough, screams of pain from Radio 4 whose budget is being cut to help pay for it. The chairman of the BBC, Sir David Clementi, justified it thus: 'Radio needs to move forward otherwise we would still be having *Listen With Mother* or *Workers' Playtime*. All radio needs to evolve. We do need to make sure we are appealing to younger audiences. That is partly about content, and it's partly about making it easily accessible, which I think Sounds is starting to do.' The BBC reckons that by 2022 podcasting's share of the UK listenership will rise to close to fourteen per cent.

The BBC is right to be alarmed by what its audience research tells it. Recent figures show BBC Radio Network News and Current Affairs had its lowest 'reach' since 2009. ('Reach' means the total number of people listening to a specific programme for a specific time during any given period: usually a week.) Average hours per listener fell to their lowest levels on record. Among young audiences, both reach and time spent hit new lows. For news, the greatest year-on-year declines came among those aged between twenty-five and forty-four.

There was a time when the BBC was the big beast of the media jungle in Britain. Now its competitors are international giants – Netflix, Spotify, Facebook, YouTube – whose financial resources dwarf its own. The BBC's annual spend on television content was small change compared with a tech giant. That makes it hard, if not impossible, to compete in the new globalised media market.

In the summer of 2019 the Media Nations report carried some pretty bleak statistics. Viewers of all ages were watching 50 minutes less scheduled television a day than they did in 2010. 'Traditional' viewing by people aged from 16 to 24 halved to 85 minutes a day over that same period. The most popular television service with young people was YouTube: more than an hour a day. BBC1 came fourth, with only 15 minutes. Nearly half of all UK households subscribed to at least one of the streaming platforms and the figure is rising remorselessly.

It was not entirely bad news for the BBC. BBC1 was the most-watched video service for all ages and the two most popular programmes were *Line of Duty* and *Bodyguard*. But, as the report noted: 'To counteract the overall drop in broadcast viewing since 2017, about 34 additional series of *Bodyguard* would need to have been broadcast in 2018.'

The BBC is so worried by the decline in young audiences that it is changing the nature of some of its journalism. And not always for the better. Sometimes it appears that the organisation is pulling in two different directions at the same time.

The top news priority in the BBC's Annual Plan for 2019–20 was to 'increase younger audiences: continuing to develop our offer for underserved and younger audiences, including podcasts for on-demand and our "voice" offer for news on smart speakers'. The second priority is 'Upholding trust and impartiality: reasserting our belief in the core values of impartiality across our news output, ensuring we remain true to those values and strengthening our commitment to explaining what events mean and why they matter.'

It's not difficult to identify the reasons for the consistent downward scores in the public's perception of the BBC's impartiality. It's partly the increasing distrust of institutions in general and the rise of other media outlets; partly, the polarisation of politics; and partly because of self-inflicted wounds such as Savile. But at least the BBC can take comfort in the findings that suggest trust in the BBC scores more highly.

'Trust' can be difficult to measure. A company selling fridges earns its trust if the fridge you've bought works well and when it does go wrong there's a man at the door to fix it on the same day you've made a complaint. It's not quite that easy for an institution like the BBC.

We can safely assume that viewers trust, say, David Attenborough. We believe him when he tells us plastics are polluting our oceans, and that is reflected in the viewers' trust in the BBC. We can also assume that a programme like *Love Island* does not do a great deal to boost the trust levels of ITV2. But news, inevitably, is the real test.

And what matters is not just that our coverage is seen to be as impartial, fair and accurate as is humanly possible. The selection of the stories we choose to cover matters hugely too. This is where the BBC's commitment to attracting more viewers comes in. The danger is that the hunt for that younger audience may have unintended consequences. BBC News Online is one battleground. It's where so many 'stories' are based on a range of subjects that seem to be little more than clickbait. On 5 December 2018, in the middle of a story on the murder of a young British woman in New Zealand, the reader was invited to show an interest in:

- Giant snail raises £231k for hospice
- Viewing in thigh-high boots discovery
- Plastic dog on jelly wins spoof arts prize

Let's take another selection from one day in random months:

- September, under its 'Must See' heading on the front page: 'Gamer with terminal cancer achieves "Ultimate goal"'; 'Seven foot snake falls from attic hatch' and 'The unanswered questions from *Bodyguard*.'
- November: 'Downing Street cat gets a helping hand' and 'Why I send pictures of my genitals to women.'
- December: 'What's Christmas like with 11 kids'; 'Taiwan helps man who ploughed into Ferraris'; 'Britain's "favourite Christmas film" revealed' and 'I've fixed my botched lip filler.'

Not quite John Birt's mission to explain, perhaps – though it's true that sometimes vestiges of it remain, albeit leading to an unfortunate juxtaposition of stories: 'Why Saudi Arabia and Iran are bitter rivals' appearing next to 'Is the taboo around male make-up disappearing?'

A personal favourite was: 'Are you a man with a cat? Share your pictures and experiences by emailing haveyoursay@bbc.co.uk. Please include a contact number if you are willing to speak to a BBC journalist.'

In 2018, Dame Frances Cairncross was asked by the government to examine the sustainability of high-quality journalism. One of her recommendations was that the BBC's regulator, Ofcom, should review the extent to which BBC Online content acts as a substitute, rather than a complement to, the offerings of commercial news providers. She also wanted the BBC 'to ask whether, in its pursuit of younger audiences, BBC News Online goes beyond the BBC's core public purposes, and inappropriately steps into areas better served by commercial partners'.

Matthew Parris is in no doubt. He wrote in his *Times* diary:

Here are seven things you hated about the BBC website home page on Friday September 7:

- 19 unmissable moments from the Proms so far
- 9 hearty and healthy slow-cooker recipes
- The 7 most influential books in history
- 9 people who have made amazing charity donations
- '5 reasons I love raving in my wheelchair in Ibiza'
- 12 whopping mistakes spotted in top TV shows
- 5 celebrity lookalikes we can't tell apart

There may have been more; I lost the will to live. In its 'Wider still and wider/Shall thy bounds be set' itch, has the corporation lost its marbles? Should licence payers' money be spent on an assemblage of shrivelled clickbait droppings when the popular tabloids do this sort of thing perfectly well already?

The '19 unmissable moments from the Proms *so far*' was a little puzzling. By definition you'd have missed them already. And the stories are sometimes written in a bizarrely confiding style – such as this article on universal credit:

Your name is Tony Rice. You're the sort of bloke who gets along with everyone. Always making people laugh. Ever since you left school you've been in and out of all sorts of jobs. Manual labour, mostly – builder, dustman, crane driver, painter and decorator. Hawker Siddeley, the aerospace company – you like it there, until the factory shuts.

You split up with your girlfriend so you ask your mum to put you up until you can sort out a flat. Save a few quid. You're very close to your mum and dad. They're your best friends, really. Your dad has lung cancer and needs a bit of looking after. You take him for a drive most days because he doesn't like staying in all the time. He's like you, not a man to sit about. At one time he worked three jobs, all at once. Still does half an hour each morning in the garden.

So you're back in the council house in Chingford, north-east London, that you've called home since you were eight years old – even after you left. Your sisters have moved out and had kids of their own but you want to take care of your mum and dad, same as they took care of you.

Impartial journalism? I don't think so.

Another temptation the BBC sometimes finds hard to resist is social engineering. Its job is to hold up a mirror to society and reflect back to the audiences what it sees. For good or ill. It should not try to create society in its own image. It should not try to place its powerful finger on one side of the scale of social justice. That is for each of us as individuals and for our democratically elected representatives to do.

The BBC has an absolute responsibility to report on what's happening, to draw attention to injustices and wrongdoing, but it is for others to put them right. Newspaper columnists and campaigning journalists are expected to have opinions and express them forcefully – the more forcefully and the more controversial the better. Newspapers should be applauded for conducting worthy campaigns. BBC journalists are different. They are required to provide facts and analysis. Which is why I raised my eyebrows slightly when the BBC announced it had created the new post of LGBT correspondent and the man appointed said: 'I'm looking forward to being the mouthpiece for some marginalised groups but really allowing them to tell their own stories.'

It was the use of the word 'mouthpiece' that jarred. Obviously the BBC must give a voice to minorities but it must not act as anyone's mouthpiece. That's what lobbyists and public relations people do. To confuse the two is to undermine the job of a journalist. Imagine a defence correspondent announcing that he sees himself as the mouthpiece for the armed forces. Or the health correspondent as the mouthpiece of the NHS. Or even, heaven forfend, the royal correspondent as the mouthpiece of the royal family.

All news operations come under pressure from vested interests all the time and, given that the BBC is the most powerful news provider in the land, it will get more stick than most. That's fair enough. Indeed, it's inevitable. But now the pressure is coming from within as well as outside the walls of New Broadcasting House. One relatively recent phenomenon is the growth in the BBC of groups of employees who conflate and, perhaps, confuse their own interests with those of the wider world. The logic seems to be that if they feel strongly about a given issue, the BBC should not only listen to them but modify its output to reflect their own world view.

A generation ago they might have been listened to politely and then shown the door. Today they don't need to talk to their bosses: they use Twitter or whatever happens to be their favourite social media platform. Social media offers an organisational ability and a public avenue for criticism, but also collective identification and a sense that the BBC should reflect a certain world view, rather than be obliged to look at all angles of the debate.

One small example was an edition of *Question Time*. It included a question from a member of the audience who was worried that it might not be morally appropriate for five-year-old children to be taught about LGBT issues. Some members of the BBC's LGBT group, including a business presenter, took to Twitter to complain that the question should not have been allowed.

The director of BBC News responded by sending all staff an email reminding them, at some length, that they're entitled to their personal views but they are not allowed to parade them on social media. Quite right too. She could also have told the group not to be so silly and suggested that it probably wouldn't look good for an organisation whose very essence is the ultimate democratic gift of free speech to engage in censorship. But had she done that it would have caused great offence – and that is no longer allowed in the modern BBC.

The great American Supreme Court judge Oliver Wendell Holmes may be best known for pointing out that free speech does not include the freedom to shout fire in a crowded theatre, but he said something even more relevant in a modern context. It was the principle of freedom of thought: 'Not free thought for those who agree with us … but freedom for the thought that we hate.'

What worries me is that the BBC is changing. We have become susceptible – from within and without – to pressure groups in a way that I have not seen in my fifty years in the corporation. Whether it is change for the better is for listeners and viewers to judge, but they can do that only if we have an open debate. And that's the problem.

Take a speech made in 2016 by the man who was then head of diversity, inclusion and succession at the BBC, Tunde Ogungbesan. Here is part of it: 'We have moved away from the normal areas of diversity, gender and ethnicity, and expanded it to include sexual orientation and trans, class, religion, thought processes and social economic diversity.'

Diversity is one test of a truly civilised society and the BBC has been trying hard to improve its track record. The proportion of black, Asian and other ethnic minorities in the workforce is above the 2011 census ratio of the population as a whole. The representation of some minorities exceeds the national average. Mr Ogungbesan claimed that almost two per cent of the organisation had said they are transgender which, as he put it, 'is very, very high'. Indeed it is. Official figures suggest that's about four times as high as the proportion of trans people in the UK as a whole. But it seems it is still not high enough. Ogungbesan noted it was much higher in areas where the organisation was committed to 'supporting employees who choose to transition, including providing paid time off for medical appointments, treatments and surgical procedures'. Gender-neutral lavatories have been installed. He also said more lesbians are 'needed'. A strange word in this context, perhaps.

And it may worry many that 'thought processes' should be included in 'normal areas of diversity'. There is a magnificent statue of George Orwell standing at the entrance to New Broadcasting House. He might well have had a thought or two about that.

Daily Mail

19 March 2014

The BBC is managed by a group of men and women who are brilliant at three things. The first and easily the most important is persuading their superiors their job is vital to the well-being of the corporation even if no one is quite sure what that job actually is.

The title offers little help. The grander it is, the less it means but it will almost certainly contain the words 'strategic', 'governance' or 'director'. Preferably all three.

Their second is avoiding taking any decision for which they can be held responsible. They do this by surrounding themselves with clever young people who do all the work and get all the blame when something goes wrong. If it goes right, naturally the director takes the credit.

And their third is to demonstrate by thought, word and deed their unswerving loyalty to the man at the top of the organisation: Baron Hall of Birkenhead.

Not that he is ever accorded that title. He is referred to only as 'Tony', the better to give the impression they are the closest of friends and Tony hangs on their every word.

Their principal activity is holding endless meetings at which nothing is decided, but a great deal of time and coffee are consumed and an even greater deal of management jargon is spoken. The more opaque and meaningless the jargon the better. That way, accountability can be avoided and responsibility ducked.

If no one really understands what the hell is going on, no one can be held to account for anything. Their contact with the real world beyond London W1A is limited, if not non-existent.

Now at this point dear reader (or should I address you as 'dear licence-fee payer'?), you'll be wondering why I, as a more or less loyal servant of the BBC, have decided to sign my professional death warrant with such a savage attack on the organisation that has provided me with a pretty decent living for nigh-on forty-five years.

The answer, as you may have guessed, is that the BBC I have described is a fictional organisation. It is the creation of some clever scriptwriters for a new BBC2 comedy series beginning tonight and starring Hugh Bonneville as Ian Fletcher, 'Head of Values' at the BBC.

I'd be lying if I said there weren't some of my colleagues who will be punching the air the morning after the programme is broadcast and shouting: 'Spot on! They've got the bosses bang to rights!'

It would be odd if they didn't.

I doubt there is a large organisation anywhere in the world where senior management is loved by all (or even most) of its workers. Or where the workers do not think there are too many overpaid bosses.

Why should the BBC be any different? I am on record as saying the BBC is over-managed. It always has been.

The BBC bureaucracy is alive and kicking. And it's not just me saying that. It's Tony Hall, too.

One of the first trips he made when he became director general was to the US to see the Google and Apple operations. Back in London, he wrote this: 'To launch an initiative, one of our colleagues had to speak to two people at Google. To get *agreement to do the BBC's first eBook, someone at the BBC had to speak to more than two dozen.'*

There's not a programme-maker in the BBC who wouldn't say Amen! to that. Back in the 1980s, I returned from filming a famine in East Africa with some powerful material.

I rang the office of the controller of BBC1, Michael Grade, and asked his secretary if he could find the time to look at it because I thought it would make a decent documentary.

Half an hour later, I was sitting in Grade's office. He put his feet on the desk and watched the first ten minutes.

'OK,' he said.' I'll get it scheduled for a few weeks' time.' And so it was.

That same process thirty years later would take many months and about as many meetings as Eisenhower held to plan the Normandy landings.

Mercifully, Hall wants to change that. He says the BBC's meeting culture hampers creativity.

He wants to halve the number of pan-BBC boards and steering groups and light 'a bonfire of the boards' to speed up decision-making and release some of the resources wasted on bureaucracy for programmes.

Anyone who thinks it will happen overnight does not know the BBC.

Yet tonight's programme is an encouraging sign. An organisation that can take the mickey out of its own management quite so ruthlessly shows it's got the message. And that's a start.

18

Goodbye to all that

Writing this book has been a strange experience. It's not that I'm new to the game. I have written seven books before this one, millions of words for newspapers and magazines, and more BBC programmes than I can shake a stick at. But this is the first time in half a century that I have written a single sentence for publication in one form or another without the tiniest fear, somewhere in the back of my mind, that the BBC might not approve.

The rules are perfectly clear. If you are employed by the BBC as a journalist you have to submit to a higher authority everything you write for publication. Fair enough. If there were no rules we could cheerfully take the BBC shilling and earn a few more by expressing our own opinions on whatever subject we chose and if that meant stepping over the line between analysis and opinion … so be it. After the Hutton crisis we news presenters were banned from writing regular newspaper columns on current issues full stop. For nearly five years I'd had a weekly column in the *Sunday Times* but that came to an end after Hutton. We all moaned about it of course and some subversive souls tried to get around the ban but I suspect most of us could see that the BBC might have had a point.

So it felt very strange embarking on this book knowing that I was free. I had finally taken the decision to retire from *Today* and would no longer be employed as a BBC journalist. No longer would I have to submit to the BBC Thought Police my subversive musings on everything from the nation's favourite bird to whether all politicians are, indeed, liars. More to the point I would be free, for the first time since I signed on the dotted line in 1967, to tell anyone who might be interested what I really thought about the BBC:

- its failings and successes;
- its idiosyncrasies and its prejudices;
- its stultifying, jargon-ridden bureaucracy;
- its belief in the magical powers of the latest barmy management theory and the consultants peddling it;
- its persistent belief in the face of all evidence that every management email must contain at least one use of the word 'exciting' and another of the word 'passionate';
- its simultaneous delusions of grandeur and lack of confidence;
- its fear of its political masters;
- its even greater fear of the politically correct brigade and the most fashionable pressure groups – usually from the liberal left, the spiritual home of most bosses and staff.

There's nothing we BBC worker bees enjoy more than telling each other how wonderful everything would be if only we were in charge of the hive. Maybe it's like that in all large organisations. But there are a few things that make the BBC different, if not unique.

It's a pretty basic rule of business that the bosses earn more than the workers. That's not always so in the BBC and sometimes for perfectly good reasons. You would expect a star like Graham Norton to earn vastly more than his producer. The programme would not exist without him. There is only one Graham Norton and he IS the programme. You might expect star football players to get a decent fee for chatting about a match. Whether that justifies paying Gary Lineker £1.75 million a year is questionable at best. Some might say ludicrous. And to continue paying that amount only a matter of months after it was announced that people over the age of seventy-five who are not on pension credit would lose their free TV licences is verging on the suicidal.

And then we get to my own department. News. Presenters on the main news programmes make the editors look like paupers. At my peak I was paid more than four times as much as my editor. And that does not include all the extracurricular gigs: chairing conferences, making speeches, writing books and newspaper articles and so on that come with the job. True, the editors don't have to get up at 3.30 in the morning but most were usually in the office soon after six and on call until late at night. Presenters finish at nine.

Then there's the question of who gets the credit. If *Today* misses a big story – or misjudges it – the editor is blamed. If the programme is boring, ditto. If it lands a big interview or fixes what turns out to be a fascinating discussion the kudos almost always goes to the presenter. In simple terms, if something goes really well the presenters get to bask in the glory. If it goes badly the editors invariably carry the can.

You could argue that that's inevitable. In the theatre the audiences rises to applaud the actors on stage who've been entertaining them for the last couple of hours rather than the director or backstage crew who've been working on the production for months or even years. It's obvious why. The performance itself is all we see. It's the same with *Today*.

You hear the presenter conducting a brilliant interview at 8.10, exposing the pompous minister for the devious chancer he is, demolishing his every point, reminding him that he'd said precisely the opposite only a few months ago, rubbishing his claims to prove his economic brilliance with unchallengeable statistics – and it is all done with that impressive calm and courtesy and modesty for which we presenters are so renowned. The plaudits should be ours and ours alone.

Or should they?

I wrote earlier that one of the iron laws of producing a programme like *Today* is that there is an inverse relationship between wanting an interview with someone – specifically with a politician – and actually getting it. The (unwritten) law states that the more *we* want to interview *them*, the less *they* want to be interviewed by *us*. Huge credit, therefore, to all the overworked and underpaid producers down the years who refused to take no for an answer when they were bidding for a tricky interview against the odds. The qualities needed are summed up in the 'Three Ps': persistence, pluck and sometimes even a dash of perjury. It takes a brave soul to phone the minister at home at 5 a.m. knowing that he has a reputation for eating young producers alive and also has the director general's personal number on his speed dial.

Their reward for succeeding is pretty modest: promotion to senior producer. That means they will be entrusted to work all night with just one producer and then, when they are utterly knackered at six in the morning, have to spend three hours in a live studio doing one of the most high-pressured jobs in the business: putting *Today* on the air. In my closing months on *Today* I asked some of my colleagues (about thirty-two years too late) for their thoughts on the best things and the worst things about being the night editor on *Today*. The best things first, in their own words:

- Those nights when there is some big story – a big political resignation, a massive human-interest story, maybe Mandela dying – and *Today* gets everybody we bid for ... exclusively.
- When the presenters come in and look at your running order and realise it's going to be a brilliant programme ... so good they can't find anything to moan about although they'll have a bloody good try.
- The morning when a massive story has broken overnight because a Cabinet minister at the heart of the Brexit negotiations has resigned at midnight and the first thing the presenter says when he walks in is something like: 'So who've we got to talk about the resignation then?' and you

say 'Actually nobody ...' and he snaps 'Pathetic!' and you say '... because we've got the minister himself!'

- The nights when you feel you're at the centre of the world. You know half the country's going to be listening in the morning to find out who won the election or the referendum or who'll be the next president of the United States.

- It's probably the same thing that keeps us all at the programme – the feeling (or fear) that we'll never do anything that matters as much.

And these were some of the worst:

- Utter exhaustion ... compounded by anxiety and stress ... partners probably bear the brunt of this.

- That pit-of-the-stomach moment in the handover meeting when you realise the day team have had a nightmare day and you have four lead slots to fill, everything else is crap too, and you just want the day editor to hurry up and stop talking while you get on and try to repair the mess.

- The cringing embarrassment of having to tell the poor guest who has schlepped their way into the studio on a freezing morning and told his family he's going to be on the *Today* programme that the news has changed in the last half an hour and he won't be.

- Political parties being unreasonable ... rarely in an Alastair Campbell shouty way but just lower-level resistance/ obstruction.

And here's how it was summed up brilliantly by one of our best night editors, Adam Cumiskey, who left *Today* a few years ago:

Those evenings when you arrive for work at 8 p.m. to discover that the day editor, who is well rested and has had a lot of resources to call on during the past twelve hours, hasn't really bothered to put much of a programme together for you. The clock is ticking and you know you will have to rebuild the programme from the bottom up. You're tired and have probably only had a couple of hours of broken sleep during the day. The way to fight this lethargy is to really shake the programme up or through a crazy amount of caffeine or calories. This means you really hit a wall at about 3 a.m. You start to doubt all your instincts, you become essentially a vessel where judgement and energy are pouring from your body. In those small hours you really start to doubt your gut feelings (in all ways). You feel your spirit and your body disintegrating. Then the presenters arrive with their own characters, strengths, insanity and weaknesses. This gives you a defibrillatory jump-start. You realise that you should be in bed asleep rather than face a savaging or at least a pretty rigorous test from someone who, unlike you, has just got out of bed after a decent night's sleep and is raring to go. This is when you often find that your editorial judgement is going to be tested to the limit and if you're lucky the craft of programme making and the osmosis of news absorption from the years you've been put through this will see you through.

By the time you get on air you're flying, fuelled by an intense adrenaline-pumped desire to get over the three hours in the most creative way you can. If you're lucky it works and you reach 9 a.m. relatively unscathed and with more positives than negatives. If not you head home for four hours sleep and try to do a better job the next day ...

When I read that I felt seriously guilty. It should be compulsory reading for all wannabe night editors – except that it might put too many of them off – and definitely all presenters.

As for their bosses, the programme editors, it's they who ultimately carry the can. They decide the tone, the texture and the content of the programme. Being the editor of *Today* is a bit like being the controller of Radio 4. It doesn't matter what you do;

there will always be someone, somewhere, who will accuse you of destroying their lives. By and large, regular listeners do not like change – which is both a blessing and a curse. It's one of the reasons why *Today* has held on to its core audience for so many years. It has become a part of their lives. But when new editors come along they invariably want to make changes. They want to make their mark. And that's not what many listeners want. Pity the poor editor who decides that maybe *Today* should give a little more coverage to the world of theatre, for instance. The cry goes out from the shires: 'Dumbing down! I do not listen to a current-affairs programme to hear a bunch of luvvies prattling on. I listen to it for news and serious debate, dammit!'

Of the eight editors I have worked with I have had flaming rows with almost all and become good friends with most – often the same. I failed to have a flaming row with my last editor Sarah Sands, the only one who joined from outside the BBC, but not for want of trying. There are some people in this world with whom it's impossible to have a real row and she's one of them. She came in for a lot of stick when she joined the programme because her critics claimed she was one of those who loved luvvies and hated news. It was rubbish. It's possible to be interested in both and she is.

Ceri Thomas served the longest and I mourned his departure. God knows how he survived so long given the hours he put in. I suspect it's because he loved the job – especially preparing for big political interviews. We were sitting one morning in his little glass cubicle in Television Centre arguing about how best to hold Tony Blair's feet to the fire and Ceri – usually a pretty undemonstrative sort of chap – gazed out across the newsroom and declared, almost reverently, 'God! This is absolutely the best thing about this job!'

For some editors the worst part of the job was talking live into the presenter's ear during the big interview. In my early years on the programme I tended to get a little heated. Too heated. I wanted to make my mark, to prove that I hadn't got the job just because I'd been on the telly for the best part of twenty years. I wanted to show that I would take no nonsense from any politician trying to duck my question or answering a question I'd never asked – which was, of course, most of them at some time or another. So I did a lot of interrupting, even occasionally raising my voice a little. In other words I often went over the top and sometimes, to my great shame, lost my temper. That's when the editor really should intervene and warn the presenter to back off. Some did, some didn't. I rather wish I'd been warned off more often but I like to think that as the years went by I calmed down of my own volition.

Trying to gauge the temper of the audience is tricky. You know if you've gone seriously over the top because they tell you. But mostly they're pretty tolerant and clearly there are an awful lot of listeners who want their political leaders to be hauled over the coals. So where should we strike the balance?

After presenting roughly 5,000 editions of *Today* I'm still not sure I know the answer to that. I'm not even sure that *Today* is doing the job it's meant to be doing when it covers the political scene. That might sound disloyal but if it's true I'd have to accept an awful lot of the blame. After all, I've been presenting it for about twice as long as anyone else. So let's try to be a bit more specific.

It may be stating the bleed'n obvious but the first requirement for *Today* is that we have to tell the listener what is going on in the world. That is the *sine qua non* of all daily journalism. When dictators take over a country the first thing they do is occupy the radio and television stations and close down any newspaper that is not sympathetic to them – and there's a very good reason for that. Controlling information is an essential step towards exercising power. As the Chinese are discovering, it's much more difficult in a digital age, but even the ubiquitous social media has yet to reach the spread and influence of a trusted broadcaster like the BBC.

Next we have to put that news in context, to give the listener some perspective. That's more difficult. For my money, the BBC massively overplayed the fire at Notre Dame Cathedral in April 2019. An important story, of course, and irresistible for television given the spectacular pictures. But not important enough to dominate the news for as long as it did. And definitely not 'tragic'. Nobody died. Perhaps if the great cathedral had burned to the ground I'd have felt differently – but it didn't and it is being restored. Many others will disagree with me. That's inevitable.

News judgement is not an exact science. It's a bit of an improvement on astrology or tarot cards but not much. We sometimes get it wrong – not least by overplaying London stories simply because that's where most of us national hacks live. There's an old journalist maxim that says all news is local: a thousand dead in a disaster in a remote part of China is equal in news value to the girl next door breaking a leg. It's not too far from the truth.

In the pre-digital era we boasted that if you listened to us every day you did not need to read a newspaper. It was nonsense then and it's nonsense now – if only because newspapers have opinions and *Today* does not. Nor should it. Newspapers can campaign and *Today* cannot. It can give a voice to campaigners but it must provide balance. There's a difference.

A more credible boast would be that if you listen to *Today* you should know what's happening in the world and be able to put it into some sort of context. Its job is not just to deliver the news, it is to explain why it matters and to provide analysis.

Politicians wield power and our job is to hold power to account. It's not easy to do that if you get sucked into the political vortex. MPs thrive on the oxygen of Westminster. Many of them lose sight of the world outside. Indeed, the worst of them – a small minority I suspect – don't much care about it. All that matters are the internecine battles and their next promotion. It is a world that provides endless material for journalists and writers of satirical novels and producers of TV dramas. It is seductive and thrilling. And it is mostly entirely irrelevant to the real world outside.

The danger for the *Today* programme and especially for its presenters is believing that just because a political story is thrilling for us, it is also exciting and relevant to the listener. The longer I've been presenting *Today* the more uneasy I have become about the relationship between us and them. At first it's all rather exciting – especially if you've been a reporter on the road for as long as I was. In that job you have to try to find the people in power and then persuade them to talk to you. When you present *Today* they often come to you. It's easy to believe that you're more important than you really are.

Always at the heart of politics is the struggle for power: who has it and who might seize it from them. The real world is all about jobs and pay and schools and hospitals and rubbish collection and tax and knowing that your children are safe when they're out on the street. But in the political ecosphere a spat between a couple of ministers might easily become the story of the day even if, as the old saying goes, they're not even household names in their own household. Similarly an arcane argument over an obscure piece of parliamentary procedure assumes far greater importance than it deserves.

We make another mistake too. If there is a crisis in the school system or a shortage of GPs the first instinct is to talk to a politician for the big interview rather than a teacher or a doctor. The logic is that you're more likely to get a 'news line' that way – even if it's possible to predict pretty accurately what the minister will say long before they have even opened their mouths. But it's faulty logic.

You might wonder why, if I'm right about this, I haven't been making a fuss about it. God knows I've been there long enough. There are lots of reasons – none of them terribly convincing. One is that it's fun interviewing politicians. Mostly anyway. Another is that it gets you talked about and, just like politicians, we hacks are not exactly averse to a bit of publicity. And the other may be that we, along with everyone else, have become victims – willing victims – of the age of celebrity.

In 1946 Winston Churchill made a joke about Clement Attlee, the man who defeated him after the war for the job of prime minister. 'An empty taxi drove up to 10 Downing Street,' said Churchill, 'and Attlee got out.'

Not terribly funny perhaps, and anyway Attlee had the last laugh. He went on to become one of our truly great reforming prime ministers. But it worked at the time because Churchill had a point: Attlee was virtually unrecognisable to the general public. And he was perfectly happy with that. He neither sought nor relished celebrity. Is it possible even to imagine saying that of any modern politician who seeks high office?

Even serious programmes like *Today* are not immune to the curse of celebrity. It's tempting to say *especially* programmes like *Today*. Too often we have behaved rather in the way a late-night celebrity chat show on one TV channel might compete with a chat show on another. Who's got the biggest star for their show? Who can get their star to make the most outrageous comments about some other star? Whose star delivers the liveliest performances?

In some ways we might actually have been able to learn a thing or two from our light-entertainment colleagues. They're probably much better than us at spotting when their audience has had more than enough of one topic or, indeed, of one 'star'. In fairness, they have a much wider and deeper pool to fish in. Graham Norton is able to range across fifty or so years of film stars, pop singers, soap-opera actors and basically anybody who's ever done anything remarkably clever or brave or unusual or just plain silly. They all really want to be on his show because they need the publicity and they're being paid pretty well to do it. And, of course, this is their big chance to show the world how witty and entertaining they can be.

When there's a big political story making the headlines and *Today* is casting around to fill the star slot the producers' options are rather more limited. The big stories usually involve serious embarrassment in one form or another for the government, which means the producers' first choice will almost certainly be a member of the Cabinet and most of them would rather drink a bottle of bleach than volunteer. Why run the risk of making a fool of yourself and damaging your own chances of one day becoming party leader – a dream most of them privately, if not publicly, nurture – when you can sit back and listen to one of your colleagues doing it instead? For 'colleagues' read 'competitors'.

In other words, the poor old producer is having to ask them or their spin doctors to do something for which – unlike the chat-show guests – they won't get paid and don't want the publicity because they have roughly zero chance of making themselves more popular. Often the best they can hope for is to survive. And if that means winning the coveted Oscar For the Most Drearily Repetitive and Unrevealing Interview of the Year ... that's just fine. Indeed, for some it is the objective.

Not for nothing was the former Chancellor of the Exchequer Philip Hammond dubbed, with heavy irony, 'Box Office Phil'. He was, in other words, a cautious chap who almost never gave away anything of news value. When I was new to the game I remember moaning to a politician after a particularly unforth-coming interview with him that there hadn't been much point in doing it. His reply was along the lines of: 'Sorry about that but I wasn't doing the interview for *you*. I was doing it for *me*.'

So where Norton and his team will feed his guests agreed lines which they will seize on to deliver their pre-planned moments of spontaneous merriment, the *Today* presenter has the opposite role – and this is where I have become increasingly uneasy. As I suggested earlier in the book, the success of the 8.10 is too often judged on whether it has unsettled the politician and trapped them into saying something they had not intended to say, and not on whether it has succeeded in moving the debate forwards. Some would use a different verb for unsettle: ambush.

You may say: 'Surely that's your fault, Mr Humphrys. You're the one asking the questions so why do it? And haven't you come to this realisation a bit late?'

Guilty as charged m'lud, but let's remember the New Testament says there will be more joy in heaven over the one sinner that repenteth than over the ninety-nine righteous men who need no repentance. And anyway, I'm not exactly at the sackcloth-and-ashes stage just yet. But I do wonder whether it's time for a rethink. I'm not alone in that. Various BBC News bosses have been worried about it for years.

There's usually a pretty clear correlation between how much they worry and where they come in the corporate pecking order. Relatively junior producers tend to cheer (albeit quietly) from the sidelines when a presenter seriously duffs up a senior politician. But the higher up the promotion ladder they climb, the more cautious they tend to be. The calculation is that it's much smarter to be considered a safe pair of hands than someone prepared to take the occasional risk for a good story. Sadly, it's not only the top bosses who take that view. Too many wannabe editors become increasingly cautious the closer they get to the editor's chair. If there is such a thing as a corporate news culture it's too often based on a philosophy of safety first.

One of the brilliant exceptions was Ceri Thomas. When he left *Today* he was promoted to a senior management job which, predictably, he hated. He was a serious journalist who wanted to keep being a journalist. So he opted to move down the management ladder (possibly the first in recorded BBC history to do so) and become the editor of *Panorama*. His big test came when he challenged a story to which BBC News (and most other national news organisations) had given enormous coverage. It was a truly terrifying story: a string of claims were made by a police informer known as 'Nick' that a wide group of the most powerful people in the land – from the former prime minister Ted Heath and the former Home Secretary Leon Brittan to the nation's most distinguished military commanders – had been part of a paedophile ring. A senior police officer described the claims as credible and true. One of those claims was that they had organised the murder of some of their victims, including a young boy allegedly run down on his way to school.

Scotland Yard took the claims so seriously that they set up a full-scale inquiry under the code name Operation Midland. It was to cost £2.5 million. Far more importantly, it was to destroy the reputations and, in some cases, the lives of some of those accused. There was, though, a fundamental flaw with the claims. They were complete garbage from start to finish: the work of a fantasist named Carl Beech who is himself a convicted paedophile.

Ceri had his suspicions from the beginning. He was deeply disturbed by the BBC's news coverage – the way the police accounts were accepted uncritically, its reliance on deeply flawed investigative work by a news website, and sympathetic interviews with 'Nick' – and ordered *Panorama* to find what he was convinced was the truth.

He was running an enormous risk. If he'd been wrong it might well have ended his career at the BBC. But he was right and the *Panorama* programme he and his team eventually delivered was a model of powerful, painstaking investigative journalism. In July 2019, five long years after Beech made his outrageous claims to Scotland Yard, he himself was convicted of twelve charges of perverting the course of justice and one count of fraud. He was sent to jail for eighteen years. By then Ceri Thomas had left the BBC.

When Evan Davis moved from *Today* in 2014 to take over *Newsnight* from Jeremy Paxman he criticised the combative interviewing style as 'overdone', 'worn out' and 'not a particular public service'. He said a culture of broadcast journalists 'getting the scalp' and 'tripping people into gaffes' had created an 'arms race' between politicians and interviewers. And anyway, he suggested, it's counterproductive: 'Politicians get better defences as interviewers get better attack techniques. Politicians now sound defensive and boring instead of making gaffes.'

Evan acknowledged that 'on a good day Paxman and Humphrys can do great interviews'. So far, so good. But then he added: 'That style was fresh once and it has just become less interesting as everyone [has] seen it more and more used.' Aggressive political interviews had helped create the 'remarkable situation we are in

… when you have a private conversation with a senior politician you come out more impressed than when you see them in public'.

Is that really 'remarkable'? Aren't private conversations always different from public conversations? Would we really expect politicians to say in public what they had just told us in private? I wish! It would make for some wonderful radio and the politician would be regarded as a hero. For about five minutes. Then his colleagues in Westminster would treat him as though he had a very nasty and very contagious disease and that would be the end of him.

In my early years on *Today* I remember being rather flattered if a politician was really candid with me in the privacy of the green room. He might agree enthusiastically that the government's policy on dog walking was completely barking and the prime minister had only approved it because she had a visceral dislike of dogs. All very embarrassing for the PM if it were to be made public. But of course it would not be because the moment they're in the studio and the green light comes on the ministers revert to type.

Embarrassing? Certainly not! The PM was showing her customary sound judgement and had taken a great deal of advice before reaching this wise position.

All these years later I'm still mildly disappointed when, say, a candidate for the leadership of his party tells me in the green room that the favourite for the job is a complete plonker, a proven liar and philanderer, who would lead the country to ruin and then, in the time it takes to walk into the studio undergoes some Damascene conversion. Would he serve in his Cabinet, I ask? Yes, of course he would, he assures me – without so much as the tiniest wink. But that's politics for you.

Evan's approach to politicians when he took over *PM* in 2018 was different from how I remember him when he joined *Today* in 2008 – at least in tone. He seems to have set out to be informal and friendly. His interviewees have become less like remote figures of authority who are there to be held to account and more like old mates who happen to have dropped by for a chat. He wanted to establish a different relationship with them – sometimes, in my view, rather bizarrely so. When the battle was raging for the leadership of the Tory party he invited the contenders to go for a stroll in the park with him and his much-loved dog Mr Whippy. Some accepted, some didn't. I can see what he hoped to achieve: a way of breaking through the formality of the set-piece interview and establishing a more relaxed relationship. Maybe the politician would be less on his guard, less defensive, more likely to give us a glimpse of the real person behind the political mask. I thought it failed.

That wasn't because Evan isn't a good interviewer – on the contrary, he's one of the best: clever, immensely well informed and genuinely curious – but because it was so artificial. We were invited to believe we were eavesdropping on a chat between two old friends but we were not. And anyway I don't want the audience to think we presenters and the politicians we interview are best mates. Or even friends. Evan often uses their first names on air. I have always refused to do that and I wish they did not use ours. It was, I think, Paddy Ashdown who started it some thirty years ago. Sadly it spread. It gives the listener the wrong notion of our relationship. But it's a losing battle.

Some of my former colleagues also think it's OK to wine and dine politicians. Again I don't. I can count on the fingers of one hand the politicians I've had lunch with (never dinner) and I stopped doing it completely some twenty years ago. It's different for political correspondents who need to be on the inside, privy to the latest gossip and ideally ahead of the pack when a story breaks. The lunches are, of course, strictly off the record. That's the whole point of them.

But presenters do not need to be insiders. On the contrary. When we want to know what's going on we ask our immensely well-informed colleagues such as Laura Kuenssberg or Norman Smith. Our own relationship with the politicians is completely different. An off-the-record chat over a glass of decent wine might just possibly give you an edge in an interview but it probably won't – precisely because it is off the record and you can't refer to it. And anyway I've yet to meet the politician who will tell you stuff (strictly off the record old boy) that does not in some way advance his own cause. I suspect that politician has yet to be born.

Something else happened on *PM* after Evan arrived. He asked the listeners how *they* wanted political interviews to be carried out. And then he delivered what he called the Ten Commandments. Here's a flavour (with my thoughts in italics afterwards):

- allow more space for the interview. *Well ... sometimes. But not always. It depends entirely on what is being said and how important the subject is. Sometimes the interviews aren't too short: they're too long.*
- deconstruct what's happening during an interview ... for example pointing out when a question is not being answered. *Obviously they should point out when questions are not being answered. I think mostly they do.*
- achieve accountability through 'enlightenment and revelation' rather than head-on argument. *Who could possibly argue against 'enlightenment and revelation'? But sometimes you need a bit of an argument to get there.*
- focus on big strategic questions, not just silly ones. *Depends what you mean by strategic. Sometimes 'silly' questions can be revealing. If a politician doesn't know the price of a pint of milk that might tell you quite a lot about him.*
- make sure the goals are clear before we start. *Of course ... but what if the politician has a different goal and it turns out to be worth following up?*
- inform the audience about contentious factual points. *Again obvious – but often the 'facts' are contentious for a very good reason.*
- interview important politicians on days when they are not in the news. *Why? Why not interview teachers or doctors or*

*scientists or plumbers or town planners or police officers or
bankers or musicians or foster parents? I really dislike this one.
Politicians get more than their share of airtime as it is. And if
they are 'important' they will be interviewed.*

- in discussions explore what the two sides agree on and not
only where they disagree. *Why?*
- show more of our 'working behind the scenes' … explain
what we've tried to do and who we've tried to speak to.
*Again why? If a politician refuses to speak to us we use the
'empty chair' technique – as* Today *did with Boris Johnson
endlessly during the leadership contest. That mattered. But
mostly it doesn't – and I suspect the audience has more to worry
about than the day-to-day problems of radio producers.*

You'll have spotted there are only nine commandments here. The
tenth is a promise to review the project and listen to the listeners'
thoughts. As you will have divined by now, I'm not overly
impressed by these commandments – but my real problem is with
the underlying principle. I'm not sure why interviewers should
expect the audience to tell them how to do their job. Perhaps that
sounds arrogant but it's not meant to be. I've always read all my
letters and emails and, believe me, there have been an awful lot of
them. Often they're simply bonkers but, more often, they're
thoughtful and I take them seriously. Inevitably there is a huge
range of opinions. Two people will listen to the same interview
and one will think it was tough but fair and I should be congrat-
ulated while the other will think it was a ruthless, self-serving
stitch-up and I should be sacked forthwith. So who's right?

The problem is, there is no right or wrong way to do an interview. If you book a plumber to install your boiler you would not
expect him to seek your opinion. He's an expert. Interviewers are
not. Almost all of us are generalists and interviewing is not a
discipline: it's an acquired skill. You can't be 'trained' to do it. We
all learn on the job. When 'ordinary' listeners get a chance to fire
questions at politicians they almost always do a pretty good job

of it. Maybe they'd struggle a bit to do a decent 8.10 interview but they might very well get the hang of it with enough practice. There's a very good reason why journalism should not be described as a profession or even a trade. It's because it's not. You don't have to be qualified – just competent. If I do a rubbish interview you might switch off, but it's hardly likely to ruin your day. If the plumber gets it wrong and the boiler blows up it probably would.

Let's be clear: I am not saying I believe we've got it right and anyway it really doesn't matter. We haven't and it matters a lot. In my own case I could probably count on the fingers of both hands the number of times I have ended an interview patting myself on the back. And the more important the interview, the less likely I am to have been satisfied with the way I've handled it. What I *am* saying is that the BBC cannot hand the problem over to the listener. The so-called 'Open Politics' approach of suggesting to them ten commandments seems to me at best a bit of a gimmick and at worst an abdication of responsibility. This is our problem – not the listeners'.

When the BBC's late, great political editor John Cole retired he reflected that he 'did find himself from time to time irritated by the fact that aggression in some cases has taken over from the desire to elicit information and ... to force the interviewee to face up to any contradictions there may be in his position or any apparent weaknesses'.

So what should we be trying to do on *Today*? What we're really after most of the time is that accursed 'news line'. Something that might get picked up in the day's news cycle and the next day's papers with a credit for the programme. Ideally something that the poor bloody victim might live to regret when the party's director of communications grabs them by the collar as they come out of the studio. They know that their job is to sound plausible and coherent and, above all, stick to the party line even if it requires them to argue that black is white. Especially when it requires them to argue that black is white.

John Birt may have been a bit unworldly but it's hard to argue with his central criticism: too many interviewers (present company included) are too often more concerned with making headlines than with helping the audience understand the issues at stake. Obviously those aims are not mutually exclusive, but no interviewer ever got a bollocking for making headlines in the next day's paper.

One of the most famous television encounters was between Jeremy Paxman and the former Home Secretary, Michael Howard, when he was running for the Tory leadership in May 1997. Everyone knows that he posed the same question twelve times without a satisfactory answer (actually, the numbers people put on it vary, but everyone remembers it). The BBC's own history website tells us: 'The refrain of "Did you threaten to overrule him" subsequently came to denote a high-water mark in the style of persistent, robust, but cordial interviewing technique pioneered by Robin Day and others forty year earlier.'

The problem is that most people can't remember for the life of them what the interview was about. (It was about the details of a meeting between Howard and the head of the Prison Service, Derek Lewis, regarding the dismissal of the governor of Parkhurst Prison, John Marriott.) All that's remembered is that Howard could not answer the question and resorted to increasingly desperate lawyerly formulations to avoid giving a direct answer. Some years later he reflected on the interview: 'I'd been campaigning all day, I hadn't remotely been thinking about Derek Lewis or prisons, I'd been thinking about the Tory leadership ... This is not an excuse but perhaps an explanation, the end of a long day when you're tired ... I wasn't able to go back over the history and so I answered in my own way. But I mean the questioning was slightly absurd because what I was not supposed to do [in office] was to overrule Derek Lewis and I didn't overrule Derek Lewis and no one has ever suggested that I did.' It's quite possible that Howard had a point.

The former BBC director general Mark Thompson says political debate has become even fiercer because of the Internet. As he put it, words can hurtle through virtual space with infinitesimal delay and a politician can plant an idea in 10 million other minds before leaving the podium. The result is 'a fight to the political death, a fight in which every linguistic weapon is fair game'.

An interview on *Today* is not often a fight to the political death, but there can be a fair drop of blood spattered on the studio carpet at the end of some. If the politicians gave more straight answers to straight questions the interviews would be less confrontational but it takes two to tango. It's not that there's anything wrong with a bit of confrontation but without sharing Evan's prescription I do have some sympathy for his analysis and I have come increasingly to believe that there may be some real downsides to the adversarial interview. It may add to the public's growing unease with the political system.

When Tony Blair gave his farewell words as prime minister in the House of Commons in 2007, he said: 'Some may belittle politics but we know it is where people stand tall. And although I know it has its many harsh contentions, it is still the arena which sets the heart beating fast. It may sometimes be a place of low skulduggery but it is more often a place for more noble causes.'

A politician's gloss, you might say. But what if Blair is right? Let's take Brexit, the greatest parliamentary crisis in my fifty years at the BBC. Certainly there has been plenty of 'low skulduggery'. Many MPs twisted and turned to further their own selfish ambitions. Many more refused to compromise and stuck to their entrenched positions in the face of all the dire warnings of the terrible fate awaiting the nation. Skulduggery indeed.

But hold on a minute. Why do we almost routinely describe politicians' ambitions as selfish but never our own? What exactly is wrong with relatively unknown junior ministers believing they are capable of holding the greatest elected office in the land? Perhaps they are – or at least some of them. Why should they be scorned because they don't have the background we tend to associate with prime ministers?

We decry those politicians who soften their previously hardline stance and offer a compromise. And we decry those who stick rigidly to their guns. Politicians often do 'stand tall' – notwithstanding the Brexit debacle – and their beliefs are often firmly held. It's at least possible to argue that the Brexit shambles happened precisely because so many MPs were driven by what they believe is in the interest of the country rather than their own base political advantage. Yet, by the very nature of the adversarial interview, we too often feed the preconception that they're dodgy characters who are only in it for themselves.

The BBC's founding father, John Reith, was evangelical about its role. It should 'carry direct information on a hundred subjects to innumerable men and women who will after a short time be in a position to make up their own minds on many matters of vital moment'.

Obviously no BBC boss would get away with that sort of patriarchal, paternalistic approach today. The notion that without the

BBC 'innumerable' men and women would be incapable of making up their own minds would be ridiculed, and rightly so. The boss would be out on his neck five minutes after he'd said it. But Reith's ambition was laudable: the BBC should be a trusted deliverer of information.

Perhaps both sides, politicians and the media, are caught up in a contest neither can win. The politician 'succeeds' by clinging to the party line no matter how fed up the audience is with hearing it over and over again. At best it's a draw. Or the interviewer succeeds by driving a wedge between politician and party line – in which case it's entirely likely that the audience neither knows nor cares. And if we do manage to get a so-called news line? These days news can travel round the world and back at the click of a mouse. An interview on *Today* can be dissected and debated, diced and sliced, on a host of different platforms. Was this a slip of the tongue, or did we shine some light on a genuine issue? Commentators and experts can be wheeled in to give their view. More politicians opine. By the end of the day we may be no wiser. And then the process starts again with a different day and a different interview.

This has consequences for us all.

In his memoirs, Ken Clarke criticises the 'hysterical 24/7 chatter that now dominates political debate'. Next week's headlines, he argues, are given more priority by governments than serious policy development and the long-term consequences for the nation. 'Media relations and public relations are now regarded as the key elements of governing,' he says. It is, he concludes, a disastrous way to run the government of a complex modern nation state.

I wonder if there might be even more serious implications. Do we damage politicians by helping to lower their reputation in the esteem of the public? Do we fail to explain – or even try to explain – the complexity of the issues that they face? And if the answers to those questions are yes, then surely we create the conditions in which cynicism about politics and politicians can thrive.

Note I say cynicism and not scepticism. We should all be sceptical: it's healthy. But cynicism is the enemy of democracy and the rise of populist movements and decline of mainstream parties across Europe seems to show that the gap between politicians and citizens is growing, not shrinking. Research suggests that 'the government' – regardless of the party in power – is perceived to make bad decisions. In the UK, government trust levels are lower than the global average. Young people tend to distrust the government more (only twenty-seven per cent trusted the government in 2018), and around ninety-three per cent feel that their views are not well presented by people in politics.

Have we unwittingly helped to create the conditions for this unhealthy state of affairs?

It was in the United States that the phrase 'Beltway politics' was first used to describe the disconnection between politicians and real people. Washington DC was inside the Beltway and it was there that politicians squabbled endlessly with each other, seemingly regardless of how ordinary people outside lived their ordinary lives. It was where lobbyists practised their dark arts, where Congress bowed its mighty head before even more powerful and infinitely more wealthy business leaders. The voters peered into this murky world from outside and did not like what they saw. One beneficiary of this disconnection, a few decades after the 'Beltway' phrase was born, was Donald Trump.

Trump's opponent in the closing stages of the 2016 campaign was Hillary Clinton, but what he was really running against was what Clinton personified: the political system. He was the outsider and she was the quintessential insider. By every conventional measure she was infinitely better qualified than Trump – but he had a weapon that no previous presidential challenger had been able to command in the same way: social media. Trump had a direct line to the American people – or, at least, enough of them to get him into the White House.

In this country we may not have Beltway politics in quite the same sense – if only because the lobbyists and the wealthy donors have less influence – but the disconnection between people and politicians is growing here too. And social media is playing its part. This is why the role of the BBC has never been more important.

The Twitter image is seductive: birds tweeting away gaily to each other and simultaneously bringing joy to the hearts of those who listen. The reality has proved altogether darker. What was sold as the greatest aid to communication since Gutenberg, enabling the voices of ordinary citizens to be heard, has offered the mob something it had never had before: a guarantee that its often malevolent voice will be heard not just within its own circle but way beyond. The idea that an MP going about her job should be threatened with rape because she believes in something different from her moronic political opponent is not just a threat to her but to the very concept of democracy.

The notion of fake news might be mildly amusing when its claims are obviously bonkers. It might sometimes even harm the cause of those who spread the stuff. Trump's boast about the size of the crowd at his presidential inauguration was an example of that. He claimed it was the biggest there had ever been and his staff continued to insist it was true even after every network in the States produced the pictures that showed it was rubbish. That might help persuade those who are open to persuasion, but not the tens of millions who believe the so-called mainstream media is a hostile force lying endlessly to protect their own privileged status. That's when we should get worried.

In Britain there are some worrying signs too – albeit on a different scale. Members of both main Westminster parties – those who have not given up in despair – seem disillusioned with their leadership as never before. As Professor John Gray of the London School of Economics has put it, we are witnessing an unprecedented meltdown in British politics. The working class feel alienated because they believe no one is listening to them any longer and those people who voted to leave the EU feel betrayed. The danger is obvious – and we see it in pretty stark terms in one

European country after another. As Gray puts it, when the main parties cannot give the voters what they want they turn to the extremes to vent their anger.

I voiced my concerns earlier about the BBC engaging in social engineering. It is none of the BBC's business how society interprets the rules by which it chooses to live – still less should it bow to pressure groups who might want to change those rules. Cultural change is a continuing process and it's the BBC's job to report it – not to influence it. But the way in which the nation conducts its political debate is very much the BBC's business because it is an integral part of it.

It goes without saying that its first responsibility is to expose the fake-news peddlers for what they are. There's really only one way to do that: build and retain trust. For all its weaknesses and failings, that is what the BBC has been doing for the best part of a century. And if that sounds absurdly simplistic … so be it. The key is always trying to separate fact from speculation and never pretending to be privy to some great truth denied to others.

The second bit – the analysis – is pretty straightforward too. It's the job of seasoned journalists like Katya Adler or Mark Easton to tell us what those facts mean, to analyse their significance. Sometimes they'll get it wrong but that's because they are journalists, not prophets. The journalist who never gets it wrong has yet to be born.

The third bit is trickier. It's the tone of the debate.

Every presenter who has ever faced a politician across the *Today* microphones has to decide what tone they are going to adopt. The temptation – sometimes irresistible – is to imagine oneself wearing the robes of an Old Bailey judge or at the very least the wig of a prosecuting barrister whose job is to prove the defendant guilty. I write from personal experience. I've done it more often than I care to remember. And I usually wish I hadn't. If we treat the politician like a suspected felon, why shouldn't the audience do the same? Is that what we want?

Yes, there will be times when a bit of tough cross-examination is called for: times when there is pretty clear evidence that the politician is deliberately trying to mislead the audience. It's probably true that some of us (again I include myself) should have been more robust when we were questioning claims made in the referendum campaign by both sides – often diametrically opposite claims. By definition they could not both have been telling the truth and they deserved to be exposed more thoroughly than they often were. The problem with that, as I mentioned earlier, is that when they know they're bang to rights they tend to stay well clear of the studio. It's on those occasions I envy the judge. How wonderful to have the power to be able to subpoena the witness, let alone the accused.

And smart politicians (just like smart journalists) will use every trick in the book to dodge the nasty stuff. I had just one interview during the whole Brexit campaign with the star of the Leave camp: Boris Johnson. It happened to come on the morning when the nation was getting very exercised about the claim writ large on the side of their campaign bus that if we left the EU we would have £350 million more to spend on the NHS every week. It was nonsense and of course Mr Johnson knew it was nonsense, but I never got the chance to challenge him properly. He was on a dodgy line from the West Country and every time I tried pressing him he would affect not to be able to hear me – so the interview got nowhere. It's strange how often politicians suffer from temporary hearing loss or unexplained technical problems when the going gets really tough.

Yet the politicians are not often on trial for some heinous crime and if we interviewers treat them as though they are, it's reasonable that the audience will do the same – or at least a sizeable chunk of the audience will. And therein lies the problem. Trust breeds trust and the opposite is true. Maybe we should allow the politician to do a bit more explaining and spend a bit less time forcing them to protest their innocence.

A former *Newsnight* editor once argued that a new contract

needed to be drawn up between broadcasters and politicians to allow for a more open and informative format. He called interviews with frontbenchers 'an arid, ritualised affair'. Twenty years after John Birt's speech about political interviewing, we're still talking about the problem without reaching any conclusion.

So am I repenting of half a lifetime spent interviewing politicians in the guise of devil's advocate?

Not entirely.

Party politics is, by definition, based on opposition – albeit a little less robust than it used to be. In the House of Commons, there are two red lines running along the length of the Chamber between the two sides and it's said that these lines are two swords' lengths apart to prevent MPs duelling. Now they rely on verbal duelling, debating skills and occasionally a bit of rather childish name-calling.

In the model interview we test the argument, spot the flaws, challenge sloppy thinking and specious claims. We also aim to give the listener some pointers to the politician's character. Can they be trusted or do they sound devious? Are they willing to engage in serious debate or just trying to pull a fast one?

Programmes like *Today* and *Newsnight* are fundamentally different from twenty-four-hour news channels or the TV and radio bulletins. Politicians know that their key message will be contained in a twenty-second sound bite and they will need to say the same thing to half a dozen different outlets to be sure of getting the message across. On longer programmes the interviewer must get behind the obvious message, give the audience a deeper understanding of the issue at hand, and help them reach an informed judgement. But how effective are we? Do we provide a proper alternative to the hamster wheel of news-channel coverage, where journalists run very fast in order sometimes to stand still?

Increasingly, I have my doubts.

* * *

When I joined the *Today* programme in 1987 none of these thoughts even entered my mind. I wanted to make a reputation for myself. I wanted to prove that I was at least as tough as any of my predecessors as well as becoming the conscience of the nation. Preposterous, I know, but it was a long time ago and I was very naive. After I'd been presenting the programme for about ten years I had lunch with a politician who'd spent half his life in Parliament and had decided he had had enough. I asked him how he thought interviewing had changed during those years.

'I can't really complain,' he told me, 'but I remember a time when we politicians were given the opportunity to think aloud. We can't risk that any longer. We'd be taken apart. That's a pity.'

He was right. In my decades on *Today* I struggle to recall a single interview with a senior politician, let alone a prime minister, in which they said something along the lines of: 'Hmm ... the opposition may be right about that ... perhaps we should take it on board.'

Nor can I remember when I have said the equivalent of: 'Ah ... fair point ... I was probably exaggerating when I said ...'

So let me try to sum up my concerns after thirty-three years of political interviewing. It's true that the news climate has changed and the relentless twenty-four-hour news cycle, combined with the incessant and often witless babbling on social media, militate against thoughtful debate. But even allowing for that *Today* presenters and their stablemates do have questions to ask themselves. Does an interview always have to be so combative? Does there have to be a winner or a loser? Does it have to be a zero-sum game?

If it does, the loser might very well be the public. If we interviewers succeed – albeit unintentionally – in convincing the listener that all politicians are liars, the real loser is our system of representative democracy that has served the nation so well for so long.

But perhaps I am too gloomy. Maybe that's what sixty years in journalism does to you. Reporters are strange creatures. We are accused of endlessly searching for human frailty so that we may expose it – and sometimes succeeding. We deny the charge that we are interested only in bad news. Don't we give endless coverage, say, to the arrival of a royal baby or a royal marriage? Indeed we do, often to the point of brain-numbing tedium. But we give more to a royal divorce. Yes, we seek out the bad news. Of course we do. We are more interested in the single plane that crashed rather than the thousand that landed safely.

We need to be where bad things are happening and, like most old hacks, I have had my share of them. I have seen an American president driven in disgrace from office, countries devastated by earthquakes or ravaged by war or brought low by famine. There is nothing more soul-destroying to report on than famine. It is perhaps the greatest evil of all because it strikes first at children. What remains most vivid in my mind, though – and I make no apology for returning to them – are the children of Aberfan. They were victims of a great crime: the exercise of power without responsibility.

But I have seen the other side too: the triumph of courage and compassion when disaster strikes. The sheer decency of countless people who sacrifice their own safety and even their own lives to help others. The sense of duty shown by many politicians who could earn far more money and lead easier lives outside politics, but genuinely want to help make their country a better place.

On the most personal level, I owe a huge debt of gratitude to the BBC. Flawed it may be – just as all of us who have worked for it or run it are flawed in our own ways – but I have not a shred of doubt that this country is richer for its existence.

And it could not exist but for the loyalty of so many millions. It's true that we have tested that loyalty to breaking point more than once and it faces competition today the like of which it has never experienced since its first television broadcast in 1936. But I remain convinced that it occupies a special place in the nation's heart and we would be the poorer without it.

When I joined the *Today* programme I wondered how long its great audience would tolerate me. It turned out to be much longer than I expected. I am in their debt too.

But after thirty-three years on *Today* I can't deny that I'm rather looking forward to tomorrow.

Illustrations

All images courtesy of the author unless otherwise stated.

Cartoons
p. 138 Mike Tyson. *(Mac)*
p. 143 'Let's stop now, John. They've been grilled enough.'
p. 161 Jonathan Aitken. *(Nick Newman)*
p. 174 Sent by the Labour Party. *(Mac)*
p. 263 Hutton Inquiry. *(Martin Rowson)*
p. 387 *Today* programme. *(Martin Rowson)*

Picture Section
Queuing at Cardiff train station, 1945.
Trinity Youth Group excursion.
Working for the *Merthyr Express*.
Liverpool dock strikes.
Interviewing kids on a street in Cardiff.
Reporting on Aberfan. *(ITV)*
The Aberfan disaster. *(Staff/Mirrorpix/Getty Images)*
Reporting on the Troubles in Northern Ireland.
Outside the White House at Richard Nixon's resignation.
Watching Nixon at a US convention.
Sledging and with family in snowy Washington DC.
Meeting PG Wodehouse.
Making a documentary on Joshua Nkomo in South Africa.
Covering protests in London.

Popping champagne in the BBC TV newsroom.
The BBC newscasting team in London. *(United News/ Popperfoto/Getty Images)*
The papers desk with Sue MacGregor and Roger Mosey. *(Jeff Overs/BBC News & Current Affairs/Getty Images)*
On air with Brian Redhead. *(Jeff Overs/BBC News & Current Affairs/Getty Images)*
On air with Sue MacGregor.
With John Cleese.
With Jim Naughtie outside the old BBC Broadcasting House.
In the *Today* production office. *(Jeff Overs/BBC News & Current Affairs/Getty Images)*
Interviewing John Major.
With David Cameron.
With Jimmy Carter.
Standing with Tony Blair.
On air with Tony Blair.
Attempted decapitation with John MacGregor and Terry Wogan.
Basra palace with Major-General Barney White-Spunner. *(BBC)*
Talking to British troops in Basra. *(BBC)*
John Humphrys portrait. *(Chris Floyd)*

Every effort has been made to trace copyright holders and to obtain their permission for the use of copyright material. The publisher apologises for any errors or omissions in the above list and would be grateful if notified of any corrections that should be incorporated in future editions of this book.